DANCE
UNTO THE
LORD

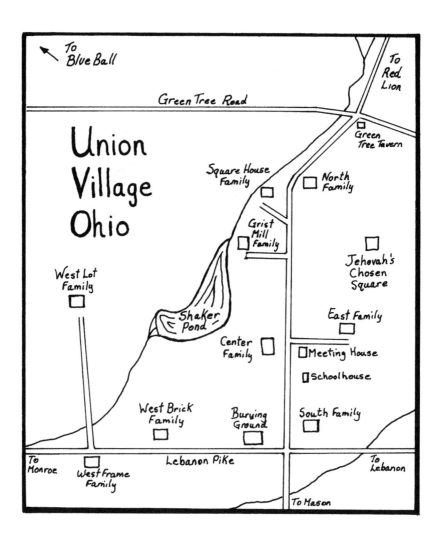

To
Blue Ball

To
Red
Lion

Green Tree Road

Union
Village
Ohio

Green
Tree Tavern

Square House
Family

North
Family

Grist
Mill
Family

Jehovah's
Chosen
Square

West Lot
Family

East Family

Shaker
Pond

Center
Family

Meeting House

Schoolhouse

West Brick
Family

Burying
Ground

South Family

To
Monroe

West Frame
Family

Lebanon Pike

To
Lebanon

To Mason

GEORGE DELL

DANCE UNTO THE LORD

THE OHIO STATE UNIVERSITY PRESS

COLUMBUS

Frontispiece map by Vicki Tieche.

Library of Congress Cataloging-in-Publication Data

Dell, George, 1901–1992
    Dance unto the Lord / George Dell.
        p. cm.
    ISBN 0-8142-0886-X (cloth) — ISBN 0-8142-5084-X (pbk.)
    1. Ohio—Fiction. 2. Shakers—Fiction. I. Title.
    PS3554.E4436 D45 2001
    813'.54—dc21

                                                           2001001845

Text and cover design by Diane Gleba Hall.
Cover illustration by Jennifer A. Tieche.
Type set in sabon by Sans Serif Inc.
Printed by Thomson-Shore Inc.

9 8 7 6 5 4 3 2 1

Contents

Foreword

THE LATE eighteenth century gave rise to a variety of newly founded religious groups, among them The United Society of Believers in Christ's Second Appearance, nicknamed "shaking Quakers," which was further abbreviated to Shakers. This group originated in England around 1747. Their doctrine was expanded by Ann Lee, called "Mother Ann," who left England and arrived with a group of disciples in New York in 1774. The first colony in the new world was established at Niskeyuna, New York (later renamed Watervliet). In 1787 the first formally organized colony was established at New Lebanon, New York. The Shakers renamed this colony Mount Lebanon, and it became the center of the Shaker ministry.

At the beginning of 1805, attracted by the Kentucky Revival and particularly by the "New Light" schismatics who had split from the Presbyterian Synod of Kentucky, the Shakers sent out missionaries to the west. Richard McNemar, the pastor of the Turtle Creek congregation in southern Ohio, and Malcolm Worley, a landowner in Turtle Creek, had both been instrumental in the Presbyterian schism. The Shaker missionaries arrived at Worley's home in the land between the Miami Rivers on March 22, 1805. Worley became the first western convert to the Shakers. He was followed shortly thereafter by a slave, Anna Middleton, and then by Richard McNemar. By the beginning of 1807 the Shakers had acquired an entire section of land made up in part of Worley's and McNemar's farms. The first Meeting House was erected in 1809. Union Village had begun.

The property acquired by the Shakers was in the western portion of Warren County. The main part of the Village was on Ohio Route

741 north of its intersection with Ohio Route 63 west of Lebanon. The South, Center, East, Grist Mill, Square, and North Families were all built along Route 741. At the height of its prosperity, Union Village encompassed 4,500 acres and over one hundred buildings.

The Shakers established several other colonies in Ohio and there were also colonies in Kentucky and briefly in Indiana. Union Village was the largest of all the western colonies, but unfortunately there is little left of it today.

GEORGE DELL was born in Middletown, Ohio, in 1901. As a youth, he watched in awe as great teams of draft horses pulled wagons filled with soberly dressed Shakers down the streets of Middletown for their once-a-year visit to "the world." Dell was entranced by the Shakers' Puritanical appearance, which contrasted greatly with that of the hundreds of foreigners and Kentuckians who had been attracted to the mills of Middletown. As he grew older, Dell walked the several miles from Middletown to see the Shaker colony, but by then, the Shakers were gone—the colony was closed in 1912, and only the buildings and ghosts remained to tell their stories.

In 1918 Dell moved to Columbus to attend Capital University. He soon found the stalls of the secondhand booksellers and began to acquire a collection of publications of the Ohio Archaeological and Historical Society. Some of the volumes contained articles about the Union Village Shaker colony. Dell intensified his search for books that told more of the Shaker story. On visits home to Middletown he made forays out to Union Village, which had been taken over as the Otterbein Home, and was able to go into the buildings to see the double sets of stairs, the great kitchens, and the austerity of the Meeting House.

For the next fifty years, Dell was involved with education—his own and then that of thousands of students he taught at Capital University. During those years he made many trips to Middletown to visit his sisters and frequently made short stops at Union Village en route. Dell retired from teaching in 1970. In 1973 he began writing *Dance unto the Lord,* a story that would ensure that Union Village would not be forgotten.

VICKI TIECHE

Chapter 1

T HEY HAD been at work since early morning, and now it was getting muddy again, for it always seemed to get muddy when the
sun stood over the forest trees. And, as usual, they had accomplished little—it seemed the patch of corduroy through the low spot
on the Swamp Road would never be completed. It was Richard's job
to drive the oxen, the Robinsons' own oxen, Midge and Frank, the
finest team in that part of the country, saving only the great beasts
the Shakers cherished. And it was Richard's job also to see that the
Berzinskis didn't abuse the oxen when they took over with their
crows and pikes to get the fifteen-foot length of oak or ash or hickory into place. Harmon Berzinski, the old man, was up in the woods
with Richard's own father, but the two Berzinski boys, Herman and
Jake, both of them giants, had the job of setting the logs across the
road and getting them tight enough that a horse couldn't drive his
hoof between them.

Richard hated the Berzinskis, all of them, saving only one, and
he thought that they deserved his hate. They must be foreigners
from their name, and they looked like foreigners, with round faces,
reddish hair, high cheekbones, and squinty eyes. All but one, the last
one, Ruth, who looked and acted something like a human being, despite the fact that she was abused by the whole tribe. Richard loved
Ruth, or he thought that he could love her, if he ever got the chance.
Ruth had black hair and her face was not Mongolian, her eyes were
not yellow but brown, and she was never profane or abusive. It was
a pity that the tribe ran her from dawn to dark, the two big cows,
Asenath and her dim-witted sister Rachel, neither of whom had ever
married, acting like Ruth was some kind of dirt under their feet.
Ruth did what cleaning was done in the Berzinski cabin, she boiled

the pot and fixed the vittles, and she had to wait on table while all the rest of the Berzinski hogs ate. That was a God's mercy in a way, for Richard knew that Ruth scraped and wiped off the tin dishes after the meals were over. The plates weren't clean, but they were cleaner than they would have been if Asenath had had to clean them. Most of the Berzinskis helped, of course, for they licked their dishes with their tongues before they left the puncheon table, slurping with great gusto and taking no particular care to keep their noses out of the gravy.

"Come on, boy, come on! Get the dam' log down here!"

Richard didn't pay much attention, and he didn't goad the oxen. Inch by inch and foot by foot the great round of oak was dragged nearer and nearer, and finally the beasts mounted the wooden platform already half buried in mud. Richard stopped them then and unhooked the log chain.

Jake blew his nose with his fingers and stepped up with his pike. "Guess maybe you might as well get your ass on up to the house," he said lugubriously. "Eatin' time. Sun's over the big sycamore, an' that means it's eatin' time."

"I'll have to go on back up to the woods and tell them," said Richard.

"All you got to do's holler."

"They can't hear when they're sawin'."

At that Herman let out a beller like a wounded bull. "Guess maybe they'll hear that," he said. "Git them critters out o' here so's we can swing the stick around."

Richard got the critters out and kept on going across the platform of corduroy already laid. They had chinked it with mud, but it was still a little rough in places. It wouldn't be rough for long—the droppings from the trees and mud from the wagon wheels going over would soon make it a passable road. It was a shame that it couldn't reach clear on down to the Lebanon Pike, but that was too far, a good quarter mile away. However, the corduroy would make the Robinson acres a great deal more valuable and accessible because their land lay across from and beyond the Berzinskis and abutted the thousands of acres owned by the Shakers of Union Village. It had been old Harmon Berzinski, however, who had insisted on the corduroy, because without it he couldn't very well get up to his north field.

At the top of the rise the Berzinski cabin came into sight, really two eighteen-by-fifteen-foot cabins, with a shake roof in between. The north cabin had been the first one, and it went clear on back to Jefferson's, or even Washington's, time. No one knew anymore who had built it, but there the Berzinski kids had been born, and there they had lived like wild foxes until the country began to get a little more settled. The south cabin had gone up only eight or ten years ago, and was now used for pigs, chickens, and the Berzinski cow. Both cabins had good fieldstone fireplaces and chimneys, at least for the first eight feet, after which, like everybody else's, they were nothing but daub and wattle. Like most other cabins in the country there was a single door on each, and a single window opposite the door that was covered with oiled paper but could be sealed tight during the winter. The Robinsons had finally got glass for their windows, but glass was hard to come by, and it was treacherous stuff to bring up from Cincinnati.

It was inside that the Berzinski cabin was something of a mess, for it had nothing but a dirt floor, although the floor was always so littered that a person couldn't be sure that he was standing on dirt. There was everything imaginable on the floor, old clothes, a smelly bearskin, potato peelings, dried cow paddies, and any litter the Berzinskis pushed off the table. Three corners of the cabin were taken up with beds, rude slab and cornshuck beds, each of them anchored to the side walls and to a heavy fork driven into the floor. Ma and Pa Berzinski slept in one, the two giant boys in the second, and all three of the girls in the third. Since Asenath and Rachel were both immense, Richard figured that Ruth had a sorry time of it, because she had to sleep between her two sisters.

Richard drove the oxen to an open shed that also served for a barn, and brought an armful of hay so that they could eat. That done, he dawdled a while, although his sweaty skin began to feel cold in the March air. He didn't want to go into the cabin before someone else appeared—it just didn't seem decent. Actually he would have preferred going home to eat, although that would have taken a while. His father and he had tried that at first, but the Berzinskis had protested because that meant losing more than an hour right out of the middle of the day. Richard knew what was in his father's mind—he didn't like to eat Berzinski filth either. But he had never said a word about his qualms, only gently nodded his head and acquiesced as he almost always did. Richard admired him for that. His father was a gentleman—not a high-falutin' born gentleman like some of the braggarts who came down the Ohio River from the East and paraded around as if they owned the whole West—but a natural gentleman, with instinctive courtesy and kindness. His father was educated too—it was he who had taught Richard to read and write and had instructed him in the mysteries of numbers. He wasn't a churchly man, but from things he had said from time to time Richard thought that he must have come from a churchly Pennsylvania family. Presbyterian he had been, and Presbyterian he might have remained if the Shaker missionaries from Mount Lebanon, New York, had stayed out of the Ohio country. It was a curious story, and Richard had heard his father tell it many times, how just about at the turn of the century the great Kentucky Revival, begun pretty much by Presbyterian preachers, had induced the Shakers in New York to send out what they called missionaries. They came about 1805, three of them, Issacher Bates, John Meacham, and Benjamin Seth Youngs, walking all the way from New York State with a single packhorse and wandering down through Kentucky and into Tennessee and back to Columbia on the Ohio River. It was an easy step from there to the Presbyterian congregations on Turtle Creek, Clear Creek south of Franklin, Bethany east of Lebanon, and Big Prairie at the mouth of Dick's Creek. The curious thing was that the Presbyterian congregations had swallowed the Shaker propaganda hook, line, and sinker. The congregation at Turtle Creek (Union Village they called it now) had gone over to the Shakers in a body, their preacher, an intelligent and godly man named Richard McNemar, almost the first convert. Then Malcolm Worley, a rich farmer, had deeded the Shakes his land and stock, and so had a lot of the others. And then, from Union Village, the Shakers had branched out, to a place they called Watervliet near the little town of Dayton, and to one named Whitewater, which was clear out west of Cincinnati and near the Indiana line. They had reached farther than that, to Pleasant Hill and South Union in Kentucky, and clear up to North Union, near the town called Cleveland, which was on the lake. But they hadn't been able to gobble up Abraham Robinson. Richard's father only shook his head and sighed whenever he talked about the matter. It wasn't true, what the Shakers said; it couldn't be true. All men were predestined—it said so right in the Bible. Those who were called and chosen were sanctified, and that was the long and the short of it. And Jesus Christ hadn't appeared a second time in the shape of some English woman who had been named Ann Lee. And it wasn't sinful to marry and have children—God said that right in Genesis. "Be fruitful and multiply and replenish the earth." Anything else was but human error, and people who went against the Bible would likely be damned.

The cabin door opened then and Asenath came out and stared at Richard while he stood with his hands on his hips. "What you starin' at, boy?" she wanted to know.

Richard blushed. "I was just thinkin'," he said. "I guess everybody's comin' up for dinner."

"Well, you won't git it thataway," said Asenath. "You want your dinner, you better come inside."

And with that she picked up a wooden bucket and slopped back in.

Richard stood on the little Berzinski hill that looked out over the west woods. A flock of crows were noisy back in the trees, and high in the sky a lonesome buzzard was soaring on seemingly lifeless wings. It was a bright day, and bright days in March had to be cherished. But it was a shame they had to eat at the Berzinskis.

INSIDE THE Berzinski cabin there was a sort of gray twilight, lit only by the lambent flames of the great fire, over which a black smudged pot was boiling with some sort of stew. But that was not the dinner—dinner was already on the plank table, something that was said to be fried squirrel, and, of course, the inevitable pone and gravy. The men sat at the table; the women had effaced themselves as much as possible, although there was really no retreat in the cabin. The old witch (that was how she was known, for her skill in simples was rumored throughout the whole countryside) sat beside the fire in a hickory chair, her face as inscrutable as if it had been carved in Egypt. Mrs. Berzinski's was a name to conjure with in the community for some five miles around. And the cabin was some attestation of her skill—great bunches of borage, basil, fennel, camomile, dogbane, purslane, parsley, mullein, tansy, and perhaps a hundred other herbs hung helter-skelter from the cabin beams, so much so that passage across the cabin was precarious. The chief fame of the old witch was that she was a skilled baby-jerker, and ten or a dozen times a year someone came howling in the night to fetch her to some remote cabin. On such occasions she gathered her apron full of rags and whatever herbs she thought she might need and went spectrally out the door of the cabin. And spectral she remained throughout whatever sort of bad trip there might be. Her face as thin as that of a hawk, she looked like some sort of doomsday woman, and in simple truth she was as much feared as honored. She subscribed to no school of medicine except perhaps the oldest: that of believing that there was always some available specific for purging, treating snakebite, causing milk to flow, or ridding a sufferer of a monstrous big bellyache. In consequence this was her main occupation in the world, and from spring to late autumn she was always in the fields and woods culling out the leaves, twigs, roots, and barks that she knew—or thought she knew—were efficacious.

The two cows, Asenath and Rachel, some twenty-five and twenty-seven years old, kept out of the way of their mother, and now sat far back in the shadows on the other side of the fire. Asenath, particularly in late years, had decided that she must be her mother's understudy, and on most occasions went with her when there was a new baby to be torn into the world. But Asenath did not have, and never would possess, her mother's skill. The spark of whatever genius was necessary, whether from God or the Devil, was simply not in Asenath's possession. Cow-eyed, she stood and stared, or sat and stared, and only when she was told what to do did she seem to have the slightest ability to do anything. Her mother did profit from her strength: when there was white walnut to scrape, up or down for emetic or purge, Asenath wielded the knife with something of maniacal energy. The same was true of digging seng roots, or sassafras. All that Asenath lacked was inspiration, and the light of Heaven had simply never descended on her head. Wrapped in a blanket and immobile on the far side of the fire, her thick lips open and her doll eyes staring, her long hair a mantle around her shoulders, Asenath might have been mummified. It would have been a God's grace if she had been.

And whatever Asenath was, Rachel was, except that Rachel had no skills whatsoever. Rachel had been born dull-witted, and though she could follow like a puppy, that was about all she could do. Once, long years ago, Rachel had borne a child, and since no one else had come near her, it was inferred that one of her brothers was the father. No one had ever made the direct accusation, and mercifully the child had died. It is doubtful if Rachel even remembered that she had once been a mother.

And so they sat at table, Harmon Berzinski at the head, or end, then Richard's father and Richard on his right side, and the two big louts Jake and Herman on the other. They ate noisily, and wordlessly, the business of life being in getting some partially warm food down into their bellies. And noiselessly Ruth moved back and forth between the fireplace and the table, and although Richard pretended not to watch her, he could not help himself. Harmon, her father, complained about everything. The damn squirrel tasted like rat. What was the matter with the pone that it was so gritty? And why wasn't the maple syrup any sweeter? Since these were rhetorical questions Ruth never tried to answer any of them. The other three women sat and stared either into the fire or into space, the men were loud and profane, and like a shadow Ruth's shape kept flitting back and forth across the firelight. Richard studied her face, but it betrayed nothing. Nor did she seem to be in the least apologetic that her feet were bare and her long hair simply pushed back over her shoulders. It was almost as if she were leading a dual life, one outward, one inward behind the passive mask of her face. Richard wondered if he'd get a chance to have a word with her before they left, but that seemed an improbability, since he would have to linger until everyone else was out the door. And he wanted that word—he wanted to renew old acquaintance. He knew Ruth: she was both gay and light-hearted, and thoughtful. She was smart, too. For some two or three years a wandering schoolmaster, Mr. Ellers, had taught a class in the old Presbyterian church, and Ruth had been the smartest of the seven kids in class. They had both been about ten or twelve at that time, and they had been able to go to school only during the autumn and spring, since the winter roads were impassable. Then, for some obscure reason, Mr. Ellers moved to Lebanon and tried to start a singing school. Richard knew that from hearsay. But the singing school had petered out, and as silently as he had come, Mr. Ellers had vanished. And so had almost all hope of getting any kind of an education.

Richard was suddenly jolted from his abstraction—his father and old Harmon seemed to have provoked some sort of quarrel. If not quarrel, then simple difference. Richard was not afraid—his father was circumspect, and wouldn't lower himself enough to quarrel with one of the Berzinskis. But Harmon had started to pound the table with his fist, and his face was getting red.

"O' course they ought to be burned out!" he was shouting. "What we really ought to do is get a whole mess o' fellers and wipe them off the face o' the earth. All that they're doin' is gobblin' up the whole dam' country. Lookat Marshall—he had to sell out. And jus' try and git them to do somethin' for you. Take a load o' corn up to their damn grist mill, or ast to have some planks sawed. Or maybe you need some blacksmithin' done, or a rim comes off'n one of your wagon wheels. You tryin' to tell me the Shakes'll help you?"

Harmon glared, and half pushed up to hang over Richard's father, but Richard knew his father could not be bullied.

"You don't understand," Mr. Robinson said quite casually. "It's only a matter of who comes first. I don't blame the Shakers if they want to use their own machinery and shops for themselves. When they're not too busy, they'll help you, if you ask them right."

Harmon snorted. "An' jus' how in the hell is that?" he wanted to know. "You don' think I'm goin' to git down on my knees and kiss anybody's ass, do you? Take the mill down at Morrow or over at Lebanon. All you got to do there is get in line an' wait your turn."

"You don't understand," Mr. Robinson said again. "You're missing the whole idea—I mean the whole idea what's behind the Shakers. They don't want to live in the world. They don't truck with it any more than they have to."

"They send out their peddlers an' sell their dam' seeds and brooms, don't they?"

"They're good seeds and brooms. Nobody has to buy them. Personally, I think they're doing me a favor."

At that Harmon snorted and swept his hand so violently in front of him that he sent a few of the tin plates flying. "You jus' ain' got the sense God give little green geese!" he said. "That ain' the way I live. Way I live is try to do a little for the other feller, and expect him to do a lot more for me. An' I don't want nobody mixin' up my mind an' tellin' me I'm goin' to be damned because I don' believe in some silly female who said she was Jesus Christ. Seems to me God knows that He ought to wipe them off'n the face o' the earth."

Mr. Robinson got up from the table. "Maybe we better get back up to the woods," he suggested. "Maybe we can work off some of our temper thataway."

Harmon's face was black, but he got up, and after him Jake and Herman. Richard pretended some further interest in his plate. The three older women still sat immobile, and Ruth stood with her back to the fire, her long linsey-woolsey dress clear down below her knees. Richard dawdled as long as he could, and happily noticed when he moved towards the door that Ruth had made a step or two in his direction. That fact gave him courage, and with the doorlatch unfastened he swung suddenly and made a motion for her to come nearer. When she did, he was so pleased that he found himself speechless.

"You want something?" he heard her say.

His face flushed. "I'd just sort of like to see you again, Ruth," he said softly.

He was pleased to see the color mount to her cheeks, and that gave him courage to continue. "Maybe tomorrow, up in the woods," he suggested. "It's Sunday tomorrow. Could you come on up?"

The light seemed to go out of Ruth's eyes, and she shook her head ever so slightly. "I don't think so," she said softly. "I'll try maybe, but I don't think so."

And with that he had to go. Jake and Herman were already halfway down the hill with their axes and pike poles, and the two older men were walking apart, as if they didn't want anything more to do with one another. Richard went back to the oxen out under the shed roof and got them under way. It would be a cold afternoon, and only work would make it seem tolerable.

THAT NIGHT at home there was more discussion about the Shakers and their strange doctrine. They sat in the circle of firelight, the iron teakettle boiling on the hob, a giant maple log burning, and the three of them relaxed and well content. As usual Mrs. Robinson had wanted to know all the events of the day—she was lonesome during the winter when she was pretty much confined to the house, although she did insist on doing the milking. It was better during the summer when she could get out to her garden and posies. And she always had a fine garden, calico beans and corn and a great patch of potatoes, and greens and herbs. Mary Robinson cherished the garden stuff, and she dutifully salted and pickled and put a lot of things up in stone jars. But her greatest joy was her posies, and posies she had, although the Johnny-jump-ups and hill daisies perhaps made braver bouquets. There were cabbage roses planted outside the cabin, and they had always come through the winter, and there were marigolds and phlox and tansy and all such things.

"Well, I didn't agree with him," Richard's father was saying. "He's the kind that would like nothing better than to get up a mob and go over to Shakertown and burn down a few buildings. He ain't got no more sense than that in his fool head."

"They're good people," said Richard's mother piously. "They don't do nobody no harm."

Richard looked at her as she sat knitting another wamus or scarf or whatever it was. At forty-five his mother's luster had faded, although she was still good-looking. But her yellow hair had tarnished, and her figure had become too full. She was several years past forty-five now. He loved his mother for her industry and courage, but what he liked particularly was that she seemed to have a level head. His father was level-headed too, but there had been occasions when he had wanted to do something outrageous, like pull up stakes and move on out into Iowa. From the way he told it the corn grew fifteen feet high out in Illinois and Iowa, and all the farmers were getting rich. His mother never at first demurred, only gently reminded him that they had a very good living in Warren County. Then, a day or so later, she would point out to him the enormous hazards in selling out what they knew was a good farm and going out into the prairie country. She doubted that there would be wood to burn. And they'd have to give up their sugar trees, and Heaven knew if they'd be able to buy short sweetening. Maybe in St. Louis, but St. Louis might be two weeks away. That is, if they had any ready cash. It did seem a sort of shame. Richard's father never admitted as much, but his wife's doubts somehow cleared his mind. The venture into Indiana or Illinois or Iowa would be mentioned a few times more, almost wistfully, and then it would be completely forgotten.

"What I don't understand," Richard found himself saying, "is why they think what they think's true. I mean the Shakers. How do they know what they say is true?"

"They don't," said his father promptly. "But, to be fair, neither does anybody else. Nobody can prove his religion's true, Catholics, or Jews, or nobody. He just thinks so."

Richard chewed that over in his mind a little while he reached down and patted old Mose, who was curled against his knee.

"If he don't know it's true, why does he think so?" he demanded. "Don't we even know there's a God."

"We think so," said his father promptly. "It stands to reason that there ought to be some sort of power behind this universe. All those stars up in the sky, and the sun and moon and everything. And mountains and the tides, and things like that. Even the seasons. They always come back again, just as if somebody was telling them to."

"Then what's so different? I mean what's so different about Shakers. Don't they have the same right to believe what they can't prove as anybody else?"

His father sat and stared for a while then. "They think they can prove what they say," he said finally. "They believe Christ came again, and lived right over in New York with them. Ann Lee. I don't know very much about her, but I guess she was a good woman. People say she was married back in England and had a whole passel of young 'uns. Most or all of them died. Then she felt some sort of awakening inside her and she began to preach and prophesy. And then she came over to this country with the disciples who believed in her, and they finally got on a good farm at Mt. Lebanon, New York. That's where the people come from who started Union Village."

Richard only stared into the fire and kept on patting the dog. "When did she say marriage was sinful?" he at last wanted to know.

"I don't know when precisely," his father answered. "What she taught was that Adam and Eve were the father and mother of the physical man, and Jesus Christ and herself were the father and mother of the spiritual man. You see, the Shakers believe that God is both male and female, or neither, whichever you want to believe. But they're always quoting the passage in the Bible that says, 'God created man in His own image, in the image of God created He him, male and female created He them.' So you see, that says it in a way; if Scripture's right in saying His image is both male and female."

"You don't think of God that way, do you?"

His father smiled. "I don't see how it's possible," he said. "I don't know what being male or female would have to do with God. I think of God as Beauty and Power and Compassion, and all kinds of things like that. I think of God when I see sunrise and sunset, or watch the woods break out in the spring. Or see almost anything growing. I think of God as something or somebody able to help me out when I get in a jam. That's the way I think of Him."

His mother looked up from her knitting and smiled. "I think of God as the Power that's able to bring babies into the world," she said. "That's what I thought of when you were born, Richard. I thanked God."

Richard's father got up from his hickory chair then and fetched The Book from the stand over near the corner bedstead. They read a chapter every night, and they were slowly working their way through the Pastoral Letters. It all seemed mysterious and strange to Richard, almost impossible, that there could have been life so long ago, and that there had been such depth of persuasion and such conviction of truth. If he were honest, he would have to say that he didn't understand Jesus Christ at all, didn't comprehend how men would risk all and dare all to bear witness of Him in an alien and hostile world. And, if it were true, that He had been God, and that God had moved among men, then it might be true that He had come again, only this time in women's form. But it didn't seem possible.

Abraham Robinson opened the big book and slowly started reading, and with that Richard stopped patting the dog and saw his mother fold her hands and close her eyes. "I exhort therefore," read his father, "that, first of all, supplications, prayers, intercessions, and giving of thanks, be made for all men; for kings and for all that are in authority, that we may lead a quiet and peaceable life in all godliness, for this is good and acceptable in the sight of God, our Savior, who will have all men to be saved, and to come unto the knowledge of the truth."

ON SUNDAY Ruth waited a long time, biding her opportunity, but it seemed as if her opportunity would never come. Sundays in the Berzinski family were a fright, for the men insisted on lying around the house, drinking corn liquor, and spitting tobacco juice. And on winter Sundays, when there was little opportunity to go out, there were just too many bodies in the way for Ruth to do anything.

Despite that fact, the whole tribe insistently complained of what they wanted done for them. Rachel hugged the fire, as usual, but Asenath was always indisposed, and rarely got out of bed until after noon. Harmon perhaps was the worst of the lot; all he could think of doing was swilling liquor from his big stone jug while he sat at the table and made insane remarks about everything.

Opportunity—what little opportunity offered—came when the sun was two hours past the meridian. For some unknown reason Mrs. Berzinski suddenly had a peremptory demand for some moss, preferably green moss, although dried would do. She had been cooking a brew in the little kettle, although no one knew, or cared, the reason. Now suddenly she began clamoring, and approached Herman to go out and look around the barn. Herman paid no attention to her whatsoever. Asenath came next, and Asenath simply remarked slumbrously that she didn't have no coat fitten to go out in the weather. Harmon was sleeping drunk and lay over the table. And for some reason, probably because she was brewing the little pot, the old witch thought she couldn't go after the moss herself.

By that time, the time of final refusals, Ruth had worked her feet into the only boots she had, and was throwing on her only coat, an old gray woolen affair that Jake had once lined with deerskin. The coat was still serviceable, although it had little comfort and no beauty whatsoever, but it was all Ruth had. Actually the coat belonged to no one—it was the outhouse coat, and so used by all the women in turn. When she turned from the fire and finally saw Ruth dressed, the old witch snorted. "You look around out there," she ordered. "Look back o' the privy. All I want's a handful." Ruth said nothing. Once she was out of the cabin she knew that no one would be able to see her, and she meant to head immediately for the north woods. Heaven knew that she needed a breath of fresh air, even though the time for meeting Richard Robinson might be long past. He'd most likely have gone out soon after dinner, and, if Ruth could read his mind, he would have headed west and north. There was a great stand of white oaks, hickories, and beeches over near the Shaker acres, open woods, where one's face wasn't always lashed with briers. Better yet, it was something of a secret spot, since it was in a slight cup of the hills, and ringed around by the almost impenetrable blackberry jungles. There were junipers there too, great and small junipers, and although they were very prickly, Ruth loved their dark green against the winter snows.

Ruth went down the hill and over the patch of new corduroy along the road, and then beyond the bridge swung hard left following an icy little stream that was edged with frost. The woods were frozen into silence; there were rabbit and fox tracks aplenty, but not one creature moved. More curiously, there were no birds in the trees or in the sky. Sometimes in summer the whole sky would be darkened with passenger pigeons, and in autumn the wedges of geese would dart arrowswift across the sky. But this day acted as if it might be a weather-breeder—it was too spectrally still.

Ruth crossed through Copperhead Hollow (the copperheads, if any were left, were fast asleep in the cold rocks), then bore north until she came out onto one of the Robinson fields. There were still a few corn shocks standing there, and as usual the ground around them was littered with the telltale evidence of raccoons, rats, and mice. Then, beyond Robinsons', came the great woods, not yet Shaker, although it was said that the Shakers had their eyes on it. Ruth was torn plenty then, but she kept on her course, crossing the great woods diagonally, and aiming for the more open stand of beech and white oak. Once—or perhaps more than once—she and Richard had gone there for a moment's silence and peace, and with a woman's intuition she judged that if he were out at all, that was where he would be.

But at last, when she came to the end of the thickety woods and climbed over the rail fence that some forgotten pioneer had split out to mark his holding, she saw with disappointment that there was no one in the beech woods. Ruth went down the gentle hill nevertheless, and started across through the trees. Beyond the beech woods, ringed in by more of the thick brush and trees, was what was called Jehovah's Chosen Square. Once—and only once—Richard and she had been fortunate enough to see the Shakers dance there, wheeling and whirling, singing and droning in their chests, and making what they called a joyful noise unto the Lord. Ruth had been only fourteen at the time, but she had thought the proceedings very strange. The Shakers danced every Sunday, of course, or almost every Sunday, but always in the Meeting House. But not in winter, when the Meeting House could not be heated. And, as far as Ruth knew, there was no way of reasoning when one of the chief Elders would ordain that on some particular summer Sunday they would dance in Jehovah's Chosen Square. It had happened in all of the summer months, and it had even happened after the leaves came down in October. The Square itself was not too large, perhaps less than two hundred feet across, but it was kept carefully mowed and cleaned of all brush and debris.

But Richard was not in Jehovah's Chosen Square. Hidden in the surrounding thickets, Ruth looked out carefully, and felt her heart fall. It would be a long way home, and the members of her family would be so angry with her she could not imagine what would happen. Her father and mother never beat her. But Herman and Jake were not that kind, and Asenath might very easily knock her down, particularly if it became time to get supper. That was Ruth's job, and no one in the family was in the least interested in taking it away from her.

Ruth headed straight for the Robinson barn buildings, going through the thick woods, and on through the briers and field of corn. There were two Robinson barns, a good log that harbored the horses, cows, and oxen, and a long lean-to divided for sheep and hogs. The Robinson house, or cabin, was some hundred feet farther east. Ruth had never been inside the Robinson house for the simple reason that she had never been invited. She had heard folks say that it was real cosy in there. But the Robinsons were clannish, and didn't seem to take to strangers. They did their share in barn-raising and things like that, but they never came down the road asking for favors.

Ruth slowed down as she got near the end of the big cornfield. She really didn't know whether she wanted to go on or not, and in truth she didn't know whether she wanted to have any truck with Richard or not. He was a nice boy—he looked good with his brown eyes and ash-brown hair that fell down about his shoulders. And he was big enough too, not so big as Jake or Herman, but big enough. She wouldn't really mind having him for the father of her children. But that was part of the trouble—the Robinsons were so stand-off-ish that she doubted they'd ever accept her. What they didn't know was that she didn't ever mean to have another Berzinski pig sty. She'd have a clean cabin—or a little brick house if they ever got able to burn some of their own clay—and there would be flowers about the door, and maybe going all the way around the house and yard.

Hollyhocks would last for years, and they looked real sassy and homey in summer. And there would be geraniums too—they lasted over the winter if a person dug them and hung them upside down. And inside there would be a puncheon floor, and big round rag rugs on it, and the fireplace would be swept with a turkey wing every day. And then, after the babies came, there'd have to be a cradle and a trundle bed, and maybe a big highboy shaped out of dark cherry wood that would hold the cups and plates.

Ruth saw Richard then—he came around the corner of the big barn and stood for a moment looking back towards the woods before he spied her. The moment he did he came running and vaulted the rail fence that ran across the yard. She was prepared for that, but she wasn't prepared for his embrace. It was the first time she had ever been hugged by a man, and it fairly crushed the breath out of her. But she liked it—she liked it a lot.

"You tired?" Richard was standing over her, looking down at her eyes, and Ruth knew he wanted her to say she wasn't too tired.

"I guess maybe I could go on for a piece," she said. "I been clear back to the Square. You weren't there."

He grabbed her hand and swung her around.

"I was there," he said as they started to walk back to the woods. "I been there twice, once before noon, and once after. I thought maybe you couldn't come."

Ruth laughed a little, and he put his arm around her and carried her on that way.

"You don't know how much I been wanting to see you," he said. "I been so lonesome this winter I don't know what to do. We don't have anything to read. There was a *Western Star* Papa got over in Lebanon, but I been through it so many times I can say it by heart. That's all, except the old Speller we had with Mr. Ellers. I know all them words."

"We had a book once, but Herman threw it into the fire," said Ruth. "It came all the way up from Cincinnati. It was by some man called Milton."

Richard knotted his brows. The name was faintly familiar, but he couldn't place it. But he would have liked to read that book by Milton. He would like to read any book. He had read in the big red Bible, but the excitement had worn out of that a little.

"What I been thinking," he said after they had come through

the briers and then out into the beech wood, "What I been thinking is that it's getting time for us both to wonder what's going to happen to us. We can't just go on living at home. How old are you, seventeen or eighteen?"

Ruth flushed a little. "You're nineteen, and I'll be nineteen in June," she said. "Same as always. You're just five months older than I am. Why?"

Richard kicked at a clod. "Just that it's about time we start thinking about settling down," he said. "Long about that time in life people have to think about getting their own place. You know what I mean."

Ruth smiled and nestled close. "I don't know what you mean unless you're asking me to marry you," she said. "There's nothing different about that. I always intended to."

It was Richard's turn to be a bit frightened. "I never said so," he countered. "I never asked you."

"You always asked me," said Ruth. "You walked up and down the road with me, and you acted like you owned me. Even when we were only twelve or thirteen. And I didn't mind. I liked you to like me."

Richard stood and stared, not at her, but clear across the woods to the tangle of trees around Jehovah's Chosen Square. "You don't put no truck in what the Shakers say, then," he said. "You think it's all right. To live together."

"I don't believe in no nonsense," said Ruth.

"You don't think the world is coming to an end. That's what some of the preachers say."

"Ain't nothing we can do about it, if it is, is there?" asked Ruth. "It's been here a powerful long time."

Richard picked up a fallen branch and began switching it around in the air.

"I really don't know how to go about it," he confessed. "Once you're eighteen, you don't have to ask nobody. But we would have to have some way to live. Some way and some place."

Ruth nodded without lifting her eyes. It was all too true—there was just no way to get a start. A new family needed a few acres, and some tools, and the help of neighbors in running up a cabin. And they needed something to eat until they could get a few crops in. Or—they needed money. But neither she nor Richard possessed a copper, let alone the dollars necessary to see them through a hard first year.

"All that matters right now," said Ruth, "is whether or not you love me. I mean really. Do you?"

"I want you," said Richard truthfully. "I don't know if I know what love is. I expect maybe it grows if a person just gives it a chance."

"It grows," said Ruth with assurance. "It festers up like a boil, and then it breaks."

Richard had to smile at that, and when she saw him smiling she herself laughed. "It just come to mind," she said. "I couldn't tell aforehand that it wasn't fitting."

They walked back hand in hand, only this time they bore south, so that Ruth would come out of the woods nearer home. And there were no assurances at parting. Ruth did remember, after she had gone down to the new corduroy, that she had been expected to bring back a little patch of moss. She found it on one of the bridge rails, and went on up towards the cabin. She had begun to wonder what the family would say or do to her.

THAT NIGHT, after his father had carried the Book back to the shelf and returned to the fire for the few minutes they always spent there before they went to bed, Richard blurted out his secret. "I was back in the woods with Ruth Berzinski this afternoon," he said, and tried to control his voice so that it would not sound guilty. His father said nothing, and made no sign that he had heard. His mother went on with the knitting that she had picked up just as soon as they had finished saying the Lord's Prayer.

"I knowed you was gone," she said finally. "I could have stood some help with the milking, since it's Sunday, and seem's as how you didn't have much else to do."

"I was back in the woods," Richard said again. "Ruth and I like each other. We're thinking about setting up, if we can find a way."

At that his father made some sort of head noise. "There ain't no hurry," he said. "What your mother and I want is for you to have a chance to make up your mind. You haven't met any girls."

Richard certainly didn't think that was very fair.

"I can't think that that's my fault," he said. "I'm always at home. Maybe if I had a job in the mill down at Morrow or over at Lebanon, or even got on the canal way over in Middletown I'd have a chance. But Ruth's the only girl I know."

"That's the trouble," said his mother immediately. "She's the only girl you know."

Richard felt a bit angry. "She's all right," he said a bit truculently. "Ruth's all right."

His father simply nodded his head a few times.

"She may be and she mayn't be," he said. "There's no way for you to know. One thing's certain, however—she's a Berzinski. And the whole passel of Berzinskis aren't all right. In fact, they're just about all wrong."

"Ruth's not like that," said Richard. "She's not like the rest of them."

"She's got Berzinski blood in her, hasn't she?"

"She's not a Berzinski in the way she acts and talks," Richard defended. "And she does all the work over there."

His father nodded. "She does that," he said. "And she does seem like a good girl. But I don't want you making up with her before you know your own mind. Besides that, getting married isn't as easy as it sounds. Where would you live?"

Richard flushed. "I was thinking that maybe she could come here," he said. "I mean, until we get a start. We wouldn't like anything better than to have our own house."

His mother put down her knitting at that. For a long time she sat and stared in front of her, and then, almost inaudibly, Richard heard her words: "We'd have to say good-bye to our home," she declared. "No two women ever belong under the same roof. It's different with men—they can get out so that they're not running into each other all the time. But women are caught inside, and have to run into each other. One wants to do a thing one way, and the other wants to do it another. It just won't work."

"Your mother was a Henderson, don't forget that," said his father. "That's why you are what you are, why you got such a good head on your shoulders. The Hendersons come through the Gap and on up into Kentucky way back in the last century."

Richard became angry inside. He had heard the story of the proud Hendersons a hundred times, had been weaned on it. His father's folks were likely as good, but nothing was ever said about them. It was always the Hendersons, with their rifle-shooting and cabin-building and raids against the Ohio Indians. And somehow they had been able to grab onto thousands of acres of good bottom land.

"I just thought I'd tell you," Richard said, and stood up to stretch himself before the fire. "I figured you ought to know how Ruth and I think about each other."

His father nodded his head. "You think on it," he advised. "Not for just tonight. I mean for maybe a year or two. And ask yourself how you'd feel being married to the whole pack of Berzinskis. Might even drive you out of your mind."

That was all that was said, and the next morning and the days following nothing was said. And Richard didn't have an opportunity to see Ruth again. And so the winter wore away.

BUT IF the winter wore away, the hurt in Richard's heart did no such thing, and the more he thought about the matter, the angrier he became. Or if not angry, hurt. It was just not fair that there was no way to get a start in life, no way to go ahead when one knew full well what he wanted to do, and what was probably best to do. There were black slaves in Kentucky and all through the South, and in the north there were their counterparts, white slaves who received for their labor exactly as much as the black slaves, board and bed. And the owners of the slaves, and in the North that meant the parents, were always bragging about how well they had managed, when the simple truth was that much of what they gloated about was the product of their children's labor.

He thought again and again of running away. Not running, simply leaving. The trouble was that Ruth would probably not come with him, even if he were so imprudent as to ask her. And, even without her, it would take years to save up enough money to get a start. He'd have to go to Lebanon or Middletown, or probably even as far as Cincinnati, and once there he would have to find a job quickly so that he could support himself. And in the meantime Ruth would have to stand all the Berzinski abuse, and if Harmon got it into his head to marry her off to some lout, then there'd be a pretty penny to pay. The worst of it was that he couldn't see Ruth so that he could have a talk with her and lay any plans. Somehow or other the Berzinskis must have learned where she had gone that winter Sunday afternoon, and it seemed as if they were not permitting her to go far outside the cabin.

And so the lambs were born, and in April there were suckling pigs, and the frost went out of the fields, and Abraham Robinson got his seed corn ready and from time to time dropped a word about getting the ground ripped up so that they'd be able to plant when the dogwoods bloomed. And the freshets ran, and the dandelions covered every inch of the ground with their bright golden discs, and Richard carted the manure out to the fields under the high cumulus.

And, on a day in late April, without actually realizing what he was doing, Richard Robinson rolled up an extra woolen shirt in his heavy coat, and hid the bundle out under the clove bush by the lane. And that night, long after the house was still, he got up and sneaked out, patting old Mose fondly when the dog whined a bit. By morning he meant to be in Lebanon, and after that the gods would have to offer whatever they would.

IT WAS really a big little town, the few streets rutted and muddy, the only claim to fame being perhaps that the Golden Lamb was a convenient distance from Cincinnati, so that it had become a baiting place for man and beast. There were a few good houses, on Main Street mostly, and there was a brickyard, a chandler's shop, a general store, and a few other stores huddled in yellow brick and slab constructions. But there were many vacant lots, with criss-cross paths through them that led to hidden cabins and frame houses. Richard had been in Lebanon many times, but always before he had looked at it almost as if it were nothing but a picture in front of his eyes. Now he was looking at it in a different way, as a sort of Mecca that might offer him some reward for his pilgrimage. Lebanon, however, did not seem to understand his demands or desires. And the most peremptory one, that he was hungry and would like something to eat, Lebanon did not understand at all.

There had been a companion on the last of the miles into the town, a bluff and hearty old fellow who was named John Cheeseman, and who was driving in with pigmeat to sell on market. John Cheeseman had gone his own way when he let Richard down at the main pike, but in the next few hours Richard ran by him several times as he made his way up and down the wood sidewalks. He purposely hadn't told John Cheeseman any truth about himself, but Cheeseman had a pretty good head on his shoulders, and when Richard came by for the third time he asked him if he had had his breakfast. Richard lied and said he had, and John Cheeseman immediately concluded that there was no reason he shouldn't leave his stand for a quarter hour to have a drink and a bite of something to eat. The hams and the loins he had brought with him probably wouldn't be any worse for the few flies they attracted while he was gone.

Cheeseman knew the town like the inside of his hand, and led the way catercornered from Broadway and on over to a little shack on Sycamore Street. Richard stood moon-eyed and waited three steps away from the door while Cheeseman knocked, but there was not long to wait, for a rather pretty girl in a pink dress came, and immediately let out a scream of recognition. "Uncle John," she shouted, and threw her arms around Cheeseman's neck. John Cheeseman folded her in his arms and ran his big yellow mustache over her cheek. "How about your Mommy?" he inquired. "She up yet, Kathy?"

"She ain't up, but come on in," said Kathy, and swung the door wide.

The cabin was decent, and one end of it, the end where Mommy still presumably slept, was curtained off by some sort of yellow and pink cloth that fell from the loft to a foot from the floor. Because of that aperture Richard could see Mommy's bare feet moving around behind the curtain, and in due time they started reaching for a pair of felt slippers on the floor.

John Cheeseman settled himself onto a stool while Kathy stood in front of him and looked at him in a curious way, as if she wanted to know why he had come so early and knew that it wouldn't be good manners to ask. John Cheeseman, however, got out his pipe and soon had the room billowing with smoke.

"What we want's a little bit of breakfast," he told Kathy. "You suppose maybe you could fry us up a few cakes?"

Kathy giggled. "We was expectin' you for dinner, Uncle John," she said. "I don't know whether we got any cornmeal or not. I s'pose we have."

Cheeseman seemed not to be anxious. "You just get some

ready," he ordered. "A whole big stack. Richard here's hungry, and so am I. It's sort of chilly out there sittin' along the street, and I left home before even the roosters was up."

The curtain parted then and Mommy appeared, a buxom woman, not at all uncomely, and definitely the mother of Kathy because the two looked very much alike. Both of them had yellow blonde hair, and both of them had eyes that were a little too close together.

"You know you shouldn't come around here so early in the morning, Papa," she said, but she lovingly pushed Cheeseman's hat onto his forehead and tousled his hair. "How's Mamma—is she all right?"

"Fine as frog hair, Milly," said Cheeseman. "Got her a little misery in her back, but she allays does come through the winter with that. Where's Frank—he left already?"

"Frank's down in Cincy," said his daughter. "Got him a notion that there might be some stuff from the East on some of the steamboats coming down the river now. You know, curtains, and hats, and dresses, and all kinds of trash like that. Time to sell 'em is in spring, when people are fixin' up their houses and sewin'."

"This here's Richard," said Cheeseman. "Don't know the last of his handle, just met him on the pike comin' in. He's hungry."

Milly looked hard at Richard. "What's he doing in town?" she inquired.

Cheeseman only smiled, and patted her rump. "You know you ain't got no right to ask things like that," he reproved. "What he want's is breakfast."

Milly shook her head knowingly.

They ate, prodigiously, and Milly even got out a little store tea instead of the spicebush and sage everybody was accustomed to. "Don't have no coffee," she apologized. "Had us a pound that we saved for company, but it's hard to get and comes high. Maybe by Easter I'll persuade Frank to get me another pound."

Once breakfast was over they sat for a while while Cheeseman replenished his pipe. Only then did he ask the question that Richard had been too afraid to ask: whether Frank could possibly use Richard in the shop. He had not succeeded in getting the question out of his mouth before Milly shook her head negatively.

"Things is slow," she apologized. "All Frank does most of the day is sit around. What he's talking about is getting a horse and going peddling through the country. Kathy could look after the store."

Cheeseman nodded his head. "Just thought I'd ask," he explained. "Young fellow needs a job, best thing to do is ask everybody."

"He's got any sense in his head, he'll go right on down to the City," said Milly. "That's the place—things is a-doin' down there. Maybe get a job on one of the riverboats. Or start buildin'—they're buildin' a lot of stuff down around the Canal basin." And then, directly, as if she had finally decided to acknowledge Richard, "What's your name, boy?"

Richard told her.

"Why'd you run away from home?"

"I didn't run away," said Richard. "I just left. I got to find a way to make some money."

"Who don't?" asked Milly. "You just tell me, who don't."

John Cheeseman got up after that. "Had me a few hogs I butchered durin' that cold snap we had at the end of March," he explained. "Larded them down, but it's gettin' a little too warm to keep the stuff so I brought it in to sell on market. What'd you rather have, loin or a ham?"

Milly wrinkled her nose. "I don't like fresh ham," she said. "Plain truth is I don't like hog. Not anymore. That's all we get, hog. What I want's a good roast out of the middle of a big bull."

"Who don't?" Cheeseman imitated her. "I'll bring you up a loin when I come back for dinner."

They went out then, unceremoniously, but the way back up to Broadway through the sparkly grass didn't seem long with food in their bellies. When they came to the stand Richard held out his hand to say good-bye, but Cheeseman fumbled in his pocket first, and when he clasped Richard's hand he left a round silver dollar in it. "Want you to have it," he said. "You'll need it to eat on. And what Milly told you is what I think you should do too. Pike here runs right on down to Cincinnati. Start walkin', and afore long somebody'll pick you up. And once you get there, look around down along the river. There's always a lot of work there where the steamers are loadin' and unloadin'."

Richard had tears in his eyes when he left and started walking south. He had never met a man as generous as John Cheeseman. Prince, that's what he was, and he was a prince because he was a true democrat.

UNDER THE sun the pike became muddy in no time, so that in some places Richard found it expedient to do what stagecoach passengers sometimes had to do, coon the fences to get beyond the worst sloughs. But the pike was comparatively straight—it ran on and on unceasingly, and each step brought him nearer to the lodestar, Cincinnati. Richard really knew nothing of the city, although around the fireside he had heard tales of the Indian Wars. It seemed that there had been a fort there once, and that the settlement was called Losantiville, the town opposite the mouth of the Licking. General St. Clair changed all that—he built a fort and called it Fort Washington, and he renamed the city Cincinnati, after the Society of the Cincinnati to which he and General George Washington belonged. But St. Clair had been unlucky then, and had suffered a savage defeat when he went too far north after the Indians, and it had remained for Mad Anthony Wayne to beat the tribes in the Battle of Fallen Timbers. Richard had heard such tales wide-eyed, particularly when he had been a small youngster, but it seemed that the Indians were completely gone now, and in truth he had never seen one. So Fort Washington was torn down because it was no longer needed, and was in the way of the progress of the city that began to ascend the banks of the Ohio, first to the first level, then to the second high ground, and now, if one could believe the travelers, clear on out to the surrounding hills. Somehow or other the Miami and Erie Canal got down through the hills and emptied into the basin in the city, and that would have been the way to get down to Cincinnati, by coming down on a canalboat from Middletown. Richard had thought of the possibility, but canalboats cost money to ride, and when he knew he simply could not get a dime he had decided to make off for Lebanon instead.

Now, six or seven miles down the road from Lebanon, he began to be very apprehensive. But the people he met on the roads should have given him confidence. They were generally loud with their shouts of greeting, and the passengers in one of the stages even waved at him. What they didn't know when they waved was that they were going to have a desperate time ahead, for a mile back Richard had cooned the fence for a good two hundred yards. Whether the four horses could pull through that quagmire was an open question.

At Mason he stopped for the nooning and bought a hunk of cheese and a piece of bread that the woman sliced off a huge loaf she held on her hip. Richard thought she cheated him too—she wanted a whole dime for the bread and cheese. His stomach, however, declared otherwise—she had given him a good bargain.

Then, only a quarter or half mile out of Mason, he again stumbled on a piece of luck. Two women had been driving a light chaise and one of the wheels had come off, so that the vehicle was hanging over the road while the two females stood over near the edge and seemed to be agonizing about their fates. Richard retrieved the wheel—it was lying on the edge of a puddle ten or twenty feet back—and peremptorily ordered the healthier of the females to hold it while he tried to raise the shay by grabbing the axle and lifting it into position. That didn't work, because there was no way for him to lift while the females got the wheel on. With that Richard started scouring the ditches for wood or stones sufficiently large to hold the rig up while the wheel was worked into place. He found both wood and stone, neither very serviceable, but with the women thrusting the stuff under while he lifted they did finally manage to get the wheel back onto the axle. Then came the hard part—the long search back the road to find the nut to hold the wheel in place. That took an hour, but just when they had all despaired, there it was lying as bright as a copper penny in a spot of ground that was not muddy at all.

After that Richard unceremoniously got up and drove, and although they were all so crowded they couldn't get their bottoms onto the seat, they made do. The horse was a good one, a coal black mare with a star on its withers, and they covered at least five miles before the women announced that they had to turn off the road. They were profuse in their thanks as Richard got down, and that led him to muster up his courage. "You couldn't use me, where you live, could you?" he found himself asking. "I can do most anything you want done."

At that they became very apologetic. "We got us a man," said the elder one who had ringlets around her ears. "We'd like to have you, but we got us a man. And we don't need much done." And when Richard just stood and stared, "So, you see, there's just no way we could use you."

Richard nodded. "How much farther is it?" he asked. "I mean down to Cincinnati, how much farther is it?"

At that they seemed flabbergasted, as if they didn't have the least idea. "It's a far piece yet," said the younger one. "It takes about two hours to drive in from here. It must be a mile."

Richard had his own notions about the mile. If it took two hours to drive in, then it must be five miles, or six or seven miles. But at least that gave him a notion.

The sun was beginning to bend down the sky by the time he came to a big plant that evidently burned brick because there were piles of bricks standing all over the yard. Worse, the weather had turned, and it looked as if it might rain and get considerably colder. Unfortunately there was no help for it but to hike on down the road, having his eyes open for whatever prospect offered. He'd like to get in somewhere for the night, particularly as he had begun to feel bone weary, but if worst came to worst, he thought he'd simply wrap himself in his coat and huddle down under a tree. From all he had heard plenty of men had done the same.

THE NIGHT was an agony, huddled as he was between two piles of lumber in the yard of some big sawmill. All through the night he woke at intervals, and all through the night the sky was a witch's revel, through which a quarter moon flickered from time to time. And it was cold, beastly cold, so that his bones felt frozen to the ground. In consequence Richard was up before first sun, and in the pre-dawn light he was out again on the road. Now all the movement there—and there were a great many heavy farm wagons moving down into the city, each with its lantern or lanterns—seemed spectral, as if the men and horses really existed only in a dream. Fortunately there was still a little of the bread and cheese left and Richard ate it as he walked, but no matter how hard he looked for a well or pump there was no place he could find to get a drink. He was a little afraid to drink, unless he found some natural spring, for there had been much talk of cholera moving up the big river from New Orleans and so coming on up the Ohio. No one seemed to know what caused cholera, but there was some talk that it was caused by bad air or bad water. People did all sorts of things to ward it off, burn smudge pots and sulphur, and whatever else came to hand. Since the burning didn't seem to work, it must be caused by bad water.

At sunup Richard startled—the City lay down in the hollow of the hills just before him, and several church spires thrust up into the morning light. And beyond those must be the river, for the darker bulk of the Kentucky hills lay beyond, and the great Ohio had to be in between. That sight, of the legendary city he had always heard about and had never seen, was like new life in his agonized muscles, and he perceptibly increased his pace, at least for the first quarter mile. More houses began to appear now, most of them small bricks and frames, and lights became perceptible behind the windows of many of the houses. Better yet, far away in the dark, there were shouts, as if teamsters and drovers were calling to each other. Richard could make out none of the words, but it was good to know that other men were alive. He started talking to himself, aloud, something he sometimes did out in the fields at home when he knew he would not be detected. He knew some passages from the Bible by heart, a few of the Psalms, and a little of what was called the Sermon on the Mount from Matthew, and now he went on savagely, thrusting his feet hard in to the mud while he half shouted, *"Blessed are the poor, for they shall inherit the earth. Blessed are the peacemakers, for they shall be called the children of God. Blessed are ye, when men shall revile you, and persecute you, and say all manner of evil and things against ye falsely."*

A woman went by wrapped in a shawl, and when she heard him, tapped her head. Richard shrugged and kept on. Despite his weariness he felt good—he had come down to the Queen of the West—Cincinnati.

Chapter 2

IN THE MORNING sunlight the world was a bright new penny, and once he got his muscles warm Richard felt good as he plowed down off the hills. For a while the way led along cinder paths and through mud, but nearer the center of town there were board walks and brick walks in some places so that gradually he wore the mud off his shoes. Then came the concatenation of really city streets, Vine and Elm and Race and Main and a dozen others, with tall brick buildings, sometimes three stories high. And now he began to read the shop names, "Pfatz" and "Hinkle" and "Zondervaan" and "Grasz," and finally "Mueller's." Richard passed that place and immediately went back—there was a scrawled sign on the window that said Crullers and Coffee, 10 cents. Even then, as he tripped the latch on the door, he almost turned back, for the place was full of people, some of them important looking and very well dressed, with hats and scarves and gloves and all the more elaborate male accoutrements. Some of the men had on beaver hats, well pulled down over their ears, and at least half of them wore string ties. Richard probably would have turned back, but he could not, for two rough-looking workmen were pushing close behind him, and he was fairly swept into the long room. Once in, he went around the mob and slunk clear to the back of the room where there was a vacant place at the counter. And there he sat while everyone else was served, until finally the watery-eyed counterman spotted him and shouted, "What's for you?" Richard was startled, so much so he couldn't get words out of his mouth. That brought the fellow a little nearer, and again he repeated, "What do you want? Got a lot of good sausages this morning. Want some sausage?"

Richard timidly ordered his doughnuts and coffee, and in

another minute the steaming mug was on the counter before him, and beside the mug two doughnuts that looked as if they had been swimming in fat. He ate, his head down, his ears alert to the blur of laughter and conversation. It seemed as if there was constant turmoil in the room; people came and went fast, gulping their breakfasts as if they had much more important business in the world. Richard knew what that business was—they all had jobs, and were rushing to meet the seven o'clock deadline. How much he envied them.

But he felt better when he was once again on the street. And now he began to look with anxious eyes at the stores and signs; they were mystical and formidable. "Fine Foods–Gottfried Keller," "Imported Haberdashery," "Riegel and Riegel, Imports," "Adolph Wentz and Son, Carpets and Furniture," "Wentlow, Spitz, and Swank, Investments and Lands" a few of them read. Richard could imagine how dumb he'd look going into any one of those places and asking for a job. They wanted people who had been to school a long time and were both crafty and knowledgeable, and they simply wouldn't look at a country bumpkin who only wanted to sweep the floors.

It was better as he went down nearer the river; here the places of business were not nearly so pretentious, nor did the proprietors hang curtains and gold signs in their windows. "Hardware and Findings" read one wooden sign, "Chandler" another, and one only "Hay and Grain." Here, in the older and shabbier part of town Richard began to feel more at home, so much so that when he passed a door that read "Bottles and Glass" he very boldly stepped inside. He was amazed—the place was no store at all, but it did exhibit rows on rows of bottles and carboys, some in amber glass but mostly green. The room was dark and low-ceilinged, and there was no one in attendance, but from a second room in the back that seemed to be mysteriously dark Richard heard the sound of someone moving about. He coughed ostentatiously, in hope that someone would come through the door, but no one seemed to notice, so that after a time he got up enough courage to walk back and look through the door. What he saw first was what looked like some kind of charcoal furnace, and then, finally, his eyes made out the form of a crippled little man who seemed to be blowing through a long pipe. And, at the end of the pipe, there was a blob of white-hot glass that the fellow kept turning around as he blew into the neck of his pipe. Richard watched in amazement—he had never known how bottles were shaped. But the dwarf paid no attention to him, although Richard knew that the fellow must have seen him standing in the door. Only after some minutes had gone by did the man with the pipe appear to be satisfied, and then only after he had performed some magical trick and so severed the pipe from the new green bottle. But he came no nearer; he only stood back in his web of shadows and stared like a frightened rat.

"I come in to see about getting a job," Richard finally shouted at him. "I need a job."

The dwarf kept staring with his animal eyes, but he said nothing.

"I came in after a job," Richard said again. "Can you use me?"

At that the dwarf shook his head, ever so slightly at first, and then very emphatically. Richard began to get the impression that the man couldn't talk, and he also got the impression that he was definitely not wanted in the establishment. He began to retreat, and once he was in the center of the main room, he turned and almost ran out the door. He hadn't counted on anything so frightening.

But after that it was easier to go into places and ask, and after that it was a forenoon of No-No-No. There were jobs—jobs for people who had already learned a trade. Furniture makers, tool makers, boot and shoe builders and repairers, weavers and dyers— they were all in demand. So, in one dirty establishment down near the river, were butchers and meat-packers. But everyone wanted experience, and no one seemed willing to teach a neophyte a trade. By mid-afternoon half of his dollar was gone—he had had neckbones and sauerkraut for lunch in a very dirty inn at the bottom of Main Street. Richard didn't prefer sauerkraut and neckbones, but the stuff was good, particularly if one didn't mind a few hairs and a little dirt. After that the sense of panic began to grow upon him; it would be only a few more hours until dark, and he certainly didn't want to pass another night in the open. He began after that to solicit everybody he met, and he even tried to ask directions from the rough crews working down on the Landing. Those fellows, blacks and whites alike, seemed not even to know what he was talking about when he asked them how to go about getting a job. They looked and acted like animals as they wrestled hogsheads and bales around, all of them big in body and a bit stooped or hunched, as if they might have been cavemen in the rocks.

Coming up from the Landing Richard got up to Race, and on the corner of Race and a shabby little street that seemed to have no name, stood a blacksmith shop that seemed to be busy from the number of carts and wagons out in front. The place had once been painted red, but was red no longer because the paint had streaked down and left only splintery gray wood. "MacCready," said the sign, and Richard went in through the open double door and saw the first familiar sight in the day, a good forge and bellows, and a whole raft of fellows who were either shoeing horses or waiting for their horses to be shod. Richard picked out the first of them and repeated his question. The man had a horse's hoof in his leather apron and did not look up, but he did say very emphatically, "You'll have to ask Mac. Go on back there—he's the one in the back."

Mac was an old man with gray ringlets clustered around his scaly brown scalp, but despite his age he seemed to be working as methodically as all the rest of them. He was finishing up putting shoes on a fine bay, and not far away from him stood a lady with violets on her hat and a shimmering long green skirt that glistened in the light of the forge. Mac didn't look up when Richard got close, but the lady looked at him and smiled. Richard thought he had never seen a more beautiful woman in all his life—she looked like a goddess. Because of her he half stammered when Mac did finally raise his eyes and see him standing on the other side of the bay.

"What I want's a job," said Richard immediately. "I need a job real bad."

Mac paid no further attention, but went back to driving nails into the shoe. Finally, after some moments of rumination he did look up and survey Richard's face. "Know how to shoe horses?" he asked. "That's what we do here."

Richard had been through the ordeal too often to care much anymore. "I don't know how to shoe horses, but I do know horses," he said. "And I could learn, and you wouldn't have to pay me until I knew how. I'd like to learn how."

Again the lady smiled, and this time she twirled her reticule and came a step nearer. "You're fresh in the City, aren't you?" she asked sweetly.

Richard felt ashamed. "I just come in this morning," he said. "But I mean to stay. I don't mean to go back home."

"What I need," said Mac, "is not really another blacksmith, although God knows I could use one. What I need's somebody to stay here nights and keep me from being robbed. That's what I need."

"What you need, Papa, is a good long rest," said the lady. "That's what you need."

Old MacCready looked at his daughter and snorted. "Been working all my life," he said. "What keeps me young, workin'."

"Perhaps the boy wouldn't mind staying here at night," said the lady. "You haven't asked him."

"I wouldn't," said Richard swiftly. "I need a place to sleep—I ain't got no place. I wouldn't mind sleeping here at all."

Mac went away for a knife and came back and pared the last hoof a little. He seemed to be preoccupied, so that Richard and the lady simply stood and stared at each other. It seemed that both of them wanted to talk and were afraid of intruding on the other. Mac came back at last, and when he did he addressed his daughter more than Richard. "Well," he said, "I guess if he wants to try it, he kin. Ain't much of a job. There's a place to sleep up in the loft, but what I'd rather was that he slept right down here on the floor. That way he'd be more likely to wake up if anything starts to happen at night."

The lady took over then. "You haven't told him what you'd pay him," she said. "What would it be worth?"

"I'd give him two dollars a week," said old Mac, "twenty-five cents a night and twenty-five cents more to red up on Satiday. Ain't much, but I ain't got much to give. He wouldn't have to pay for any room."

The lady looked at Richard and smiled. "That would be to start," she said. "Perhaps you could learn how to shoe horses, and then I think maybe Papa'd pay you a little more. Do you think you could get along on two dollars?"

What Richard didn't tell her was that two dollars sounded like a small fortune. He'd have to beg if he meant to eat during the first week, but he thought he might screw up his courage and ask for an advance after a day or two. Mac would probably let him have a dollar.

"I'd like to try," he said. "I'd like to try a lot."

Mac said nothing more, and after her father had led her horse out and hitched it, the lady disappeared. Richard felt out of place, and no one paid any attention to him whatsoever. Once or twice one of the three other fellows in the shop came back to the water bucket or went out the back door to relieve himself, but no one seemed to have the courage to talk to him. But it seemed they all knew he was going to stay on because by some sort of psychic energy they communicated as much to him.

It began to get dark, and the shop cleared out. Then, when it was almost black outside, the fellows all hung up their leather aprons and disappeared. Mac was the last to go, and before he went he took Richard up into the loft where there was some sort of metal cot with some old horse blankets on it. Mac motioned to the blankets, and Richard got the sign and carried them down the ladder. It seemed he would sleep on the floor of Mac's tiny office, where there was just room enough to stretch out between an enormous rolltop desk and a pine table that was stacked with all sorts of bric-a-brac.

"Want you some supper, you can go next door," said Mac before he left. "Ain't much of a place, but the stuff's clean. You got money enough to buy some supper?"

Richard said he had, and without more ado Mac went out the door and started to walk home.

Richard hooked the door behind him, and turned to survey the spooky room. The fire in the forge was almost dead, but in the little light the rows on rows of horseshoes hanging on the wall glinted like some sort of pagan symbols. He thought he'd wait a little while and then go next door to see how much he could get for a quarter.

SUPPER WAS good—it was some sort of meat and potato stew with hunks of what must have been old root-cellar carrots and turnips thrown in. And there was bread and butter, plenty of bread and butter. Richard sat at the counter for the very good reason that that was the only place to sit, for the square wood tables with metal legs were all occupied with a rag-tag, miscellaneous jumble of white and black men who looked as if they were some of the dockworkers. Some of them had their own bottles and shared them conspicuously, but there was neither beer nor liquor for sale in Mrs. Zimmerman's eating place. There were two pimply girls who carried out the bowls of stuff from the kitchen, both of them Mrs. Zimmerman's daughters obviously, for they had the older woman's bleached hair and pudgy stomach. But they were dressed in good calico that came clear down to the floor, and they moved with amazing swiftness for such big animals. Mrs. Zimmerman stayed behind the counter and served the pie, and she served plenty of it, but pie cost another nickel and Richard didn't think he could afford it. It was good dried apple, and the chunks were huge.

After that there was nothing to do but go back to the blacksmith's shop. Richard felt almost glad to get inside—once night shut down the city went black. Down along the Public Landing there were still some torches, but in the city proper it seemed as if all the buildings were dark. Later, when the moon rose, the Kentucky hills could be seen black on the other side of the river, and once or twice during the night Richard got up and pressed his nose against the glass. It seemed almost unreal that he was here; it was almost as if he were some sort of discarnate being caught out of time and space. Inevitably his thoughts went home to the hill acres, and when they did a half lump rose in his throat. His father and mother would not understand—they could not understand. And, sooner or later, the news that he was gone would be communicated to the Berzinskis, and Ruth would not know what to make of it. That was the prime danger, that Ruth would think she had been deserted, and might begin to despair of her lot. Richard thought of ways in which he might get in touch with her, but there was actually no good way, short of going on back himself. That he was resolved he would never do. The Berzinskis would probably not try to marry Ruth off immediately, and there was always the chance that Ruth would run away herself. Richard somehow did not want her to do that—it was too risky. It was hard enough for a man to make his way in the world.

About midnight, as nearly as he could judge, someone went down the walk outside with a lantern, and an hour after that there was a fearful yowling in the street, as if drunks were coming back up the hill from the Landing. Fortunately no one tried to get in through the door. Richard had pulled the big hook snugly into the hasp, and had moreover taken the precaution to arm himself with a good short blacksmith's hammer. Despite that assurance, he slept fitfully and was awake long before dawn. There were streaks of cerise in the eastern sky this morning, and through the little dawn light fitful shapes began again to hurry on down to the Public Landing. The torches down there looked as if some new steamer had pulled in to the wharf, and the workday had started early.

Well, it was a good beginning, he assured himself of that. He didn't mean to stay on forever as a watchman; he meant to hang around in the daytime and gradually learn the craft of the blacksmiths. He had thought it all through in his own mind; first he'd learn to hammer and shape iron, practicing whatever tricks there might be, then he'd try his hand at hinges and shovels and various kinds of tools. And inside of six months he'd be a master smith, for the very good reason that he was young, had strength and energy, and the will to excel. Then if he decided to stay on here, old Mac would have to pay him more. And there was no good reason why he shouldn't be paid for two jobs, and sleeping in the shop made him able to get along without paying room rent.

Then, after he'd saved up a hundred dollars—and the way to save it faster was simply not to buy anything—he'd go back up to the old neighborhood and somehow get word to Ruth that it was time for them to go away together. And they'd go far enough, maybe out to Indiana, where he could set up his own shop. And then they'd rent a cabin, and as soon as they were able, run up their own house. They'd have five or six children, and the family would be able to take its rightful place in life.

It wasn't only a dream—everything of importance that had ever happened in the world had been only an idea at first. That was what a man had to have, the courage and imagination to dream hard enough. And then to make other dreams, just as soon as the first had been realized. That's the way it would be, right on until both Ruth and he had to hobble around on canes. And then, perhaps they'd have to leave off dreaming, and let their children take care of them.

BUT THE days went on, and it was Maytime, and with Maytime the world was so much regenerated and fresh that Richard sometimes could not abide the dreary darkness of the blacksmith's shop. Old MacCready was good to him—he had no complaint about his treatment. And Red and Ruggles and simple Simon, the bald-headed man next to MacCready in age, were good to him, and he had no complaint about that. But the giant buttonwood tree that overhung the shop and was now coming into leaf made him long for the buttonwoods along Turtle Creek, and when one Sunday he took a walk far out into the north hills there were dogwoods hanging on all the rocky slopes. Worse, the fields were green, and it was plowing time, time to stagger along after Midge and Frank and see the black earth turn under the share. His father would need him now, for in late years Richard had done more than half of the plowing and planting. And the Johnny-jump-ups would be making the roadside blue, and the trilliums and springbeauties would have enchanted all the open woods. Thinking of that made him think of the old witch and how she would be out scouring the woods for her simples, and when he thought of the old witch he inevitably thought of Ruth. They might be keeping her prisoned, her father and Jake and Herman, and the old cow Asenath. And that thought made him mad, and he became madder when he realized that there was nothing he could do about it.

Wandering the streets of the city, and lolling about the Public Landing in the sun, with its enormous commerce and endless drays and the great teams pulling bales and boxes up the hard climb into the city, Richard often cursed himself for a ninny. He should be a part of this traffic, that he knew; he should be making five dollars a week and saving up so that he could at least dream of making his dreams come true. And he should be going upriver and downriver on some of the barges or steamers, and he should have great ambitions in the world. And the disgusting truth was that he was nothing, a cipher, so contemptible that people didn't even take the trouble to talk to him.

Ordinarily he went back to the shop after he had had a cheese sandwich or a bowl of noodle soup for lunch, and through the long afternoons he begged Red and Ruggles for jobs to do. And, though they were reluctant at first, they didn't discourage him. In fact, old Mac seemed to approve, and one day he went to some secret hiding place and came back with a leather apron that he tied around Richard. "Might as well as save your clothes, boy," he said apologetically. Richard grimaced a little at that—his clothes were a sight, and his old clodhoppers weren't exactly the kind of shoes the other men wore. Most of them wore half boots, boots which seemed to be made of some sort of supple yellow leather, and didn't squeak when the men walked. Richard had seen some of them in a bootmaker's window on Elm Street, but the price had been five dollars. He didn't know how he would ever be able to afford so expensive an item.

Then, one day, the lady came back, and when she saw Richard in the shop she seemed to be surprised. "I didn't know you were still here," she said when she saw him standing beside Ruggles. "Papa never said."

Richard was apologetic at once. "I been trying to learn how to shoe horses," he defended himself. "I'm learning."

She didn't seem to approve too much of that. "I thought that maybe you'd find something better to do," she said. "You don't look like the kind of man that shoes horses all his life. Have you looked around?"

Now Richard knew he was definitely on the defensive. "I been down to the Landing a lot," he said. "They don't seem to want anybody down there."

"I don't mean that," said the lady. "I thought that perhaps you'd be learning a trade. Can you read and write?"

Richard felt abused. She didn't know—she had probably had the benefit of some private teacher. She hadn't learned all her polish in MacCready's home.

"I can read and write a little," he said. "I can read the Bible, most of it. Course, some of the words I don't understand."

"Can you write?"

"I'm best at numbers," said Richard. "But I can write a little. Trouble is I never practiced."

She looked away a little, and Richard thought she looked sad. He felt awkward standing at the side of the room with her, both of them trying to keep out of the way, and after a little while he found an excuse to move away. But that night, after all the rest of the fellows had gone home, old Mac called him out under the buttonwood and said, "You ain't too busy Sunday, my daughter Laura wants you to come on out to dinner."

Richard was flabbergasted, and old Mac himself looked puzzled. "Don't know why," he said. "It's just women—they get these fool notions. Guess there wouldn't be any reason you'd have to hang around here Sunday anyway, not in the daytime. What do you usually do on Sundays, go to church somewhere?"

Richard thought that he ought to know that nobody would go to church in the kind of clothes he had to wear.

"I just usually take a walk," he said. "I got to get to know the town a little bit better than I do."

Mac seemed interested and ran a hand over his brown head. "I'd do the same thing if I was young again," he said. "Get lost sometimes myself, all them houses going up way out in the fields. I been in Cincy most all of my life, and I ain't never seen it like it is now. Must be ten–twenty thousand people here, so many they're just battin' into each other. And they make prices high. One of them lots over on Race Street sold the other day for five hundred dollars. Hell of a lot more'n it's worth—it was bought for only about two dollars. But that's what people will do, crowd into each other. Laura don't know it yet—she lives almost right next door to me up on Vine—but I'm thinkin' o' movin' out myownself. Got my eye on something up in what they call Walnut Hills. Got grapevines all over it right now, but it don't have to have. Trouble is the fellow that says he owns it don't seem to have clear title. All he wants is fifty dollars, and that's a dam' sight too much, but I'd give it to him in a minute if I thought I wouldn't be rooted out ten years after I went in."

Richard thought Mac probably should be brought back to the business at hand. "I don't think I know where you live," he said. "I know where Vine Street is—I been on Vine Street a few times."

Mac nodded his head. "It's a sort of far piece," he said. "Got to walk out almost to the canal. Then you'll come to three red bricks all together, and a stone's throw on the canal side a big yellow frame house with two chimbleys on it. That's Laura's house. Mine is the middle brick. Lived with us for a while after she got married, she did, but then she got tony when her man started to make money. Whole hell of a lot of money, so much they don't know what to do with it. Thinkin' now about buildin' way on out, but if they got the sense God gave little green geese they won't 'cause you can't get either in or out in the winter when it gets real snowy or icy. I've told them that a dozen times, but they don't listen too well. Still talkin' about it."

It was all Greek to Richard. "What's her husband do?" he wanted to know. "I mean your daughter's husband."

"Commission merchant," said Mac promptly. "That's what he

calls himself. What I call him's a damned robber. Never lifts his hand, only gets in a lot of stuff on consignment and then marks it up so that people have to pay him a pretty penny to get it. Goes East three or four times a year, up the river to Pittsburgh, and then maybe on over the mountains to Baltimore and Philadelphia. Goes in style, too. Nothin' in this world but the best for Arthur St. Clair Bentley. That's what his folks named him when he was born. That's a heller, ain't it—Arthur St. Clair Bentley! Had me a handle like that I'd feel like takin' a straight razor and slittin' my throat. But Laura, she don't seem to mind. In fact, she had her some little cards printed, and that's what she's got on them: Mrs. Arthur St. Clair Bentley. Every time I see one of the damned things I feel like pukin'."

Richard didn't feel that way, but he was envious. It didn't seem right for some folks to have too much while other people had too little. It was one of the tricks played by birth and luck, not the result of any merit.

"I'll try and be out," he said. And then, when Mac seemed to have forgotten what they were talking about, "I mean Sunday. I'll try to find your place on Sunday."

At that it was Mac's turn to look discomfited. "Ain't my place you're a comin' to," he said. "You go there, you won't find anybody at home. It's the big yellow house where we're going to eat. Every Sunday—Laura makes sure that we get a good bait in our stomachs every Sunday. Bentley ain't home for weeks on end, and she says she needs company."

Richard was wondering what he could do about his shoes. And whether he shouldn't try to get a bucket of water and wash down during the night. He had a notion he smelled. Better than that, but worse too, he might take one of his dollars and buy himself a clean shirt. He had seen some in a shopwindow somewhere, on Race or Third Street, or somewhere.

"I'll try and be there," he said as Mac got his lunch bucket out of the office. "I'll find it somehow."

Mac went out without another word. And the next day was Friday, and Richard suddenly made up his mind that he'd wash Saturday night, and see to it that he had a new blue shirt to put on.

THE BENTLEY house was gorgeous—it had pine floors, not the stupid old walnut or ash that most people had to put up with. The pine was a rare item, and had to be carted across country and then brought down the river. Some people said it came all the way from New Jersey, wherever that was. And there was a lot of scrollwork in the Bentley house, and the walls were plastered, with dadoes going around the whole top of the room. It didn't heat, of course—nothing heated in the wintertime, but as another evidence of wealth Bentley had installed some sort of iron stove that stood in the parlor and had a pipe going over to the big chimney. Richard had never seen such a device, and wondered how effective it might be. Today there was no need of the stove, for it was warm outdoors.

The lady had met him at the door, and she had called him Richard. He was so taken aback by that that he got his feet tangled up in one of the rugs and almost fell over while she was still holding his hand. "I'm so glad you came out, Richard," she was saying. "Just go right into the parlor, Papa and Mamma's in there. But wait a minute—I want you to meet my daughter." And she began to call, "Nancy, Nancy, come here a minute."

Nancy came, a willowy little girl who might have been fifteen or sixteen. Richard held out his hand, and Nancy finally took it, but he knew from her looks that he must have done something wrong. He had read in a book once that a gentleman was supposed to bow, but he hadn't the least idea what that meant. "I'm glad to meet you," Nancy was saying. "Mamma's told me about you. Your name's Richard, isn't it."

"Richard Robinson," said Richard, and felt himself go faint. He didn't know what was the matter with him, but the girl somehow made him ill at ease. He began to wish that he hadn't come.

Inside the parlor he met Mrs. MacCready, who was introduced simply as Mamma. She was a puckery little old thing who looked a lot more decrepit than her husband, and she wore a little blue bonnet on her head that was tied under her chin. "Sakes alive!" she kept saying. "What a big boy you are. Sakes alive!"

Richard didn't know what to do, and after a moment Mrs. Bentley somehow indicated a rocker on the far side of the room. The girl Nancy was gone—she had probably gone down the center hall and disappeared into the kitchen. "Dinner won't be long," Mrs. Bentley kept saying. "You comfortable, Mamma? You can put one of those pillows behind your back where it hurts. Papa, give Mamma one of the pillows on the sofa. You can reach them."

They settled, and Mrs. Bentley waited until she thought they were as comfortable as they were going to be. "Well, dinner won't be long," she said again. "And it's not much, only a goose. I got it on market Friday and need a lot of people to help eat it up." And with that announcement, she too disappeared into the kitchen.

It was deathly still in the parlor after she had gone. Richard saw a shelf of books on the far side of the room and would have loved to examine them, but he thought he didn't dare. He sat like a ramrod, afraid to rock back and forth, afraid to look at Mr. MacCready, afraid of almost everything. He was already speculating how well he'd be able to use a knife and fork. At home they generally just gave everyone a sharp knife and used their fingers. But this wasn't home.

The gilt clock on the mantel ticked, and the hands pointed to almost half-past twelve before Nancy reappeared. "Mamma says it's time to come out now," she said. "Richard, you help Grandma so she don't fall. And, Grandpa, you'd better spit out your tobacco, you know there's no spittoon in the dining room."

Grandpa did. They walked towards the center hall and then back to the dining room, which was evidently right behind the closed room at the front of the house. Richard heard that room referred to later as the library, and he knew what a library was. If they were real rich, and they seemed real rich, they might even have a hundred books in there. If so, no wonder they kept the door shut, and probably locked.

Mrs. Bentley sat at the head of the table, her father and mother to her right, and Nancy and Richard to her left, Nancy nearest the kitchen. Once down in their seats there was a little flutter of conversation, most of it about Grandma's aches and pains, and then just when Richard was thinking that he probably ought to reach for the bread, an agonized moment while Mrs. Bentley turned to her father and said, "Papa, we're waiting."

Papa said grace, not very articulately, but too long. Then they waited while Mrs. Bentley carved the bird. Nancy served mashed potatoes on the plates as her mother handed them to her, and for vegetable there was a side dish of stewed rhubarb. Mrs. Bentley served the rhubarb once she was done with the goose, and at long last they all settled down to the serious business of eating. No one passed the bread, and no one but Richard seemed to want it. He was afraid to reach.

It was curious the way the Bentleys ate; they did it almost apologetically, and insisted on talking the whole time. Old Mac would get his mouth full and then his daughter would ask him a question that he had to choke to answer, or she herself would describe some of her strange experiences in the City. It seemed she drove out almost every day, and she was never tired of trying everything new under the sun. She had even been in Covington and Newport, clear across the river; a number of younger folks had gotten up a party one night and gone over in rowboats. To hear Mrs. Bentley tell it, both Newport and Covington were enterprising towns, although, of course, much smaller than Cincinnati. Much smaller.

And then, like a pistol flash, there was a quick end to comfortable eating. "Richard," said Mrs. Bentley apropos of nothing, "You haven't said anything. I don't believe you can talk."

Richard hurriedly gulped down what was in his mouth.

"I guess I don't have much to say," he admitted. "I been eating."

Mrs. Bentley smiled. "We're all eager to know about you," she said. "All about you. Tell us about your home. I think you said your father farmed."

Richard was angry that he always flushed. "We got us a little place up on Turtle Creek," he said. "Ain't much, only about a hundred acres. It's near Shakertown, if you know where that is."

Mrs. Bentley seemed puzzled. "I've heard about it," she said. "They're the people who believe the world is going to come to an end soon, aren't they?" she asked. "Or what do they believe?"

"I don't know what they believe, but they dance," said Richard. "Dance every Sunday indoors, and outdoors sometimes during the summer. Got them a meadow all enclosed with woods that they call Jehovah's Chosen Square. That's where they sometimes dance during the summertime. And when they do they sing or just make loud noises."

Mrs. Bentley laughed aloud. "It's funny," she said. "People do all sorts of silly things when they claim they're worshipping God. But I never heard of Jehovah's Chosen Square."

"Ain't got the brains God gave them," said her father. "You

want to know what's the truth in religion, you follow John Wesley. He was the man who knew."

Mrs. Bentley did not rise to the argument. "I guess we'll just have to be tolerant," she said.

"There's no sense in saying what isn't so," said Nancy. It was the first words she had spoken at table. "There's got to be some truth, and a person can't agree to just any old thing."

"The Catholics say they got it," said old MacCready. "Come on down to the shop sometimes, and parade around as if they think they're better than anybody. Got a chip on their shoulders, all them Catholics have."

Mrs. Bentley changed the subject. "What do you raise on your farm, Richard?" she asked. "Is it mostly corn?"

"Corn and pigs," said Richard. "Course we have other things. Wheat and barley, and we always have a flock of sheep. And Mamma has a big garden. She puts up a lot."

"I wouldn't mind having a good watermelon right now," said Nancy. "It's hot today. How about you, Grandpa, would you like a slice of watermelon?"

Grandpa looked up over his glasses. "Got enough right here on this table," he said. "Don't seem right for some people to have everything they want, and some people to have nothing."

And again Mrs. Bentley changed the subject.

"Nancy," she directed, "I think it's time for cake. And bring in the big bottle of wine—Papa always likes wine with his cake. I'll get the coffee."

Grandpa did like wine—a little too well. Richard saw him drink one waterglass full, and then another. Grandma had a sip of wine and finished off with coffee, and Richard thought he had never tasted anything like this coffee. It certainly wasn't made out of roasted acorns. As for the cake, it was the best he had ever eaten, all covered with some sort of caramel icing so that it seemed like eating candy.

After that Mrs. Bentley got her parents back into the parlor, and when she saw Richard looking vacantly out the window she called Nancy and told her to take Richard out and show him around the neighborhood. Richard got a bit stiff at that, but he went along, and Nancy chattered once they were away from the house. He had never met a girl like that—she seemed completely natural. And she didn't seem to be trying to make up to him either. All her talk was about Mr. Smithgarn, who was teaching her music, and the horrible school she went to where some old fool named Bates insisted they had to read Caesar to be educated. And Nancy didn't want to be educated, at least not in that way. She knew her numbers already, she could write a good hand, and everybody had always said she was a good reader.

That last remark made Richard sad. "You got to have books to learn to read well," he said. "That's the trouble with me—I never had any books."

That brought Nancy up short. "Good heavens!" she exclaimed, and stamped her foot a little. "We got lots of books, lots of books we'll never use again in this world. Take some home with you. D'you ever read about Robinson Crusoe?"

Richard confessed he hadn't.

"Well, you take that," said Nancy. "We'll find other ones. But you got to read about Robinson Crusoe. And then, when you finish that, you got to read *The Vicar of Wakefield*. Mamma says it's her favorite, so you can't keep it, but you can read it."

They walked up as far as the canal, and saw two of the big white boats, the *Oregon* and the *Miami*, being pulled along by mule teams in tandem. That made Nancy think of another secret desire. "That's where I'm going some day," she declared suddenly. "Up the canal. Do you know how far it goes?"

"I think it goes to Dayton," said Richard. "Leastway, it goes as far as Middletown."

"Then that's where I'm going to go," said Nancy. "You want to, you can come along with me."

It was a wicked afternoon, a very wicked afternoon. Richard had never imagined that there could be a girl who was so little repressed.

LYING AWAKE that night, the late, bawdy sounds from the waterfront loud about his ears, Richard was confused and a great deal dejected. He didn't understand Cincinnati, he didn't understand Cincinnati at all. What he didn't understand was that no one understood Cincinnati, an infant suddenly become an overgrown colossus. Cincinnati was all things to all men, a conglomeration of contradictions, a study in contrasts.

Cincinnati was gray cobblestones, particularly on the Public Landing, and on the hard climbs up from the Landing, cobblestones, pigeons, shelled corn, yellow-red brick stores and houses, with all sorts of gimcracks and dadoes on their facades. Cincinnati was mud, manure piles, the great public market, pigs, dogs, and sheep in the streets, and waterfront dives that slopped out beer and Kentucky whiskey. Cincinnati was rivermen and ruffians in the streets, tall, lean, and tough men, some of them with their dirks only half hidden. Cincinnati was endless steamboats nosing in at the Landing because there were so many of them they could not come alongside. Cincinnati was Madame Trollope's Folly, St. Peter's, and the white steeples of the Protestant churches. Cincinnati was slaughterhouses and iron-mongeries down by the river, and the dark pall of smoke that in winter sometimes hung over the town from a thousand chimneys. Cincinnati was horses, great dray horses able to pull tonnage up the hills, and trim fillies that Negro slaves, themselves rented from Kentucky, drove hitched to light buggies and landaus when fine ladies paraded their flounces and furbelows in the May afternoons. Cincinnati was bald-headed bankers with high hats, brewers with red noses, countrymen come in to sell geese, eggs, and chickens, Catholics telling their beads in St. Peter's, canalmen breaking heads in waterfront saloons, migrants from New England and Pennsylvania on their way downriver, fortune hunters trying to pry up anything half loose, land speculators out to swindle anyone. Cincinnati was gilt homes, harness bells, throaty steamboat whistles, and the silver tongues of sleighs in the winter night. Cincinnati was the sun coming up over Eden Heights and Mt. Adams, lacquering the heads of the great elms and buttonwoods in the valley, and prying even into the sour shanties that the madams down by the river kept for the fancy trade. Cincinnati was schmierkaese, headcheese, and sauerkraut, and the enormous tonnage of neckbones and spareribs thrown into the Ohio to feed the catfish because they could not be consumed by the populace. Cincinnati was Lane Theological Seminary and Professor Stowe, who had married one of the Beechers, and whose wife Harriet was bitterly displeased by the traffic in Negroes she had discovered in the West. Cincinnati was privies in all the backyards,

flamboyant washes hung out every Monday morning, and thin burial hearses with black-plumed horses. Cincinnati was a maelstrom,
an unexpected turbulence in one of the river pockets, when floating
down from Marietta one had passed a hundred like it in which only
sleepy cows grazed.

Cincinnati was dirty, barbarous, rude, crude, and in spots filthy,
but there was pulsating energy in all its barbarity. Cincinnati was, in
short, a sort of future crammed down into the ring of hills that represented the past, that reminded one of the forgotten old Indian
Wars, and of General St. Clair and his now demolished Fort Washington, from which he had marched so bravely to be butchered.
Cincinnati was hope, promise, fortune, love, everything that the
heart desired, a city called the Queen of the West, and certainly destined to be a regal Queen.

And, lying in the dark, Richard realized that he had none of
Cincinnati's fabulous treasures, and that there was little hope of ever
making his dreams come true. There was, in all sincerity, no real reason why he should be, or stay, in Cincinnati.

THE DAY at the Bentleys, and the following mornings and afternoons
at the Bentleys, did little to lighten his temper. Mrs. Bentley, once
Richard had eaten Sunday dinner with her, seemed to know a hundred reasons why she should tell her father to have Richard come
out to help her. They were good reasons—there were chores to do
about the place. Mrs. Bentley did sometimes employ a rented Negro
slave, but only to drive her out in the afternoons. For some strange
reason which Richard never learned, that was all she would permit
Ash to do, and Richard reasoned, however erroneously, that she did
not want to load the man with any heavy work. Ash was about
forty or forty-five, a tall man with a good figure, and with the most
inscrutable eyes Richard had ever seen. The eyes seemed both to be
dull and to smoke, and somehow they looked right through you.
Ash was the soul of courtesy, and he actually talked rather well, but
he told not one word about himself or his past. In fact, he avoided
company, and if Richard should go out to the stable while Ash was
there, the slave always found some reason to leave. There was a bottle green coat and a green straw hat that were kept in the stable and
that Ash always put on before his forays into the town, but when he

came back he took time only to unharness and rub the horse, and then he seemed to melt away. Richard didn't notice Ash's disappearance at first, and then he did notice, and after that he purposely watched to see how Ash got away from the place. It was easy, Ash simply skipped lightly over the back fence, and dropped down into the streambed of the little gully. Down under the thickets he was hidden from sight, and where he went was anybody's guess. But Richard did know one thing: when he left Ash always had a shiny silver dollar clamped into his palm. The dollar was his own; the rent for him Mrs. Bentley likely paid to whoever had farmed out the Negro from the Kentucky side of the river.

Richard's jobs were mostly cleaning, but there might be variations. Mrs. Bentley was no gardener, but she did sometimes want her beets and potatoes hoed. And she always wanted the whole back end of the yard cleaned out—it was full of scrub willow, hazel coppice, and just plain thorny blackberries. The trouble was that she had no suitable tools—all she could find to give Richard was a hatchet. And with the hatchet he made little progress, but he did make some. The mass of cuttings, once they were dried, were burned out near the gully. Mrs. Bentley never again ate with Richard. When he was there through the noon hour he ate in the kitchen, and once or twice, on a sweaty afternoon, Mrs. Bentley came out into the backyard with a glass of something that she called punch. It was generally sour and not bad-tasting stuff, and it was always a little cooler than Richard expected because the Bentleys had a good deep well.

Richard never saw Nancy again, and he purposely did not inquire about her. It seemed that she was somewhere at school, in the town or out of the town he didn't know. But Nancy must have whispered something into her mother's ear, because one day soon after the dinner at her house Mrs. Bentley called Richard to the house and presented him with a book that was called *The Vicar of Wakefield.* "Nancy said you'd like to read this, Richard," she said. "Would you?" Richard was afraid to confess that he would, and must have stammered, because she said, "It's yours, and you don't have to return it. I bought it especially for you because it's my favorite novel and I don't want to let my copy get out of the house." The Vicar was followed by Nancy's first choice, *Robinson Crusoe,* and Richard found that unbelievable. Once he had the books he bought a few candles and carried them to the blacksmith shop with him, and after that he must have read two hours a night, lying flat on his belly on the floor of old MacCready's office, the candle anchored to the floor near his book. It took several weeks to get through *The Vicar of Wakefield* and *Robinson Crusoe,* and after that, just when he was assured that reading was one of the greatest fulfillments a man could have, Mrs. Bentley dampened his spirits by lending him something called Pope. It was a book of poems, and Richard couldn't make head nor tail out of the volume. The lines all seemed to seesaw back and forth, and it didn't make any difference where you turned in the book—it was all the same. Richard had had a few poems in his Reader, but it was nothing like this, and though he fought valiantly he had to give Pope up.

"I don't know what's the matter," he told Mrs. Bentley the next Wednesday. "I just don't know what he's saying. I don't get anything out of it."

Mrs. Bentley smiled sweetly. "I was afraid of that," she said, and took the book from him and put it on the kitchen table. "I was afraid that you might not be ready for Pope. You will be some day, but I guess we'd better read some other things first."

There was never anything as good as *Robinson Crusoe.* Richard tried to plow through something that was by an author named Scott and that was all about Jews and knights and duels and castles and things like that. Scott wasn't as hard as Pope, but he seemed to have a hard time getting anyplace and once or twice when he had been trying to read Richard discovered that he had fallen asleep. Once he had even knocked over the candle, but mercifully it had gone out.

So June lingered, and the flies were bad, so much so in the smithy that a person couldn't sleep at night. Worse, Richard had to keep the big doors closed so that he lay in his own sweat and couldn't get a breath of fresh air. He thought of going back to the farm a hundred times, but somehow he felt he didn't dare. His father was a proud man, one who didn't take an injury lightly. And, rationalize as much as he dared, Richard knew he had injured both his father and mother. His father was too old to do all the farmwork, particularly in those years when the crops were heavy. And they had been heavy in the past, sometimes prodigious. Both 1843 and 1847 had been good corn years, so good that the Shakers at Union Village bragged that they had gathered over ten thousand bushels of corn in each of those years. After that the rains weren't quite right, but they were good enough, and the Robinson farm seemed to drain well. Richard had even counted on the fact that when his father and mother got too old to work he would have to take over the management. But not without a woman to help him, and if they wouldn't have another woman in the house, then that dream had to be at an end.

He might go on downriver—he had thought of doing that a hundred times. People talked about a big town down at the falls of the Ohio, and other people were always saying how good things were over in Indiana country. For that matter, once he got on a flatboat or steamer, there wasn't any real reason why he should stop. Maybe go clear on down to what was called St. Louis, or beyond that even, float down the Mississippi to New Orleans. He had enough money now—he had managed to save up twenty dollars. The money, all in silver dollars, was in a glass jar buried under the dirt floor of the smithy, and he dug it up every Saturday night after MacCready had paid for the week and he was alone in the shop. And when he dug it up, he always made certain to blow out the candle first. He had no difficulty finding the jar in the dark, and since his whole hoard was in silver dollars, he could easily count the money. As a matter of fact, he counted it every week, and with each succeeding week marveled the more at his good fortune. He always saved back one dollar for pocket money, but that was a foolish bit of insurance, for the money Mrs. Bentley paid him through the week was always enough to get him through. The trouble was that when he was working for Mrs. Bentley he couldn't be working at the forge, and he was making good money there now, for old Mac paid him ten cents for every horse he shod. It added up in the course of a week.

He had to buy some new pants—his old ones got so dirty and torn that he was ashamed to be seen in them anymore. His shirt fared better because he never wore a shirt at the smithy. It was neither too hot nor too cold in there in summer because for some unaccountable reason the smithy seemed to keep cool, despite all the heat from the forge. Actually, Richard sometimes consoled himself, it wasn't a bad life, and if he kept on educating himself he might be able to catch on doing something better in a few years.

However, that meant, or probably meant, that he would never go back for Ruth. And that was one thing he did mean to do, and as soon as he had a hundred dollars saved up, he would.

Chapter 3

THERE WAS something wrong. It was quite apparent that there was something wrong, but Ruth didn't at first know what. Richard was not with the men when they came in for dinner. She thought that maybe he was just down with a spell of chills and fever from getting too cold in the woods. She didn't dare ask, and she knew different when she saw his father's face because old Abraham Robinson looked gray and almost ill. Moodily the four men took their places at the table, and as soon as they did she ran to fetch the big iron skillet of fried hominy from the fire. Then the storm came.

"Jedus Chriis'!" screamed her father when he saw the hominy. "That all we got to eat?"

Ruth kept her mouth shut, but the old witch came to her rescue. "You want meat, you go out and shoot some meat," she said evenly. "Can't give you what ain't in the house."

"You could wring a chicken, couldn't you. Stead of sittin' on your ass all day long an' foolin' with them yarbs."

Mrs. Berzinski stared him down.

"I catch you foolin' with my chickens, it'll be the last thing you ever do fool with," she said. "Them chickens lays eggs."

Harmon slumped back down at table and spooned a mound of hominy onto his tin plate.

"All we git any more," he grumbled to Mr. Robinson. "Work all day long an' all we git's corn hominy fried in hog fat."

"You want some meat, go out and shoot some meat," his wife said again.

"You know dam' well there ain't nothin' runnin' in the woods."

"They's foxes and polecats," said the old witch. "That's a heap more'n you deserve."

They ate in silence, all of them cowed. Once she had the skillet on the table there was nothing more for Ruth to do, and she went back to the fireplace and stood in the shadows behind Asenath. One thing was certain—Asenath was some sort of wall, and they couldn't stare through her.

Ruth felt her heart pounding harder when the idea suddenly touched her brain that Richard might have run off. She wouldn't know why—the Robinsons always seemed to get along so well with each other. But, hearing the men talk, she knew for sure that he was gone because they kept making plans without him. It seemed as if there had been a little trouble that morning because Mr. Robinson had appeared alone with the oxen and had insisted that he was the only man who would drive them. That meant that Herman had to go up into the north woods with his father to cut down trees and lop them, and that Mr. Robinson always had to stop a while after he dragged a log down because Jake couldn't get it into position by himself. And that meant that in the whole morning they had managed to position just three tree trunks, and they were all a little mad. But they couldn't get along without the Robinson oxen.

The idea struck her that Richard might have gone over to the Shakers, but she thought she knew that he wouldn't do that. He had always said that there was no sense in their religion, although he had been generous enough to admit that a man's religion was his own concern. Ruth hadn't the least idea what he was talking about because she had never known a thing about religion. It seemed as though in the old days there had been a few churches around, and there were still one or two in Monroe and, she supposed, in Lebanon. She had never been as far as Lebanon and so didn't know, but she had once gone to Monroe when the whole family traipsed over there for some reason. Monroe was the most town she had ever seen, and though she must have been no older than seven or eight she remembered that she had thought it of giant size. There must have been fifteen or twenty cabins and little houses in Monroe. And there was something they called a church.

"You wring me one o' your damn chickens for supper or I'll do it myownself when I come back in." It was her father talking as he hung menacingly over her mother's chair.

"You wring a chicken, you'll get chicken with pizen in it," said her mother quietly. "That's what you want, that's what you can have. An' then your innards'll burn out and you'll die in your own puke."

They glared at each other, but Ruth knew her mother would win. She always did. There'd be fried hominy for supper again because it was all they had left. There wasn't even any meal in the house, and there was nothing to trade for meal. Given meal, she could bake some pone on the board and serve it with the last of their long sweetening. But without meal it would have to be hominy, and after the hominy was all gone, it would have to be nothing. Unless Jake or Herman went out with the gun and shot something they shouldn't, maybe a hog or sheep that belonged to someone else. They had been known to do that, and several times a gang of men had come up to the house and said they'd like to look around. Once, several years ago, some of the farmers had gotten really ugly. But Jake and Herman always destroyed the hide and most of the carcass, and brought home only big hunks of meat. What they couldn't use immediately they hung in trees down along the swamp.

Ruth thought she'd ask Asenath a few questions that afternoon, but that depended upon getting a chance, and it depended also on Asenath's knowing something. Chances were that Asenath didn't know anything more than she herself knew—there was just no way for her to find out. But Asenath was shrewd, and she had something of her mother's gift of what they called second sight. Asenath sometimes knew without knowing how she knew. She'd say dumb things—or wise things—right out, slurring her words a little in a sort of slow drawl. "They's some men comin'," she'd say, or "Fixin' to git us a big snow tomorrow." Almost invariably some men would stop in at the cabin, or the sky would oblige Asenath and fulfill her prophecies. But how or why she said what she did Ruth could never understand. It was worse sometimes when Asenath went with her mother at night and there was a new baby to be brought into the world. "Ain't no sense in goin'," Asenath might say. "That baby's goin' to be born dead." It often was—it obliged Asenath by being born dead. And that gift, or whatever it was, made Ruth afraid of Asenath, although she was not above using her when it might be profitable to do so. She kept out of Asenath's way, just as she kept out of her mother's way and the ways of her father and brothers. It was not the same with Rachel—Rachel didn't have her wits, and for that reason Ruth treated her like a big sleepy dog. She combed

Rachel's hair almost every day with a wooden comb, and whenever Rachel had to go out to the privy Ruth went along with her. She sometimes wondered what would happen to Rachel, what could happen to Rachel. Maybe the best thing that could happen would be an early death, but Asenath had never prophesied anything like that. It was almost a shame that she hadn't.

THAT NIGHT the Berzinski world came perilously close to an end. It had been a chilly day, and the men had been out working on the corduroy. At somewhere an hour or so before sundown Ruth had thrown a little corn to the chickens, and then, with growing darkness, she had put another skilletful of hominy on the coals at the front of the wood fire. She was afraid to do so, because she had seen her father in rages before, and it was not a pretty sight. But there was nothing else in the house to eat, and she knew that when the men came in they would be screaming for food.

It was near blue dark before they finally came, and there had been no sundown because the sky was gray and it looked as if it meant to drop snow. Ruth lit the whale oil lantern and set it on the table, then got out the tin plates and wiped each of them off with her apron. The really sticky particles of food were not to be dislodged so easily, but there was no way to wash the dishes.

Then, finally, they came in, with the door flung open wide so that the cabin chilled off, and there was a great deal of snarling and spitting at each other. Harmon paraded right to the table and flopped down on the stool at the head, and Herman and Jake soon did the same. They made a sight as they hunched there, all of them huge, all of them with piggish squinty eyes and a brush of reddish stubble on their cheeks and chins. The old witch, sitting at the side of the fire as usual, made not the slightest sign she had seen them, but Asenath finally stirred herself and got to the table, and after that Ruth led Rachel over. Rachel always ate a little, never very much, and she ate in the only way she knew how, with her fingers, generally smearing her face so much that it had to be wiped off afterward.

Ruth saw, as she bent to the fire, that her father was staring straight ahead, as if he hadn't the slightest notion what they had to eat. She carried the skillet over timidly, and, half afraid for her life, reached it over Jake's head and plopped it down at the head of the table. And at that Harmon pushed back immediately, and tried to grab the skillet with his hands. As a result he got burned.

"Goddamn it!" Ruth heard him shout. "I told you this noon I ain't eatin' no more of that hogfood. Where's the supper. I told you to wring a chicken." And he stood staring like a drunken man, and at last, when it seemed no one meant to contradict him, he grabbed the old lady's cap off her head and with it carried the skillet to the hearth and dumped the hominy in the fire. That done, he stomped back to the table, and put his mouth down right alongside his wife's ear. "Now you go on out and wring me one of your chickens!" he ordered.

The old witch simply stared straight ahead of her.

"You heard what I said," Harmon shouted.

She paid no attention, and Ruth remembered afterward that she had seemed completely calm. "They's lots o' things'd kill you deader 'n a stone," Mrs. Berzinski said calmly. "I ain't fixed on the one I'll use yet but I will. You just touch one o' my chickens an' you'll see."

Harmon straightened up, and for a long time stared at his wife uncomprehendingly. Then, a slight sneer on his face, he smiled a little. "Less'n I git to you first, you old sow," he said calmly. "Just you remember that—I might git to you first."

And with that Harmon grabbed up his coat again, and ten minutes later drove their only running horse out to the road. They all knew where he was going, either to Lebanon or Monroe. That meant that he either thought he could get credit or had at least a quarter in his pocket. There was a good inn at Lebanon, as well as a number of whiskey joints that generally provided free bread and cheese, but there was little at Monroe. However Harmon went there from time to time, and without actually saying so they all imagined that he must know some cheap woman of the town that he could cotton up to.

After he was gone, they simply all sat and stared at each other. The hominy burned bright in the coals because of the hogfat it had been fried in, and Jake at last went out and came back with an ear of yellow corn that he started shelling into the skillet. Herman sneered when he saw what Jake was doing, and at long last got up and took down the rifle from its pegs over the fireplace. He fiddled with the gun for a long time, finally got some lead and powder from a hidden niche between the logs, and without a word put on his coat and went out into the dark. They all knew where he was bound—to the Shaker land. It wouldn't be the first time he had brought home a Shaker sheep or pig.

Then, when they had built up the fire because of the growing cold, they heard the buggy in the lane again, and thought it was Harmon back. It wasn't—it was some frantic young farmer who said he had driven all the way down from Red Lion. It had come his wife's time, he said, and they needed somebody to help bring the baby. The old witch sat for a moment in silence, almost as if she had not heard the man, who was wild-eyed with fright. "When'd she begin?" she finally asked. "It come on right afore you left home?"

"I don't know when," said the fellow. "Maybe this afternoon. She was tossin' and hollerin' when I come in."

When she heard that, the old witch moved, and so did Asenath. What went into the yellow bag no one knew, but Asenath gathered a whole armful of half-dirty clothes while the old witch swiftly and silently moved under the rafters, picking handfuls of stuff from the dried herbs hanging there.

"You didn't give her nothin' to eat, did you?" she asked swiftly.

"Didn't give her nothin'," said the fellow. "Just got the horse and come. It's a far piece."

"What is it, her first?"

"She had one afore," said the man. "It died."

They went out the cabin door without another word, and in the dark Ruth heard the man whipping his tired horse unmercifully. She imagined that her mother would be sitting on Asenath's lap—that was the way they ordinarily traveled when there was only a little two-seater to carry them.

After that there was only silence in the cabin, silence and the little sounds Jake's corn made as he roasted it at the fire. Ruth sat in the shadows behind Rachel so that Jake could have enough room to work, and she began to think about going to bed, since that was the only way to keep warm. Somehow she felt numb, not with cold, but with hate and disgust. She knew that people just didn't live this way, the way they lived, and things had gotten so much worse of late that she didn't know how she'd be able to endure it very much longer. The inevitable thought reoccurred to her—to run away. It was perhaps the only way out, the only thing to do. But it was easier for a boy than for a girl. Girls ordinarily didn't have any way to get along out in the world, and everyone was suspicious of them, but people could generally find something for a boy to do. Richard Robinson hadn't come back home with his tail between his legs. Ruth wondered where he had gone, wondered more if he would ever come back. She had enough sense to know that she wasn't the only woman in the world, that after a time Richard would meet other girls. And then what would happen to her? The thought was so bitter that she bit her lips, so hard that she drew blood.

It got colder as the night wore on, and she kept listening for her father to come back up the road. No one came. And Asenath and her mother would likely be out all night—it generally took all night. Ruth wondered then if she'd ever have strength enough to bear a baby. The thought was disgusting to her—she had heard too many stories about bloody childbirths. And about dead babies, and freaks, without hands or eyes or sometimes with too many fingers or toes. There probably was some explanation, unless the total explanation was that a malevolent God had so designed events and was getting even with people. That last thought chilled her; it seemed too probable, since there was no other way to explain floods and ice storms and long spells of drought in the summer when the crops dried up. It would be pleasant to have someone tell her something about what people called God. Ruth couldn't imagine what He looked like, or where He was. People said "in Heaven," as if that meant something, and they always looked up, but all Ruth saw when she looked up was sky and stars. She had heard about the book called the Bible that people said told all about God, and she had once seen a Bible, but she had never had one in her hands. Some day, she resolved, she'd have to get her one of those books, and then read the whole thing if necessary to find out what the mystery was.

That thought brought another thought—that the Shakers said they knew what God was all about. From the evidence of Union Village Ruth had to agree that they might. Everything seemed to prosper there, the orchards and grain fields and cows and pigs and sheep and gardens and everything they had. Beyond that, the evidence of her own eyes, and the other grudging evidence she had picked up from hearing people talk, Ruth knew nothing, but her mind told her that God had prospered the Shakers and certainly hadn't prospered the Berzinskis. Ruth had to agree that the Berzinskis deserved nothing. She had tried to be loyal to her family, but her sense of loyalty was running out, and in fact hardly existed anymore. There was only one thing wrong about the Shakers—they didn't believe it was right for children to come into the sinful world and for that reason they wouldn't let men and women live together. Something deep down inside her told Ruth that that was wrong. But she could live like that, if that was the way God wanted it. The thought had often teased her to run away to the Shakers. Lots of people did, if what she heard was true, and lots of people got mad when anyone did. Parents had been known to take horsewhips and go after their children, and there had been mobs go to Union Village and demand that someone be given up. Only, a person didn't have to come back after he came of legal age, and Ruth knew that she'd be nineteen in another month or so. That was probably what she should do—go to the Shakers the day after she turned nineteen. But that would mean giving up Richard, and that would mean living and working in a sort of prison. The thought was not appealing.

Ruth got up then and led Rachel over to the bed so that she could get her under the covers. It was hard to get Rachel's dress over her head because she couldn't or wouldn't help, but Ruth finally got her under the blankets. There was a buffalo hide too, a mangy, smelly buffalo hide that they sometimes used to help keep warm in winter, and when Ruth saw that Rachel's teeth were chattering, she threw the buffalo skin on top of her. She had started to take off her own dress when by chance she glanced over at the fire and saw Jake's greedy eyes fixed on her. Trying to see more than he should see very likely. Ruth blocked him—she simply kicked off her slippers and got into bed with her dress on. It was good to snuggle up to Rachel because Rachel had started to get warm. After that, in the stillness and dark, the firelight flickering across the naked beams, she knew a moment of peace. She even said a prayer, at least a few words that any benevolent Deity would have accepted as a prayer. "Oh, golly, I sure hope there's some way I can get out of this," she said to herself. "I sure hope there's some way."

That was the last she knew—she was asleep when Jake came prowling over to stare down at them. So was Rachel.

THE UNITED SOCIETY, or the United Society of Believers, or the United Society of Believers in Christ's Second Appearance, had been in Union Village, or what was now called Union Village, since 1805. There had been little land at first, only Malcolm Worley's farm, and then, after the conversion of Richard McNemar, the Presbyterian preacher who had taken part in the Kentucky Revival, and particularly after most of Preacher McNemar's flock had also listened to the voices of the three missionaries sent out from Mount Lebanon, New York, there had been a great deal of land. Now there were over four thousand acres, half of it tillable, half converted to grazing lands or left in woods and streams. There was a sawmill and a grist mill; there were woodworking shops and forges; there were tan pits, boot and shoe shops, dye vats, carding, spinning, and loom rooms; and of course there were great numbers of barns to shelter cows, pigs, geese, turkeys, chickens, sheep, and oxen. There were also numerous dwellings, some of them very large, the North, Center, Brick, Square, South, East, West Frame, West Brick, West Lot, North Lot, and Mill structures. There were also three buildings on the south road which were called the Children's Order and the Gathering Order.

The Ministry, those first in the Ministry at Union Village, lived in apartments over one end of the Meeting House; there were First and Second Elders on both the men's and the women's side. In addition to these, there were family Elders, always two of both sexes. And in addition to these there were numerous Deacons and Deaconesses, always the same number of either sex, unless the Deacon or Deaconess happened to have some particular skill. So there were kitchen Deaconesses and house Deacons and Deaconesses, and there were shop, garden, woodlot, orchard, loom room, dye vat, and perhaps a dozen other Deacons and Deaconesses.

The men and women lived together in the separate houses, and they were gathered together into the several Families, but although together they were always separated. There was a table in the dining room for the women and one for the men; there were separate wings in the houses and separate stairways for the men and women; there were separate crafts and tasks, depending largely upon strength and skills. The women made the wine, which was used only for medicinal and never for sacramental purposes; the women presided over the washhouses and the fruit and vegetable cellars that were dug into the ground behind each of the great brick dwelling houses; the women worked the oil presses, gathered and dried herbs, and were busy in the clothing rooms from which each member was issued two separate suits of clothes a year. The men worked the fields, took care of the barns and stables, chopped the wood, ground the grain, made the furniture and brooms, and made the maple syrup and sugar, sometimes as much as five thousand pounds in a single year. It was the custom for every man to weave his own hat, and some of these were beautifully made, although in winter the Society sometimes provided fur hats for the men. The women wore caps always, and there was a separate cap loom. The men were obliged to shave their beards once a week, although there were always those who said beards in men were designed to ward off weakness of the eyes and throat.

The women were always addressed as "Sister" and the men as "Brother," unless they happened to be Deacons or Elders, when that title of respect was accorded them.

The women planted extensive gardens, and both men and women busied themselves in gathering seeds of desirable plants, which were then guaranteed to be fresh and good and were peddled for miles around. Boots and shoes were of the best leather, and the skins employed were dye tanned in Shaker tan pits, to which other servitors dutifully brought in tons of oak bark. The dyes employed in the dye rooms were all dark or drab, as was fitting. The wood shops made all the necessary furniture, and made it very plain and right, using only the best black and white walnut, and other hardwoods, although now and again cedar was also employed.

It was the business of selected women in the several Families to see that the gardens grew and prospered, although no flowers were planted, either in the gardens, or around the houses, since such employment was idle and smacked of vanity. There were always acres of potatoes, corn, cabbage, beets, and there were always hundreds of bushels of apples and peaches brought into the Families. These were dried and stored, or made into peach leather or sauce. There were also gooseberries, currants, and rhubarb in the gardens, while raspberries and wild blackberries were gathered from the fields.

On the south road stood a schoolhouse for the children, where Webster's Speller, the New Testament, and the skill of the teachers were the only aids the children had in learning, and in the schoolhouse the boys and girls were taught separately until they learned to read, write, and cipher.

There were also one or two annual recreations for the Family members, sometimes visits to neighboring towns for a day, picnics in the woods, or the annual harvest festival when many of the members went out to the fields and woods and sang and danced the loaded wagons home. There was also a beautiful custom among the separate Families, at least of the young singers from the separate Families, of making their own Christmas hymns and rising in the pre-dawn light on Christmas morning to ride in sleighs to the separate Families and serenade them with their new hymns. There was also the Yearly Sacrifice, an open confession of hidden sins to another member, and there was the annual footwashing, which generally happened in the quiet rooms on Christmas Eve.

There were almost no books in Union Village, and there were few if any newspapers, although now and again one from Lebanon or Cincinnati would find its way into Union Village and be scanned by those who desired to read—and could read. There were no dentists or doctors in the Village, although in duress one might be summoned from a nearby town. There was also nothing that spoke of the world, or was in the least worldly. No slave or partner in business could belong to the Society, which was of free men only, and then only those who were willing to surrender all their worldly possessions when they joined the Society.

There was also no compulsion. Children were not forced to join the Society, nor were they ever stolen away or in the least abused, and adults could leave Union Village whenever they liked, although there could be no restoration of the property they brought with them when they came.

And the good word, that Jesus Christ had appeared again in the person of Ann Lee, was spread wherever the Elders saw missionary activity profitable. So Watervliet, near Dayton, had been established in 1810, North Union near Cleveland in 1822, and Whitewater, over near the Indiana line in the dry forks of the Whitewater River, in 1824. In addition missionaries had been sent to the Shawnee Indians when it seemed that there was a work of God among them.

Despite the difficulties of travel, there was a great deal of intercourse between the Societies; it seemed that the Ministry at Mount Lebanon was always sending leaders and converts west, while Union Village kept going and coming to and from its colonies at Watervliet, North Union, and Whitewater. Pleasant Hill and South Union in Kentucky were also visited, although West Union, in Indiana, had to be discontinued and the members scattered because the West Union ground was malarial.

All in all, the Shaker way was an enormously successful and memorable undertaking, and those who were firm in the faith knew that, short of the Millennial dawn, it was the Kingdom of God come to earth.

THE SHAKERS, or Shaking Quakers, believed quite simply in the God of the Bible, and in Jesus Christ, the Son of God. They believed, however, that since God was dual, both male and female, Ann Lee, who had lived a life in Golgotha before the revelation of her Ministry came to her, was the second Christ, the female Christ. And it was true, at least true to their satisfaction, that Ann Lee, or Mother as they preferred to call her, had said many wise things, although she had not walked on water or healed the blind and palsied. They believed also, or so it seemed, in the imminent end of the world, and in preparation for eternity they were determined to lead quiet and decent lives in thought, word, and deed.

There had been evidences of God's presence, or at least they were so convinced. In about 1815 there had come a mighty upheaval which afterward they called Wartime, when it seemed that Holy and mighty angels were causing all sorts of psychic aberrations among them. Children said wise things, and sometimes acted very foolishly, and those who had the "gift"—and they believed everyone had the "gift" or inspiration to do something creditable—were torn by forces they did not understand so that they both preached and prophesied. After that fearful time was past, there was reasonable quiet again, but after a dozen years or so the psychic manifestations began again, and it seemed as if certain chosen were both seeing revealed wonders and were the tongues to reveal these things to their fellow men. Men and women, and sometimes children, were propelled across the Meeting House floor, or sometimes outdoors across fields and fences, and some of the chosen instruments spoke in strange tongues that could not be understood or interpreted.

There was nothing particularly strange about all of this, for others had predicted the end of the world, and the Millerites had been fervently praying and patiently waiting for the cataclysm of fire when all the elect would be caught up in the clouds. And in various places there had been reported spirit rappings, rappings that often led to no intelligent communication.

The Shakers were patient and bided their time. When the weather was warm enough to gather in the unheated Meeting House they met there every Sunday for preaching and exhortation, and that was always followed by the dance, because Scripture declared that one should dance unto the Lord, and the dance had probably been the first mode of worship. The Shaker dance was hardly more than a shuffle, but in addition to the shuffle there was also the Square Step and the Lively Step, and these were sometimes used at the inspiration of the spirit. The dance was sometimes accompanied by a hymn to Mother, but the exultation was most often what other people declared to be a sort of drone that seemed to come from the chests of the believers.

Shakers believed in a godly, righteous, and sober life, and there was never any real levity. The Meeting House floor at Union Village was sometimes wet with tears, but neither there nor in any one of the giant Family houses was there ever the voice of unstifled laughter. Nor was there ever much relief from piety except in daily work. There were no books to read, and reading was discouraged. There were few newspapers that were brought into the Village, and after a time these were forbidden, since they were a trial to faith. There was never any exhibited anger, for it was unseemly. There was little affectionate conversation. One addressed one's fellows as Sister Martha or Sister Miranda or as Brother William or Brother Paul, one's superiors as Deacon Branscomb or Eldress Margaret. And one said whatever one had to say in measured syllables, for there was no call—or more properly no "gift"—to do otherwise. Any evidence of worldliness was a confession of sin, and too great levity was proof that the soul within was scant and starved.

In consequence of such repression, all one's energies had to be expended on tasks assigned by the House Elders or Work Deacons, and in doing tasks well and thoroughly the Shaker Families took delight. Everything was of the best, or was designed to be the best. And everything was plain and simple, chests and bedsteads, tables and chairs, sleighs, brooms, wagons, clothing, whatever the Shakers created. The Shaker believed in quality because his life was itself quality, and the tasks assigned by God through His chosen Ministry were to be performed patiently and efficiently. Shakers did not believe in making "good" bargains; they believed in giving more than they promised. Nothing was sold to the world outside that would ever be found to be cheap or shoddy. The seeds peddled through the surrounding counties had to grow; the brooms must be made of the best broom corn, be heavy and full, and be properly bound; the gloves, caps, and stockings that were sometimes sold to the world had to be the best wool or leather. The ministers of God could not think otherwise.

The Shaker tables were plain, but the food was abundant and it was nourishing. Meats were eaten, of course, but pork was always a bit discountenanced, and after a few decades it was forbidden. Orchards were set out that contained a thousand trees. No wines or hard liquors were permitted to be consumed, unless for medicinal purposes. Spicebush, sage, and sassafras teas were the only beverages served at table, although for a time coffee and store tea had been permitted. There were a hundred spices because the Families all had extensive herb gardens. Cider was drunk, and nuts from the woods, walnuts and hickories and butternuts, were cracked and passed around in wooden bowls at Christmastime, when some genteel commerce between the sexes was permitted in the Family Meeting Rooms. And whatever the community could not itself supply was purchased by the Trustees in the surrounding towns, but this only after the various Deacons had requested the Trustees to make such purchases, and the need for them had been thoroughly studied.

And the days were alike, and melted together, and the months coalesced, and the years ran, and the various Ministries, always appointed by the Elders at the parent community at Mount Lebanon, New York, succeeded each other. The burial ground became full of bodies that slept in unmarked graves, and the world was first skeptical and brutal, then polite, and finally contemptuous. But the Society endured and everyone thought that the Great Day could never be far in the future. Mother would come again—the hymns declared as much—and when she came she would expect to find her children ready and full of light.

It was a decent faith, a hopeful faith, and those who walked the ways of piety had faces as serene and untroubled as the cows that grazed in the wide pastures and never inquired about the stars.

RUTH DID not know all these things, of course. There had always been Shakers in her world, and she really had not enough schooling to inquire about anything. But the thought of running away to the Shakers had become a persistent thought, and after that one bad night she had spent in the cabin with Rachel and Jake the thought was like an explosion in her head.

For it had really been a bad night, with her father, mother, Asenath, and Herman all gone on devious tasks. All that night Jake prowled through the black cabin, and by some psychic sense Ruth knew whenever he came near the bed where she and Rachel were lying. Sometimes in the dark she could even feel his gulped gasps for breath as he stood over them, and when she could not hear him she could smell him, for Jake smelled only slightly better than a polecat. Ruth fought herself to keep from sleeping, for there was always a chance that Jake would get it into his head to crawl into the bed with them. Ruth really was not afraid for herself, but she remembered what she had been told, that Rachel had once had a child. It was too obvious that Jake was, or might have been, the father, although Ruth sometimes wondered if it could not have been either her father or Herman. Jake was the worst of the lot, but the other two were not much better.

The night was long, too long, and it seemed as if no one would ever get home. Her mother and Asenath would not, of course—her mother always stayed the whole night through, and when she did finally come sometimes left Asenath behind to care for the new mother and child. And there was no sense waiting for her father—he was likely passing the night in some woman's bed. That left Herman, and since she knew Herman had gone out to shoot something that didn't belong to them, she thought he should be back by midnight. He wasn't.

Somewhere in the frost a fox barked and seemed to be too near. The chickens were shut up in a wooden coop, but there was a chance that a fox might be able to work his way inside. Ruth thought once or twice of getting up and going out, but the night was so cold and her clothes so inadequate that she simply couldn't make the effort. And, because of Jake, she didn't want to leave the cabin, not for a minute. The fox came nearer, then seemed to be on some other trail, for its bark diminished, and Ruth dozed off into a catnap. It seemed only minutes after that that she heard a bumping and scuffing outside the cabin, and at long last Herman came back. Ruth heard the thump of whatever he had been carrying as he threw it on the table, and then Herman went over to the fire and started scraping the coals. Jake joined him there, and as they added pinwood to the coals the flames finally danced up. After that the two of them worked together until they had the chimney blazing.

Ruth slept then, although she knew she'd have to be awake if her father drove home in the early light. He'd want his meat, and Ruth would have the sorry task of taking the butcher knife and cutting up whatever Herman had brought home. She hated butchery—it made her sick in her stomach. It made her sick too to know that they always had to go out and steal. It seemed to be the only way the Berzinskis could get along. And people complained about them and shunned them for probably that very reason—that they knew the Berzinskis were thieves. It shouldn't have to be that way; with three strong men to work they should be able to do better. But they never had done better, not as long as Ruth could remember.

The sound of a horse in the driveway made Ruth come to her senses—it seemed probable that her mother was home. She was. The cabin door opened and Mrs. Berzinski seemed to seep through the door, her gray hair down her back and her dirty dress dragging behind her. Ruth heard her snort when she saw the meat—it was what she almost always did. Ruth thought then, for perhaps the hundredth time, that her mother despised them all, the whole rag-tag pack and parcel of them. Including herself. Her mother might just take it into her head sometime to poison them all—it was her constant threat. There were plenty of things in the fields and woods that were said to be poison, even some things that grew in the garden. Like white snakeroot, or ginseng, or the red love apples that some people grew for show in their gardens. Some people said the apples were deadly poison.

It was a task to get up, but no task to dress because she had never undressed. Ruth shook her long hair out, rubbed her hands over her face a couple of times, and went over to the table. "She have her baby all right?" she asked her mother.

"She had her baby," said her mother drily. "It's never all right. Bled like a stuck pig."

Ruth had no stomach to inquire further. There was blood all over the table where the skinned carcass of a middle-sized pig was lying. In the small light the glazed eyes seemed to look at her as if she were the culprit and not Herman, who was slumped in a chair by the fire, at last fast asleep. Ruth felt slightly dizzy, and went over to the water bucket in the corner to get a dipper of water to quiet her nerves.

IT WAS FULL spring again, and Ruth realized that she could go any time she wanted to or decided she had to. Every day now her mother left the cabin soon after sunup, and she ordinarily came home with her plunder near dark, sometimes with her apron loaded with the precious things she had found in the woods. What these were Ruth never knew; when they were dumped out on the table they looked like trash. Mrs. Berzinski cooked some of the stalks and roots in a small iron pot she kept for that express purpose, but the most she hung up against the rafters to dry. No one in the family ever had the courage to inquire exactly what the bunches of wilted stalks and grasses were, or what they were good for. And Mrs. Berzinski offered no explanations. What she would not tolerate, however, was that anyone in the family should knock any of her herbs down, and if someone unwittingly did, there was always a razor-sharp comment and a nasty look.

With the warmth of May things seemed a little better—at least it was possible to get away from the cabin a little while almost every day. Once the garden was plowed—Harmon always did this task without complaint, probably because it was one he had done all his life—the seed dropping and planting was up to the women, and sometimes even Rachel came out with Asenath and Ruth to help their mother. Rachel always stood over near the rail fence and looked vague and uncomprehending, but Ruth thought she was not too unhappy, and there was at least sun on her head and shoulders. So the rhubarb came up and was stewed into sauce, although it was hard to get enough sugar to sweeten it, and Mrs. Berzinski dried a small armful of the stuff. Then the violets and dandelions were over all the hills and tucked into every crevice of the earth, and the thousands of wild junipers, or cedars, as they always called them, seemed somber in the sunshine. The men went plowing every day, and one Friday Harmon went away and when he came back he was dragging a cow behind the buggy. No one dared inquire where he had gotten the cow, but she was fresh, and after that they had milk. They made cornmeal mush and ate the milk and some of the maple sugar sweetening on the stuff, passing around the only two brown bowls they possessed.

And there was meat—after that one bad night Herman kept them supplied with meat. Some he said he got by helping other farmers butcher, but no one in the family was that green—all the butchering had been done before the ice went out of the streams. It was probable that Herman had discovered certain farms that he could raid for slabs of bacon and fat hams.

On a day in May Ruth finally did what she had wanted to do for a long time—she seized her opportunity, since Asenath was around to take care of Rachel, and slipped up the road to the Robinsons. As she expected, Mr. Robinson was out in the fields somewhere, but fortunately Mrs. Robinson was behind the house in her garden. She had a cherry red sunbonnet on her head, and wore long stockings on her arms to shield them from the sun. And, when she saw Ruth coming, she pretended to be very busy—she was setting out cabbage plants that they had raised in the hotbed from Shaker seed, and the bending over repeatedly was giving her an awful misery in her back.

Ruth drew up at the garden fence and stood there for a long time while Mrs. Robinson pretended not to see her, but when Ruth started talking to the dog and patting him Mrs. Robinson knew that the game was up.

"O, I didn't know you were there," she said as she inched herself to her feet. "You folks all well."

"Good as can be expected, I suppose," said Ruth. "You get through the winter all right?"

Mrs. Robinson thought she did not have to answer that sort of interrogation, not from one of the Berzinskis.

"I ain't as young as I was once," she said. "It gets me in the back, this does. I used to be able to stick in a hundred of them without feeling puny."

They stood, both of them wanting to ask questions. Mrs. Robinson thought that Ruth might know where Richard had gone, and Ruth thought that there was a good chance Richard's mother might know the same thing.

"You all get through the winter all right?" Mrs. Robinson threw back at Ruth.

"About like always."

"Meat hold out?"

Ruth fought herself to keep from coloring.

"About like always," she said glibly. "We made a good bit of sugar when the trees run. What we're eating is mostly mush. It's good with maple syrup."

Mrs. Robinson wasn't confused or deceived. Abraham had discovered only two or three weeks ago that someone had raided their smokehouse—they had lost two hams and two sides of bacon. Anyone could have taken the stuff, of course, but anyone wouldn't. The inference led straight to the Berzinskis. Now Abraham had set an old bear trap in the shack, an evil thing with four-inch teeth in its iron jaws. Mrs. Robinson was so afraid of the trap that she wouldn't go within ten feet of the smokehouse.

"Richard ain't here anymore, is he?"

There, it was finally out, and the direct question had to be answered in some way, or in no way at all. That too would be an answer. But Mrs. Robinson didn't even try to answer; she only dropped the hoe she had been holding, and when she turned away Ruth knew that she was crying. It was several minutes before she wiped her eyes on her apron and half turned around.

"You don't know where he went, do you?"

Ruth shook her head. "I didn't even know he was gone until I didn't see him anymore," she said. "I don't know where he went."

Mrs. Robinson only stood and stared at her.

"It was about you," she finally said. "Maybe you know that. It was about you."

Ruth didn't know how to answer that.

"I don't know anything about it," she said. "I didn't know he meant to go away. He didn't say so."

"It was about you," Mrs. Robinson said again. "He was sweet on you, and his father and I didn't want him to get married so soon. That's what it's all about."

Ruth felt a lump in her throat. If Richard was gone, it was likely all over, whatever there had been between them. And it could be that he meant never to come back. It was her turn to cry now, and she felt two tears sneak out of the corners of her eyes.

"It wasn't me wanted him to go," she finally managed to get out. "I wanted him to stay right here so I could see him once in a while. He was all I had."

At that they both cried. "It was all his father and I had too," said Mrs. Robinson. "And if it hadn't been for you, he'd be here right now."

Ruth saw no sense in prolonging the agony, and when Mrs. Robinson turned back to her wilting cabbage plants, she unceremoniously pushed away from the fence and started back home, the old dog Mose trotting along beside her.

So that was it—he was gone and gone for good. And if he was gone, then the probability of his coming back was not very great. Possibly by this time he was miles away, and very possibly he had found someone else to love.

Ruth walked down the road woodenly, so dazed that she didn't even see the scarlet redbirds flirting around in the hawthorn trees. There was nothing ahead of her now, nothing to hope for. Nothing.

Chapter 4

T HE GARDEN prospered, although in June it was already necessary to bat the bugs off the rows of potatoes. But the beets were up, and the corn was well out of the ground, although it looked as if it badly needed hoeing. Probably the best indications of wealth to Mrs. Berzinski—for the garden was always called hers, even though Ruth and Asenath did almost all the work in it—were the clumps of milfoil, tansy, bergamot, chicory, and camomile. There were chives too, and onions, and a whole host of lesser herbs she had brought in from the fields and transplanted into the plot, things like buckthorn, Queen Anne's Lace, butterfly weed, and blue vervain. For some reason that only she knew, she had also laboriously toted in Jimson weed and pokeberries, although these last were so common that there was no sense in harboring them. All in all, it was not a really good garden—it had not been manured properly—but it was not a contemptible one, and the old lady generally passed the mornings out in the open, her head bound in a square of red cloth and her teeth clamped hard on a corncob pipe into which she had stuffed raw tobacco.

Ruth did most of the heavy work, and although she liked being in the open, she did not like that necessity of also doing all the cabin chores. But Rachel was unable to help, and Asenath always acted as if she thought she would demean herself if she cooked or cleaned anything.

So things went along, and the sun grew high in the sky, and the fields grew up in tangles as they always did. There was wheat to cut in June, poor wheat with grass and weeds all through it, but Jake and Herman got it bound up into sheaves, or at least said they did. They'd bring it into the barnyard and knock the grain out of the

heads sometime in July when they got good and ready, and after
that, if they could summon up enough energy to carry some of the
stuff to the mill at either Lebanon or Monroe, there'd be flour. In
some years they just didn't get around to the task, but despite that
fact Harmon always planted a couple acres of wheat.

It was better in the barnyard—a few of the hens had gotten
broody, and Mrs. Berzinski had dutifully given them the chore of sitting on eggs. So there were bright new chicks running around, and
there was even a goose that somebody had found wandering around
up in the wild land. Year after year Harmon talked of turkeys, but
there were never any turkeys, and it was probably just as well, for
turkeys were particular critters. Not only that, but there were still a
few wild turkeys around, and Herman was generally able to shoot
one or two of them in the fall.

So things looked good, reasonably good. But there were other
signs too, more ominous signs. Harmon was never at home on the
weekends, and somehow they all knew that he was passing his time
with the woman in Monroe, whoever she was. No one was ever curious enough to do any spying, but each Friday night Harmon went
through the misery of shaving himself with the old razor that had
two bad nicks in the blade. He'd wet his face with lye soap and
curse and swear while he stropped the razor, but he did generally
manage to hack off some of his bristle. He also always managed to
hack off some of himself, and he was ordinarily a bleeding mess for
a few hours after he had finished shaving. However, his mood always seemed lighter when he was going into Monroe, and once or
twice on Monday mornings he even brought back a few presents,
once some sugar cookies and once a bucket full of frogs. Harmon
said he meant to eat them, and he expected Ruth to kill and clean
them, but she adamantly refused. That made Harmon angry, and he
slapped her hard, something he had rarely done. However, Ruth did
not clean the frogs, and at long last they were dumped down into
the creek.

But all that summer Ruth waited and languished. Richard
would come home, she thought, would definitely come home sometime. He wasn't the kind of man who simply deserted. Ruth found
several occasions to go over into the woods and cut back of Robinsons, but there was never the slightest evidence that anyone was
around. The house and outbuildings looked deserted, although there

were a few fields planted and the cows were still grazing in the meadow out behind the barn. The Robinsons were still alive, she knew that, for now and again the Robinson wagon came down the road and headed off somewhere, and once or twice Mrs. Robinson had been with old Abraham. The Robinsons never looked in when they passed; it was almost as if they had declared in their own minds that the Berzinskis no longer existed. They were evidently still sore about the loss of their hams and sides of bacon.

The hot days came, and with the hot days life seemed a little simpler, although there was still plenty of work to do. They were eating potatoes now, little green potatoes that tasted green, but were enough to keep the walls of the stomach spread apart. Better than that, Jake and Herman had found a job in Lebanon, and once there, they did not come home for weeks. That meant fewer mouths to feed, and somehow the women found it easier to get along when the men weren't around. Ruth had no real idea what Jake and Herman might be doing, and she knew with assurance that whatever it was they would never bring any money home with them when they finally came. But it was a blessing just to get shut of them.

However, with the waning of summer, her apprehensions grew again. She just couldn't pass another fall and winter in the miserable cabin. First they would all have to endure the rains, and then in the bright autumn sky the geese and ducks would fly south, and then the chill would come, and they'd be starving cold for endless months. She grew miserable at the very thought, but generally had sense enough to scoff at herself, for the chaffinches were still on the sunflowers and the autumn asters had not yet begun to show blue. However, the thought recurred again and again, and the only escape she could think of was in going away to the Shakers. She didn't know how she would like that—it was too much like being buried, but there was always the chance that the Shakers knew more than she did and could lighten her mind about a lot of things.

The worst thing was that there was no one to talk to, no one to confide in. They were all too busy, her mother with boneset and Joe Pye and weeds like that, Asenath with whatever ghosts she communicated with as she sat staring into space, the menfolks with whatever meanness they were dreaming up at the moment. Asenath was probably the only one who would have listened, and once or twice

Ruth tried to get her into a talking mood, but Asenath never said two words together, so that Ruth finally let her alone.

Then something happened that made her change her mind in a hurry—Herman came back from Lebanon with a nasty mean woman who had lost almost all her front teeth. Herman never said she was his wife, and it was apparent she was not, but that night they slept together in the corner bed where Jake and Herman had always slept together. Ruth expected either her mother or her father to be angry, but it seemed as if they didn't care that Herman was sleeping with the woman. In the mornings Lily—that was her name—always woke up in a snarling mood, and was always after Herman to do this or do that because she felt so bad she couldn't wait on herself. Herman always ignored her, of course, not paying as much attention to her as he would have to a basset bitch, and after a time Lily would get hold of herself. But Herman did manage to get bottles for her, brown bottles full of something that made the woman's face flush. For a half day after that she'd go around drunk, and then fall down somewhere and sleep off her stupor. Herman seemed to think it funny whenever he found her lying on the floor or half fallen off the table. He'd cackle and point to her for a long time, making sure that everybody acknowledged the fact that she was blind drunk, and then he'd finally pick her up in his arms and throw her on the bed as unceremoniously as if she were a sack of corn. After Lily came it was noticeable that Harmon was away from the cabin for longer times—sometimes now he'd come back on Tuesday instead of Monday morning. The wheat had not been thrashed out, of course, and now the corn would never get cut and shocked. Once or twice Ruth went up to the fields herself, but the corn wasn't ready to be ground, and the wheat had all been smashed down and covered with weeds.

She decided then to go, having no regrets except, perhaps, for Rachel. But Rachel was hardly living; she existed, if she existed at all, in some sort of dream world swarming with apparitions that she could not understand or bring into focus. Ruth thought she would die, how soon she didn't know, but Rachel would surely die. It might be a mercy if she did. As for Asenath and her mother, they'd get along as well as they ever had, and both of them had some sense of mission in the world. People came to the cabin sometimes when somebody was down with chills or colic, and they generally brought something with them in payment for the potions or simples the old witch sent along with them. And there'd be new babies to bring into the world—one could be sure of that. As for Herman and Jake, and particularly Herman, now that he had his doxy with him, Ruth didn't care if she ever saw either of them again. Her father, in spite of his constant meanness, she didn't hate quite so much; he had evidently had a desperate time in the world. For years it had been evident that all of his kids hated him, although they depended upon him as their final support in every crisis, and it had long been evident that the family had worn him beyond endurance. Once she went away Ruth didn't ever want to see him again either, but she thought that time would soften her memory of him and make it less bitter.

There were no plans to make—she had nothing to take with her. She'd have to go to the Shakers almost as naked as the day she was born. She owned nothing in the world, neither shoes nor coat nor a decent dress to wear. She would be washed clean—she'd see to that by stopping somewhere along the brook as she cut across through the woods. She meant to go that way because she didn't want to be seen on the roads; she'd plunge into the woods, make her way west, cut north then to say good-bye to the Robinsons' place, then head west again and go in through Jehovah's Chosen Square. There wouldn't be anyone dancing in it anymore—the leaves were starting to come down, and through the winter the sacred place would sleep in its consecration.

Ruth decided to go on Sunday afternoon. Her father would be gone, Jake was still away, and Herman and his whore would likely be out gallivanting around somewhere. It was likely that her mother would be out of the house too, for with winter coming on she generally took advantage of all the good days to add to her supply of medicines that would have to last through the winter. She'd likely be crawling around somewhere in the woods looking for toadstools or wintergreen berries, or picking another bouquet of pennyroyal. That would leave Rachel in the cabin, but there was nothing that could be done for Rachel. Day after day, hour after hour, she sat in her chair and stared into vacancy, and whoever came in first would find her there, completely unaware that everyone was gone.

It would be Sunday afternoon, as near the middle of the day as she could find time to slip away. Ruth's heart jumped a little when she thought of the enterprise, skipped a beat when she thought of just walking into Shakertown and asking for help. But that's the way it would have to be, come what might.

THERE HAD BEEN several Ministries in Union Village, all of the First and Second Elders and Eldresses being appointed by the first, and dominant, Society in Mount Lebanon, New York. First, and perhaps most conspicuously, had come the good David Darrow, who had been First Minister of the Society from its founding in the West in 1805 until the time of his death in 1825. Under David Darrow the Society had been enlarged to nearly five hundred souls, and he had brought it from log cabins to good frame and brick dwelling places. Mount Lebanon had helped, of course; it had sent out many confirmed members and many guiding lights. The first sawmill was built in 1807, only two years after the foundation. Then the East, West, North, South, and Center Families were established, and suitable dwellings built. The land was cleared, and greatly added to by wise purchases and outright gifts, and the converts were put to work at their separate skills, so that the Society was self-supporting and self-sufficient. Weavers, dyers, tanners, spinners, cabinetmakers, smiths, wheelwrights all were deputed to do what they could do best, and although there were defections, mobs, lawsuits, and the attempt of the government to force military impressment upon some of the members in the War of 1812, the Society came through all its ordeals. The Church at Union Village did more than this; at the advice of Mount Lebanon they enlarged their work and established new communities at Watervliet, North Union, Whitewater, and even attempted one at West Union in Indiana. It seemed that the blessing of Almighty God was on David Darrow, and he was so well beloved that he was called Father David. He was only seventy-five years of age when he died.

After his death it seemed that Union Village lay for a while in a condition of shock, and it was not until 1829 that Solomon King was appointed First in the Ministry, with Joshua Worley Second, and with Rachel Johnson and Nancy McNemar First and Second on the women's side. Solomon King was to be First for only six years, but under him the Shakers counted eleven Families at Union Village, with a total membership of a little over five hundred souls. The

North, South, Center, East, and Brick Families were considered the Church, but the Square House and Grist Mill, both mill families, came also under their governance. The West Brick and West Frame were composed of members who had not yet been absorbed into the Church proper. The so-called North Lot and West Lot groups were "Gathering Orders," for those living there had not been accepted into full membership.

David Meacham headed the Ministry formed in 1835, but he was replaced after a single year by Freegift Wells, under whose Ministry there began again many spirit manifestations that proved that holy and mighty angels still watched over the chosen.

Freegift Wells was a good man, a thoroughly pious and godly man, and those who aided him in the Ministry were also of the chosen. Freegift looked with disfavor on all that had to do with the world, and it was noticeable that under his leadership there were improvements in piety. Newspapers were banned, and the "yearly sacrifice" was insisted upon, this last being the open confession of all one's sins. Freegift was a man troubled by the enormous pride of the world that many of the members still exhibited, and in his whole Ministry he bore witness to the spirit, and spent long vigils in the hope that the voice of Mother might direct his acts.

RUTH DID EXACTLY as she had planned—she waited until all were out of the house save only Rachel. At the last moment she thought that she should leave some note to indicate that she had gone away of her own volition, but there was nothing in the cabin to write with, and nothing to write upon. The least she could do was make her bed, and that she did, tossing the cornshuck pillows, and straightening the quilt. She looked around then, and she could hardly believe that she never meant to come back. Given enough food to eat, and enough discipline among the members of the family, the cabin could be a pleasant place, one that she would be loathe to leave. But there were circumstances she could not change, and the thought of another winter there was frightening.

No one saw her—she was sure of that. Asenath had made some sort of mission to the garden, and her mother was out in the woods somewhere, as she had known she would be. The men were gone, had been gone all weekend, and Herman had taken his light of love with him. Ruth was rather sure that somewhere they would find another bottle, and that the woman would be sick all the next day.

She cut west along the tiny stream that came down out of the hills, stopping for a while to wash her legs and arms and face, then swung north for her last look at Robinsons—there was no one out in the garden or farmyard. After that she boldly made her way into the rows of Robinson corn and walked between them towards the west woods. Once she got that far she was pretty sure she would be safe, for there was just no reason for anyone to be in the west woods. Her mother never came that far.

Ruth stopped under a beech—it reminded her of the times when she was younger and had been there with Richard. Almost every fall they had gathered hickory nuts in the woods, good shellbarks, and they had sometimes gone home with nearly a bushel. There were hickories today; a few had already fallen and the squirrels were busy collecting them and carrying them to the trees. Ruth watched a long time while a family of red squirrels alternately chattered at her, and made off with their pillage. Some people shot squirrels, but Herman never had—he said they were not worth powder. Ruth was glad of that—she could not have borne cleaning or eating squirrels. They were too much like spirits of the woods. There seemed to be something sacred about them.

There was one last stop—on the edge of the thicket that enclosed Jehovah's Chosen Square. Ruth knew that this was the final place where it was likely she could change her mind and turn back; after she entered Shaker land she would swiftly be through the Square, and then beyond that she'd be out in the open fields. If she ever got that far, she knew she'd never come back.

She had no precise plan, but the great North Dwelling was only a good half mile on the other side of the Square. Since she hadn't the least idea where to go, and since the North was somewhat isolated, she thought she'd go there. And if they didn't want her there, then they could tell her where to go. She didn't know anything about Shakers, but she imagined they'd be kind, although she was coming at an awkward time. She had heard that the Society was always skeptical about Winter Shakers, those who came in the late fall simply to escape the winter weather and who then left in the early spring.

It seemed only a moment she stood there, although the moment was likely prolonged to a full ten minutes. Then, when she came back to her senses, she was frightened for the last time. Even as she started working her way through the thicket she kept telling herself that she'd turn back. And as she kept telling herself that she'd turn around and go home, she kept working on through the thicket, until at last the Square stood open before her.

Once she got that far she no longer hesitated and even ran until she got out of the clearing and into the thicket on the other side. There was no turning back now—there was only one thing to do, go forward with a bold face and learn what fortune could bring. Whatever lay ahead could not possibly be as bad as that which lay behind.

THE FIRST THING Ruth noticed as she came in along a lane that led through two fields of standing corn was the barns and outbuildings, and beyond the barns and outbuildings a small knot of female Shakers in caps who were congregated in front of a smaller shed that was pretty well hidden behind a stand of dusty-yellow hollyhocks. Ruth knew at once that the shed must be a necessary, a large privy. She was certain of that fact when she saw a male Shaker, walking very sedately as if he refused to admit he was in a hurry, go towards the similar necessary on the other side of the lot. The females seemed to be chattering together, although in muted tones, and once one pointed to a big mound in the ground. Ruth looked too, and saw that there was a wooden door in the mound, and that there were limestone steps leading down to the door. She rightly inferred that the mound must be one of the root cellars or apple cellars. She had slowed her pace considerably now because she was puzzled where to go. There were two back doors to the North Dwelling at the tops of little sheltered porches, and she could see another door on the north side of the building, and it seemed as if the man must have come from that door. The back doors should lead to the kitchens, she knew that, but it seemed probable that it would be a breach of courtesy to go in through the kitchen.

Ruth decided just to stand, and to wait until some of the women returned to the house. It was not long. The three or four in the privy came out and nodded to the five or six women standing outside, and after that they seemed to form ranks of twos and start around the back of the North Dwelling. Happily they were coming towards the wellhead where Ruth was waiting. But they wouldn't look up; they walked as if they might be prisoners, with never a word, never a smile, never a simple glance of acknowledgment.

"Can you tell me where to go?"

It was her voice, although it sounded unreal.

"I want to know where to go," she said again as she fell into step beside them. "I've come to join."

At that one of the younger ones, whose face looked sunburned beneath her dainty lace cap, giggled a little. But she didn't speak—she seemed to be waiting for a large red-faced woman who was considerably older. The large woman had a peeled potato for a nose.

"I want to join up," said Ruth again when it seemed they didn't mean to stop. "That's what I'm here for."

The red-faced woman stopped at that, and when she stopped all the others halted. "You'll have to see Eldress Anna," she said. "But you can't join here—this is the North, and we belong to the First Family in the Church Order."

"What'll I do then?"

"You'll have to see Eldress Anna," said the large woman sharply, "That's what I told you: you'll have to go talk to Eldress Anna."

Ruth followed them, and it seemed they meant to go in through a woman's door on the north side of the building. She was ignored, but by this time she had decided that she might as well be hung for an ox, and when the ladies went in through the door Ruth followed them.

Inside the North Family building it was not very light. The group marched up some steps, and came to a great hall that ran the length of the building; then the Shaker women turned off to the left and headed for a wooden staircase that led up to the second story, and probably to the third. Ruth knew she didn't dare go up there, and so was left standing. She didn't mind very much—her reception had not been very cordial. For a long time she stood and stared, first up one direction of the large hall, then down the other. There were doors at both ends, wooden doors with many panels. And there were closed doors all up and down the hall, and behind the doors it seemed no one was stirring, for there was not the slightest sound.

But there must be people there, because Ruth knew that the North Family had perhaps a hundred people in it.

She started to whistle a little, very softly, but the whistle sounded eerie in the hall, and she decided that perhaps she must not. After that there was nothing to do but wait. She waited, perhaps for a quarter hour. Then she heard steps, and the steps were coming down the stair at the west end of the hall. She saw him then, a man, first his shoes and legs, then his Shaker coat, and finally his face and straw hat. In the wan light the face looked something like a sick moon when the night is watery. Ruth fairly ran to meet the fellow, although it was possible he meant to walk towards her. He was surprised—she saw that—but he stood his ground.

"I don't know what to do," she said boldly. "I came over here to join the Shakers, and nobody will talk to me. I don't know what to do."

The man smiled a little, at least his eyes smiled, and that was the first evidence of any welcome she had received from the whole of Union Village.

"I guess I don't really know what you should do either," he said. "Most people go right on down to the Gathering Order. That's on the south pike, if you know where that is."

Ruth had decided that she was not going to declare that she knew a thing about the Shaker community.

"I don't know whether I could find it or not," she said. "I'm a stranger here."

The man smiled again, and Ruth saw that he had good teeth. Most people didn't once they had passed the age of twenty-five, and he looked all of forty or forty-five.

"I guess maybe you'd better talk to Brother William," he said. "Elder Abernathy is gone, and Eldress Anna is probably asleep. You come along and I'll see if Brother William's in his room."

They walked down the hall towards the front of the building. Ruth was hoping Brother William would be in, because Eldress Anna and Elder Abernathy sounded much too formidable.

Brother William came immediately when the round-faced man knocked on his door. He was a tall man, his face tanned, his eyes light blue even in the little light in the hall. "You want me, Brother Matthew?" he inquired when he saw the moon-faced man in the door. And then his eyes took in Ruth, and he looked puzzled.

"Here's a girl come in," said Brother Matthew. "I don't know what I should do with her. I'm still a little bit strange myownself."

"She should go down to the Gathering Order and ask for Sister Samantha," said Brother William.

"That's what I told her," said the round-faced man. "But she's a stranger—she don't know where it is."

"You could tell her," Brother William suggested. "It's not too far, only about two miles. You could go across by the lane."

The round-faced man shook his head. "It's near time I got to go out to the cowbarn," he said. "I've got a duty."

Brother William seemed to understand that perfectly. His blue eyes glinted a little and his face grew thoughtful as he seemed to consider whether he might be the appointed instrument to see that Ruth got down to the Gathering Order.

"I guess I can," he said at last. "I meant to go over to the wood shop and see that everything was ready for tomorrow, but I don't have to." And then to Ruth, "You wait here. I have to get my hat."

Ruth waited and the round-faced man waited with her, and when Brother William came back in a moment he had his summer straw hat set firmly on his head. Moreover, he was carrying a good, thick, knobby cane in his hand.

"Thank you, Brother Matthew," he said, and dismissed the round-faced man. And then to Ruth, "We'll go out this way. No sense in walking around." And with that he motioned to the west end of the hall and started walking in that direction.

Ruth walked with him, and was almost blinded by the sunlight as they stepped out the door. Brother William walked ahead slightly, as if that was the appointed way, and Ruth dutifully fell in a half step behind him. The cinder path ran down to the road through the North Family lawn. The lawn was rather pretty for it had recently been sheared by sheep.

AND THEY WALKED. At the road Brother William turned south, as Ruth knew he must, and for a long time they went on in silence between the great fields of yellowing corn that seemed to spread in all directions. It was different when they came to the houses somewhat clustered in the Village proper; at that point Brother William started to tell her what the separate structures were called. So he pointed out the Brick and Center Houses, and the beloved white Meeting House, where he said the Ministry lived, and almost as an afterthought he pointed across the corn with his cane and said that the Grist Mill and Square Families lived out in that direction. However, said Brother William, the Grist Mill and Square really belonged to the First Family. Ruth was thoroughly confused, but she thought she dared not ask questions.

In the Village proper there were a great many more signs of life; everywhere, it seemed, men and women were going about whatever duties they had appointed for the end of the day. Brother William was apologetic. "There's some things a person can't help doing, even on the Sabbath," he said. "All the pigs and sheep and chickens and things has to be taken care of."

Ruth nodded her head knowingly, but Brother William still seemed not to be satisfied.

"It's Holy Mother's will," he said. "The Ministry always tries to do what's right."

Just south of the main buildings Brother William cut off the road and found his way across the ditch by walking a plank that had been conveniently laid there. "It's a lot closer this way," he explained. "We can just cut right across the fields and go down the run a little ways."

Ruth followed happily—she felt completely concealed once they got the protection of the corn. So the whole phalanx of weathered barns and farm buildings was left behind, and they were again in the kind of world Ruth understood best, particularly so when they came to what Brother William called the run. Some of the original forest trees still stood along the run, great elms and sycamores, and even a cottonwood or two. And there was a tiny stream that could sometimes be seen through the autumn yellow daisies that grew head-high. Brother William guided her through the worst tangles by holding the weeds and flowers back with his cane, and he seemed unnecessarily courteous, so much so that Ruth wondered if she dared ask him questions.

"I guess I don't know what the Shakers really believe," she ventured, hoping that she might be able to provoke Brother William to talk a little.

Brother William wasn't talking. "That's the purpose of the Gathering Order," he said. "It will all be explained. After it is, if you choose to stay and sign the Covenant, you may, and if you don't want to you can go away in peace."

"You believe in God, don't you?" Ruth tried again, but Brother William was firm.

"It will all be explained," he said again. "You'll have plenty to eat and a good place to sleep and work to do with your hands. And it will all be explained to you, every jot and tittle. You'll learn all about Holy Mother."

Ruth decided not to agitate the matter any further. She had decided that she liked Brother William, and now she began to decide that she didn't like him. Compared with Jake or Herman, she'd have to say that he wasn't really a man. Instead he seemed something of a bloodless cipher, half an angel and half a kettle of boiled dandelions. That was probably the trouble with the Shakers, that they were all waiting for something to happen that was never going to happen. Holy Mother, whoever she was, wasn't going to fly down again and light on one of their barns.

The West Frame building finally came in sight, after Brother William had gone off the path and led the way through an apple orchard that was hanging heavy with fruit. Ruth was hungry and wanted more than anything else to pull some of the apples—they would probably be sour, but she had really had nothing to eat during the day. She hoped they would not be too late for supper at the Gathering Order.

Brother William went up onto a small unpainted back porch and opened the door without knocking. There were people in the room, all of them women, and only two or three of them with Shaker caps on their heads, and they were all busy preparing cheese and cutting enormous loaves of white bread and setting out jams and jellies. Brother William went right up to one of the caps, an old woman, probably over fifty, whose once yellow hair was not very well secured under her head lace.

"Brought you another one, Sister Samantha," he said. "She come in to the North this afternoon."

Sister Samantha simply nodded her head, and kept on stirring what looked like vinegar into something that looked like spinach.

"Come in for the winter, did she?" she inquired of Brother William knowingly, her head bent all the while over the table.

"Nay, I don't think so," said Brother William. "Find her some clothes and a place to sleep. And give her something to do."

Sister Samantha nodded without reply, and tasted her vinegared spinach. It must have been all right because she wiped the spoon on her apron and put it back on the table.

And with that Brother William went back out the door like a gray shadow, and was gone. The six or seven girls and women in the kitchen kept on doing industriously whatever they were doing, and Ruth stood up against the wall in order to be out of the way. It seemed as if she was welcome, half welcome, but it didn't seem as if anyone was overjoyed that she had made the first step to come into the fold.

The kitchen was bare, drab, very efficient. The wood surfaces all seemed polished, even the floor—there was not a speck of dirt or dust on anything. At the side of the kitchen, backed up against the chimney, was a great iron monster that must be a cooking stove, and in one of the corners stood an eight-foot-high clock that monotonously ticked off the duration of eternity. Ruth had learned to tell time, although they had never had a clock in their cabin. It was almost five o'clock, and it seemed to her reckoning as if the women were counting on serving supper at five. It would not be too soon—by that time the front of her stomach would almost be touching her backbone.

IN THE LEAN late summer first dark, a granddaddy bullfrog sometimes thumping from the nearby stream, and a thin moon climbing in the east, they sat around the center table in one of the big square rooms while Sister Samantha read a passage from Scripture and exhorted them in her own homely way. "Be sober, be diligent, for your adversary the Devil walketh about as a roaring lion," Scripture had said, and Samantha, who must be some sort of minor Eldress, was now embellishing the words. "It means that you got to be busy all the time and not to ask questions," she said. "Do what you're told to do, whether you know why or not, and keep busy every minute of the time. And don't think foolish thoughts, 'cause if you do, the Devil's likely to be seen whispering right in your ears. Everybody's got something to do in this world, whether it's milkin' cows, makin' cheese, or helpin' the garden. Mother knows what you're a-thinkin' every minute o' the day, and if it ain't right, then Mother won't ever think to call you her own. I knew a man once—that was afore I had ever heard o' Mother, but I was a good church member, and so was he, for all that matter. Went ever' Sunday, an' took communion, an' did all them things. Ever'body kept on sayin' that he was a good man, but he wasn't a good man atall because he wouldn't work worth a penny. Just let things grow up about his ears, and finally the sheriff had to come an' take his kids away. That's what it means, somethin' like that."

Ruth sat and stared. There were a dozen of them in the room, or nearly a dozen, all of them sitting on straight hickory chairs and pretending to be interested as they stared at Sister Samantha in her little puddle of lamplight that spilled out on the square center table. The walls of the room were bare, although they had been dressed with lime, and the wide ash boards in the floor had been scrubbed unmercifully. There was one redeeming feature—underneath the one window there was another little table, and on it a potted fern. The fern was Samantha's, and her refusal to throw it away had cost her status in the Shaker community, for it was an evidence that she could not entirely forswear the lust of the eyes. The fern had been her mother's, and possibly her mother's mother's, and somehow it had survived transportation clear across the mountains. So Ruth sat and stared at the fern while her mind told her that Samantha was revealing no great secrets.

They had eaten well, bread and strawberry jam and yellow cheese and cottage cheese. The stuff that Samantha had been tossing in a wooden bowl was called salad, and what it was Ruth didn't know, but it tasted something like grass, and she ate it down, although most of the other neophytes had refused to touch it. After that she had been taken in charge by a large girl named Clema Porter, and Clema, once they got upstairs into one of the six sleeping rooms, seemed to be human. "Guess you can wear this, Ruth," she said, and handed over one of her own dresses. "They'll have to make you some shoes—they do that up in the village. Tell Samantha that you need some and she'll have you measured."

Ruth wanted to ask questions, but decided to wait a while, particularly after Clema pointed to a bed in the corner and told her that she guessed that was the one Ruth would have. Ruth tried it and thought she had never slept on such a bed in her life; it was soft and didn't crack like cornshucks every time she turned. But beyond that comfort the sleeping room was really austere and Clema said that it was already cold in the mornings. "Just wait till winter gets around," she said. "We'll freeze to death. No place to warm bricks or anything. We'll all freeze to death."

Ruth thought she would be able to stand it, but she didn't tell Clema so. Clema looked soft, a bit too fleshy and soft, although whatever fat she had should help to warm her. But Ruth knew that a person had to move in cold weather—he had to make his blood run downhill and uphill. That was the only way to fight the icy days.

That night, when they all prepared for bed at half-past seven, Ruth was surprised when she saw most of the girls kneel down by the sides of their beds. She had never seen anybody pray, didn't have the slightest idea what they might be doing. But she meant to cooperate, and when she finally made up her mind to get under the blanket, she too knelt down at the side of her bed and shut her eyes. It was a sort of good feeling she had, kneeling that way, with her forehead touching the blanket, and she almost went to sleep. As it was, she decided to kneel down every night, at least until she discovered what the act was all about.

IN THE WEEKS that followed Ruth learned a great deal about the Shakers that she had never known before or even guessed. They seemed to be good, pious, and rather stupid people, since there was a blandness about the faces of all the real Shakers she met. There were not many, perhaps only a dozen or so, but there seemed to be a regular going and coming of persons from the other Families every day, and on one occasion some two dozen men appeared in wagons for the apple picking. They stripped the orchard in little more than two days, and they left behind several of their deep white oak baskets filled with red, yellow, and very large green apples. Ruth realized then that the West Frame house had no great earth mound behind it and so probably had no way to keep its own fruit and potatoes. Later she was to discover that there was something of a raw earth cellar, and that it was well stored with various things, including the covered crocks that held cheese.

All through the apple-picking the women in the West Frame had been somewhat sequestered, and at the end of two days Sister Samantha was beside herself in trying to invent new tasks. The house was already so clean—it was cleaned everyday—that there were no longer surfaces to scrub, and the kitchen crew welcomed no intruders. So, for the better part of two days, the rest of the women sat and stared, and unfortunately could see very little from the windows, where there was from time to time at least the benison of a shout or the sound of tangled voices as the teams drew big wagons between the orchard trees. Then, as abruptly as it had begun, the apple picking was all over, and the women were emancipated again. This meant that those who were assigned to the garden might go again among the cabbages and rows of late beans, and at least look at the sky and get lungfuls of fresh air.

Ruth was happy that she was one of the garden crew. There were five of them—Ruth, middle-aged Patience Blake, a leggy young female named Flossie (that was all Ruth ever heard her called), a young wife named Mary Hawthorne, who was in her twenties and was still crying because she had been separated from her husband, and a woman who looked fifty and who was constantly complaining of a stitch or crick in her back. Frankly they did little in the garden—in late October there was little to do. Most of the potatoes had been dug, although there were some weedy rows that were still to be uprooted, the cabbages had all gone to round maturity, and the corn was withered. There was a long row of red beets, and there were chives and parsley and a few onions that had not yet been gathered in. So all day long the five of them pretended busyness and now and again chopped at a weed with their iron hoes. They weren't fooling anybody, of course, not even Sister Samantha, but they were at least out of the house, and that was where Samantha preferred to have them.

The idleness gave Ruth plenty of time to think, and it was then that she started adding up her first judgment about the folks in the Society. They were clean, patient, and seemingly willing. They were almost all uneducated—half of them could neither read nor write. They were all a bit confused, and they were all more than a little fearful, for the dire prophesies they heard murmured every day did their nerves no good. Mother was coming, she was coming in the clouds of glory to gather her saints. That supposed fact was dinned into the heads of every one in the West Frame every night when

Sister Samantha led in what was called Family Worship. Sister Samantha herself Ruth judged rather unkindly; she was a do-er, and no one could deny that, but it seemed to Ruth that life was short enough that one could afford to stop and stare awhile. The Shakers didn't seem to have much sense of wonder or of admiration. Birds were birds and beasts were beasts, and no one looked and marveled at the chains of geese that were flying about the sky, or even thought to pat the neck of a cow. Without being much of a philosopher Ruth began to feel that there was something wrong about the incessant worry about one's immortal soul. God—whatever God there was— if He had created men and women at all, must have put them on the earth for some purpose better than to wear out their lives in self-torture. There was so much to see and do in the world, so many places where one might be expected to be happy. The Shakers weren't happy, not unless they were happy in that world many always withdrew to, and even then they must know a kind of happiness that never showed on their faces.

To be very truthful, Ruth knew that this wry judgment was not completely true about the few women she knew in the Gathering Order. There they were not all saints, at least not yet, and some of the girls and women didn't mind talking about their bitterness. Clema Potter and Mercy Bivvens were both completely discontent: Clema because she confessed that she'd like to find a man and settle down somewhere to have a few kids; Mercy because after the death of both of her parents she had suddenly found herself alone in the world. Clema was tall and strong, a really handsome young woman, with dark straight hair that fell to her waist when she sometimes pulled off her cap and shook her head. She had made a confidante of Ruth almost from the first night, and while she kept prudent lips whenever she was in the presence of some of the pious, it was only so that she could vent her anger more openly afterwards. Clema had come to the Shakers because her father and mother had come, and she told Ruth she hadn't known what she was getting into. For some unexplained reason neither her father nor mother had been made to wait while they were schooled in the Gathering Orders, and Clema frankly didn't know what Families they were in. Up in Franklin her father had been a sort of carpenter and a sort of jack-of-all-trades, and her mother had been the best cook in the whole community. But then—they were past forty, they had both seemed to get religion, and the first thing Clema knew they had been talking of selling everything they possessed and coming over to the Shakers. Clema had been unable to help herself. There had been a man—there had been several men, but Clema hadn't liked any one of them enough to marry him, and had been waiting until the right man came along.

As for Mercy Bivvens, that was another story—smallpox. Mercy was slight and very pretty in a doll-like way, but her gray eyes looked frightened and she seemed oblivious of her porcelain beauty. She was almost as small as a child, and she seemed to weigh hardly anything, but she was well put together and always made people look back at her, as if they couldn't believe what they had just seen. Mercy's people had lived down near Mason, Mercy said, in a brick house that her father had built himself. And they had raised lots of things on their farm, including tobacco, and Mercy had been used to running over the hills with her dog Lindy. And then, in one week's time, it was all gone, and her girlhood was over. The neighbors had even taken the dog away, and before a family named Fry had carted her up to Union Village Mercy had heard the report that some farmer had shot Lindy. That report might not have been true, but it was true for Mercy, since she had no way of proving it false. Mercy actually was helpless—she had never helped much, either on the farm or in the kitchen. All her memories were of roaming over the hills, running as light as thistledown, gathering violets and spring beauties in the spring, bringing home bouquets of Joe Pye and sloe thistles in the fall. Mercy had never realized that she was being indulged; she believed that life was good and was to be loved. Now, after only a month of her desolation, Mercy walked almost as if she were asleep, and at night when Samantha read the New Testament and went into one of her long rambles in explanation Mercy just sat and stared, as if she was trying to see clear to infinity. Ruth had marked her that first night, but had known nothing of her story. When Clema told her the next day, Ruth went out of her way to be kind to Mercy, but Mercy seemed to be totally indifferent to either kindness or rudeness. She seemed stunned, almost as if she were no longer living in the world.

The other three sisters in the sleeping room were totally different, and Ruth couldn't find herself very much concerned with any one of them. Naomi Spinsterwald was slight and had reddish hair, Lucy Hawks was a stringbean with sharp inquisitive eyes, and

Clementina Richards had a blotchy face and nondescript hair that hung lifelessly behind her waist whenever she took off her cap to go to bed. Those three Ruth thought would very likely in time make good Shakers; they all seemed somehow as if they had been born to be forgotten. Naomi confessed one night that she was afraid she was damned. There was no reason—the idea had just crept into her head, and she didn't know it could be traced back to a howling circuit rider. She told about the circuit rider, of course, with a sort of desolate rapture in her eyes. After that the thought of damnation had eaten into her brain, and she had come to the Shakers as a last resort, in hope that they might be able to lighten her misery. Clementina Richards was cowlike, and with her face would frankly have no chance of ever being married. There were pimples all over her cheeks and chin, and from the first day Samantha had started dosing her with mullein and tansy tea. The teas might have been poorly chosen; at least they had done no good. Ruth didn't like to be near the girl, for purely selfish reasons, because she was afraid that the pimples might be poison and communicable. Clementina talked, whenever she talked, and that was seldom, in a sort of singsong, as if she were repeating something that she had memorized and half forgotten. Her memorization, if any, was not from one of the great masters, for what she said was trash. As for Lucy Hawks, the sixth person who slept in the large room, she looked as if she alone might be destined to become one of the chosen who, given a little luck, might some day be First or Second in the Ministry. Lucy had sharp eyes, and she kept her tongue tied, but she had an enormous amount of energy, and whenever there was a common task to be done, no one could keep up with her. She had no friends; at least no one dared intrude upon her. Lucy seemed not to mind at all. Ruth asked the others where she had come from, but no one knew, and one day the word went around that Lucy was a sort of spy, planted among them to learn who really was eager to embrace the Shaker faith. Ruth didn't believe that report for a moment, but she nevertheless withheld all information and confidences from Lucy. There just seemed to be something too imperative about her.

And so the days passed, and one morning a whole host of men came in with corn knives and cut and shocked the corn, and after that they could see clear up to the Village. There was no sense in looking; all they saw across the lonesome fields was a gray smear of buildings on the far horizon. On some days the smoke went straight up from the great dwellings, and on windy days it blew down across the houses. And one night there was a great fire, and everyone in the house thought that one of the village cowbarns might be on fire. It wasn't, they learned later; because the night was not windy the South Family had decided to burn some accumulated trash.

And so the days went, monotonously, unrealistically, as if they were not actually living in the world any longer. And each night Sister Samantha gathered her flock together and made some pious exposition of something she didn't know anything about. The discourses rather got on Ruth's nerves, and she knew that Clema was furious. Once, after they had gone upstairs, Clema exploded—but only to Ruth. "She's nothing but a damned old fool," Clema said that night, and furiously ran a wooden comb through her long hair. "She's a damned old fool."

Ruth said nothing, but that night neither one of them knelt down beside her bed. Somehow the gesture seemed inappropriate. Then, in the dark after the candle had been pinched out, they could both hear Mercy Bivvens lying in her bed and sobbing bitterly. Somehow the sound made the cold chills go up and down their backs.

TONIGHT SISTER Samantha was running an exposition upon the wickedness of what she called the Adamic Order. It seemed that there was Adamic Order and Church Order, and Adamic Order was, if not totally wicked, then highly undesirable. There was something greatly worse than the Adamic Order, if one could interpret Sister Samantha's sighs and groans, but she refused to explain, no matter how much Clema Porter pressed her to do so. So they all sat in a ring, as usual, and as usual the older females had all congregated in one of the dark corners. Well away from the little light of the whale-oil lamp they were almost shadowy back there, but at least they maintained order and asked no questions.

"So it all come from that," Sister Samantha said for perhaps the hundredth time. "Adam sinned with Eve, and then Cain and Abel was born, and Cain killed his brother. It all come from that."

"I don't know what you're talking about," said Clema Porter suddenly. "How did Adam sin with Eve."

Sister Samantha took hold of her steel-rimmed glasses and pulled them off her nose.

"Adam did what he shouldn't have done," she said as she leaned in Clema's direction and shook her head. "Nobody's supposed to do what he done."

Clema was not to be put down so easily.

"It don't mean anything to me," she said. "If you know what he done, then I think you should say so."

At that Sister Samantha seemed to shake her jelly so that she sank back into her chair.

"Men an' women's made different," she said. "I don't want to talk about it. Maybe some day you'll know what I mean, and then you'll feel ashamed of askin' questions."

"Adam just lived with Eve, didn't he?" asked Clema. "That's what it says in the Bible. An' it says that God told them to be fruitful an' multiply. I don't see how they could multiply unless they lived together. That's the way pigs and cows are born."

Sister Samantha began to grow angry at that, and now she emphasized her words by shaking her finger in Clema's direction. "What we got's a new revelation," she said, and her voice trembled. "It all come to Mother after she had been through sin an' had come out safe on the other side. Men an' women ain't supposed to live together."

"But it says they should right in the Bible," said Clema. "Be fruitful and multiply. That's what it says right in the Bible."

"It's a new revelation, I told you," screamed Sister Samantha. "Them as wants to live in the world can live in the world, if'n they do it only when they want to have a baby. That's what's called the Adamic Order. But Church Order's higher, an' in Church Order nobody lives together at all. An' that's the way all the saints live because Mother told them that's the way it was supposed to be."

"Who told Mother?" asked Clema evenly. "Maybe she didn't know what she was talking about."

Sister Samantha gasped at that and now she got red and trembly. "You're a-goin' to hell, young lady," she screamed at Clema. "I don't know whether you're even worth prayin' for anymore. You're a-goin' to hell."

Clema seemed almost indifferent—at least she was not in the least excited. "It just don't make sense," she said again. "Maybe you don't understand it the way you ought to. Adam and Eve had to live together for any of us to be here at all. If they hadn't, then we'd never have been made."

Sister Samantha refused to answer, and instead fell on her knees, the invariable sign for all of them to fall on their knees and join her in the repetition of the Lord's Prayer. Tonight, however, it seemed she could hardly get the first words out of her mouth, and after they all broke in together, Samantha stopped entirely. The prayer over, she labored to get up, and that was always a job, even when she wasn't mad. When she finally did get to her feet, Clema had long vanished upstairs.

That night they were all very quiet in the big bedroom. Lucy Hawks was in first and pulled the covers clear over her head. Clema took her good-natured time, but she too had her chin thrust out, and Ruth could tell she was thoroughly mad. All the rest of them acted apologetic, as if somehow they had been unwilling witnesses. Ruth wanted to say something but didn't know how, and thought she'd best wait until morning. Lying in the dark and shivering a little because of the frosty night, she reviewed in her head everything she had learned, or thought she had learned. Carnal intercourse, according to the Shakers, was sin. But as Ruth understood it, men and women who couldn't ever hope to be good Shakers might live together if they met only for the purpose of having babies. After that they were supposed to act like strangers towards each other. But if they did live together repeatedly, then according to the Shakers they were committing sin. It all made sense—a little bit of sense. Sister Samantha had simply gotten mixed up—she hadn't been able to make a reasonable explanation. Not that Ruth thought Clema needed any elucidation. Clema was smart as a whip, and she had simply been trying to get the old goat muddled. That was what Clema called Samantha, an old goat. Ruth had to admit that the term was not a bad one—that was about the way she thought of Sister Samantha herself.

THERE WAS, in late October, much coming and going, to and from the other Families, and that provided sufficient excitement to keep them all half contented. Nor, it seemed, was there ever any preliminary announcement of things that happened, but Sister Samantha must have been used to the regimen, for she took everything quite casually. One morning, for instance, she told the whole group at breakfast that they would all be busy in the kitchen that day, at least for a time, for the big cabbages must be gotten in and sauerkraut laid down in the great stone jars in the cellar. And that's what they did all day, or most of the day, peeling the cabbages back and looking for slugs, and then slicing them with ten or a dozen knives. The mound of cabbage piled up in the center of the table until it looked as if it might fall off onto the floor, and only then did Samantha begin laying it down in the twenty-gallon jars. First there must be a layer of cabbage and then one of the salt scooped from the large bag that two of them had dragged into the kitchen, then another layer of cabbage and another layer of salt. Ruth had never eaten the stuff, and in anticipation she thought that it did not look too appetizing, but Clema and Lucy and some of the others assured her that it would be all right if only enough fat pork were cooked with it. The jars would get scummy, they said, but that didn't matter a bit, for the scummy water could be drained off.

That day, as luck would have it, a wagon drove in from somewhere up in the Village, and three men got out to take a barrel of cider down cellar. Everyone said that there had been quite a lot of cider made that year, so there was more than enough to go around.

Then, on the twenty-second day of the month, Samantha announced quite calmly at the end of evening prayers that she would again want them all in the kitchen the next day—they were going to make the necessary apple butter to get them through the winter. There would have to be bushels and bushels of snits—and she didn't define snits. They all learned the next morning. A big wood fire was first started out near the garden and well away from the sheds, and then Samantha commanded them all to go down to the cellar and bring up all the apples they could carry in their aprons. And then around the tables in the kitchen, they peeled, and cored, and cut into fine pieces, until again there grew such a mound as the cabbage had been. After that Samantha took charge: the big iron kettle was brought out of one of the sheds and hung over the fire coals, several bushels of snits were dumped into its capacious maw, and Samantha herself brought two gallons of cider from the basement and dumped over the apples. And that was just the beginning—all day long Samantha stood over the kettle, and as the apples boiled down other bushels of snits were added and other gallons of cider, and near four in the afternoon more spices than Ruth had ever known existed in the world. The spices must have been brought by the men from the Village, for Samantha produced a great wrapped bundle that no one had ever seen before and acted as if she had to guard it with her life. There were handfuls of what was called stick cinnamon and mace and a whole double handful of cloves, and what else Ruth didn't know. But after that the stirring began in earnest, and it began to look as if the apple butter would not be done before their woodpile was exhausted. The evening chill began about five, but Samantha said not a word about supper, and there were a few who began to grumble. Samantha paid no attention whatsoever. Her blowsy hair blowing outside her cap and her squinty eyes staring, she kept lifting wooden spoonfuls of the stuff and then letting them fall back into the bubbling mess. The apple butter looked black now, or almost black, and soon after that Samantha commanded the legion to bring out the brown and black crocks that had been washed and ranged on the kitchen table. Whoever had the crock in her arms had to hold it while Samantha used a big dipper to fill it within an inch of the top, and by that time the crock was getting hot and heavy, so that they were all glad when the last one of them had been carried indoors. But the kettle was clean, or almost clean, and Samantha proudly pronounced that that ought to be enough to last the winter. There really was no supper that night, but they all carried out big slabs of bread and spread them from the stuff still clinging to the walls of the kettle. There was also cheese, of course—there was always cheese.

Then, in early November when the weather had turned brisk, the first butchering must have taken place up in the Village, because again there was a wagon in the rutted lane, and men brought down great slabs and hunks of meat that were hung in the cold cellar. There was not too much of it, of course, no hams or slabs of bacon, for those must be cured for weeks before they could be used. But there was sausage, a whole mound of sausage and fresh loins, and some awful stuff that was called headcheese. Spirits picked up perceptibly when they saw all the meat—they had been meat-starved for a long time. That night there were pork chops for supper, as many pork chops as anyone wanted to eat, and the next morning there was fried sausage for breakfast, again as much as anyone wanted to eat. Samantha was eager to get the meat all used up; she kept sniffing at the weather every morning for a week while they ate themselves fat. After that it didn't seem to matter what was served on table for a time, and they went back to their customary potatoes and beans. But all the old-timers said that there would be more meat, meat all through the long winter. Never so much at a time again, for when the fields got hard and the frosts plated all the streams they could all stop worrying about spoilage.

As everyone expected, the weather did turn warm again, and one Friday night Sister Samantha announced that they were all to be up early in the morning because they were going to go up to the South Family and help in the harvest gathering. Those few who knew what she was talking about seemed to feel good about that, although most of them had not been in the Society that long. Questions brought prompt replies; all day long they'd shuck corn and toss it into convenient farm wagons, and when they finally came in at night they'd pick up all the pumpkins they could find and throw those on top of the last loads. Since most of them had never husked corn, nobody seemed to have the least idea that the harvest gathering might not be as joyful as it was supposed to be. Some of the men even had trouble with the stubborn corn and wore what they called husking pegs on their right hands, but the rest of them might have to anticipate bruised hands and knuckles.

The day, when it finally dawned, was gray and there seemed to be even a hint of snow in the leaden sky, but at seven o'clock they were all out on the road marching along on the Lebanon Pike. Ruth thought it strange that they did not go right across the fields, but Samantha wouldn't hear of it. Two by two, Mercy Bivvens marching with Clema and Ruth with Naomi Spinsterwald, they went east until they came to the intersection of the pikes, and from that point marched north to the South Family. They weren't shivering any longer by the time they got there; in fact, they were sweaty, for Samantha hadn't dawdled on the road despite her bunions. It seemed as if they were expected at the South, but no one came out to meet them for a long time, and no one had the courtesy to ask them in. So in the wan light they all stood in the backyard in a clump, and after a good quarter hour was passed the men began to come out of the house and go down to the barns to hitch up the teams. By that time both women and men in the South were coming out, and they promptly made for the barns so that they could ride out to the fields. Samantha caught on—she led the girls with her down to the barns. "You all stay together now," she admonished continually. "No matter where you are out in the fields, you all stay together." No one paid any attention to her; it looked as if it might be impossible to stay together.

There might have been some order in the procedure that followed, but there was no apparent order. A wagon would pull from the barn, and ten or a dozen people would jump on it, and then another wagon would appear, and the same thing would happen. Ruth got on the third wagon, and insofar as she knew, no one else from the Gathering Order did. Jolting back over the rutty lane, and shivering a bit, Ruth managed to steal a glance or two at the men and women in the wagon with her. They all seemed well wrapped up in their cocoons of clothes, and most of them had woolen mufflers around their necks. Ruth did not know the mufflers were designed to keep the chaff from getting onto their sweaty skins. She herself had no such protection, and it didn't seem as if she were dressed quite as warmly as the regular Shakers.

After that, it was fun for a time, and then almost pure misery. The corn was stubborn—it would not come unshucked in a hurry. And her wrists began to hurt and her skin began to chafe, and with the sun only three hours high she didn't know how she'd get on to the end of the day. But something was being accomplished—the wagons had begun making a steady procession in to the cribs and back out to the fields again. When one left all those who had united to fill it joined others who had not yet gotten their wagon full, and sometimes it seemed as if the yellow mound in the wagon swelled right in front of one's eyes. Ruth did her share, but by ten o'clock she was not doing too much. The day had turned fine, fine for November, and by high noon the sun was even shining. That made things seem a little better.

Then it was time to march back to the South for dinner, and dinner on harvest days was always something special. Ruth managed to find Clema and they went in together, and Clema's hands were beginning to blister just like Ruth's. The Sisters and Brothers who evidently belonged to the South went in through the back doors of the big house without the least invitation to those in the Gathering Order to follow, and that finally left the Gathering Order standing alone by the stone wellhead. Clema was beginning to get angry, and under her breath she was saying every mean thing she could think of. Clema was also embroidering her remarks a little—with profanity. All the Sisters of the South were "stingy bitches," and the Brothers "damned hoptoads." Ruth had to smile in spite of herself. She was cold and hungry and it did seem as if their work might be paid for with a little kindness.

It was Sister Samantha who finally took the bit in her teeth; when no one came out from the big Family, Sister Samantha shooed her charges together and boldly entered the back door. It seemed as if she knew where she was going and what she was doing, for she led straight to the end of the women's table, where there were at least a dozen unfilled places. Samantha pulled out a chair, fell on her wobbly knees beside it for a moment, and presumably said a prayer. They all followed her example, although it was doubtful if all of them said prayers. That ceremony over, Samantha sat right next to one of the South Sisters and boldly told her to pass something. The Sister did—she passed what was left in a brown bowl that had held hominy and sausage. Samantha passed the bowl to Arly Parks, one of the older women who sat next to her. And Arly reached it on to Celia Johnson, who was as starved and pinched as Arly. Celia cleaned out the bowl, and plopped it down in the center of the table. After that Samantha sat and glared, and no one moved a muscle to help any of them.

As it turned out, it was just a matter of waiting. One by one the South Sisters finished, and knelt down again at her chair before she left the table. When the Sisters were half gone, Samantha didn't hesitate; she simply got up and began passing down the dishes. There were pork chops, bowls of hominy and sausage, butternut pickles, peach jam, and plates of bread. Samantha wasn't satisfied with that—she also brought down most of the plates of cheese. The Sisters who were still eating sat and stared straight ahead of them, eating as timidly as rabbits. Samantha could probably never hope to become one of them, for she ate with gusto, flapping her big lips and sucking at the bread when she couldn't bite it with her broken front teeth.

That was almost the end of any joy the Gathering Order had in the harvest festival. The afternoon was a long agony—the sun went back in again and a chill wind began to blow out of the southwest.

But the big wagons kept on driving towards the cribs, and the shuckers kept getting nearer and nearer the cowbarns—they had started at the far end of the field. The sky was going gray before it was all over, and by that time even the men looked as if they would be glad to limp home.

No one came out to invite them into the South House to get warm, and Samantha didn't seem to expect it. As soon as her fifteen were ready, she formed them in two's and started the long march back down the pike. Only this time they didn't go so fast because Sister Samantha was perceptibly limping. Once back in their own house, the first thing to do was build the fire, and it wasn't until two hours later that Samantha said that anyone who was hungry could go out in the kitchen and eat.

There was little worship service that night. Samantha dutifully put on her steel-rimmed spectacles and stumbled over a few words from the Gospel of John, and after that she simply told them all to go to bed. It was quite apparent why she did not try to kneel—her legs were so stiff that she would never have been able to get up again.

THERE WAS ONE other invitation before winter set in—they were all told that they might come to the last service in the Meeting House before it was closed up for the winter. Since there was no way of heating the place, it had to be shut up in the bitter weather, and all through the winter the several Families would worship together in their own Family Rooms. So in a way the last service of the year was always a bit sad, although everyone tried to make something special of it. The hymn writers generally had prepared a new hymn that would be sung. And the First Elder and Eldress in the Ministry would ordinarily say a few words, and exhort to chaste and decent lives in thought, word, and deed. After that the dance would start, and sometimes the dance would go on for a good hour. And sometimes there might be spirit manifestations, or some chosen instrument might speak in voices. No one ever attempted to interpret the tongues, and there seemed no need to. When holy and mighty angels inspired the chosen instruments, what they said was forever sealed in Eternity.

At the Gathering Order there were a great many whispered

comments about the first visit to the Meeting House, some of them not too complimentary. Mercy Bivvens begged off—she said she could not go because she was hurting inside. No one believed her, of course, not unless "hurting" meant that she was crushed, bitter, and pathetic. Day after day Mercy dragged around, and her once childish beauty was no more. She had become too thin and frail, and she took joy in nothing. When they had gathered corn from the big South field Mercy had sat the whole day along one of the rail fences, and not even Samantha had gone near her. Now it seemed better to leave her behind when they marched up to the Meeting House, for the service could be nothing but a long agony to her.

This time Ruth determined that she would march with Clema, for there was no one else in her little group that she could tolerate. Those who slept in the other rooms, almost all of them considerably older, wanted to march together, of course, and the younger women would have had it no other way. For all her blotchy face Clementina Richards had a little joy of life left in her, and even Lucy Hawks didn't seem quite certain that she wanted to wear out her life being a Shaker. Now and again Lucy would pucker her face and stick out her tongue, and although she generally did everything that Samantha suggested, she seemed to do it unwillingly.

As for herself, Ruth didn't care very much whether she went to the Meeting House or not. The way Samantha talked, it was meant to be something of an indulgence—they would have some first revelation of the joys prepared for them in the Shaker heaven. They would not be permitted on the floor, of course; like outsiders who sometimes came in from Franklin and Middletown and Lebanon, they would have to sit behind the railings that walled off the visitors. But the young Sisters—and probably Brothers, for the members of the male Gathering Order would also be there—could see the dance and witness the pleasure they might expect when they were finally considered acceptable enough to sign the Covenant. That would be only, of course, after they had well proven that they were of devout lives.

There was a great deal of work in getting ready for the big day—all dresses and caps had to be washed and pressed, all capes brushed, and all shoes washed off clean. Then they must be lessoned by Samantha, who told them repeatedly everything she knew of Shaker meetings. They were to keep their eyes open and the mouths shut. They were not to shout or hum, they were not to fidget in their seats, and they were not to be too curious with their eyes. Those were marks of the world, and outsiders sometimes proved so disorderly that they had to be asked to leave. Samantha certainly didn't want anything like that to happen.

THERE HAD BEEN a great bustle of preparation before the Sabbath. Sister Samantha seemed to want to inspect everything, dresses, shoes, caps, collars, capes, and bonnets, and she was very critical. Whenever there was a mud stain around the hem, the dresses and underskirts had to be sponged off, or washed. The boots had to be clean, and rubbed with tallow until they were completely water-proof. Samantha was so thorough that she even insisted on inspect-ing the handkerchief that would be tucked in the sleeve.

She had gone further than that: on Saturday night, instead of the usual family worship, she had given complete instructions as to how they were to march, where they were to sit in the Meeting House, and how they were to conduct themselves. If there were hymns, they could not, of course, be expected to help in the singing, since they did not know the words. But once the hymns started they could hum if they liked, and Mother would be pleased with that. They were never to laugh, and never to swivel their heads around. There would be dancing, and they were not to join in the dance, since they did not know the steps. But if they conducted themselves decently, they would undoubtedly be filled with rapture, for there was nothing like Union Meeting. "There's a peace," said Samantha, and wiped her hand across her face unctuously. "There's a sort o' peace of God that passes all understanding."

While she talked on and further intoxicated herself the rest of them sat vacant, with staring faces. Ruth thought it strange that Clema asked no questions, but tonight at least Clema sat with her hands folded in her lap. It was the older women who seemed most eager; some of them were leaning forward half off their chairs all the while Sister Samantha talked. One, a starved rail of a woman who always looked like a sick hawk, wanted to know if the visit to the Meeting House meant that they would soon be accepted in Church Order.

"It don't mean that atall," said Samantha immediately, and her words were a little threatening. "When they think it's time the El-ders speak, but they don't think it's time yet. They don't think any of you has purged away the lusts of the flesh."

Ruth wondered how Samantha knew, since none of the Elders ever came to the Gathering Order, and Samantha sat there day after day like a chicken on a nest of eggs. It was possibly only a matter of time; perhaps everyone had to spend six months in one of the Gath-ering Orders before he could even hope to join the Church. Ruth re-ally liked that. What she had seen of the inside of the North Family dwelling, and what she had observed of the pious faces in the har-vest fields did not lead her to expect any beauty or comfort once she was sent to one of the big houses.

"We'll have an early breakfast, right after six," Samantha had said. "There'll be bread and eggs and not much else cause it's a holy day. Then we'll start up just as soon as we do up the dishes. I want you all to be there early—I don't want you traipsin' in after meeting has begun. You all get cleaned up first thing in the morning."

They didn't even say a prayer that night. Clema put her arm around Ruth's waist as they started out the door, and whispered something that Ruth could not understand. They were out in the hall before Ruth dared ask, and this time it was plain enough.

"I said she makes me sick to my stomach," said Clema. "When-ever she starts talking I want to puke."

On the evening before the great day Mercy Bivvens went to bed right after supper, and by the time the rest of them got upstairs she was pretending to be asleep. All of them knew that she was not asleep, and all of them with good hearts wished she were. Mercy was likely lying with her eyes open under the shelter of the covers, and she was likely staring uncomprehendingly into the long vacancy that lay ahead of her. All of them in the big bedroom were very quiet that night as they prepared for bed, and the cold ash floorboards did not even bring out the customary protests. It was always an agony to get into bed, and the best thing to do was simply not undress at all. One needed everything she could get hold of to cover her until the bed began to get warm.

Lying in bed, thinking of little Mercy in anguish on the other side of the room, Ruth had many misgivings herself. This was really not what she wanted to do with life, to give up all the things of the world, all human relationships in order that she might save her immortal soul. Her immortal soul was with her right now, and it wasn't happy. The Shakers were good and provident people, and there might be some truth in their religion, but they hadn't as yet proved as much. And whatever they were, they didn't seem quite like normal people—they were much too withdrawn. She thought of the day at the South Family when no one had been able to invite them in to eat at the common table. The invitation should probably have come from one of the Elders in the Family, and without it no one else was empowered to be gracious. But that was no way to live: one had to be able to make his own decisions. Some of them might be wrong, of course—some of the Shaker decisions were also probably wrong—but at least one would have the joy of knowing that he was doing the best he could with whatever strength God had given him.

Mercy was crying now—rather, wailing helplessly—and Ruth heard Clema hop up and go over to her bed. In the dark Clema was whispering something, and she was likely also holding Mercy in her arms like a mother. Ruth had a good feeling about that, but she knew that Clema was powerless to bring Mercy out of her misery. Life did nasty things to people at times and sometimes to good and gracious people. And the wicked sometimes prospered. It just didn't make sense, not a bit of sense.

How long Clema stayed at Mercy's bed that night Ruth didn't know—she was so tired that she fell asleep. But in the morning Clema was still huddled there, sprawled across the edge of the bed, a blanket over her shoulders and head. And Mercy was at last sleeping, and in the little light it looked as if she were made of candle wax.

Mercy did not come down to breakfast in the morning, and despite repeated entreaties refused to get out of bed. First Clema went up after her, then Ruth, and finally Samantha pulled up the steep flight of stairs, grumbling on every tread. Standing down at the bottom of the bare stairs Ruth and Clema could hear her haranguing, but her loud mouth did no good. Mercy had evidently decided that she could get along without Union Meeting, and that was the way it would be. Samantha's spite, of course, would come later—she'd make Mercy pay a pretty penny for being so self-willed.

So in due time they marched, as they always marched—like wooden soldiers. It was frosty in the fields and along the wayside ditches, and by the time they came to the crossroads where they would turn north their faces were as red as cherries. But Samantha was determined and led the way like some bunioned lieutenant, walking on the sides of her feet and rolling a little with every step. Sometimes she slowed down a little, and then they all had to lag for a time; and then Samantha would seem to be filled with new determination, and fairly begin to claw at the frozen mud. Once beyond the crossroads they had a slightly better path beside the road, for that part of the land seemed gravelly. And by that time there was something to see: big farm wagons, pulled sometimes by four horses, were moving down in the direction of Cincinnati. The teamsters had probably come from as far away as Red Lion, or maybe even beyond Red Lion. Ruth didn't know what might be up there, but it was plain the road led somewhere.

As Samantha had intended, there was no one in the Meeting House when they got there. Samantha had a privilege, and she knew just where she wanted them to go, right in the southwest corner and up against the visitors' gallery, since from that spot they could see all the dancing best. Someone had taken a great number of the hickory and oak chairs down from their pegs and placed them in blocks on the floor, but Samantha borrowed chairs until she had all her charges cluttered against the rail. "Now fold your hands in your laps and be quiet," she said again and again, probably to every single one of them. The older women looked a little scared, and promptly seemed to freeze. It was easy to do that in the Meeting House because they could all see the plumes of frost as they breathed.

There was nothing then for what seemed a long time, save a little scratching on the floor upstairs at one end of the hallway where the First and Second Elders in both Ministries lived. Ruth had always wondered about them—she couldn't imagine what they would look like. Probably like pale-faced saints, with no more blood in them than would fill a good-sized mosquito. Lucy Hawks sneezed then, and Samantha was horrified; she made a gesture with her hands and whispered something that was inaudible. But Lucy kept on sneezing until she had her sneeze out. After that it was like a tomb again, although from the Family lots not too far away from the Meeting House came from time to time the sounds of squeaky pumps or cows bawling. Even those sounds seemed good—they proved that there was a little life left in the world.

Then, finally, it came—the sound of tramping, the rhythmic thud of a hundred feet as they hit the ground in unison, and the sound got louder and louder until it crept right down the road and up to the closed doors of the Meeting House. It was the North, and the North always prided itself on being first in the church. There were some ninety-two of them, unless Ruth missed her count, and the men and women were about equally divided, though there did seem to be a few more women. The women marched down the length of the floor and sided into chairs at the left; the men came behind and filled the chairs at the right. Then there was silence again, save for a few coughs. The North sat as immobile as statues, and Ruth felt Clema's finger dig into her ribs. She didn't dare acknowledge Clema, but she knew what Clema was thinking—that they all looked like mechanical dolls.

Probably five minutes passed, and now there was unceasing clatter and turmoil at the door. Ruth knew that Clema was looking for her mother and father, because she hadn't the slightest idea what Family they had been put into. But the Grist Mill and the Square Families, both small, came in, and then the South, and Center, and finally the Brick House and East. No one in Samantha's group knew them apart, of course, but Ruth did know that Clema hadn't seen her father or mother. Either they were not there, or they were indistinguishable in their Shaker drab.

The room was filled now, although there was no one in the visitor's gallery, probably because of the frost. Samantha had said that people sometimes came in there and caused disturbances and had to be asked to leave, generally smart young bucks who had driven over from the nearby towns. There was a long silence—and the silence was silence, so much so that one could close his eyes and think the room was empty. Then someone—Ruth didn't know where he came from—stood up in the front of the meeting room and made some weird sounds in his throat, and almost immediately a hymn started. The tune wasn't bad, at least not too bad, but the words were all about Mother and how she was coming soon to catch her children up in the clouds. The voices were strong enough, and they were even a bit harmonious, but the singing was doleful and languorous. It didn't seem from the sound as if the Society was too joyful.

Once the hymn was done, someone who must have been one of the Elders read a long passage from a black book, and the words were so strange that Ruth knew that the book must be the Bible. She didn't understand much of what the man was reading: it was all about Israel thinking it had been deserted but that Jehovah would redeem it in His chosen time. The Elder read well—he could pronounce the words as if he were used to them, but he read so that every word sounded alike and there wasn't the least music in his voice. Once he had finished, the Elder put down his black book, and then he started to say things that he was making up as he went along. Mother was watching, he said; she knew what every single one of her children was doing at every moment of time. And so did the holy and mighty angels know, and it was their business to help the pure in heart. But those who had sinful thoughts or persisted in sinful acts might find themselves alone; Mother would know their sin and perhaps send their guardian angels away. There were a number of sinful things that some members of the Society were still doing. They were still reading newspapers, and that was worldly sin, since it showed a hankering after the lusts of the flesh. And some of them were shirking their work, so that the looming or the dyeing or whatever didn't go on as well as it should. And they were all probably eating too much meat, and even pork on Sundays. Going through the Village the Elder had even seen a woman with a gold pin stuck at her throat, and that was vanity and the pride of life. Be not deceived, God is not mocked, and God would never have permitted His Christ to appear again in Mother's form if He did not want them all to believe in her and become members of the redeemed. The world would be consumed with fire—that was prophecy, and the world was so wicked that the fire might come at any moment. And when it did and all the saints would be caught up into the clouds, they would have nothing to complain about if they were left behind because they were too sinful. Just last week a messenger had brought another letter from the Elders at Mount Lebanon, and the Elders there blessed them all and warned against the pride of life and the sins of the flesh. And if they hoped to see the blessed morning dawn, then it behooved them all to regenerate their lives, confess their sins, and offer themselves as acceptable sacrifices to the great God in Heaven.

Ruth felt a little shivery—the man had been so sepulchral when he talked that he had gotten on her nerves. It might be true, some of the things he said. Certainly the Berzinskis had gone after the lusts of the flesh, and they had not been blessed. They passed in a file before Ruth's eyes as she sat there, her father Harmon, then Jake and Herman, then her mother and Asenath and poor Rachel. Of them all Rachel was probably the only one who was living without sin, and that only because she knew nothing and could understand nothing. And she herself was not faultless; even while she heard the words the Elder was speaking her mind had been offering all sorts of objections. Her mind told her that the man was talking without authority, that he could not know the things he pretended to know. And he acted as if people had been created only so that they could be little animals, kept on a leash by God. Ruth knew practically nothing about the man he called Christ, who must have been one of the Jews, but it seemed that the New Testament had been written about Him and not the one they called Mother. Mother, it seemed, hadn't been dead too many years, and that was probably why they believed in her more than in the first Christ. Ruth simply didn't know. It seemed logical that there might be a God, but she couldn't define her idea in any way. Somebody had to be responsible for everything that was, all the cows and flowers and people, and everything. But you could look clear up into the stars on a clear night, and there was no sight of what they all called Heaven. And no one she knew had ever seen angels flying.

She came back to her senses to realize that the men were hanging the chairs on pegs along the wall and clearing the floor, and when they had finished that the men first and then the women stood in two big clusters at the opposite sides of the rooms. All of the chairs would not go on pegs, and those left over had to be pushed hard against the walls. Then, once that was done, they all started lining up, the men on the north side of the room, and the women on the south. And now they all began to make some kind of humming or bumbling sound in their throats, and without visible signal they started moving, both men and women making two separate long lines that curved and returned at the gallery end of the room. And now the humming became louder, and the movements faster, so fast that some of the older women gave up and dropped out to sit in the chairs against the wall on the women's side. It seemed to Ruth that the marchers were all dragging their feet, or shuffling a little, but that went on for only five minutes or so, and then they went into ranks and started another step that was like skipping. And while they were skipping they started singing again, only this time some other song that was faster than the one they had sung before. It was impossible to know what they were saying, but whenever she could catch a word or two Ruth thought it sounded like the other song. At least the word "Mother" was distinguishable, and "For Mother is washing her lambs and her sheep."

How long the dance went on it was impossible to know; it seemed a short time, and it seemed a long time. At least it was long enough for sweat to stand on some of the faces, but the eyes of the people dancing towards her always looked the same, half glazed, as if they were not completely aware of themselves. Ruth wondered how she could ever expect to become that way, and the thought was just a little nauseating. It might be the way angels danced—if they had legs, but angels were supposed to have wings, and if they had wings they would most probably get their recreation that way. Ruth thought that if they could promise her a pair of wings she'd be more eager to join them. It would be fun to have big white wings, and to go floating like some of the big geese she had sometimes seen in the autumn sky.

It was perhaps noon when the dance stopped—at least it seemed that way. Then, suddenly, they were all in two blocks again, and the same man who had preached got up in front and held up his hands while he said something. All that Ruth could understand was "Go in peace."

They went in peace, marching again like soldiers, and emptying the room from the rear. Samantha waited until they were all out, and then she finally wobbled to her feet, and motioned for them all to get up. Samantha had tears in her eyes and seemed to have a lump in her throat; she had probably guessed that she was paying a high price for keeping her mother's fern. The Lord had afflicted her with a heavy burden, all because of a little lust of the eyes.

Once they got out to the Pike they could see the marching lines, the Center and Brick Families already up to their houses, the North marching woodenly down the center of the road; then when they turned south, there was the South Family going into its yard, and the East Family far down the Pike. But they'd not march again like that, if what Samantha said was true—not until the spring. All through the winter the Meeting House would be sealed up, and the four prisoned Elders and Eldresses would have to huddle against their separate stoves. It might be March, or even April, before they all came together again. Ruth was sentimental enough to think that that was a shame, in a way. Think what one would think about Union Meetings, the Shakers very likely did a lot of good. One step they had danced for a time, the Square Step, looked as if it might be fun, and the Lively Step was at least lively. But the silly sighing and humming in their throats didn't add up to much.

Samantha had a hard time getting home, and her laggard pace slowed them all a great deal. There was nothing to see now—the fields looked desolate, although they were still full of corn shocks that had been put together again after the harvesters had stripped them. These would be carried in sometime during the winter because they were needed for fodder. And wheat would be planted between the shocks, or had already been planted, and whenever the snows melted off in the winter thaws the fields would look emerald green. And then the round of the year would begin again, and new corn-fields and potato fields would be planted, and they'd have to do everything all over again, make maple sugar, shear sheep, harrow, hoe, butcher, and keep forever busy with their looms and dye vats. It all seemed fruitless in a way, like going around on a track and never getting anywhere. But that was the way life was, everything and everybody went around on a track, and all one really did was get older.

The last quarter mile two of the older women took hold of Samantha's arms and helped her along—the trip to Meeting had been almost too much for her. And now the frost had melted out of the road, and it was yellow mud in some places and runnels of water in others. It took them all a long time to get to the West Frame.

And when they did it was almost like coming home; they'd get in out of the wind now and there would be a fire in the kitchen, and they would all be able to get warm while they ate.

It was Clema Porter who discovered that Mercy Bivvens was no longer in their room—Clema had run right upstairs as if she had had some kind of premonition. She was standing by Mercy's empty bed when Ruth came into the room—Ruth had gone up to take off one of her woolen petticoats that was dragging on the ground. Clema just stood beside Mercy's bed and stared. "She's gone, Ruth," she said at last. "Mercy's gone. I had a notion she'd do it."

Ruth didn't dare to ask questions. It was a cold world out there, and there was just no place to go. It would be a blessing if Mercy had not wandered too far.

CLEMA SAID before they left the bedroom that she was going out to hunt for Mercy just as soon as she had had a few bites to eat. Ruth knew that was the thing to do, but it seemed unlikely that they would find her. Mercy had taken her cape—they learned that, and so it seemed possible that she would have walked towards Monroe on the pike. But when Ruth mentioned her surmise, Clema shook her head. "She's not that strong," she said. "She's so puny the wind would blow her away out there. I think she's right around here somewhere, maybe in the woods along the creek."

Neither of them said a word to Samantha, who seemed to have recovered sufficiently to be supervising the kitchen. There would be little to eat, nothing that was hot, but they never ate very well on Sundays. Samantha probably thought that the Sabbath day called for fasting, or that since Sunday was never a day of work they needed little. So there was always bread and cheese, or very rarely meat, if there was any meat left over from Saturday night. There were also on Sundays Samantha's remedies for everything imaginable; she was always trying to dose somebody with oil of wintergreen, or with boneset or mullein or tansy teas. And Samantha always had camphor and goose grease and sulphur, and seemed to be happy when she could detect some signs of cold in one of her charges. She was bitterly unhappy when the charge said that she didn't want to be rubbed. That sometimes happened, although the older women generally consented to the sacrifice of their flesh.

Ruth and Clema had decided to say nothing about Mercy—on Sundays Samantha always disappeared into her room after some quarter hour, leaving the clean-up crew to tidy up the kitchen, and until sundown on the Sabbath she was never seen again. Samantha always said that she was meditating, that that's what the Sabbath was made for, but they all had a good idea that she was sleeping. At least her eyes always looked blurry when she reappeared again in time to direct the kitchen crew what to set out for supper.

Clema waited until she was sure that Samantha was securely sealed in her room, and then she fairly dragged Ruth upstairs with her, both of them tiptoeing on the stairs. Clema got out of some of her heavy petticoats because she didn't want them dragging along behind her, and Ruth followed her example. They did take their capes—it would likely be cold out in the fields and woods. But, as a last gesture of defiance, Clema threw her Shaker cap onto the bed. Her hair tumbled down behind her back, and she looked better that way, and Ruth again followed her example. Even then both of them knew that the women in the kitchen would know something was amiss when they went out the back door with their hair flying in the wind. That was a shame, but it could not be helped, and there was no one in the kitchen who had the least authority over them. All that the people in the kitchen could do was run to tell Samantha, and that seemed extremely improbable.

Once out beyond the sheds that stood behind the West Frame, Clema headed right across the frozen garden. But that seemed futile, because if Mercy had gone that way it seemed as if there should be tiny tracks in the mud. Ruth pointed that out, and Clema agreed. After that, as they pushed through the horseweeds and got down nearer the creek they both kept looking for tracks. There were a few tracks, of rabbits, and field mice, and even some big boot tracks, as if a man had come that way. But the boot tracks were frozen deep, and probably had not been made recently.

It was a bright afternoon, and once they got used to the chill in the air they both realized that the gaunt trees were beautiful in a spectral way. But the field flowers were all long gone, and the goldenrod and asters furry and beaten down. A flight of bluejays played up and down the little creek, flashing their wings against old sycamore branches, and once a squirrel made some sort of whirring sound far in front of them. But beyond that there was nothing; the day dreamed in a sort of frozen solitude.

"I don't think she came up this way, Clema," Ruth said after they had gone a quarter mile.

"I don't either," said Clema. "Only reason I think so is that there's no place else to go. Where would you go if you were trying to get away?"

Ruth couldn't answer that question. It would take them a good hour, or the best part of an hour, to get up as far as the grist mill and sawmill, which lay off northwest of the Center Family, and by that time a good part of the afternoon would have been spent. Mercy might have been picked up by somebody who had come after her and carried her away in a rig. Clema mentioned that, but the thought was so improbable that they didn't even discuss it.

They were squarely behind the main Families in Union Village now, and they both knew that they might be seen by inquiring eyes. For that reason partly, and partly to get out of the cold wind for a while, they ducked into an empty sheep house that stood near the creek. Looking out from that covert they both swept the fields and what they could see of the Village with their eyes, but nothing moved except the blue plumes of wood smoke coming up from the few chimneys. "You think we ought to go on?" Clema asked then. "I don't think she could have got this far."

"I think we'd better go on up," Ruth answered dolefully. "While we're this far we'd better go on up as far as the mills."

"They'll see us. The people in the mill houses will see us."

"I don't much care if they do," said Ruth. "You don't care, do you, Clema?"

Clema scoffed. "I hope they all choke," she said promptly. "All I know is that I'm goin' to get away from this damned place. I can't stand it." And then, after a moment of silence, "What'd you think of church this morning?"

Ruth only made a gesture with her hands. "I never saw so many holy people together in all my life," she said.

"You goin' to stay here? I mean, with the Shakers."

"Not if I can help it," Ruth answered promptly. "I don't think they know anything. Not what they say they know."

Clema seemed to hesitate a little at that, and then, as her fingers dug at a loose iron nail, she said slowly, "Why don't you come with me? I'm going to clear out. I got an Uncle Thorpe who lives up near Franklin. He's my mother's brother, and he gets drunk, but it's the only place I have to go. He wouldn't mind if you came along with me."

It was Ruth's turn to hesitate. "When do you mean to go, Clema?" she asked.

Clema only shook her head. "Soon's I can," she said. "Thorpe don't like me much, an' I don't like him atall, but once I got there he'd have to put up with me. I can tell you one thing: Thorpe don't give a damn for preachers. Says they're all alike, all barkin' up the wrong tree. Thorpe gets thrown out o' all the camp meetings. Always gets drunk, an' then they drive him away."

"I don't think I better go with you," Ruth said then. "I mean, if you go."

"You got any reason?"

Ruth hesitated. "There was a boy I liked a lot," she said finally. "He might come back, and then he wouldn't know where to find me."

"He know you're with the Shakers?"

That was the trouble, and Ruth confessed it. "He don't know atall," she admitted. "I don't know where he is, and he don't know where I am. And I don't know how to let him know."

Clema only whistled a little. They stood a long while in silence, and then Clema suggested that they go on, at least until they came to the mills. She didn't care if they were seen.

They walked again, stumbling over the frozen clods in the old cornfields. But they were careful to stay near the creek, so that they could be half concealed by the head-high horseweeds. The gaunt weatherbeaten mills came nearer and nearer, and at last they could both see the race and the dam. Beyond the dam they knew there would be some sort of mill pond, and neither one of them dared speak of the thought that was in her mind. It would be impossible to know if Mercy were in the mill pond unless her body had floated to the surface, but they'd both be reassured if they could see nothing.

Ruth led now, very cautiously. Once some women came out of one of the Mill Family houses, and after five minutes or so they seemed to have started a fire in what must be the wash house. All that night they'd keep the fire burning so that there would be plenty of hot water on Monday morning. It was the regimen in all the Families, and even Samantha had them start the wash fire on Sunday night.

The sky had darkened a little, and now there was no sun, only a sort of gray pall that seemed to hang over the frozen world. And now they were both walking timidly, and the nearer the mill pond they came, the shorter their steps seemed to be. And then they saw it, and both felt their hearts skip. There was a skim of ice all around the edge of the pond, and open water in the center. And nowhere was there any sign of Mercy.

They didn't dare speak—they could only look at each other. "She never got this far," said Clema at last. "Thank God, she never got this far."

For some reason Ruth wasn't so sure. "It won't hurt us to walk on up to the north end," she said. "I don't think she got this far."

This time Clema took the lead, almost as if she wanted to get her duty done, and as they went along very quietly they both kept staring at the icy water. There was nothing, nothing at all. At the far north end of the pond there was a tiny wooden landing, and tied to it a very primitive boat. Once they saw the landing, they both knew that at that spot they would turn back to the Gathering Order. And they'd have to go back the same way they had come, because the creek was so high that it was impossible to find stepping stones across it. And there was nothing on the other side anyway, nothing but sheep pastures, and the sheep were now all in the barns.

And then, at the last moment, they both saw at the same time. Mercy's tiny shoes were in the bottom of the boat, and they had to be Mercy's because they were as small as a child's. At that sign Clema screamed, and started to cry, and Ruth felt the tears coursing down her own cheeks. There could be no reason for Mercy's shoes to be in the boat unless she were in the water.

THEY RAN for the Mill Family House, which was on the east side of the Grist Mill, although there was no sense in their running. And once there Clema rushed right on in, and found as usual that there was only emptiness inside. The Mill Family members were all keeping their rooms on the Sabbath, and simply did not want to be disturbed. They started shouting then, and it seemed to take a little while before doors were timidly opened. A big man finally appeared. He had circles under his eyes and he was trying to draw on a black coat. Once in the hall he simply stood and looked at them, as if he were having a bad nightmare.

"There's nothing on fire, is there?" he finally asked, and when he spoke the skin on his forehead creased into a dozen furrows. "What's the matter?"

Clema started to talk, but other doors were opening and other men coming out into the hall, so that she was not heard. Then, when everyone seemed ready to listen, Clema seemed to have lost her voice.

"She's in the pond," Ruth told them. "Mercy's in the pond. She's drowned."

At that the doors on the Sisters' side went shut again, but the men seemed to come awake. "Who's drowned?" asked the big man, who was evidently the miller. "How do you know anybody's been drowned."

"Her shoes are in the boat," said Clema. "Mercy's shoes are in the boat."

The big man wasn't too sure. He hated women, and most of all he hated hysterical women, and in his opinion all women had the ability to get hysterical over nothing.

"Now hauld yer tongue, hauld yer tongue," he kept on saying. "You got no gift to say things as ain't so."

That made Clema angry. "You can go look for yourself if you're so damned smart," she said. "We know what we know, and we know that Mercy's shoes are in the little boat."

There were more questions. The miller was shoved aside by a gaunter man who was addressed as Elder Samuel. Elder Samuel seemed to want to get at facts from the beginning: he wanted to know who they were, what Family they were from, and who Mercy was. And why did they think she had fallen into the pond.

"She didn't fall into the pond," said Ruth. "She was unhappy. She threw herself in."

Elder Samuel's brows knit at that, but he began giving orders, and half a dozen of the men went back to their rooms for heavy coats and then marched off. By this time their faces were frozen into masks of immobility—they seemed to know what sort of distasteful task was ahead of them. They could drain the pond, of course, but that would take a long while. And they could use long poles and homemade hooks to probe and grapple. But even then the body might elude them; it might be that it wouldn't be found for days. And the girl might not be in the pond—everyone thought of that. But in that case there was no reason why the shoes should be in the boat.

An older woman came out of her room then, and joined Elder Samuel. "You'd best send them back home," she said the moment she came up to the group. "They got no business being here."

Ruth rather liked the woman—she had a face that was perfectly calm. She looked as if she would be a good manager, even about holy affairs.

Elder Samuel just stood and stared—it seemed for a long time. After a time he asked more questions, and both Ruth and Clema took turns at answering. Mercy had been sent to the Gathering Order because her people had suddenly died of smallpox. And someone had shot her dog, and she had loved her dog more than anything in the whole world. He had been a long-nosed collie. And she had never been happy, not for a single moment. No, Sister Samantha hadn't mistreated her. But she hadn't been too sympathetic either.

The Elder just stood and shook his head, and after a long time the white-haired woman told him again that he had best send the girls home. Someone could hitch up and drive them—all the men weren't out probing the pond.

It seemed to be a long time before Elder Samuel agreed, and when he finally did, he said he'd drive them himself. And when he went out to hitch up, the Eldress put her arms around the shoulders of Ruth and Clema and led them to her own room. It was again a gaunt and empty room, but there was a crocheted rug on the floor and an open Bible on the little table beside the bed.

"There's no cause to grieve," the Eldress kept saying. "These things happen, and we don't know why they happen. God in His infinite wisdom looks after His own, and He might have known that there was no call for Sister Mercy to live on in this sinful world. God looks after his own."

They were not much comforted, but Ruth was able to stop her tears first. Eldress Anna was the first Shaker she had met who seemed to be a human being, and to have the love of God in her heart. Ruth thought that she wouldn't mind it so much if there were a person like that she could take her troubles to.

Elder Samuel was finally prepared and drove up to the back door of the Grist Mill House, and Eldress Anna went along to the rig. "You tell Sister Samantha just what happened," she kept repeating. "She's got a good heart—she'll understand. You tell her just what happened."

Neither Ruth nor Clema thought that it would be possible to tell Samantha what had happened. Samantha would never understand—

she would think only that Mercy had been headstrong. But that wasn't it at all. When a person's heart was broken she was no longer responsible for anything she did. And Mercy Bivvens wasn't going to hell. Eldress Anna had known that, and Samantha would have to know it too.

It was not a long drive home, in fact it seemed too short, for neither Clema nor Ruth wanted to go back into the West Frame. Mercifully Elder Samuel came along in with them, and it was he who told Samantha. And because of something in the way he spoke, Samantha seemed very humble. "I should have known better than to leave her alone," she kept on saying. "I should have known. But I thought she'd get over it."

That night it was like a funeral in their house—no one ate very much for supper, and everybody seemed to be walking on tiptoe. They'd never hear anything more about Mercy—they all knew that. There would be no Shaker funeral—Mercy had not been a member of the Society. Her body would simply be wrapped in a sheet and put into a rough box, and then they would carry it to an unmarked grave far out on the edge of their cemetery. In a way it was all they could do for her, and no public mourning would have helped anybody in the least.

Chapter 5

WITH THE ONSET of real winter there was a change in the quality of life in Union Village. Though ability to cope with winters may have been touch and go at first back in 1805 and the years
immediately after, four decades later there was a solid, unchange-
able, and seemingly casual adjustment to the rigors of the frost. By
the end of November all the fields were bare, and all the year's in-
crease had been gathered into cellars and barns. Later, with the
complete hardening of the earth, manure would be carried out to the
fields, but that seemed only a minor task because it occupied only a
relatively few people. From the end of November on most men and
women rarely, and sometimes never, stepped far outside their
dwellings. In the big brick houses, however, the spinning rooms,
loom rooms, cheese rooms, seed rooms, and minor shops were forever busy, and in the major shops that had their own buildings cold
weather seemed only to add zest to labor. So the mills sawed lumber
and ground grain unceasingly; the cabinet makers forever assembled
tables and beds, chairs, chests of drawers, and both low and high-
boys; the wheelwrights shaved spokes and shaped rims; and the
forges turned out nails, hinges, locks, scythe blades, hoes, footscrap-
ers, and whatever else might be demanded.

There were minor nooks and crannies in the Village, of course—
in fact, minor nooks and crannies in each one of the big houses.
Each of the Families had its own pharmacopeia, housed in its own
proper cubicle, and each pharmacopeia had a custodian who pretended to be expert in neither allopathic nor homeopathic medicine,
but instead relied on old herb remedies that represented the accrued
wisdom of the race. One could count on several constants in each
such collection of medicines. Joe Pye roots were good for fever,

boneset for colds, and camomile to purify the blood. Tansy and spikenard were pronounced efficacious for almost all ills of the flesh. Butterfly-weed roots were good for pleurisy, and common speedwell was thought to be able to cure almost all maladies. In addition there had been fermented in each family a few gallons of wines for medicinal purposes, generally grape and currant and elderberry. And in addition to wines there were unguents and salves, and medicinal seeds that were thought to be anodynes. Moreover, each house had, either in kitchen or medical office, generous supplies of sassafras and sage, sometimes the inner bark of white walnut, and always large bunches of dried mullein, peppermint, spearmint, and pennyroyal. The kitchen proper added many herbs all its own, borage and anise and fennel for salads, marjoram and basil to season poultry, parsley and caraway seeds for eggs and cheese, rosemary and thyme for meats, and dill to give a piquancy to old vinegar. For drawers that contained linens and clothing, however, there was only one proper perfume, lavender, and each one of the great Families always nurtured a large bed of lavender in a corner of the house garden.

When the great snows fell the Village might look almost frozen into immobility, but nothing could be further from the truth. The house roofs would stay white with snow and the rime and icicles would hang from all the sills, but inside the great structures there was constant activity, and that best pleasure in life, useful work well done. For the House Deacons and Work Deacons tried to match skills and temperaments to necessary crafts, and they were not pleased if any member of the Society was himself displeased with his occupation. Some people liked to dress meat, and some liked to spin and weave, some to scutch flax, plane wood, hammer metal, pour beeswax candles, or grind flour. Some liked best to sort and wrap seeds in brown paper, some to stitch brooms, sew leather, or even to ply their constant knitting needles. Some were quite content to cook food, some to care for the animals in the stables, and some to brave all sorts of weather in carting dung or felling trees in the winter woods. And some, a very particular few, the Trustees, Ruling Elders, House Elders, and principal Deacons, had more genteel occupations. The Trustees handled all monies and signed all contracts. The Ruling Elders meditated on spiritual things—and decided which persons should be transferred from Families to Families, or be sent to

Whitewater, Watervliet, and even North Union. The Deacons some-times acted in only a supervisory capacity, although in most of the shops and workrooms they did as much as any of the others.

There was little frivolity in Union Village in the winter—mirth was unseemly. And there was little reliance upon the wisdom of the outside world, and those few members who did sometimes glance at stray newspapers were looked at with arched eyes. Probably half the members in the separate Families could read and write—a little. A slightly larger percentage could cipher a bit. A good many had read in, or even through, the New Testament, but almost no one the en-tire Bible. There were few entire Bibles in the Village, although the Ruling Elders had access to one. There were also no Shakespeares, Bunyans, or Miltons, despite Milton's great theme. In the school-house, which stood down near the Children's Order on the south pike, there were a few innocuous books, very few, and then those only that pretended to teach something about the arts of arithmetic. Two teachers were supplied for the two schoolrooms, one for the girls and one for the boys, since the sexes must be kept apart. Sister Lena Gasper had for many years introduced the young girls to the rudiments, Brother Ralph Baines for fifteen years, and after him Brother Matthew Poggs, the boys. There were ordinarily no young-sters in the school over the age of twelve, and in truth the children of either sex were not many, since as time went on it seemed as if fewer and fewer families surrendered their acres and came to join the Order.

On the whole the winter life was very pleasant. One could keep reasonably warm in the big houses if one wore enough clothing, the food was good and plentiful, and the dining rooms sometimes steamed from the adjacent kitchens. Every night there were, or might be, gatherings in the Family Rooms. Sometimes baskets of ap-ples were passed around, although cracked walnuts and hickories were ordinarily reserved for the Christmas season. In the Family Room the Sisters sat on chairs lining one wall, and the Brothers on chairs that had been taken down from pegs upon the wall opposite. There might be from time to time a few miscellaneous comments, such gems of wisdom as "Brother John Knobs 'as got a crick in his back," or "Sister Ruth Bowles is feelin' poorly." There was, how-ever, no general conversation. In the lamplight from the center table the faces against the farther walls always seemed like pale and oval green blobs, but they were quiet faces, passive faces, faces that seemed to reflect the assurance of eternity. Sometimes a song was sung before the members broke up to end the evening, and sometimes one of the Family Elders came in to dismiss them with a prayer.

It was quiet in the Families by eight at night, and only when someone was lying in one of the sick rooms was the darkness likely to be disturbed by lamp or candlelight. The Families slept, for most of the members would be up by five in the morning. And breakfast would be served at six, and a new day would be ready to run its course, a day exactly like the one just dead, and the one that was still to come.

Winter was responsible for certain discomforts and hazards, of course. It was cold in the bedrooms, and there was often ice on the ironstone pitchers in the morning. And the herringbone walks to the backyard necessaries had to be repeatedly shoveled off, and covered with ashes and cinders from the fireplaces. In the morning, also, the backyard pumps and horse troughs would often be frozen solid, and though the horse troughs could be freed with an ax, the pumps required a great deal of hot water from the kitchens. Frostbites were probably one of the most unpleasant evils of winter, and they were not uncommon. Sometimes feet, fingers, and noses were rubbed with snow, but it was more common for the afflicted member to soak his feet in hot water. Those who had easy jobs in the indoor shops seemed never to be able to understand frostbite, and sometimes even made disparaging remarks about the stablemen and woodcutters. But the persons who made tart remarks were most often those who heated bricks at night and carried them to their beds wrapped in pieces of old woolen blankets.

There was not much travel on the main road leading through the Village in the wintertime, and sometimes after a blizzard the road became impassable. Whenever that occurred, ten or a dozen of the ox teams owned by the separate Families would be yoked to drags, and in a long procession they would break out the road, sometimes as far as the Green Tree Tavern, which stood a good mile north of the Village, and always as far down as the Lebanon Pike on the south. The ox parade was a sight, a rather joyful one, for it demonstrated power, and the proof of power somehow made the members swell with pride.

It was not uncommon in winter for travelers on the road to seek refuge in the Family dwellings, particularly when they had been caught by unexpected storms or depths of snow. There was one common way the Shaker Families treated such people—with extreme courtesy. They were fed, but always at the ends of the Brothers' and Sisters' tables. If they had to be kept overnight, they were not given beds. There was a stove in each of the Family Rooms, and there the unbelievers could sit through the night, although a member of the Family always stayed up to watch the fire. On occasion such guests had been known to discover brown bottles in the depths of their greatcoats, and they could even become loud and profane, if not downright abusive. There was never any protest, and not one word of comment to discourage such incivility, and in consequence the transgressors ordinarily learned quickly that they were expected to keep decent tongues in their heads.

Winter also quite tragically seemed to cause, or at least hasten, many disorders and sicknesses, and it always brought a few deaths. Cholera was always feared, but cholera never broke out in the Village. Typhoid did on occasions, and diphtheria from time to time took its toll in the Children's Order. And every winter someone seemed to die from what, for want of a better description, was known as "a prodigious big bellyache." And, just as unfortunately, some of the older members seemed destined to slip on the ice and break arms or legs. When that happened the arm or leg was splinted and wrapped securely until a physician could be brought in from Monroe or Lebanon. Sometimes, particularly in spells of bad weather, that took days.

In short, in winter all seemed more or less right with the world, and the members, as they went about their appointed tasks, had the joy of that best benison, the peace of knowing their day's work well done. If Mother was watching, as all the instruments always repeated, she should be well content, for it was evident that her children were making every effort to walk in her ways.

BEFORE SHE LEFT Clema tried desperately to get Ruth to come along with her. All Ruth's objections seemed silly and inconsequential to Clema. It wasn't like going to the other end of the world. Franklin was only six or eight miles away. And the man that Ruth was waiting for was likely never going to appear again. That was the way with men, if Ruth didn't know it; once a girl was out of sight she was also out of mind. And there were plenty of women in the world, so that a man never had to turn back on his tracks. "Uncle Thorpe ain't so bad," Clema kept persuading. "You could stand him. And there's nothing to keep you here, not a damn thing. You don't want to stay and become one of the Shakes, do you?"

Ruth could only shake her head, but Clema was so insistent she made her miserable.

"It ain't that," Ruth finally said lamely. "I just don't think that I ought to go to Franklin. What would I do there?"

"Do what you'd do any other place," said Clema promptly. "Look around and see if you can spot somebody who might get sweet on you. Franklin's a big town—there's more'n a hundred people in it. Maybe two hundred. There ain't no reason why you shouldn't be able to latch onto somebody."

Ruth kept on shaking her head, and after a time that made Clema mad and she slapped her. "You're just no dam' good," she said finally. "You're a fraidy-cat, and my Gawd how I hate fraidy-cats. You stay here and one day you'll do the same thing as Mercy."

Ruth stood and looked out the window. There was nothing to see up the creek, nothing but sycamore trees amber in the sunlight, although the blue bank of clouds in the west looked as if it might come on to snow. If it snowed Clema would be caught on the road. Ruth told her as much. She didn't care that Clema had slapped her. She really felt like slapping herself.

Clema came and looked, but she didn't seem frightened. "I been out in it before," she said. "Starts snowing I'll go into some farmhouse. Nobody minds very much when it snows."

"They'll know you're a Shaker," said Ruth. "You got Shaker clothes on."

"They're going to stay on," said Clema. "They're warm, and that other stuff I had is just trash. I earned the clothes—I ain't stealin' them."

After that they heard someone moving about in the downstairs hall, and they both knew Samantha was likely listening at the bottom of the stairs. And if not Samantha, then one of the pious ladies who had vinegar in their veins.

Clema left the house right after dinner, and as it happened

Samantha was already on her way to her room for a nap, and the kitchen crew didn't seem to think it strange when Clema went out the back door. At the last, just before she left, Clema dragged Ruth into the hall and kissed her. "You don't know, Ruth," she said in a sort of agonized whisper. "You stay here, an' they'll kill you. You'll listen to their sermons, and finally you'll think it's maybe true. An' then you'll join up, and that will be the end of it."

Ruth only shook her head, but she returned Clema's kiss. "Be careful," she admonished. "Don't let anything bad happen to you."

Clema shook her head, and two minutes later she was gone. Ruth sneaked into the front room after that and looked out through the lace of Samantha's fern. Clema was heading straight west for Monroe, and from Monroe she would likely turn north, unless she decided to stay there for the night. If it came on to snow she might just do that, stay in Monroe.

AFTER THAT the days seemed a lot more bitter. The roads did fill up with snow, and then the first snows melted and there was nothing but mud outside. And then the mud froze, and it snowed again. That wasn't the worst—the worst was that the days were long and desolate. Samantha was trying to teach Ruth to knit, but her hands were so clumsy that the wool always got knotted. What she would rather do was work on one of the two looms they had in the house, but the older women kept the looms tied up so that no one could get to them. There was nothing to do, nothing to read, nowhere to go, no one to talk to. Ruth fixed on Lucy Hawks as a possible confidante, but Lucy hadn't the free and easy ways of Clema. And it seemed as if Lucy had really made up her mind to try to become a good Shaker. "There just ain't no sense goin' on like that," she told Ruth once when Ruth was fretting. "Trouble is you don't really want to do nothin'. You just don't seem to want to do nothin'. You don't believe that Mother is watchin' you. How do you think she feels when she sees you mopin' around."

Ruth got out of that—she told Lucy that she had a headache. That night Lucy told Samantha, and as soon as Samantha knew she brewed Ruth some tea. And Ruth dutifully drank it. It was bitter, but it wasn't poison, and it kept Samantha from disturbing her any further.

Chapter 5

It was perhaps three days after that that the impulse came to go back home, not to stay there, of course, but to see how the family was getting along. They would at least be familiar faces, and the faces wouldn't look as if they were made out of dough. The more she thought about it, the surer Ruth became that that was what she wanted to do. It would be difficult to get home without Samantha's knowing, of course, but it might be managed. She'd walk north along the creek, then cut through the dip in the land where she'd be out of sight. That would bring her to the north road somewhere near the South Family. And from there she'd turn north again until she was through the Village, and then farther on, she'd turn east and cut through the fields until she came to the woods. And once in the woods she'd be safe from all inquiry. It would be like living again to get into the woods, and she'd go on east past Robinsons' until she came to the lane that led south to the Berzinski cabin. It sounded easy to make her getaway that way, and she never once thought of getting back. Samantha would likely have kittens if she knew she was gone, but she could be put off—Ruth would simply say that she had gone out for a walk. The fact that none of the others ever went out for a walk, and the further fact that she had spent the whole afternoon in idleness, would be held against her, of course. But she meant never to tell Samantha the truth, no matter how hard she inquired.

Wednesday was a bad day, not too cold but muddy. Ruth prudentially greased her shoes. On Thursday it came on to rain, and the rain was cold. Then, Thursday night, it turned much colder, and everything froze again. Ruth decided that if Friday was bright, it would be her day, and when she wakened Friday morning she couldn't wait for the sun to come up. And when it did it looked as if Friday would be clear and cold. There was not a cloud in the sky.

They had cabbage and sausage for dinner that day—it was one of Samantha's most usual meals. Ruth ate heartily, but not too much; she didn't want the stuff churning in her stomach. She tried to be bright at the dinner table so that none of the others would suspect anything, and she must have been too bright because Samantha suggested she go down cellar in the afternoon and sort potatoes. Ruth seemed to comply. That job would at least get her out of the house, and once out of the house she'd find some opportunity to slip off. She'd probably go down cellar for a little while, and then go back out to the sheds, as if she wanted some more baskets. And from the sheds it would be easy to drift north, and if she were lucky no one would see her.

It turned out that way, because nobody came out on the back porch and called. Ruth walked quietly, as if she weren't in too much of a hurry, and then, after she had covered a couple hundred yards she cut over to the creek. On the creek path it would be hard to see her because there were too many weeds in the way.

It was a bright and crisp day, but the wind was from the north and it stung her face. Once she turned east she'd no longer have to face it, and as soon as she got to the deep woods there would be no wind at all. And then she'd be back in her own world, which never worried a whipstick about the supposition that Mother might be watching. In fact, that ridiculous idea would be good for nothing but a round belly laugh.

THERE WERE Shaker woodcutters in the big woods southeast of the North Family, so that Ruth had to swing out of her way to avoid them. That brought her inevitably to Jehovah's Chosen Square, but today the Square looked desolate, the long brown grass matted down by the snows. Ruth cut through the Square and got into the woods as soon as she could, and the moment she did she took off her bonnet and ripped off her Shaker cap. Her hair came tumbling down over her shoulders at once, and she shook her head like a dog emerging from water. The cap she tucked into the pocket inside her cape, and thought at the moment that she'd be glad if she never had to put it on again.

As she had expected, the woods were friendly—they were always friendly. The hickory nuts had all disappeared and in the hollows of the grass between the snow drifts only the shells remained, but there were in places old black and sodden walnuts peeking out through the snow. And here and there there were still some old bright bittersweet berries. Ruth remembered then how she had yearly brought some bittersweet to the cabin, and how Asenath and her mother had always thrown the stuff into the fire as soon as they could. It wasn't worth anything, they said, and it was quite evident that they had no eyes for beauty.

It was rather slow going through the woods, and Ruth was no

longer in a hurry. Now that she was on her way home, the thought intensified that she would have to remain unseen. She would not be welcome in the cabin, and if she showed her face there, everyone would scoff at her. And if they discovered that she didn't mean to stay, then there might be a real brawl, and they might try to restrain her by force.

She was coming abreast of the Robinsons' farm now, and while she kept concealed within the edges of the woods, she did keep looking out towards the Robinson barns and outbuildings. There was the slightest chance that Richard might have come home, and if he had, then she wanted to know it. But the Robinson sheds and barn lay under snow, and only the big manure pile steamed in the frost. Once she thought she heard a faraway door slam, but that was likely only a deception of her own ears, though once she did definitely hear the Robinson dog. Old Mose was barking at something. He sounded lonesome.

Ruth cut a little south then in order to follow her usual creek path. It was more tangled with briers than she remembered, and she was well scratched before she came near the corduroy road. There she did definitely stop, looking out from the shelter of a great beech whose long arms came down almost to the ground. There was nothing to see, and there was nothing to hear except the small murmur of the water as it broke out from under the ice. That didn't seem too strange; her family was likely shut indoors. Herman and his lady, if he still had her, would be huddled up against the fire, and Rachel would be sitting there in her usual chair, staring forever at vacancy. And her mother would likely be brewing some sort of mess in the only iron pot the family had. That had always made it hard to get supper, when her mother had wanted the pot to brew one of her concoctions. As for Jake, he'd likely be sleeping in the corner bed, and her father would probably be in the other cabin where the horse and cow lived. He passed a lot of his time there through the winter.

Ruth got out to the road at last, and without actually thinking started walking quietly over the new corduroy. The logs were smothered with leaves and the leaves were rotten and covered with ice, so that the road made walking tricky. Once she had gone across the tiny creek and had started up the far rise Ruth walked so slowly that she was hardly moving, and all the while her eyes were fixed on the hill. The cabin finally came in sight, and it lay cold and bare. For a moment Ruth didn't notice that there was no smoke coming from the chimney, and when she did her heart skipped a beat. There was always blue wood smoke there, day and night throughout the winter. But today there was nothing. And the snow that covered the whole roof, even around the chimney, proved that there had been no fire for a long time.

At the lane Ruth was positive—there were no marks in the snow and it looked as if there had never been any marks. She started to climb the hill then, and when she did she saw that the cabin door was standing a little open. She felt panic at that sign—her family was gone. It might be that the Robinsons would know where they went, and it might be that not even the Robinsons would know. Her father had never been a man to take counsel or to divulge his business.

After she wedged open the door and went into the dark cabin Ruth was finally sure. The bedclothes were gone from the bed, and even the old buffalo hide was gone. The cabin had been stripped clean, and the Berzinskis had left almost nothing behind. There were some corn shucks on the floor, and kicking through those Ruth uncovered what had been her old corn-shuck doll. It had been lost for years. She cried when she saw it, and dutifully picked it up and set it into the window frame. The doll seemed to be all that was left of her life on the hill, and it was better that it stay right there in the cabin, since it was probable that there no profane eyes would ever see it.

Ruth made sure—she went into the other cabin, but it was empty as the first. They had perhaps eaten the chickens, or taken them with them. And the cow was gone, and their single horse. Things might have gotten so bad that there was just no possibility of continuing life on the old home acres. And there must have been bitterness and desolation and quarrels before they all pulled out. Ruth had not the slightest knowledge where they might have gone, but her mind said Kentucky. Her father had come from Kentucky, from some place way on down in the canebrakes. And he had always said that Kentucky was a damn sight better than Ohio. Down in Kentucky men didn't have to do everything because there were niggers to do the work. And people knew how to hold their liquor.

There was no sense in staying; in fact, it seemed to Ruth as if some compelling force within her was urging her to get off the hill in a hurry. She was crying as she went down through the snow. She had thought that she did not love them, did not love anyone in her family, and it was too early as yet to say she really did. But, no matter how bad they were, they were her roots, and without them she was truly alone in the world. And now there was no place to run if she ever wanted to get away from Shakertown.

On the way back up towards Robinsons' the impulse came to go up there very boldly and ask them what they knew. Ruth remembered very well that Mrs. Robinson had been nasty to her before, but there was a chance that she would have gotten over her spite. And there was just nothing else to do; if the Robinsons didn't know where the Berzinskis had gone, then nobody would.

There were snowy wheel tracks going into the Robinson lane, and Ruth walked in one of them. She was rather hoping that old Abraham would be in the house, because he seemed to have better manners than Mrs. Robinson. At least he had always treated Ruth very decently. Ruth went to the back door—the Robinsons had two doors—and knocked rather timidly. Most places one didn't knock—one just went in—but a person always knocked at the Robinsons. They seemed to want it that way.

Abraham wasn't at home—at least he was not in the house, and Mrs. Robinson, when she finally appeared, seemed to have no intention of asking Ruth to come in. "Well?" she said when she opened the door six inches and shoved her face through. And then, "I see you've gone and got yourself converted to a Shaker."

Ruth ignored that, almost ignored it. "I'm not a Shaker yet," she said. "Do you know where my folks went to?"

Mrs. Robinson seemed to sniff a little at that. "I never had no truck with them," said Mrs. Robinson quite definitely. "I don't know where they went to."

"Did you know they were gone?"

"It's been quiet around here," said Mrs. Robinson. "I guess that's the way I knew they were gone. It's been real quiet. And we're not missing things any more."

Ruth let the insult pass. "What do you know about Richard?" she asked boldly. "Is he comin' home? I mean soon?"

At that Mrs. Robinson's face seemed to go gray and she looked as if she wanted to cry.

"It was you who did it," she said bitterly. "If it hadn't been for you he'd be here right now. We need him, and we don't know where he's at."

Ruth felt her strength drain away again.

"I didn't know he was going," she said honestly. "He never told me he was going. I don't see that I had anything to do with it."

"It was his wanting to marry you," said Mrs. Robinson. "I guess you knew that. And you weren't the right girl. We didn't want any Berzinskis in the family. Not in our family."

And with that Mrs. Robinson very firmly closed the door and dropped the bar in place.

Ruth looked out towards the barn before she left, but it seemed that Abraham was not around. And the wheel tracks in the lane were almost proof—he had probably gone to Red Lion or Lebanon. Ruth thought Richard's father would be easier to talk to than his mother, but there was also the chance that old Abraham would himself be angry with her. There was nothing she could do about it.

It seemed a long way back to Union Village, and this time the woods seemed sterile and void of life. Ruth walked mechanically, and even tore through some of the briers. It seemed to her as if she were suddenly empty, as if she were hardly better than a bag of meal. People just did things to her, some of them nasty things, and she had no capacity to fight back. Now she felt that her last reliance was gone. She was truly alone in the world. Perhaps she should have gone with Clema, and perhaps she still ought to pick up and traipse after her. Back with the Shakers she was certain that she'd be able to eat and sleep, but she was also certain that her life would be empty. All the things she had wanted, and most of them were very real and simple things, looked as if they were to be denied. There would be no man and no babies. And there would never be a home with decent furnishings, and books, and table covers, and things like that. Just never—never.

The sky was beginning to look like first evening and the woodcutters had gone home from the woods when she passed through Jehovah's Chosen Square and came out on the old corn land. Biting her lips as she stumbled over the stubble, Ruth thought that, given the slightest chance, she'd never go back. Never go back. And all the while she thought such things, her feet inevitably brought her nearer Union Village. She got to the Pike at last, and turned south, then crossed the footbridge over the ditch and headed over towards the creek. She'd have to give herself time to make up her mind. Probably the whole winter—winter was no time to be out alone in the world. But with spring she meant to be gone, where she didn't know. She was just not going to surrender, not going to become one of the waxen old ladies one saw in the Shaker Families. And never, never, never, not in a thousand years could she ever believe that Jesus Christ had been born again, and that they had called him Ann Lee.

SISTER SAMANTHA was definitely angry, and when she got angry she kept mumbling with her lips as if she were chewing at something. They ate their bean soup and bread and butter supper in virtual silence, and afterwards the girls and women who worked in the kitchen washed up in silence. It seemed that something had happened while Ruth was gone, and it seemed as if no one was permitted to tell Ruth what had happened. But everyone knew that she had been gone, gone a very long time, and no one completely believed her excuse that she had just gone out for a walk. It must have been a strange walk, for when she came back her hands and forehead were torn by briers, and her hair wasn't even all tucked under her knit cap.

Ruth supposed that Samantha had decided to let the matter rest until family worship that night, and that was exactly what happened. Samantha read something from the New Testament about being willful and disobedient. Then she squatted back in her chair and pushed her octagon glasses up onto her forehead, after which she made a business of staring at each of them in turn. All but the older women back in the shadows. Samantha never once looked in their direction, and Ruth knew that if they were ever willful or disobedient the sky would fall in.

Samantha pursed her lips then, folded her hands in her lap, and began staring directly at Ruth. "I been here a long time," she began, "but I can't never remember anything happening in the Village like happened this afternoon. People as leave their appointed tasks to go do something else just because they want to is on their road to hell. That's what the Apostle means, and that's what the good book says, so that's what he has to mean." And with that Samantha nodded her head vigorously up and down. "It's as plain as the nose on your face," she reiterated. "That's what it has to mean."

After that there was something of a silence, and Ruth thought that that was the end of it, but it was only the beginning.

"I been here a long time—in the Gathering Order," said Samantha. "I been a good Mother to the girls and women here—you can ask anybody an' they'll all tell you that. I been a good Mother. But I ain't ever been so beside myself as this afternoon. Here was Elder Phineas Riegel askin' whether there might be somebody able to take over the schoolhouse until Lena Gaspar recovers from her pleurisy, and I tell him yes, there's a girl down cellar sortin' potatoes who can read and write. An' then when I send down cellar, Ruth ain't there atall. God knows what got into her head, but she ain't there atall. An' she ain't nowhere, not in the house nor privy nor nowhere. An' we can't find her, no matter how much we holler out the back door. An' all the while Elder Phineas lookin' at me and wantin' to know what could have happened, and I can't answer any more than a rooster with its head cut off. An' all that happened just because of what the Apostle calls willful and disobedient conduct, which ain't fittin' either in the sight of God or our Holy Mother. An' there's been no explanation given as yet, an' I don't think there is any. Sister Ruth just got feelin' rebellious because I asked her to handle a few potatoes, an' she skinned out. That's the explanation."

They were all looking at her, Ruth knew that, looking like a circle of judges before the appointed execution. Even the younger girls, Patience Blake, Mary Hawthorne, and Flossie, people who should know better. Ruth would have liked desperately for Clema still to be there—Clema would have stared them down. She herself felt helpless.

"Well?" It was Samantha again, and this time she was staring right at Ruth. "If you got anything to say for yourself, you better say it, young lady."

"I took a walk," said Ruth promptly. "That's what I told you before supper—I took a walk."

"You got your good clothes all muddy," said Samantha. "That's what you done."

"I couldn't help it," said Ruth.

"Why did you have to take a walk?"

Ruth knew what Clema would have said—Clema would have said it was because she was sick of the damned place. Ruth didn't want to say just that, but it was the truth.

"I'm used to walking," Ruth said, as quietly as she could. "I don't like to sit in the house all the time."

"You wasn't in the house—you was down cellar. You was supposed to be sortin' potatoes."

There was no way of denying that fact, and Ruth said nothing. That seemed to put Samantha on the defensive, and she pulled her eyeglasses back onto her nose and hunched forward in her chair. A long minute passed while they stared at each other, and while the other girls seemed to be afraid that the judge was now going to pass judgment of condemnation.

"Well, he's a comin' back," said Samantha at last. "He's a comin' back tomorrow morning because they need somebody to learn the girls in school their lessons. It was my fault an' I regret it—I told him you could read and write. That's why he's a comin' back. He says they don't want nobody old, but somebody like Lena Gasper was at first, who can maybe stay on fifteen–twenty years after Lena goes to her grave."

That was the end of the matter; after that they all fell on their knees and mumbled through the Lord's Prayer, although Samantha refused to repeat "as we forgive those who trespass against us." Ruth had to smile in spite of herself when she heard Samantha stop, and then resume with "And lead us not into temptation."

It was chilly in the bedroom that night—human chilly. The incivility might have been a good thing for Ruth; it made her mad, and when she got mad she seemed to come back to herself a little. In her mind the women in the Gathering Order were either victims or fools, probably a little of both. It was no defense for them to say that life was hard out in the world. Of course it was hard—that was the way it was meant to be. Probably none of them had had to live like the Berzinskis, and probably none of them knew that anybody in the world lived that way.

IT WAS PERHAPS nine o'clock the next morning when the Elder came back. Ruth was using brick dust to scour some knives in the kitchen when she saw the light wagon pull around in back of the house. The Elder looked very serious and dignified as he sat on the high box seat with the reins held in both hands, and he made quite a business of hitching to a small peach tree in back of the house, so that Ruth had a chance to get her hands cleaned. She had thought that he would come straight in through the back door and began to get apprehensive, but instead Elder Phineas Riegel walked around to the front of the house and Samantha was there waiting for him. From the unction in her voice, heard distantly, it seemed as if she was on her very best behavior.

Ruth set her cap and waited, and it was not long before Samantha tottered back to the kitchen. Once there, she shut the door behind her and glowered a little bit. "He's in there waiting," she said brusquely. "Now you mind your manners. You won't be talkin' to a dummy."

Ruth got up and Samantha followed her in through the rooms until they came to the parlor. It was the same room that was used each night for evening prayers, and Samantha's fern was very conspicuous in it, the only perceptible sign of sin in the whole house. Ruth hesitated a little when she got to the parlor, but the Elder was standing near the door holding his wide-brimmed hat in his hand, and he came forward to meet her. "I'm Elder Phineas Riegel," he said as he held out his hand. "First in the East Family. We take care of the schoolhouse because we're the nearest family to it."

Somehow Ruth liked him at sight—there seemed something warm in the man. He was certainly no beauty, but he was distinguished-looking. About fifty, and with heavy gray eyebrows and not so gray hair. He had evidently not shaven since Sunday, and there was a stubble on his cheeks and chin. His face was long and thin and his nose was long and thin, but his eyes redeemed his face—they were good green-blue eyes with crowfeet in the corners. Elder Phineas, in fact, looked as if he were—was—often out in the weather. His skin was like fine brown leather.

"I think we'd like to be alone," Elder Phineas said calmly when he saw Samantha getting ready to squat in her favorite rocker. "It won't take a long time."

Samantha seemed shocked, but she managed to waddle out of the room in the direction of the kitchen. Ruth had an idea that she would keep the doors open so that she could listen. Once she was gone, however, Elder Phineas took care of that—he walked over and shut the heavy walnut door. And having done that, he came back and stood looking at Ruth, as if he were trying to measure her in his own mind.

"Sit down, won't you?" he said at last. "We'll be more comfortable if we sit down."

They sat, on straight chairs, one on either side of the square center table that had the Bible on it. Once they were down, Elder Phineas lost no time in coming to the point.

"It's about the school," he said. "I guess you know Sister Lena Gaspar is sick. She's had the school a long time, but she may not be able to go back for a while. I'm looking for somebody young and strong who can take her place. You look young and strong."

Ruth felt a little more at ease when she saw him smile. "I'm not a Shaker," she said. "I might not be the person you want."

The Elder smiled again. "I know all about you," he said. "You're Ruth Berzinski and you took a walk yesterday back to your old home. You didn't know that they had all moved out a month ago."

Ruth blushed shamefully. There was no way the man had of knowing that, she thought. It had been almost an accident that he did know—one of the men woodchoppers had followed Ruth. And he had been watching when she came out of the empty house and went up to Robinsons. The rest Elder Phineas had learned from a seed peddler in the East Family who knew the Berzinskis and had passed them on the road. It was quite evident from the way their wagon was loaded that they were carrying all their plunder with them.

Ruth thought she should say something, but couldn't find another word to say. She didn't have to; Elder Phineas took charge.

"You can read and write, can't you?" he asked. "Not too well, but a little. Can you?"

"I been to school three terms," Ruth said. "Course it didn't last long at a time. But I can read and write."

Elder Phineas reached out a huge paw and pulled the Bible to him. He seemed to know it by heart, because he didn't have much trouble in finding the place he wanted. "Read this," he commanded, and got up to hand the book to Ruth.

It was something called Corinthians—and Ruth couldn't say that word too well.

"'Though I speak—with the tongues—of men and of angels—and have not charity—I am become—as sounding brass—or a tinkling cymbal," Ruth read. She tried to stop there, but Elder Phineas waved her on with his hand. "And though I have—the gift of—prophecy and understand—all mysteries—and all knowledge—and though I have all faith—so that I could remove mountains—and have not charity—I am nothing."

"What's 'charity?'" snapped Elder Phineas suddenly. "Do you know what it is?"

"It's giving things to people, I think," said Ruth. "I don't really know."

Elder Phineas nodded. "In this case 'charity' means love," he said quietly. "Do you know who the Corinthians were?"

"They were people who lived a long time ago?"

"Who wrote the passage you were just reading?"

This time Ruth really did color. "I guess Jesus," she said. And when she saw his eyes, she really got hot. "Was it Jesus? I don't know."

Elder Phineas managed not to tell her at the moment.

"If eggs cost seven and a half cents a dozen, how much would three and a half dozen cost?" he asked quickly.

Ruth racked her brains, but the answer wouldn't come.

"I could do it if I had a slate," she said. "That's the way we always did it in school."

At that Elder Phineas reached inside his coat and brought out a small slate and slate pencil. "I brought these along because I wanted to see you write," he explained. "No reason why you shouldn't use the slate to figure."

Ruth put down the three sevens, and the three halves, and then tried to complete the half dozen, but somehow she couldn't. Phineas didn't seem to approve too much. "How many rods are there in a mile?" he asked. "Did you learn things like that?"

Ruth had to shake her head No. Neither did she know how many gallons there were in a barrel, how many small measures there were in a bushel, or how many square rods or feet there were in an acre.

"You'll have to get things like that by heart," said Elder Phineas. "That is, if you want to help teach school. Some of the children are real smart, and the girls are always smarter than the boys. That's what you'd have—the girls."

Ruth felt ruined—she had not realized how dumb she was. "I

don't know whether I ought," she said in half apology. "I don't know whether I could ever make a good Shaker."

Elder Phineas seemed more interested at that confession than he had been at the revelation of her scanty knowledge. "What's troubling you?" he asked. "Is there anything I can explain?"

Ruth shook her head and felt miserable. "I guess it's just that I don't believe it," she said. "I can understand about Jesus Christ, but I can't understand the other."

"You mean about Mother Ann?"

That was it, and Ruth shook her head yes. After that Elder Phineas was silent for what seemed a long time. He sat with a hand on each knee, the wrists flapping the fingers up and down a little.

"You don't understand about Jesus Christ," he said at last. "Nobody does, not even the wisest men alive. It's all a mystery, and that's the way it has to be received—as a holy mystery. It's the same about Mother Ann—we don't understand that either. But it's the same thing—it was the power of God that passes all understanding. You would have known that if you had been here in the Village three or four years ago. The Spirit was upon us then. Did you ever hear people talk with tongues?"

Ruth shook her head. "I don't know what you mean," she said. "Everybody talks with his tongue."

"Not this way," said Elder Phineas. "I mean with different languages, tongues that a person doesn't have any right to know. As if I'd start talking Hebrew suddenly, or you'd start talking Greek. Wouldn't that seem strange to you?"

"I never heard of anything like that."

"Three or four years ago we had a dozen or more people in the Village talking with tongues," said Phineas. "Some of them only children. And they'd go hurling across the floor of the Meeting House as if they'd been shot from guns. I even saw John Marlin go right across fields that way, and he seemed just to roll over the fences. It was the power of the Spirit, nothing else."

Ruth felt just a little frightened. People had always said that the Shakers were crazy, but she had always thought that only a slur on them. Now she was not so sure.

Elder Phineas saw her discomfiture, and changed the subject.

"You'll need books," he said. "There's a Primer and a Speller I'll bring you. And a couple Arithmetic books." And he got to his feet as if he meant to go. When she saw that, Ruth also stood up.

"What I'd like to have is something I can read myownself," she said boldly. "I'd like to have something to practice on."

Elder Phineas didn't seem to think that strange. "Did you ever hear of a man named Washington Irving?" he asked. "I've got something by him stored in my trunk. And I think I've got something by Fenimore Cooper. They might be too hard for you, but you could try them. And in the meantime it would be a good idea for you to practice on the Holy Bible. Maybe one or two hours every day. Read it out loud so that you can get the words straight and see how they sound."

That seemed to be the end of the matter, although Ruth felt shaky. She hadn't really said that she'd try to take over the girls in the school. The worst thing was that Elder Phineas acted as if he didn't have to have her consent. Once the matter was all arranged in his own mind, he seemed to think she had to do anything he liked.

Elder Phineas went out the back way, and by opening the door suddenly managed to find Samantha in the passageway. He very likely knew that she had been eavesdropping, but he pretended not to notice. "She'll be starting next Monday," he told Samantha. "School takes up at eight o'clock, but she better be there early to get the fire in the stove going. And you'll have to pack her a lunch—she can't come home for dinner."

Nothing was said about how Ruth would get to the school, which was a little brick building right down in the fork of the Lebanon and Mason Pikes. It had been built there because it was nearer the Children's Order.

Elder Phineas did turn once more at the back door, and again he gave Ruth his hand. "You're scared now, Ruth," he said kindly, "but you won't be so scared once you catch on to it. It won't be too hard."

And with that he went out the door and closed it behind him. Samantha waited to explode until the Elder drove away, but the minute he did, she gave vent to her feelings.

"There's no sense you're actin' stuck up," she told Ruth. "Only reason you was picked was that nobody knows what else to do with you."

And with that Samantha waddled over to the table and put a

piece of raw cabbage in her mouth. They were having cabbage for dinner because some of the leaves were turning brown.

THE BOOKS appeared miraculously—one of the East Family members stopped in on his way to Monroe with a load of corn. Ruth carried the volumes up to her bedroom when she saw that Samantha's nose was out of joint. One, a little red book, was called "A History of New York," and it was by a man named Diedrich Knickerbocker. And then it was also by a man named Washington Irving. Ruth didn't understand how that could be possible. The other was a slightly larger volume, and it had started to fall apart. It was by a man who was called James Fenimore Cooper. Ruth opened each of the volumes and tried to read a little bit, but she got no sense out of what she was reading. They didn't seem like schoolbooks at all; they had a lot of hard words in them, and they both went on and on forever.

Samantha looked daggers when Ruth told her that she was also supposed to read the Bible, for perhaps as much as two hours every day. Bible reading, Samantha thought, was her own privilege, and she prided herself that no one in the house could read the Holy Book as well as she could. But if Ruth practiced two hours a day, then it might be possible that Ruth would learn to read that well too. Such a situation would be intolerable.

It had been Saturday when the Elder called, and there certainly wasn't much time to prepare for school on Monday. Nor did Samantha help—on Saturday afternoon she sent Ruth and Patience Blake down cellar again to sort potatoes. A few potatoes seemed to be soft or were turning rotten, and those had to be carried out and dumped on the garden. Ruth wasn't too sorry about the task—it got her out from under Samantha's feet. She was apprehensive about going to the schoolhouse on Monday, and all the while she was sorting potatoes she was trying to do arithmetic sums in her head. Adding wasn't too hard, but subtracting was. As for multiplying or dividing, Ruth had never even heard of the possibility of having instant answers to difficult problems. And she knew that the minute she got the real schoolbooks she'd try to figure out what they were all about.

The schoolbooks came on Sunday, and again it was a Shaker man who brought them. It seemed that they had not been in the schoolhouse, and that Elder Phineas had had to send down to the South Family for them because Lena Gaspar had carried them home. There was a little red Arithmetic, a Primer and First Reader, and a Speller. The Arithmetic and Reader didn't look too hard, but the Speller had a lot of funny words in it, particularly towards the back. Ruth thought she'd not try to do too much with the words in the back of the book, maybe never.

It was a dreary day, that Sunday. They had a little house church service in the morning, during which Samantha delivered one of her usual homilies. Then there was only dried pea soup and cold boiled potatoes for dinner. After that Samantha went to her room to meditate and the rest of them were left to find their own salvation in the cold house. Most people stayed in the kitchen—that was the only room half warm. But the swarm in the kitchen was actually pious— most of the Sisters sat on hard chairs and stared straight in front of them. There were no approvable topics of conversation on Sundays, and most of the women didn't have sense enough to speak about anything anyway. Ruth finally gave up and went to the cold bedroom, then, seeing her opportunity, crawled through a tiny door into the attic. It was dark and frigid in there, although the builders had put down some floorboards. There were two old trunks in the attic and nothing more, and before she left Ruth thought that when the weather turned warm again, if it ever did, she'd see what was in the trunks. That is, if she were still in Union Village when the sun came back.

All that day the sky was like lead, and it looked as if it might start to snow at any minute. It didn't snow, however, not until darkness started to seal the world. Then it wasn't snow but icy grit, and the windows got coated and the back porch became slippery. Supper, when they finally had it, seemed dismal—the sleet had turned to snow and the whole house was being sealed in. Ruth's heart sank— there was no way for her to get to the school in the morning except walk, and by morning the road would likely be very heavy going.

She said no prayers before she went to bed that night—she didn't even kneel down. She felt numb, stunned, almost as if she weren't really herself. Somewhere it seemed as if the girl who was known as Ruth Berzinski had been lost, and there was left now only a frightened stranger who would have to face a class of girls in the morning. It was not a happy prospect.

Chapter 5

SEVEN LITTLE GIRLS were all standing desolately around the cold stove when Ruth got to the school. It had been a hard struggle to get there, through the snow, and it had perhaps been a harder struggle for the children, for they had had to come almost as far as Ruth. They were shivering convulsively, and they had already stuffed dried leaves and a little brush into the iron monster that was supposed to warm them, but they had not been able to find the block of matches. Ruth couldn't either for a time; finally, she discovered it in what was evidently supposed to be the teacher's desk. It wasn't a desk—it was a table, a light brown butternut table. Ruth knew how cantankerous such matches could be, but she did finally manage to strike fire, and the dried leaves from the wood box caught. After that it was only a matter of nursing the fire until it got strong enough to kindle wood.

Meanwhile they huddled and shivered. Ruth had her arm around the two smallest children, two little beauties who said their names were Leda and Mary Brooks. They looked almost exactly alike, with flaxen hair and blue eyes, and although they now and then tried to smile bravely, there was something desolate in their smiles. Ruth refrained from asking questions—there was no sense in reminding the children of past circumstances that they had not been able to control. Somewhere there should be a father and a mother, at least one of them left, and somewhere there should have been a home. It was perhaps again a case of converts to the Shaker faith who had surrendered all their possessions and surrendered their children as well.

Once they got warm, it seemed the girls relaxed a little. Charity Dobson, the largest girl, who said she was twelve, told her own name without being asked. Charity was redheaded and freckle-faced, and she had a big body for her age. Carrie and Martha Harnsdorf were nine and eleven, and they were two little mischiefs who seemed happy. Until Ruth thought she had to stop them, they kept warm by running up and down the length of the schoolroom. Felicity Jackson said she was ten, and Lucy Graham that she was eleven. Felicity was sad-eyed and small for her age. Lucy was non-descript—she had nothing to recommend her but her large green eyes. Unfortunately she seemed to stammer or stutter a little.

Once they were all a bit warm, at least near the stove, Ruth relaxed a little. The girls kept their coats on, and so did Ruth—the room would have been intolerable without them. But the bonnets

Dance unto the Lord

were hung on pegs along the wall, and the chairs were dragged over nearer the stove. When they were all established there, Ruth brought back the slates that had been piled on the teacher's table. There were not enough slate pencils to go around.

"We're going to begin to count and write numbers," she told them. "Can you all count to ten?"

At that Leda Brooks shook her head sadly, but the rest of them began shouting that they could count as far as a hundred. At least some of them thought they could.

Ruth moved her chair over beside Leda, so that she could watch her closely, and began to dictate. "What I say I want you to write on your slates," she instructed. "And write carefully, so that there is no mistake. First of all 'Seven.' I want you all to write Seven."

They were eager enough, but it was plain that Leda Brooks couldn't write Seven. Ruth helped her. And then in rapid sequence she called out Nine, One, Three, Four, Eight, Six, Five, Two, and Ten. The slate pencils scratched, and the slates had to be examined so that they could be erased. And then they did it all over again, until finally the little girls had dropped out and Ruth was calling out numbers like Ninety-Five, Seventy-Three, Fifteen, and Thirty-Six. The older girls got those numbers all right too.

But the game couldn't go on forever, and the fire needed more wood, so Ruth had to dream up something else. In the silence that followed the replenishment of the stove she heard for the first time what must be the boys' class on the other side of the dividing wall. It seemed that they were singing, but Ruth couldn't make out the song. She thought that a good idea, and decided to try it herself.

"I think maybe we'd better sing a little," she told them when she came back to her chair. "Who knows a song?"

Nobody knew a song, not one. Sister Lena Gaspar must not have been a singing woman, because the girls looked vacant. Ruth was blocked—she had counted on them to teach her a song. Actually, she herself didn't know one song, not one. She had never sung, and no one she knew had ever sung. Jake and Herman would sometimes let out screams in the cabin and her mother had mumbled to herself a lot, but they had definitely never sung.

"Don't you know a Shaker song?" Ruth asked them desperately, thinking that Sister Lena might have taught them one of the Shaker hymns about Mother Ann.

They shook their heads as if they did not know what she was talking about, and Ruth was too timid to try her own voice on a homemade melody. But she decided right then that she was going to learn a song or two. It wasn't right for children not to know how to sing.

"I guess we'd better read, then," she said, and went back up to the desk to see if there were any reading books available. There were two Primers, and one First Reader. Ruth brought all three of the books back to the fire, and distributed them so that it might be possible for everyone to see one of them.

"We're going to read the Primer," she said. Turn to the first page, and I'll ask every one of you to read in turn. That way we'll see if we can read the first page."

The big girls were humiliated, and after a little while paid not the slightest attention. Charity Dobson frankly looked out of the window, and the two Harnsdorf girls started kicking each other. Ruth told them to stop that, and they did for a little while, and then began kicking all over again. And the little girls couldn't even read the Primer, at least not well. They did seem to know their letters, at least the big letters. They weren't quite so certain about the smaller ones.

And now the fire needed fixing again, and the stovewood in the box was going to run out in another hour. There was more stovewood outside, of course, a big stack of it that Ruth had noticed when she came in. It was buried deep under the snow, but it might not be too wet. They'd have to venture out and carry a lot of the pieces in after a little more time had gone by, but it might not be fun breaking the pieces loose. And only the biggest girls could go—the little ones were not much larger than a hunk of stovewood.

It began to be a dismal day, and the clock standing on a shelf at the side of the room acted as if it were frozen. Outside someone pulled a farm wagon through the drifts, its wheels creaking, and after a long time there were repeated shouts out on the road. They all ran to the windows to see what was the matter, and they all shouted when they saw the Shaker ox teams lumbering along in a slow procession. They were probably going on down as far as the East Family, and once they did that, they might turn around and break the road back to the West Frame and West Brick. At least Ruth hoped they would. Unfortunately the oxen were soon out of sight, and then there was no further excuse to look out the windows. Ruth tried slates and numbers again.

It began to be a miserable day, the longest day she had ever passed in her life. They tried a skipping game on the floor, and that seemed fun, but after a time someone over in the boys' room hammered on the wall. Ruth understood; whoever was over there thought they were making too much noise. The skipping game stopped, and they tried to read the first page of the First Reader. The older girls weren't interested and the younger ones found it too difficult.

Finally it was twelve, and they could breathe. The girls got out their brown-paper lunches and Ruth took hers from the inside pocket of her cape. The lunches were identical: bread and yellow cheese. No one protested—they were all used to bread and cheese. But Charity did start coughing and between coughs she said that she had to have a drink. There was no water in the water pail, and Ruth had not even thought of getting a bucket of fresh water. She rushed out into the cold with her bucket, but the pump in the yard was frozen solid. There was nothing to do but scoop up a big handful of snow for Charity, and Ruth did that as she ran back to the warmer schoolroom. Outside the weather had turned colder and there was a nasty wind blowing from the west. It seemed as if the sky wanted to drop snow again.

Ruth took a long noon hour, and during the noon hour the boys' schoolmaster didn't seem to mind if the girls ran and skipped around their schoolroom. Then it was finally one, and the dull business of learning had to proceed again. They counted, but this time without slates and without looking at any books. Then Ruth tried addition, holding up fingers to help the little girls. Subtraction proved to be more difficult, and Felicity Jackson couldn't understand it at all. Felicity insisted that the total number of fingers that had been up at first had to be the right answer, even though Ruth bent down three or four of them. Ruth didn't insist. She thought of demonstrating with chairs, but that would likely make too much noise again.

And then, just when she was beside herself, and when she knew she'd have to go out to the woodpile, the door opened and Elder Phineas walked in without announcement. His breath plumed as he stood in the door, and it kept on showing a little until he got up against the stove. "Cold out there," he said quietly as he rubbed his hands together. "Must be zero."

Ruth didn't know exactly what that meant, but she agreed that it was cold. Elder Phineas tried to make himself inconspicuous by going around to the back of the stove. "You just go on," he directed. "Keep on doing whatever you were doing before I came in."

Ruth did—it was the silly subtraction game with her fingers as the soldiers who were either shot or disappeared into the trees. Lucy Graham made a few good guesses, and the Harnsdorf twins weren't too bad. Most of the rest of the girls were either disinterested or completely confused. The game went on like a top running down, and finally it collapsed entirely. Ruth got up then and stood so that Elder Phineas could see her. "We don't have enough books," she said. "There's only two Primers and only one First Reader."

Phineas nodded sadly, and now he was warm enough to unwind the knitted scarf he had wound around his neck. "You could tell them a story," he suggested. "They'd like that. Tell them a story."

Ruth was blank. Just as she didn't know any song, she didn't know any story. She had heard about stories, and she guessed that's what was in the hard books by Irving and Fenimore Something, but she hadn't had time to read the books. Certainly no one had ever told her a story.

"I don't know a story," she had to confess. "I can't tell any because I don't know any."

Elder Phineas looked sad, but after a moment he went up to the teacher's table and brought back the big chair that was still up there. Once he had dragged it to the fire, he had the girls scoot their chairs aside a little so that he was right in the middle.

"This is the way it goes," he said, and remembered that he still had his hat on his head. He took it off then and placed it on the floor beside him. "I'll tell you the story of a king who lived a long time ago way over on the other side of the world. Would you like to hear that kind of story?" And he carefully looked at each of the faces in turn until each one showed at least some interest.

"Well," said Phineas, "this king's name was Midas, and he was a good king, but one who wasn't too wise. Do you know what 'wise' means?" And he put his arm around Lucy's waist and drew her a little towards him.

"I d-d-don't know," said Lucy.

Elder Phineas turned to Charity, who was three times the size of Lucy. "Do you know what wise means?" he inquired again.

"I think it means something like smart," said Charity.

"That's exactly what it does mean," agreed Elder Phineas. "So King Midas was a good king but he wasn't too smart. I mean wise. He had a big palace and big gardens and bags of money and a beautiful daughter. And in his garden he had roses, lots and lots of roses, so many roses that they were growing as far as you could see. Do you know what a rose is?

"We don't have none in Union Village," said Martha Harnsdorf promptly. "They're something bad."

Elder Phineas shook his head a little. "No, they're not bad," he said. "They just take a lot of care, and we don't have time to spare growing them. Roses are beautiful flowers. Well, Midas had lots and lots of roses. But what he liked best was his daughter, who was just about as big as Lucy there. And his daughter had long golden hair, and he loved her more than anything else in the whole world. Every night he would kiss her to sleep, and every morning he would get her up and give her the best things in the world to eat."

"Did she eat cheese like we do?" asked Felicity Jackson.

"Cheese is good for you," said Elder Phineas, and looked out under his bushy gray eyebrows. "Cheese is good for you. But Rosemary—I think it was her name—didn't eat cheese. She ate hummingbird eggs and silver flowers and things like that. She was a princess because her father was a king, and princesses always eat hummingbird eggs."

"What's a hummingbird?" This time it was Carrie Harnsdorf.

"A hummingbird is a bird that makes its wings go so fast they hum," said Elder Phineas. "They go so fast you can see right through them."

And with that he paused and wiped his brow. To her amazement Ruth saw that there was actual sweat on his forehead.

"Well," said Phineas, "King Midas did something that was pleasing to the gods and they told him he could ask anything he wanted in the whole world. Anything."

"I d-d-don't know what g-g-gods are," said Lucy Graham.

"They're angels," said Felicity positively. "That's what they are."

"Not angels," Elder Phineas corrected. "Angels are something different. Angels have big white wings and fly down from heaven."

"I don't know where heaven is either," said Lucy.

Elder Phineas looked at Ruth for a moment and Ruth thought his face was a bit gray.

"Heaven is where God is," said Elder Phineas patiently. "People always point up when they talk about heaven."

"Can angels fly just like birds?"

"I guess so," said Phineas. He shook himself a little after that, and didn't seem to know what had happened to the story.

"Let me go on," he finally said patiently. "I was telling about King Midas who had a beautiful daughter and who liked roses. And he did something good and the gods said he could have anything he wanted. Can you guess what he asked for?"

"I know what I'd ask for," said Charity Dobson. "I'd ask for some more bread and cheese. I didn't have enough for dinner."

The Elder let that pass.

"He asked for the Golden Touch," Elder Phineas announced dramatically. "That means that he wanted anything he touched to turn to gold."

And with that he stopped and looked around the circle of faces, this time evidently hoping for some questions. None came.

"So he wanted everything he touched to turn to gold," said Elder Phineas again. "So the gods said yes, and they went away. And King Midas touched one of his roses, and it was pure gold. Then he collected a big armload of golden roses. But then he wanted something to drink."

"So do I," said Felicity positively. "We don't have any water in the water bucket. Sister Lena always had it full."

"We'll have some tomorrow," Elder Phineas promised. "It's snowing too hard out to get any now."

"The pump's froze up," said Ruth. "I tried, but the pump's froze."

"You could have melted some snow on top of the stove," suggested Phineas.

"I didn't think of it," said Ruth.

Elder Phineas got up then and went to the west window. It was snowing furiously outside and there was a bad wind from the west that kept howling around the schoolhouse. Elder Phineas looked out a long time, and then turned around and walked back to the fire.

"I think you'd better get them home," he said. "Looks like a blizzard. I'll go with them—I have to get back to the East Family."

At that half the girls started jumping up and down, as if they were perversely delighted for the chance to get back out into the snow. Nobody seemed to be interested in the end of the story. All the girls started putting on their bonnets, even before they were told to, and after that they fastened their coats around them. Fortunately the drab coats were long and made out of good wool.

"If it's this bad tomorrow, I don't think you'd better come," said Elder Phineas. "No sense in trying to have school on a day like this."

Somehow Ruth agreed, although that would mean a desolate day for her. But she'd try to read Irving, and that way maybe the long day would pass. That is, if she ever got home. She'd have to go right against the wind to plow back to the Gathering Order, and the wind was a lot stronger than she was.

Elder Phineas set the damper on the stove, and then told the girls to wait until he went over to the boys' side and told them to go home. Then they'd all go together. They could all tell that he had gotten around the building all right, because there were suddenly howls and screams from beyond the walls. The boys were evidently as much delighted that school was out as the girls were.

After the cavalcade left the building Ruth waited a little while to stand up against the stove and get thoroughly warm. She had a bad feeling about her first day as a teacher, a very bad feeling. But everything had been against her, the weather, the lack of books, the frozen pump, the sluggish fire—almost everything. Sadly, however, she realized the further truth: all the things she didn't know were against her. She'd have to know a lot more to become a good teacher.

And—but this was a minor matter—she would have liked to know what happened to King Midas. That's what she'd like to have—a golden touch. If she had, it was very probable that things would change.

IT SEEMED a different world in the dark days of December. The snow in the roads packed hard, and then new snow fell, and was itself packed hard. Farm and town sleighs and sledges appeared on the pikes, sometimes bright with red and blue blankets and buffalo robes. Everywhere there were frozen ruts where unwary vehicles had ventured imprudently into what had been mud. In the Village proper there seemed to be the persistent smell of wood smoke, and sometimes the bluish smoke itself hung low over the roofs. And everything was sealed, the windows and doors and gates and barns, and sometimes it seemed even life itself. There were travelers on the road, of course, and sometimes curious travelers, even peddlers and tinkers, although neither breed got much work in Union Village, which had its own tin shop and smiths, and rarely if ever bought anything from peddlers. But the itinerants were a hardy breed, and all through the winter they would keep coming in dribbles. There were packmen with lace, ribbons, and buttons, wandering cobblers, and even scissors and knife sharpeners, and their direction always seemed to be down towards the big city, as if they all thought that fortune lay at the end of the trail.

And Ruth kept coming to the schoolhouse every blessed day, through good weather and bad, and most often she found the children there before her. She had the hang of it now, at least a little better, and she was no longer frightened, although she made no more pretenses. She had grown up ignorant, she knew that now, and she learned not to pretend to knowledge that she did not have. The schoolroom work was in a way easy—she didn't worry about that any longer. Elder Phineas had found a large sheet of slate that he said could go on the wall, but there was just no way to hang it, and it found a place standing against the wall near the stove where Ruth could most conveniently use it. And Elder Phineas had been better than that—somewhere he had managed to get hold of a few more schoolbooks. They were not all the same, but there were Readers and Primers, and two Arithmetics. The Arithmetics Ruth explored more than the Readers, and she soon discovered her limitations. There were charts and tables in arithmetic, all sorts of measurements of everything under the sun, gills, and tons, and pecks and furlongs and a lot of other hard things that a person just didn't have to know. The book was even very precise about land measurements; it seemed the men who wrote it thought everybody ought to know how to calculate the acres in triangular and trapezoidal fields, and to know all about rods and poles and chains and things like that.

It was not those gifts that made Ruth the most happy, however, for Elder Phineas found a second book by the author whose name was Washington Irving, and this one Ruth really liked. It was called simply *The Sketch Book,* and it told about London and English houses, and had some stories in it, one about a man who slept twenty years up in some big hills called the Catskill Mountains. Ruth didn't think the story was true, but she was not too sure. The other story she liked was about a silly schoolteacher whose name was Ichabod Crane, and that was a good one, because he was in love with a girl that a big Dutchman named Brom Bones wanted. And so Brom Bones pretended to be the Devil and chased the schoolteacher clear out of the country. Ruth read the story over and over. She kept on enjoying it even though it had some big words in it that she didn't know.

It was three weeks before she really met the teacher who had the boys next door, although she met him indirectly before that time because every morning when she got to school she found her woodbox filled. Ruth knew that he must have led his boys out to fill it because some of the girls told her as much, but Brother Matthew Poggs kept his distance. Ruth became apprehensive about him long before they met face to face, because almost every afternoon she could hear him licking some of the boys. There would be a whack-whack-whack, and then she'd hear the boy start screaming. She didn't like that at all, and neither did her girls. While the whippings were going on they all sat in frozen silence, and it was a good fifteen minutes afterward before anyone dared even to speak out loud.

Brother Matthew Poggs, however, proved to be quite a self-effacing individual. He was about thirty and he had catfish eyes in a scrofulous face. They met at the pump one afternoon quite by accident, for Leda Brooks had had a nosebleed and Ruth had run out to get a cloth wet enough to put on the back of her neck. Matthew was standing at the pump like an Indian idol, his head thrust back and his lips guzzling at the water dipper. "Hoddoo," he said when he saw her, and then he started to pump frantically when Ruth told him what was the matter. "Get her head back," Matthew directed. "Make her bend her head back." And not satisfied with that, he followed Ruth into her schoolroom and tried to take charge himself. The nosebleed didn't stop until it got ready to stop, but it was not for want of Matthew's trying. Ruth finally had to thrust herself in to protect the little girl, who seemed to think she was in the clutch of some monster.

And so the days labored along, and the year bent down to the dark, and every night Samantha tried to assert her authority by directing Ruth to do something she knew Ruth shouldn't have to do. Like washing up the dishes, or taking a broom out to sweep off the porches. Samantha always seemed to think that Ruth wouldn't do what she had been told to, and she always stood by truculently until the task was completed. After that she generally folded her hands in her apron and pretended piety, but Ruth casually ignored her. However, with the coming of the Christmas days Samantha wore a new face. Almost every night now, after she had read from one of the evangelists, Samantha delivered a short sermon about the Yearly Sacrifice and the Christmas Eve footwashing. She explained everything ad nauseam, saying the same thing ten or a dozen times in a row. It was fitting and proper—Samantha ordinarily began that way—that they should all rid themselves of the secret airs they were carrying in their hearts. Course, they weren't Shakers yet—they hadn't signed the Covenant. But it would be an evidence of good faith if they all did what the members of the Society did because the Ruling Elders would be pleased when they heard about it. They should all pair off in twos, and on Christmas Eve they should tell the other person of the real blackness in their hearts. And then they should get a big bowl and wash each other's feet. That's what Jesus had done, and that's how the custom had come down to them, and it was the fittin' way to show humility. And with that Samantha would purse her lips and take time to stare into all the eyes that were visible in the little lamplight. The younger girls generally stared back, but Ruth once or twice heard one of the older women sniffle. She herself neither stared nor sniffled, but she had made up her mind that she was neither going to participate in the Yearly Sacrifice, nor let anybody wash her feet. And she didn't mean to wash anyone else's feet either.

There were not many preparations for Christmas, but there were a few. In the established Families there was a big butchering in December, and now the smokehouses were hung full of hams and sides. And Ruth heard that some of the younger members of the Society were meeting secretly to practice their Christmas hymns. These, she was told, were always original compositions, and once

they were gotten by heart they would be kept ready for the early ser-
enading on Christmas morning. Whoever the singers might be, they
would have to be up in the black dark, and then they would be carried on box sleds to the other Families, where they would pull into
the snowy yards and sing long before the sun was up. Ruth thought
the idea rather appealing, and even made a few slight suggestions
that the Gathering Order might make and practice its own hymn.
Samantha put an end to that suggestion: the Gathering Order was
not permitted to intrude on the rights of the established Families.
And any fool could see that they didn't have a team and a box sled
to carry them around, even if they had wanted to go.

After that Ruth gave up all her Christmas notions, except in the
schoolroom. Elder Phineas finally found some colored paper, after
Ruth had told him three or four times that she would like to have
some, and although the colors were not good, Ruth cut the sheets so
that the girls could use flour paste to make chains of rings for the
schoolhouse windows. Elder Phineas wasn't too sure that he liked
the rings when he came in one day. "They look a little worldly,
Ruth," he said, as he kept fingering parts of the colored chains.
"They might even be heathen."

Ruth stood her ground. "I like them," she said. "And all the
girls like them. They're the only flowers we have in the wintertime."

Elder Phineas only nodded his head a little when he heard that.
"We don't dote on flowers," he said quietly. "Sometimes I almost
wish we did. A few posies in the yards might look real good."

That was all, but Ruth promised that she'd take down the rings
just as soon as Christmas was over. She decided then that she would
break the chains and send parts of them home with all the little girls.
It might be the only pretty thing in their lives.

So all seemed set, but two things happened on the twentieth day
of December that changed her world. The first was that on the way
down to the schoolhouse that morning Ruth found an issue of *The
Western Star* in one of the wheel tracks. The newspaper had evidently blown out of a sleigh, and it lay unblemished. Ruth knew
that newspapers were forbidden in the Village because they were
sinful, but something made her pick the paper up and carefully fold
it so that she could tuck it inside her coat. Where she'd be able to
read the copy of *The Western Star* she didn't know, but she decided
that she'd find the time and place. That would probably be in the

schoolhouse after all the girls had gone home for the day. And she certainly didn't have any feeling that she'd be doing anything sinful if she read it.

However, the occasion didn't come on that day, for Elder Phineas stopped into the school just about a half hour before Ruth was ready to dismiss. There was nothing peculiar about that—Elder Phineas often stopped in, certainly once or twice a week. School was never the same after he got there, because all the girls were constrained and acted afraid, although Elder Phineas made himself as inconspicuous as he could, generally by standing in the back of the room near the stove.

Today, however, he seemed to be laboring under some compulsion, and when Ruth finally told the girls to go home, and then started to get her own coat—*The Western Star* was tucked into one of the sleeves—Elder Phineas told her to sit down a bit. There was something he wanted to talk to her about, something he said he had had on his conscience for a long time.

Ruth sat down, and Elder Phineas pulled over one of the school benches that ordinarily lined the wall. After that he made a sort of cat's cradle with his hands, and seemed not to know how to begin. Ruth decided to help him.

"I know I'm not doing too well, but I'm doing the best I know how," she said. "I thought maybe their own teacher would be back by this time."

"Sister Lena may never be back," said Elder Phineas. "She's poorly, very poorly."

"What's the matter with her?"

Elder Phineas seemed hesitant. "A flux," he said finally, and that was the end of the matter. Phineas recovered himself after a few seconds of silence. "It wasn't that I wanted to talk to you about. What I wanted is to ask you if you don't think it's time."

Now Ruth was puzzled. "I don't know what you mean," she said. "Time for what?"

And again Phineas didn't answer.

"We think we're a chosen people," he said finally. "What we're trying to do is what we think is the will of God. And we abide by the revelation."

Ruth saw no reason to try to say anything to that, and after a long time Elder Phineas resumed.

"What I really want," he said, "is for you to sign the Covenant and join the Society. The way it is now you're not in a state of grace—you don't belong either to the redeemed or the unredeemed. You won't find peace until you decide to put your fears behind you and come over."

Ruth knew that she was coloring. She liked Elder Phineas, and he had been good to her. And he didn't seem to be as stuffy as most of the others—he had brought her the Irving books and the Fenimore book she couldn't read. Moreover, he had talked about roses, and almost said he liked flowers. She didn't want to offend him, but neither did she have the slightest inclination to join the Society.

"I don't have it in mind," she said, to be as gentle as she could. "Not yet. I don't have it in mind."

"You don't believe that the will of God spoke through the life and words of Mother Ann?"

"I don't know anything about it," Ruth said. "I don't see anything that's so different. Unless it's living the way you all do."

Phineas seized on that. "But that's it exactly," he said. "We live the way we do because we believe the things we do. Since we believe, we can't live any other way."

"I don't think it's wrong to have children," Ruth said boldly. "All of us were children once. If we hadn't been, we wouldn't be here."

Phineas nodded approval. "True enough," he said. "But in the wisdom of the Holy Mother it's time now that we stopped all carnal knowledge. Those that were born in sin must purify themselves, and they must see that no others are born in sin."

Ruth felt trapped. "I've thought about it and thought about it, but I guess I still don't see it the way you do," she said finally. "The way I see it, if there weren't no children, the world would come to an end."

"The world is coming to an end," said Elder Phineas positively. "There are signs in these times, just as Scripture foretold. Men of sin have called down fire from heaven, and now there are steamboats on our rivers and trains snorting across the land. It wasn't that way in Jesus' time. God doesn't want it that way. And everywhere you go you can see men walking in the pollution of their own minds. There are things I know that I wouldn't dare tell you about. Horrible things. And those things are mentioned in what are called newspapers, and so the filth is spread. Those are all signs of the times."

Ruth was miserable. "I can't do it," she said, and her hands tore at her dress. "I just can't do it right now. I just don't know enough about the world."

Elder Phineas's eyes had been bright, but now they dulled again, and he hung his head.

"Don't wait too long," he said sepulchrally. "The end of all things will come like a thief in the night. And when that great day happens, the chosen will be caught up to heaven in a cloud of glory. 'And of that day and that hour knoweth no man, no, not even the angels in heaven.'"

And with that Elder Phineas pulled himself to his feet and stood staring down at her. "I like you, Ruth," he said quietly. "That's why I don't want to see you lost. I like you."

Ruth waited until he left the schoolhouse. Somehow she felt afraid, she didn't exactly know why. The thought raced into her mind that she should have gone away with Clema Porter. She couldn't go now, not while the winter lasted. But she couldn't very well wait until spring—for all its seeming quietness Union Village seemed to be little better than a seething cauldron. Men and women tortured themselves to death in the big houses, and they seemed to like what they were doing. It didn't make sense.

The copy of *The Western Star* fell on the floor when she tried to get into her coat. Ruth picked it up at once and again hid it. She'd have to read it now, she decided that, she'd just have to read it. *The Western Star* came from another world, a world the Shakers didn't seem to know even existed.

THE WESTERN STAR was about so many things Ruth became confused. Some people were chewing the rag about something that was called a tariff. And there had been a runaway on Sycamore Street and a lady had been hurt by being thrown out of a sleigh. There was so much pork in the Cincinnati market that shippers were advised to delay sending more down to the city for a while. Any number of steamboats were tied up at the Cincinnati Landing, some of them from Pittsburgh, and some from Louisville, St. Louis, and some place called New Orleans. There were lockets and brooches for sale

on Vine Street. Fine woolens might be seen at the shop of J. Haniger.
The same was true of beaver hats—a fresh consignment had just
been received. A Negro slave named Jimby had run away—he was
six feet tall, weighed twelve stone, and had a notched left ear. All the
churches in Lebanon meant to have Christmas services, and at one a
children's choir would sing. Anyone who wanted wood sawed into
lumber might bring it to John Barnsby on Locust Street. Fine
beeswax candles were to be had from John Harnes. The Legislature
at Columbus was debating a new tax law. Stagecoaches had been
slow the last week because of the new snows, but they had all managed to get through. Somebody was a barber and tooth drawer.
Women's hats for spring would probably be adorned with some
things called ostrich plumes and egret feathers. First quality boots
and shoes might be had at the shop of Matthew Holloway on Main
Street. Good dirks and hunting knives were for sale by Jeremy Si-
monson. A barn had burned down in the alley behind Second Street.
Stick candies and lemon drops were to be had at the town bakery.
Alpacas, velvets, and serges might be purchased by the yard or bolt
from Eli Flemmer. In England it was said that children were being
shamelessly exploited in the coal mines. New York, Baltimore, and
Boston all had reported ships delayed by the hard winter.

It went on and on, the revelation of a world never guessed.
Lying in the attic and tracing the words in the *Star* by the light of a
single candle, Ruth forgot she was chilled to the bone. That was
what she wanted—what was out there, a sort of hurly-burly world
where thousands of people seemed to get along with each other
without worrying in the least that the world was coming to an end.
And it couldn't be true, what the Elder said, about the man of sin
calling down fire from heaven to propel the steamships and railroad
trains. Ruth had not the least idea about either of the contraptions,
but it seemed as if they were popular. And it seemed that they helped
to get things done.

She waited to get out of the attic until she was sure that everyone had gone down for supper, and when she finally appeared—
after the prayer was said—Samantha looked daggers at her. "You'll
keep on sleepin' until you go to your grave," she said tartly. "When
supper's on the table, it's on the table, and that's when it's intended
to be et."

Ruth didn't think it mattered very much when it was "et." There was only greasy hominy and sausage, and the hominy, as usual, tasted like lye. Samantha had ordered one of the kitchen women to make a pudding, and the pudding wouldn't have been bad if only there had been some syrup or sugar to sweeten it. Ruth took a few mouthfuls of the stuff, but it tasted like glue. That, unfortunately, was the way her world tasted at the moment—like glue.

Chapter 6

IT WAS IN early June that there came, in rapid succession, a number of changes in Richard Robinson's life. And they all happened so casually, so naturally, that in regarding them afterward he was inclined to believe that they had been preordained. The first, and smallest, change was that the number of dollars in his stone jar under the floor of MacCready's shop was now only a few short of a hundred. He had worked hard and spent little during the past year. Counting his silver hoard, as he did in the dark every Saturday night, the big outer doors securely bolted, he knew that he was a poor man no longer. If he wished now, he had enough to go back home and ask Ruth to run away with him. The thought was recurrent, but the bit of prudence in his mind always whispered that it would be a good idea to enlarge his fortune while he had the chance. Ruth would not suffer too much more since it would be summer when she could be outdoors most of the time, and by autumn he might have half a hundred more dollars. Or even more than that.

Then, one day, quite by chance he heard MacCready talking with an old gaffer who stopped into the shop from time to time. Richard knew that the old gaffer was John Gillespie, the owner of the Red Star Blacksmith Shop. The conversation had been so smothered in the sound of hammer blows that Richard hadn't been able to make any sense of it, but now he heard the Red Star man say, "I'd almost sell the whole dam' thing for a hunnerd dollars. Yessir, Mac, I'd almost sell the whole dam' thing."

Richard's ears pricked up at that, and he purposely made a silly side trip to the rear of the shop where the two were standing talking. The trip proved fruitless, however, for MacCready and the other old man shut up like clams until he had finished his business of acting like he was selecting two shoes from the vast numbers that hung on the wall. The moment he got back to his anvil, however, the two started up again. Richard knew where the Red Star was and had once been in it—it wasn't too far from where the Bentleys lived. The Red Star wasn't a bad looking place, a wood sprawl that was a little rundown, though probably not too much, but for some strange reason it didn't seem to draw customers. People who wanted their horses shod would go right past the Red Star and down the street to Atlas, or way over on Sycamore to the big harness shop. In fact, some of them probably drifted clear on down to MacCready's near the river.

That night, after all the others had gone home, Richard made a business of asking Mac what John Gillespie had been talking about. That wasn't easy—he had to avoid the direct question. "Guess maybe John Gillespie is counting on getting rid of the Red Star," he said, and tried to make his voice casual. MacCready didn't answer right away, and when Richard finally looked up MacCready was staring at him. "Now just how in thunder did you know that?" he demanded. Richard shuffled across the floor. "Just thought I heard him say something like that," he remarked casually. "Maybe I didn't hear right."

Mac didn't say anything else that night, but for some obscure reason he brought the matter up the next day. "Feller just had a hundred dollars, the Red Star mightn't be bad to have," he said as he held onto Richard's apron. "I had it, I'd lend it to you, but I don't have it."

Mac was going away after that, but this time Richard followed along after him. "That ain't what he wants for the whole thing, is it?" he asked Mac. "That all he wants?"

This time Mac did look at him hard. "Wants a partner," he said. "Red Star's doin' all right, but there's too much work for John. What he wants is a partner."

Richard only nodded his head, but he decided that he might walk around that night and see what John Gillespie himself had to say. John wouldn't be too much surprised, and in Richard's mind it was better if Mac didn't know what he was about.

As it turned out, it was a solid offer. The two of them stood on the little box porch on Race Street and John kept on spitting tobacco juice over the railing. "That's the way she stands," he kept on saying. "What I need's a new bellows, and a whole lot of other things. And the way things are I just keep puttin' them off. That's the trouble—I just can't seem to get enough money in a pile to do what I want. Maybe once I got fixed up the way I ought to be, the Red Star could get goin' again. At least that's what I keep on tellin' myself. Why? You ain't got no hunnerd dollars, have you?"

Richard pretended that he hadn't heard the direct question. He hadn't really, for his eyes had been distracted by a rather pretty girl who kept on going back and forth through the room inside the door. She looked like she was maybe twenty or eighteen at least, and she had long slim legs and good hips. Richard was never able to see her face, partly because her long shiny brown hair was hanging over her shoulders. It came clear down to her waist.

"Well, have you?" John Gillespie brought him back to attention. "You got a hunnerd dollars you don't know what to do with, you couldn't make no better investment. What you'd be doin' is buyin' yourself a sure thing. I'd split up with you two-thirds and one-third—you'd be makin' almost as much as I would out of it. It's a dam' good offer."

Richard refused to say—he told John that he wanted time to think about it. He had already started to shuffle off the porch when John thought of his last inducement. "You leave Mac, you'd have to find another place to eat and sleep," he said. "Ain't no reason why you couldn't stay right here. We got us a room without nobody in it. Got a lot of plunder in right now—it's a sort of attic. But we could get that out in a hurry. An' my woman sets a good table. Wouldn't cost you only one–two dollars a week."

Richard nodded his head. That last was really an excellent inducement, because he needed some place to call his own. Sleeping on the floor of old Mac's office had been all right for a time, although it had been deuced cold at first. And he was getting tired of eating in the hash houses down near the river. It was always the same stuff, pork and sauerkraut, fried ribs, stew, something called soup that contained whatever was left over in the kitchen, and all sorts of trash that had undoubtedly been remainders on market. It would be good to eat at a family table again.

"You better make up your mind in a hurry," John Gillespie called after him as he started out through the little yard. "Couple other fellers I talked to are actin' interested. You got the money, or know where you can get it, you best make up your mind in a hurry."

"I'll let you know end of the week," Richard promised. It had to be that way, because he wouldn't be able to dig up the stone jar with his money in it until the end of the week. At least he thought he wouldn't. If he didn't keep the money buried, the ninety-some dollars would have to be hidden in some other place in Mac's shop, and that provided a hazard.

But he wasn't sure—he wasn't sure at all. Walking back down to the river through the web of houses, he felt himself torn almost apart. If he used all his money to buy into the Red Star, then he wouldn't be able to go back for Ruth. And that's what he had always told himself that he had been saving the money for. But if he did go back to the farm, then Ruth might not want to run away with him, and he'd lose his chance to buy into the Red Star. And the Red Star probably had a future—there was just no reason why it couldn't be made into an acceptable shop. What it took in in a week Richard had no way of knowing, but it should be at least twenty-five dollars. Maybe more. And one third of twenty-five dollars would be over eight dollars a week, and that was more money than he had ever made in his life.

The fireflies were dancing over the yard and vacant lots as he meandered home, and from the river there was still the throaty sound of steamboats yawing around or meandering past the Landing. But he couldn't see that far—the Kentucky hills had faded into black. Pretty far up the sky he thought he could perhaps see the tops of them, because it got a little lighter up there, and in what must be sky there seemed to be a few faint stars.

Well, he'd think it all over. He'd think it over real well. And if he did decide to invest in the Red Star, then maybe he could go back for Ruth in the fall.

HIS DECISION was precipitated by something that happened on Saturday afternoon. That morning when old Mac came in he sidled up to Richard and said that Mrs. Bentley had asked for him that afternoon. Mac didn't know why—it was just something she wanted done, and she had told her father three or four times that he mustn't forget to tell Richard to come up. "Maybe won't be much doin' by that time anyhow," Mac had finally grumbled as he moved away from Richard's anvil. "Gits pretty slow sometimes on Saturday afternoons."

It did get slow around two o'clock, and when Mac reminded him again Richard finally took off his leather apron and put a shirt on. He was of two minds about going up to the Bentleys—he wanted to, and somehow he didn't want to. Mrs. Bentley always had a hundred things that she thought had to be done right away to keep the world from coming to an end. And most of them didn't matter, at least not very much. The herringbone walks didn't have to be scrubbed, neither did the windows have to be washed, or the floors swept. And sometimes there were ridiculous things—like climbing up and nailing a couple of shingles back on the house. Or pumping a lot of water and carrying it upstairs and dumping it into Mrs. Bentley's tin bathtub. Or taking the dog out for a walk. Sometimes when Ash wasn't around, she even wanted him to hitch up and drive her down into town. But for the life of him Richard didn't know why, because she never really made a business of buying anything, nor did she seem to have any place in particular she had to go. He finally decided, after making a number of such trips, that she was just lonesome. It *was* lonesome in the house—Nancy was never home, and Richard had begun to be uncertain that Mrs. Bentley really had a husband. At least he never appeared.

Today he dawdled on the way, taking a circuitous route to get up to the house on Vine Street. Even at that, sauntering along as lazily as he could, he was hot when he got there, and so went around the house to the pump in the backyard and sloshed water over his wrists. Working in the shop all the time, he really was not used to the summer sun, and he could hardly remember that he had once made a business of being in the hot summer fields all day long.

He knocked on the back door, but no one came, and then in answer to repeated knocks he thought he heard a faraway voice calling that he should come in. Richard did, a little slowly. Inside he saw that the kitchen was cleaned up as neat as a pin—and that was different because it was most often littered. He stood for a while at the kitchen table, wondering what he should do next, and frankly not too anxious to do anything.

"That you, Richard?"

The voice called down from upstairs, and he had to answer it.

Once he did, he heard Mrs. Bentley laugh. "Will you come up here?" she asked. "I'm in some sort of a mess."

Richard went into the hall and turned up the stairs. From the head of the stairs he could hear her puffing and churning around in the front bedroom.

"Richard, I need you," he heard her again. "Come here."

Richard went to his right and passed the room that Nancy occupied when she was home. It was only two more steps to the Bentley bedroom, and when he went in through the door he saw that Mrs. Bentley was struggling with her dress. Her hands were behind her, and the dress was half open, but it seemed she could neither get it off nor on.

"I need somebody to help me get out of this thing," Mrs. Bentley said. "The hooks are stuck."

Richard didn't know why, but he began to feel slightly dizzy. His pulses were pounding, and he had half a notion to break and run. It wasn't decent to be upstairs alone with a woman when there was nobody else in the house.

"I don't know what I can do," he said. "I'm not used to those things."

"Just get behind me and see if you can unhook me."

Richard got behind her, and then his eyes danced—the dress was half open and her breasts were hanging bare. And they were beautiful breasts, plump and full. He looked away, and then he looked back, and now he really did feel as if he might faint.

"Can you see what it is I want you to do?"

Richard didn't know how to answer that. His fingers were fumbling with the hook, but it seemed as if it had been purposefully jammed. At least it was clamped together.

"If it won't unhook, rip it. I can't stand this way all day."

Richard ripped the dress, and the moment he did Mrs. Bentley let it fall. She was suddenly naked and the next moment she had turned, and was grasping him in her arms while her lips tried to reach out to his face.

"You don't need to be afraid," she kept on saying. "You don't need to be afraid. It's perfectly natural."

After that Richard really lost control of himself. All his life he had watched chickens in the yard, cows in the pasture lots when they were in heat, but he had never imagined that when the time came he would completely lose his senses. And he did, and afterwards he couldn't remember the details of the encounter. All that afternoon—it must have been all that afternoon because the Catholic bells were ringing six before they parted—they lay together on the big bed which had been so heavily perfumed that Richard almost gagged at the essence. The thought struck his mind that he'd smell like that for days, and if he did, all the men in the shop would exhaust their vocabularies on him. And they'd all know where he had been—they were all experienced.

At six Mrs. Bentley got up and threw on a violet wrapper, and after that Richard lost no time getting into his clothes.

"We'll have a good supper," said Mrs. Bentley. "I've got steaks and melon. And you can have garden peas if you want them."

Richard couldn't believe his ears. After what they had done he thought she should be crying and wringing her hands, and instead she seemed as cool as if she were made of ice. He himself felt flushed, and as soon as he could he ran out to the pump and poured cold water over his wrists. Standing there, his heart pounding, he suddenly made up his mind that he wasn't going back into the house at all. He'd do what he had often seen Ash do—he'd drop over into the gully and get away from the house that way. And he'd never come back—he'd just never come back. And this would have to be the end of anything he had to do with Mrs. Bentley's father. Richard thought he wouldn't be able to look the old man in the face any more.

That decided another thing too—he'd dig up his money that night and go up to see John Gillespie tomorrow. And if the offer still held, to buy into the Red Star Blacksmith Shop, then that's what he'd do.

But some time, somehow, he'd have to tell Ruth, about what had happened that afternoon, and see if she would forgive him.

COUNTING WHAT he got from Mac that week, and saving out enough to live on, Richard knew that he'd be able to offer John Gillespie ninety-six dollars. He could take it or leave it, and Richard didn't much care what John decided to do. If he said no, that he wasn't selling any interest in the Red Star for less than a hundred, then Richard decided that he'd set off for home. If he said yes, then he'd stay and see how much money he could save before another winter came. But before another winter he'd go back after Ruth. She deserved it—she shouldn't have to live in the Berzinski filth. And then they'd come back down to the City together, and somehow, somewhere they'd find a way to make a go of it.

That night he felt more like a miser than ever before in his life. As usual, he put out the candle before he started digging, and as usual he was apprehensive that someone had discovered his secret and removed his treasure. But it was all there, and in the dark Richard thrust his hand into the gray stone jar and started counting the dollars into piles. There were ninety-three in the jar, and he could add three. That was exactly what he had planned. He had to fumble in the dark before he found the small leather sack that he had laid on Mac's desk. He had bought the pouch for this particular purpose, and he had at first hidden it in one of Mac's drawers. Then Mac had stumbled upon it, and tossed it into the top of the desk. It wasn't where it was supposed to be, but Richard's fingers touched it at last. After that it was easy, but he made sure that the money didn't tinkle in the leather pouch.

That night he slept with the silver under him, and when the usual Saturday night drunken sounds filled the street outside he held onto the pouch with both hands. But there was no alarm—it was only a usual Saturday night.

He decided then that there was no sense waiting—he'd walk right up to John Gillespie's house the first thing in the morning. Even before he had had a mouthful to eat. But in the morning it was ghostly going through the Cincinnati streets—there was a heavy fog that filled the valley. Fog or no fog, the City was always different on Sundays. It always seemed to be sealed in silence. It wasn't silence really, for bells tolled, and there were steamboat whistles and the usual small sounds, particularly of horse hoofs on the dirt streets. Despite that, however, there actually was something different about Sundays—as if the town were frozen in piety. But anyone who knew Cincinnati knew that it wasn't really piety.

The John Gillespie family was still at the breakfast table when he got there, and John insisted that the family make a place for him. Mrs. Gillespie grudgingly obliged. She was tall and thin but looked as if she might once have been pretty. Donald, who must have been the only son unless one was grown up and gone away, was about twelve. He had black ringlets all over his head, and he ate crullers like a little pig. And the girl Richard had seen when he stood on the porch with John sat right across from him. Her name was Fanny, and she was a real beauty. Today she had stuffed her hair into some sort of cap or net, and she ate so daintily that she made Richard ashamed of himself. He couldn't really see her, however, because Fanny kept her head bent over as if she didn't want to look at him. From time to time Mrs. Gillespie reminded her that she'd have to hurry if she meant to get to church on time.

"Well, what brings you?" asked John at last, and wiped the back of his hand across his red moustache. "Get you a notion, did you?"

For answer Richard took the pouch out of his lap and dumped the silver dollars into the center of the table. Happily they did not roll.

"Ninety-six," he said. "All I've got right now."

John's eyes seemed to bug, and inadvertently he put out his hand and started winnowing the silver dollars.

"Said a hunnerd," he said at last. "Even hunnerd."

"Ninety-six's all I got," said Richard again. "Take the rest out of my hide if you want to, but you can't get them any other way."

John finally nodded. "Trust you for four," he said, and started scooping up the dollars. Richard put out his hand and restrained him.

"There's a paper we'll have to sign," he said. "I can't give you my money if I don't get nothing back."

John didn't seem to like that. "You got my word, ain't you?" he asked, and started flipping at his suspenders. "Don't mean to tell me you don't think my word's good."

Richard felt awkward. "I guess it's good all right," he said. "Only this is if something'd happen to you I wouldn't have nothing to go on. I'd rather have a paper."

John knit his brows. "You don't mean go to one of them lawyer fellers?"

Richard shook his head. "Guess it'd be all right if we just wrote it up ourselves," he said.

John sat and stared at him after that. "I ain't much good at fig-urin' or writing," he said at last. "Maybe Fanny kin do it—she's ed-ucated. I ain't never learned."

Chapter 6

"I think maybe I could get something down," said Richard. "It don't have to be much."

But John only shook his head. "Wouldn't know what you wrote," he said.

"You can ask Fanny."

"She's got to go to church. That's the way we brought the kids up, an' that's the way we want it. She's got to go to church."

After that Richard filled the leather pouch with the dollars. "I can't do it unless I have some writing," he told John again and again. "Just wouldn't feel right about it."

When the dollars disappeared it was evident that John wouldn't feel right either. "You could come back," he said. "Mass don't last only an hour or so. Whyn't you come back for dinner. We're goin' to have chicken." And to his skinny wife, "How about it, Mamma? Be enough chicken for the young feller here?"

Mrs. Gillespie nodded her head as patiently as a martyr. "Guess so," she said. "There's only one chicken. It won't stretch too far."

John came along out to the porch. "You could stay," he said. "No sense in thinkin' you got to run away. Mass don't last only about an hour."

Richard excused himself. The bag of dollars would get mighty heavy by noon, but he would have felt heavier if he had had to sit in the Gillespie parlor. Richard remembered the day at the Bentleys' when he had tried that, and winced. He winced twice when he remembered what had happened yesterday. On sober reflection he couldn't believe that it had ever happened. He had counted on being pure when Ruth and he got married, and now he was so dirty he couldn't stand to look at himself.

THE PLACE for Richard to sleep in the John Gillespie house was truly an attic—it deserved no better name. One could stand only under the comb of the roof, and on either side the rafters slanted down sharply, so that Richard had to crawl into what was known as the bed. It wasn't much, only a couple old quilts spread over what must be wooden packing boxes. Worse yet, all the clutter that had been in the attic had been transported to the narrow hall, simply because there was no other place to put it, and now it was almost impossible for anyone to walk down the hall.

The same criticisms might have been made of the "good table" that Mrs. Gillespie set. It was largely bread and gravy, without sufficient meat to make good gravy. John Gillespie himself seemed not to notice nor to mind; he ate heartily from any dish that was in front of him, using his knife to smear anything onto the wad of bread he always seemed to have in his fist. Breakfast was ordinarily fried bread, or something very like it; dinner was fried fat side meat, perhaps with a cooked dish of dandelions or beet tops or what tasted like weeds; supper was more bread and sometimes even a skinny piece of ham. There were no desserts, and John Gillespie snorted even at stewed prunes. "Don't need no medicine," he always said when his wife timidly offered him the dish. "Work regular as a clock and have all my life. Don't need no medicine atall."

The Red Star Blacksmith Shop, however, was somewhat better than the house. It was really nothing much, just an ugly wood sprawl that had been added to from time to time, so that the additions to the main building seemed to reach out in all directions. Not in the front, however. The front of the Red Star was solid and had been painted with some sort of red clay paint, and someone now forgotten had once cut a red star out of wood and suspended it on a metal bracket in front of the shop. And that was the only embellishment, save for the paper signs that anyone seemed to have permission to nail up on the walls. Most of these signs were homemade and were probably put up by neighbors; they advertised milk, stallions at stud, needlework, homemade pickles, and perhaps fifty other things. Since most of the papers had been written in pencil they were almost illegible. But they fluttered in every breeze until they finally tore from their nails and got mucked down in the street.

The real blacksmith shop was, insofar as Richard could observe, about like all others he had seen. The bellows was wheezy, as John had remarked, and looked as if it really should be replaced. But there were two anvils, and the necessary complement of hammers, tongs, pincers, and bar iron, and the walls were hung with a thousand shoes, all of them covered with spiderwebs and dust. The floor was dirt as it should be, and there were adequate posts where horses could be hitched while they were shod. John Gillespie even had an office, and it was almost an exact replica of the office in MacCready's shop, with its old rolltop desk so cluttered with miscellaneous litter that a person could find almost anything there, unless he really wanted something particular. The something particular could never be found.

After that first day in the Red Star, however, Richard was aware of what was really wrong with the place. It needed customers—badly. That morning there had been only one horse that had lost a shoe on Race Street, and the driver of the grocery wagon didn't want to pay for anything more than the one shoe. The afternoon was a little better—a farmer brought in a team of good grays. Then, about four, a Negro drove in with a bay. Richard had to look twice to be certain that it wasn't Ash, since the buggy looked something like Mrs. Bentley's, but it wasn't Ash, not by a good many shades of color. This Negro was black, blue-black, and he had the whitest teeth Richard had ever seen. They seemed fairly to sparkle in his head.

That night Mrs. Gillespie—they all called her Mom—served liver, and the liver was still bloody when it came to the table. John Gillespie ate it heartily, and Donald ate it, and even Fanny put a few dainty pieces into her mouth. Mrs. Gillespie didn't seem to eat a thing—she never seemed to eat. Actually she looked as if she might be sustained on vinegar, and Richard had no idea at the time that the vinegar was really beer. There was some evidence later that night, however, when Fanny went out and came back with a tin bucket of the stuff. Richard was sitting out on the front porch steps by that time, and when John Gillespie came to the door and invited him in he declined. It was hot in the house, and up in the attic it would probably be so hot that he wouldn't be able to sleep. Knowing that, Richard leaned back against the side of the porch and permitted himself to doze off now and then. The fireflies were bright across the fields, and the little breeze that touched him felt as soft as satin on his cheeks. Somehow it made him think of Mrs. Bentley, of Mrs. Bentley's hungry lips. He still couldn't believe what had happened, that he had made such a fool of himself.

THE WEEK wore through finally, and John Gillespie had no fortune to divide on Saturday night. Richard's share was a miserable three dollars, just about what MacCready had been paying him every week. He winced a little when John put the silver dollars into his hand—it seemed that John thought he had a preference for silver dollars. But the ninety-six were gone, and remembering them, Richard also remembered that he still owed John four dollars. He gave him back one of the dollars. "Won't charge you for bed and board until we git goin' a little better," John said. "Been a slow week."

"It's always slow, ain't it?"

John seemed to stiffen a little at that. "Is an' it ain't," he said mysteriously. "Just can't tell about the way people bring their horses in. Sometimes they all seem to want to come at once."

Richard refused further comment, and after a time John went away as quietly as he had come.

On Sunday morning there was the usual rushing about so that the kids could get to church. Fanny, it seemed, wanted to get to early mass, not the real early one, but the nine o'clock. It took a lot of doing, because she had to fix up a little bit and her mother insisted she help with breakfast. She and Donald finally got off, and Richard watched them cut across the fields until they were out of sight. He wondered a little just what the rush was—it seemed somehow to be a little indecent. He hadn't the least idea what the Catholics believed and didn't mean to inquire, but he thought it must be some strange stuff like the Shakers believed. Well, the Presbyterians too, for that matter. They all chattered a lot about God, and there wasn't any of them who knew the least thing about God. All that a person could know was that he was alive, and that there were a lot of things he couldn't understand. Things like how babies grew inside of female animals and were finally born as pigs and calves and dogs and even human beings, and how the seasons kept on rotating so that it was sometimes summer and sometimes winter, and of how accidents seemed to happen to some people more than others—and all kinds of things like that. Of course, it was plain as the nose on your face that whatever there was had to come from somewhere. And since people didn't know the answer, they said God, and thought that there was no sense in inquiring any further. And they talked about Heaven too, and angels, and all manner of things. A lot of that was written in what they called the Bible, but the people way on back that wrote the Bible could have made it up. They couldn't have been any smarter than the people now, not that long ago.

Sunday was dismal, as it almost always was, and Richard decided that he'd wait around just long enough to eat whatever there was for dinner. After that he'd take off somewheres, probably up Mill Creek or out to the hills, or even down to the river. There was always something to see down at the river, although it didn't seem as busy on Sundays as it did the rest of the week.

The kids came home finally, and Mrs. Gillespie got the stove smoking, and in due time there were porkchops, lots and lots of pork chops. They were the best thing Mrs. Gillespie had served yet, and she even seemed to think so because she nibbled at one, and didn't look quite so much like a martyr as she usually did. Richard ate six—there were enough, and even some left over. He thought that he'd like to ask for the leftovers to carry with him, but he didn't dare. Not yet. And Mrs. Gillespie would likely want them for supper.

He was starting out of the yard, and thought he could make a clean breakaway when to his surprise Fanny came out on the porch and called to him. "Where you going?" she wanted to know. "Any place special?"

Richard hung on the wooden gate. "Not special," he said. "I'm just going out for a walk."

Fanny didn't hesitate. "Just wait a few minutes and I'll go with you," she said. "I've got to help Mom with the dishes."

Richard went back and sat on the porch, and after a time Donald came out and sat with him. Donald had a knife and was trying to cut something out of a piece of shingle. The way he whittled Richard knew he'd end up cutting himself. That had been the invariable end when he had been as old as Donald and had tried to whittle.

Fanny had on a green dress when she finally came, and she was carrying some kind of straw hat in her hand. Richard thought she looked pretty with all her hair tied in back and still tumbling to her waist. Fanny always looked pretty, but she always looked worried too. There were two perpendicular wrinkles that sat right on top of her nose. And she almost never laughed.

"You want to lead the way or you want me to?"

Richard hadn't even thought of a way. When he wandered he ordinarily just wandered—it seemed to be more fun that way.

"I wasn't going any place in particular," he said. "You know any place?"

For answer Fanny caught hold of his hand and turned him

around. "Let's go up along Mill Creek," she suggested. "There's a woods up there. Unless you want to go up along the canal."

Richard didn't, not particularly. And Fanny kept hold of his hand and led him along as if he were some sort of little boy. He didn't mind, but he did think it peculiar. Fanny didn't seem to be that kind of girl.

"You think the blacksmith shop will pay you?" she asked when they were going past some high-boarded fence that Fanny said enclosed a slaughterhouse. "I mean enough? Do you think it will?"

Richard decided to be purposely vague. "I don't know," he said. "Don't have much business now, but maybe it will. I'm not worried."

"It used to be good," said Fanny. "When I was a little girl. I can remember horses standing out in front and waiting their turn. We had more flies back in those days too."

Richard let that pass. "You go to school somewhere?" he wanted to know. "I mean how did you learn to read and write?"

"I practiced," said Fanny. "Course, I went to school for a while. But I read things and I practiced writing. Why?"

Richard had to smile when he saw her face. Her lips were a bit open and her eyes looked soft. Fanny, he decided, was a remarkably pretty girl. There just wasn't anything wrong with her, and she didn't act like she should be the daughter of the Gillespies.

"Tell you what," he said. "I'll ask you a question and you see if you can answer it, and then you ask me a question and I'll see if I can. Whoever loses has to pay the other person something."

"You mean a forfeit," said Fanny. "All right. Who were the Pharaohs?"

"They're in the Bible," said Richard. "Guess they were kings."

Fanny laughed—a little. "Half right," she said. "I'll let you try again. What are the Pyramids?"

Richard had never heard of them and had to admit as much. "Guess maybe they're kings too," he ventured.

"They're not at all," said Fanny. "They're stone buildings. Now it's your turn?"

"What is a Shaker?" asked Richard. "I mean, 'What do they believe?'"

Fanny shook her head. "I never heard of them," she admitted.

"So we're even. My turn. Who was Benjamin Franklin? What did he do?'"

Richard finally had to admit he didn't know. It seemed as if he had heard the name somewhere, but he couldn't place it. He had to admit as much. It was necessary that he get even.

"Who wrote *The Vicar of Wakefield*?" he asked Fanny. "His whole name."

Fanny had to shake her head—she had never heard of the book.

And so they walked, and now they were really out in the country, and there were men with scythes in the wheat field alongside the road. They forgot their game, and stopped to watch for a while, and Richard got hungry-hearted. That's where he should be—he knew that, but he didn't dare say as much to Fanny. And it was sort of pleasant walking with her. They were holding hands unashamedly now, and it seemed as if they both needed that added reassurance. After the wheat field the dirt road ended, but a path plunged off along the creek, and that was even better. Here and there, sometimes anchored in the roots of one of the big sycamores, there was a man or boy fishing with worms, and some of them had strings of fish too. Richard had never fished in his life—there had been no time, and no place to fish. Fanny didn't seem to like to stand and watch as much as he did.

There were some blue flowers, and Fanny gathered a few, then when they wilted she threw them away. Richard didn't think that strange—he didn't think they should have been picked in the first place. They belonged along the creek. After that they had to make their way through a mound of brushwood brought down by some flood, and after they did Fanny wanted to stop and rest a while. They did, in a violet bed at the base of a giant oak. Only one or two violets were still blooming, and those in obscure places. Fanny sat silent and looked thoughtful, and after a time Richard himself lay down with a blade of grass in his mouth.

"There's one more question," Fanny said unexpectedly. "You owe me a forfeit—you didn't answer as many right as I did."

That brought Richard to his hands and knees. "I got three right," he said. "You didn't get any more."

"I got four," said Fanny firmly. "So you owe me a forfeit, and I want you to answer a question. Truthfully."

That made Richard smile. "I might not be sure I know the

answer," he said. "I don't know the answer to most of your questions."

"You'll know the answer to this one. What I want to know is why you don't like me."

And with that Fanny herself put her hands behind her back and leaned into a bed of violets.

Richard felt just a little confused. He didn't understand women, and he couldn't for the life of him make out what she was driving at. He didn't know he was taking too long a time to answer, not until she repeated her question.

"I do like you," he said. "What ever put that idea into your head? I mean, that I didn't."

"How much?" demanded Fanny promptly. "Is it only a little or is it a lot?"

This time Richard did feel himself flushing. "I don't know," he said finally. "I guess a lot. Why?"

Fanny didn't say why. Her eyes seemed to be fixed far out in the distance, and she seemed to be thinking so hard she didn't know she looked funny.

"Do you like me enough to marry me? I mean right now. I've got to get out of that place—I can't stand it any longer. I want to get married."

Richard's heart pounded. He didn't know what to do, and he wanted to reassure her but the moment he moved over and put his arm around her shoulders she bent her face up and kissed him full on the mouth. Her lips felt like Mrs. Bentley's and he should have had sense enough to be prudent the moment he realized the fact.

He wasn't prudent—Fanny wouldn't let him be. She wanted to prove her love, prove it the only way she knew how, and Richard accepted the sacrifice. All that afternoon they lay in the grass, and happily there were no interlopers to mar their marriage. Not till the sun finally began to sink behind the trees did they remember that they had to go back home. Fanny rearranged her clothes as best she could, but her eyes were jubilant, and she didn't seem in any way ashamed.

"I don't want to get married in the Catholic Church," she told Richard blithely. "They wouldn't like you anyhow because you're not a Catholic."

"We don't have to get married right away, do we?"

"I want to get married right away," said Fanny. "Soon as I can. We'll hunt us up some preacher and have him say the words."

Richard's heart pounded—it seemed as if his dreams had suddenly come to a complete end. He didn't really know whether he liked Fanny that well, although she had been very sweet to him. But he had really meant to go back to Ruth—he was half promised to her.

He decided on the way home that Fanny would likely get the idea of a hasty marriage out of her mind. After all, women were only women, and they did get carried away with silly notions. Maybe tomorrow, or the day afterward, she'd remember, and not want to get married at all. Not unless she discovered she had to.

THERE WERE noodles for supper and they were good. Mrs. Gillespie had been rather waspish because they came home so late, but tonight Fanny carried her head high, and even sassed her mother a little. That brought the prompt threat that she should have her face slapped. Fanny didn't seem to mind that either, and promptly said, "You won't be talking that way in a little while. I won't have to take it forever."

At that even John Gillespie looked up from the table where he was already hunkering over his plate. "Long as you're under this roof, young lady, you're a-goin' to mind," he threatened. "You ain't so high and mighty that you can sass your mother right in her own house."

"Maybe I won't be in her house too much longer," Fanny said contemptuously. "Maybe I won't have to stay here."

That did bring them all up short, and for a time they simply froze in their positions and stared at each other. Mrs. Gillespie had the big bowl of noodles in her hands and was halfway between the stove and the table, Donald was already down in his place, and Richard was standing behind his chair. He felt himself going red— they had agreed on the way home that they wouldn't tell Fanny's folks right away. And, secretly, Richard was hoping that they wouldn't ever tell them. Fanny had said on the way home that she didn't want to wait until she had a miss, but since Richard knew absolutely nothing about female animals he wasn't sure what she was talking about.

"You sit down," commanded John Gillespie suddenly. "Just sit on down and keep your mouth shut."

After that they ate in silence, although the Gillespies did say their usual table prayer and cross themselves.

The noodles were good, but no one tasted them, and after the noodles there was a peach pie. Richard guessed that the peaches had come from the scrunty tree in the backyard. It looked like it was almost good-for-nothing, but it did have a few wry-looking peaches on it.

These was nothing else that night, but in the dark Fanny came out on the front porch where Richard was sitting on the steps. "I'll see about getting a preacher tomorrow," she whispered as she snuggled up against him. "There's some sort of little church down the street. I don't know who preaches there, but I'll bet he can say the words."

Richard decided that it might be time to take a stand. "Ain't no hurry, is there?" he asked. "We could wait a while."

He could feel Fanny stiffen. "You can't wait once it's happened," she said. "You don't think I want to run around for weeks until my stomach gets all swollen out, do you? You wouldn't like it if it was you."

"We just don't have to be in such a hurry," Richard protested. "Maybe there won't be any baby. It happens that way sometimes."

Fanny scoffed. "You ought to know," she said. "Since you're a man, you ought to know."

"Well, it wouldn't hurt anything to wait two weeks."

"I don't know what good it would do. Maybe in two weeks I'll start to get sick in the morning. Don't think my mother won't know what's wrong with me."

"Everybody doesn't get sick," said Richard. "And we don't have anything to set up on."

Fanny had thought about that. "We got ninety-six dollars," she said. "It's your money, and I know where Pop put it."

"You can't steal it back. That wouldn't be right."

Fanny laughed a little at that. "It wouldn't be stealing—it'll be only a sort of wedding present," she said. "Pop don't need it anyway—he ain't going to do anything about fixing up the shop. We might as well have it as my mother. She's been talking about getting a parlor organ, if she can find one."

John Gillespie came out on the porch then and squatted beside them so that they didn't have a chance for any further talk. John was smoking a stogie, and the stogie stank. Nevertheless he seemed to be enjoying it thoroughly. For a long while they sat in the dark together, John spitting into the flowerbed from time to time, until at last he got up wearily and said that it was time for bed. Maybe nine o'clock, or half past eight at any rate. Time to hit the hay if they meant to get up in the morning.

Fanny waited until her father was back in the house before she kissed Richard for the last time. "You can't sleep with me tonight, honey," she whispered in his ear. "You'll have to wait until tomorrow night, if I can get the preacher for tomorrow."

Richard only grunted, but he did return her kiss. She was a sweet girl, but she seemed a bit too crafty and designing to please him. And he hated to be forced into anything too fast, and she was forcing him far beyond his will.

"I won't do it for two weeks," he announced positively. "Maybe by two weeks we won't any longer have a notion. We don't even know each other very well."

Fanny didn't like that at all. "I'd say we got pretty well acquainted this afternoon," she said. "I don't know what more you want."

And with that she stomped inside and shut the door after her.

Richard sat and stared at the darkness. The thought came to him to bolt—to just leave everything behind him and get clear out of the city. Heaven knew where he might land, but his will would be his own—he could go upriver, downriver, or any other place he liked. The thought of staying here, at least in John Gillespie's house, somehow put lead in his stomach. He wondered again how a woman knew that babies were certain. He imagined maybe it was like horses, or cows, or anything else; there was just no way of avoiding them, once one had set the machinery into operation. That was a pretty howdy-do. But in that case maybe Mrs. Bentley was pregnant too. Only she didn't seem to be in the least concerned; she acted as if she knew a way out of the mess.

Well, damn it all, damn it all! He had played the fool, and now the whole world looked like it meant to come tumbling down about his ears.

FROM THE WAY they treated each other in the next week, Richard imagined that the two older Gillespies knew a whole lot more than they let on. Fanny alternately snapped at him and honeyed him up with open kisses, and neither her father nor her mother did anything but stare. Now and then Richard intercepted their furtive glances at each other, and when Fanny started coming over to the shop in the afternoons and lolling about John Gillespie told her emphatically to go home and stay there. Fanny did, but she pouted that night and wouldn't eat any supper. Once she even came into the attic during the night and started fumbling about his bed, but Richard refused to wake up, even when he knew that she was there, and after a time she gave up and went back to her own room.

So a week passed, and the Red Star did a little better, but not much. It was on Tuesday of the second week that Fanny came out on the porch at night and told Richard quite calmly that she had seen the preacher. He was a young man and he had a wife of his own, so he understood. At least that was what Fanny said. They were to be down at the Mission Friday night about five, and he'd say the words then. He had a book they were written in, and Fanny had seen the book. There was nothing they had to get by heart.

Richard shuddered. "You know you're sure," he wanted to know.

"I'm so sure it hurts," said Fanny. "I didn't come this month at all."

Richard didn't quite know what she meant by that, but he supposed there was some way women had of knowing. Now that the inevitable doom was settling down upon him, he even tried to reconcile himself to it. Fanny probably wouldn't be too bad. About like any other woman, fretting, and chewing the rag, and always saying that things were wrong no matter how right they were. That was the way his mother acted, and old Abraham Robinson had let the words spill off his shoulders as if they were just so many drops of rain. In fact, it was doubtful if his father really heard what his mother said. He'd go on his own way, his face a complete blank, and five minutes later he'd be out in the barn mending harness or trying to file a plow point or anything else like that. And Richard's mother herself would seem to forget what she had been complaining about. That was probably the way life was, the way it had always been clear on back to what people called the Garden of Eden.

Chapter 6

The idea of having a baby, however, was something else again—
he really didn't want a baby. Not this soon. To have babies a man
ought to have some fair expectation of the future, and he ought to
know where the money was coming from to establish a good home.
It seemed that it wasn't always that way—it seemed that people had
babies whether they wanted them or not.

"You'd better quit early Friday afternoon so's you can clean up
a little bit," he heard Fanny say. "You always smell like sweat when
you don't wash."

That brought Richard back to his senses. "What time?" he
asked, and then added, "Your father will know something's up."

"He might know already," said Fanny. "I told Mom. All she did
was shake her head up and down."

"You tell her you were going to have a baby?"

He heard Fanny gasp. "My Gawd," she said, "why would I tell
her? That's why we're getting married, so's we don't have to tell her.
Once we're married, that's what everybody expects."

Richard didn't promise that he'd be ready on Friday, but Fanny
went back into the house like a general who had just commanded an
assault on a fortress and is contemptuous how many of his men will
be killed. Inside Richard could hear her humming some hymn, and
she wasn't making much effort to keep her voice low. He watched
her for a little while as she passed in and out of the lamplight, and
for the life of him he couldn't tell what she was doing. Sorting something, or collecting something, it seemed. She'd be a manager, all
right—she was that kind of woman.

That night he finally got off the porch and meandered down
Race Street for six or seven blocks. There were lights on in some of
the little houses, and now and then he could see people sitting and
talking or reading papers. All married, that was evident—they were
all married. Maybe it wouldn't be so bad; maybe after a while they
could rent one of these little houses and get a start in the world.
Probably the only trouble was that it had come too fast, before he
had really had a chance to make up his own mind.

On the way back home, the faint glow of the City behind him,
he wondered if he really loved Fanny, or could ever really love her.
He didn't know. He thought she was pretty, but maybe not as pretty
as Mrs. Bentley. Not as pretty as Ruth, but Ruth had a different
kind of beauty. And Fanny looked like she wouldn't want to do

much work, whereas Ruth could work in the fields all day long. Perhaps love came later, perhaps it was just a matter of getting used to somebody else. Maybe it came only after two people had gone through a lot of hardships together. Maybe—maybe.

Well, he'd try. He didn't know just what the preacher would expect him to promise, but it probably wouldn't be too bad. Lots of other people had gone through the ceremony without being blighted, and perhaps he could too.

THE PREACHER was a timid and proper young man, quite young, probably still in his twenties, and he had called in his wife and his wife's mother to act as witnesses. And they weren't in the little white church at all—they were in the parlor of the tiny manse. The parlor was threadbare: it had a worn carpet tacked down to the floor, a carpet with holes in it, and there were just three wooden chairs and a stand with a lamp to serve as furnishings. The Preacher stood near the lamp so that he could see his black book, and the rest of them stood back in the shadows, Richard and Fanny holding hands in front.

It was all over as fast as a person could say Jack Robinson; all they had to do was make a few promises. Richard couldn't even remember what they were; all he could remember was that he had said "I do," and "I will." Then, when he thought the ceremony was going to wind up and get going, the preacher suddenly said, "I now pronounce you man and wife." He had hardly gotten the words out of his mouth when Fanny snuggled up and kissed Richard, and then the preacher's mother kissed him, and the preacher held out his hand. "I hope you'll be very happy," he kept on saying. "I hope you'll be very happy." However, Richard noticed that the preacher's wife didn't kiss anybody, or even offer to shake hands. She had stood back in the shadows all the time the ceremony was going on, and she had good reason to because her belly was swollen up so far it looked like she had a big watermelon in it. Richard felt better when he noticed that; it seemed as if even preachers were not above having babies.

They raced home, stopping only long enough for Fanny to give the preacher one of her father's dollars, and back at home Fanny ran into the kitchen and yelled at her father and mother. "We done it," she shouted. "We're married. I told you we were going to do it."

John Gillespie just looked over his eyeglasses—he had been reading the paper. Richard didn't mind that, but he did think the look Mrs. Gillespie gave Fanny was a little strange. "Thank God," she said as she held Fanny in her arms and kissed her. "Maybe it'll turn out all right after all."

They ate supper then, and supper was a bit special, so that Richard knew there had been preparations for the wedding feast. They had liver and onions, and for John Gillespie, who didn't like liver, there was a dish of fried brains. There were fried potatoes, too, and after that something very elaborate, chocolate pudding. Richard ate heartily and the food tasted good. It seemed that there was little difference being married—he didn't feel a bit different. Except that now he knew he'd have to look after Fanny the rest of his life.

That night, however, Fanny went to her room, and he went back to his quilts in the attic. He didn't mind—he was too stunned to feel very amorous. In the upper hall Fanny had whispered something about her bedsprings creaking, and he hadn't even realized what she was talking about. It didn't seem to matter very much.

It wasn't until the next morning that the full sense of his position came down about his ears. Fanny was up before he got downstairs, and she blithely announced that she was going out and see if she could find them some place to live. And, secretly, she showed him a purse full of dollars—she must have had at least fifteen or twenty of them. What that meant, if she ran away with all her father's money, was that Richard wouldn't be half owner or a third owner of the Red Star at all. The paper that John Gillespie had signed would be worthless without the money.

Richard worked hard that day, and gradually the hurt of having been forced into marriage diminished in his mind. This was very likely the way the world ran, and he had just been too green to know it. Probably from Adam and Eve and on down through the ages people had been getting together in a thousand different ways, and then blithely starting out together as if the world would have to make a place for them. It didn't always—Richard knew that the Berzinskis were proof of the fact—but most people seemed to manage somehow. At least after a while. His father and mother had told him that they had started out with two chickens and a spade. That was about as low as people could go, but they had made it. He and Fanny would make it too—they didn't have two chickens and a spade, but they did have young hearts and strong muscles. And blacksmiths were needed everywhere in the world, and would probably always be needed.

THE HOUSE Fanny found was a miserable little box in an alley off Pearl Street. It had no merits, except, perhaps, that it was not too far from Central Market. Beyond that, it was only a room with board walls, but whoever had lived there before had left behind some semblance of an iron stove. It smoked, but it did get hot enough to warm a pot, and a single iron pot was at first all they had to cook in. Fanny somehow supplied the rest of the furnishings—all day long she seemed to do nothing but scoot around the trash stores, where she did manage to pick up an iron bed, a bowl and pitcher, and some miscellaneous bric-a-brac, including a maple rocker and two rickety chairs. The house frankly looked nothing like a love nest, and Richard got sick at his stomach every time he stepped into the door. At first, however, Fanny acted triumphant, and if he so much as hinted a complaint, she cut him down with a sort of acerbity he was not used to. At times there seemed to be almost hatred in her tones, as if she held it against him that he had gotten her pregnant.

She gave Richard many hard moments, more than moments, for he sometimes escaped the shack in sheer desperation and went out into the streets to walk his mood away. As he remembered, it was Fanny who had been the aggressor, not he, and in memory, at least, he thought that he had hated almost every moment of that woeful Sunday afternoon. Whether that was entirely true or not, he did dislike taking all the blame. Fanny had deliberately inflamed him, teased him, and at last almost flung herself at him. And now she was certain that she was going to have a baby. He sometimes wondered if things were entirely as they seemed. He understood why she had wanted to get away from her shrewish mother, and he realized that life must have been hell for her in the house on Race Street, with nothing to do the livelong day. Maybe a girl would do anything to get out of a house that harbored the two Gillespies, but he wasn't at all sure. It always seemed as if there was something he should know that he didn't know.

Chapter 6

Of one thing he was quite certain: Fanny didn't really love him. She made gestures from time to time, and she almost always kissed him when he came home at night. But there was no warmth in her kiss, and almost invariably she'd start a tirade before the kiss had dried. She just couldn't live this way. There had to be a rug on the floor before winter came. And there should be some sort of couch to lie down on in the afternoons. The bed was all lumpy and it was hot in the afternoons. Why didn't he go down to the river and see if he could get another job at night. Or stay out of the Red Star entirely. They couldn't live on three or four dollars a week, and even when she picked up stuff from the market gutters it seemed they never had anything to eat. And they'd need heavy clothes before winter, and then when the baby came they'd need a lot of stuff, flannels and nightgowns and salves and all kind of things. Why *didn't* he go down to the Landing? There was always a lot of work to do down there, and they'd probably like to hire on another man. Somebody would. There wasn't no sense sitting at home every night, and besides that they had only one rocker. And no decent lamp to read by.

The complaints were circular; they kept reappearing as if Fanny had laced them to some kind of gigantic belt that spun upon the wheels of her mind.

Richard endured her. Most nights he tried to get in a little reading, and now that they were down in the heart of the City there was plenty to read. People sometimes even threw away newspapers, and a person could pick them up as they blew across the city streets. And there were two bookstalls that Richard had found, actually only large pushcarts that some rat-faced fellows pushed up against the curbs any place they thought there might be people to look. The books were all used and dog-eared, of course, but they were a revelation even then. It seemed that some folks had written about everything under the sun, faraway places, medicine, law, religion, education, even farming. There were love stories too, and there were always almanacs. Some of the books were so old that they went all the way back to the other century, and some of them had once been really handsome, with leather covers and gold embellishments, and all sorts of things like that. The trouble was that they cost a good bit, some as much as a half-dollar, although most of them came at a dime or even a half-dime. There were a lot of sermons that preachers had preached somewhere, and a number of travels to far places,

‹ 185 ›

and even some books that had woodcut charts in them. Richard had been surprised when he found one one day that showed what was inside the body of a man and the body of a woman. He was a little ashamed to be caught looking at the yellow volume, and every time the Jew who ran the stand looked his way he put the book down and pretended interest in something else. But he always picked it up again. A man didn't seem to be so much of a mess inside as a woman was. She had all sorts of tubes and hollows down in her belly, but Richard had to gasp when he saw a baby curled up in a big sack in one of the drawings. He had never known about that before, and he had always wondered. The worst of it was that Fanny would be like that in a little while. He turned red when he remembered that she said he was responsible.

He did go down to the Public Landing once or twice, and he found enough courage to sidle up to one of the fellows who had a paper in his hands and seemed to be marking down something every time a box or bale was wheeled by. The man didn't hear him at first, and then when he did finally hear him, he wasn't interested. "Hell," he said, "I don't do the hiring. You want a job, go and see Jim. But it ain't likely he'll take you—he's got a full crew right now." After that Richard contented himself with watching, until finally he almost got run over by a team of big grays and decided he'd better get back home.

There was one further diversion—the Market, particularly on Saturday nights. Sometimes there were good things lying in the gutters down there after the stands had been closed and the people had driven their carts away. It was hard scrounging around in the dark once all the lanterns had been taken away, but it was sometimes worth it. There were all sorts of things in the gutters, always some potatoes, and lots of times meat trimmings, and even garden stuff that hadn't been good enough to take home. Richard picked up green beans and early peas, and there were always bunches of stuff to make teas with, but neither Richard nor Fanny had much use for teas. Such things were good to trade, however, and sometimes Richard managed to trade spearmint and pennyroyal for potatoes and onions. Sometimes when he finally went home he had a big basket full of plunder. There would be a further scene at the house when he finally got there; Fanny would always wrinkle up her nose and say, "I don't know what you got those for. They're just trash."

Richard didn't think so—potatoes looked like potatoes to him. Of course, some of them were a little wrong on one end or the other, and some of them were green or wrinkled. But they'd fill the pot, and at the moment that seemed to be about the only thing that mattered.

THINGS WEREN'T going too well at the Red Star either. Worse than that, after Fanny took the silver dollars, John Gillespie never seemed to have much use for Richard, and from that moment on John paid him just as little as he could. And always gave him the hardest jobs, and those he was afraid to do himself. Some horses were kickers, and despite the fact that they had restraining straps to keep them from kicking too much, some were real nasty. Richard came home bruised more than once, and after every such episode he decided that as soon as he could find something better to do, he'd switch. But he did like working with iron; it was fun to shape it and then heat it cherry red and quench it in the trough. John didn't like it a little bit, but when he wasn't busy Richard even tried fooling with a number of things. The best were probably the weathervanes—he made two or three good roosters, and even tried a swan and a cow. The cow didn't really look too much like a cow, and nobody bought that one. But the roosters went in a hurry—they were worth two dollars, and they worked. Richard had pinioned them so expertly that they'd turn if he just blew his breath on them.

Once he got the hang of it a little bit, he even tried making shop signs to hang out in front of stores. That took a lot of work, and the letters were troublesome. It was better when there weren't too many letters. Richard turned down "Witherspoon and Slocum"—they had a beer saloon down on Elm Street that they wanted to call a "Tavern." But he made a good hanging sign for R.C. Phlinn. Dr. Phlinn (he said he was a doctor) had eyeglasses that people could go in and try on until they found something that seemed to help, and all Phlinn wanted was a big pair of iron spectacles with his name hanging under it. The thing when it was finished was heavy, but Phlinn paid five dollars for it. That was what he had promised; he said he'd give five dollars if he liked the thing when it was done. He liked the sign all right, and he paid with a five-dollar gold piece. John

Gillespie accepted the gratuity gratefully, and that was the last that Richard ever saw of it.

Richard had to carry his dinner now, because the Gillespies didn't seem to want him to come over to dinner any more. Fanny knew that, but she didn't bother to pack him anything. He ordinarily bought his lunch on the way up to Race Street in the mornings—there was a shop that sold old crullers cheap. He usually bought six, and he never had any left over after he was through washing them down with well water. He did, however, sometimes hanker for the hot soups and stews he had been able to get in the little eating places down around the river.

So, somehow, the summer wore away. By August Fanny had more or less gotten over being sick in the mornings, and she was starting to show some swelling. Not much, but a person almost had to know that she was pregnant. Richard told himself from time to time that he'd have to scout around and find out just where they'd be able to find a doctor when the time came. It wouldn't be until March—there was that to be thankful for. Fanny had told him that he couldn't be sure of that—first babies had a habit of coming any time they wanted to. It might even be February, or even January. Richard doubted that, although he didn't pretend to know anything about the mystery.

Then one day—it was on one of the stinking hot dog days in August, he almost fell over Asenath in the Public Market. She had been bending down between two stalls picking up something in her apron, and Richard wouldn't have known her in the least if she hadn't looked up just the moment he passed. The sight of Asenath froze him into immobility, and Asenath herself didn't seem in the least bit pleased. It was almost as if she disliked meeting anybody from back home, almost as if she were a fugitive. The thought raced across Richard's mind that perhaps she was. Asenath for her part stood holding an apronful of corn, her cowlike eyes almost uncomprehending. "What you want?" she asked finally. "You want anything?"

"I'm just surprised to see you," Richard managed to blurt out. "I didn't know you come way down here."

"You don't want anything, just go on," suggested Asenath. "Ain't no business of yours where I am."

Richard felt slapped, but he decided he'd never get such another opportunity. "Is Ruth all right?" he asked.

Asenath simply stared, her big bulk almost dominating him. "How'd I know?" she finally answered. "Might be all right an' she might not be. Run away, that's all I know."

That was news, and Richard remembered that he had a quarter dollar in his pocket. He got out the coin and stood holding it in his hand while Asenath turned away from him and started husking the corn. She must have felt his presence there, because after a time she turned around again. "You don't want anythin', just move on," she said again.

Richard pointed to the pile of corn. "How much is it?" he wanted to know. "I mean I might want to buy some."

At that Asenath bent up lazily and came to stand behind the counter. "It's ten cents a dozen," she said. "Sweet corn. It ain't horse corn."

"I know it is," said Richard. "Give me a dozen."

"You got a poke? Anything to put it in?"

Richard didn't have, and said he'd carry the corn in his arms. Asenath watched while he made a business of selecting the ears. He was quite casual about it, and she didn't seem to mind.

"Where'd Ruth go?" he asked, and tried not to seem too eager.

"Don't know where she went," said Asenath. "All I know is we stood it as long as we could, and then we got out. Pa and Ma and Rachel went down into Kentucky."

"Where are Herman and Jake?"

"Right here some'eres," said Asenath. "Leastway, that's where I think they are. I never saw them again after we all got off the wagon."

"You mean you're living right here? In Cincinnati?"

"Reckon I'd have to live here if I want to work here," said Asenath. "You ain't got twelve—you got eleven."

Richard wondered if he dared ask, and finally decided to take the bull by the horns. "I guess you don't do it anymore," he said. "I mean what you used to do, you and your mother. I mean about babies."

At that Asenath stood like a statue and stared out into space.

"Guess I could if I had to," she said. "Ain't no fun—I can tell you that. People don't want to pay nothin' for it neither."

"How much do you want?" Richard asked boldly. "I mean, how much do you charge?"

This time Asenath stared at him. "You don't mean you got you a baby comin'." she said unbelievingly. "Where you live?"

"Right around the corner. In a little alley behind Pearl. I don't think it's got a name."

"How far along is she?"

"I don't know what you mean. My wife's right there. We live in a little house in the alley."

Asenath looked disgusted. "What month?" she demanded. "What month's it due in?"

Richard didn't know. "Guess it started in June," he said, and felt his face burn. "Just about the middle of June."

"Ain't no hurry then, is there? Won't be until sometime in March—late March."

Richard wasn't certain. "She said it might be February," he told Asenath. "She said first babies come early."

"First babies come late," said Asenath. "They have to do all the work for all that wants to follow. Never saw a first baby come early."

Richard didn't have time to digest that. "Well, would you, then?" he asked anxiously. "I'd be able to pay you, unless it's an awful lot."

"Think about it," said Asenath. "And there's no hurry—March is a long time off. Might not even be livin' by March."

"I ought to know where to find you."

"I'll be right here," said Asenath. "Long as the stuff keeps on comin' in from the farm, I'll be right here. And when the farm stuff's over, there'll be all the winter trash."

Richard dropped his corn and got it cradled into his arms again.

"You just ain't got no notion where Ruth went, then, have you?" he asked once more.

"Reckon she went Shaker," said Asenath. "That's my first guess, an' that's my last guess. She ain't up in Shakertown, she might be pushin' up daisies somewhere. I don't know an' I don't care."

Richard thanked her—he really didn't know what for. The corn spilled out of his arms before he had gone very far; someone had put in a raised section of boardwalk over a mud hole in front of a store, and he fell over it. He never did get back his whole dozen ears of corn, because three ears spilled under a farm wagon that was standing along the curb and it just didn't seem worthwhile to crawl after it.

THE SUMMER wore away, and Richard went back to see Asenath, sometimes almost every week. And while he got no further information about Ruth, for the simple reason that Asenath had none, he did discover that Asenath could be fairly gracious. They'd haggle sometimes over what she had on the stand, apples, or potatoes, and once even puffballs, but it was friendly haggling, and Asenath ordinarily sold to him for a lower price than that she had first quoted. Her supplier, and the man who owned the market concession, was some fellow named Henry Charles, but Richard never saw Charles, and couldn't even guess what he might look like. Asenath always referred to him as "the old rat," but it seemed a friendly term. Charles, it seemed, had a farm somewhere out Mill Creek Valley, and for years he had made a business of keeping the market stand. But he couldn't tolerate people, and that was why he was never around. With time Asenath even became half friendly, and from time to time she offered Richard a bit of advice to pass on to Fanny. "She ought to walk," Asenath had declared stoutly when she learned that Fanny was spending most of her time sitting in a chair or lying on the bed. "Once her time's come, she'll wish she had." Richard relayed the message that night, and was answered with a storm. "You must think I'm out of my mind," Fanny said venomously. "Look at the way I look."

"Nobody cares how you look. Everybody'll know you're going to have a baby."

"Well, do you think I want them to know that? If you do, you're plum crazy. If you hadn't done this to me, I'd be going places."

Richard let the matter drop. But he did finally worm out of Asenath where he could find her if he needed her. She was renting a room in a wood building right off Elm. It was a filthy place, and it was all full of Italians and gutter scum, but the room was cheap. And Asenath didn't stand for any nonsense—she let them alone, and by heaven they better let her alone or they'd know the reason why. Once her tirade was done, however, she assured Richard that he wouldn't need to find her, not for a long time. And that afternoon she again told him to tell Fanny to get plenty of exercise. If she was afraid of losing the baby, she could stop worrying. Now that she had carried it this long, it was a safe bet that she'd take it all the way.

Fanny did prove helpful in one way—she reminded Richard of the slaughterhouse they had passed way out on Race Street. Now that the slaughtering season was in again, there would be plenty of pigmeat out there that a person could have for the asking. Mostly spareribs, of course—it saved taking them down and dumping them into the river. All that a person needed was a good poke, or market basket, for that matter. But a market basket would sometimes show the blood.

Richard got a bucket—he had to buy one. The next afternoon he took off early and walked from the Red Star up to the slaughter-house. The place was filthy with flies, but there were large barrels at the side of the room into which the butchers were from time to time emptying their trash. And, as Fanny had said, there were plenty of spareribs. Most of the meat had been trimmed off, but not all, and they'd be tasty. After that they ate spareribs three times a week. They couldn't keep them, of course—the weather wasn't cold enough yet to keep them. But it wasn't a bad walk up to the slaugh-terhouse, and the fellows up there were real friendly and didn't seem to mind at all. Richard got the notion that he could have a job there if he wanted one, but he got so that he hated the place. It smelled of blood—and death.

In September the first cool days came, and with the cold the cracks in their house started showing. They had known about them, of course—anyone could see that the walls were only single boards which sometimes matched so badly that a person could see light be-tween them. With the chilly days Fanny started to complain of the cold, but try as he would Richard couldn't pry her out of the house into the sun. "I'm ashamed to be seen, that's what's the matter," she shouted back at him a hundred times. "I don't look this way. My God, I can't even get my dress on any more." When she quarreled Fanny's face got ugly, so ugly that she was almost unrecognizable. Richard sympathized with her—a little bit; he knew he wouldn't want to be carrying a baby around inside him. But women were sup-posed to want children, not to hate them. Anyway, that's what peo-ple had always said.

After a week of chilly weather, and sure knowledge that the

house could only get worse, Richard bought a cheap hammer and made a business of bringing home big packing boxes that were sometimes set out behind the more important stores. Most people seemed to want the boards for stove wood, but Richard decided to nail them onto the walls. It took a while for him to make enough nails, since John Gillespie seemed snoopy, and Richard didn't want him to know how cold the house was, but once he had several hundred he started in earnest to seal the room. Fanny screamed—she claimed that he was ruining the appearance of the place. He was. But he just let her scream, and after a time she subsided. The walls when they were finished didn't look much worse than they had before, and one thing was certain—the house was a little bit warmer. Not a lot, but a little.

It was a beautiful September and a beautiful October, and then with November the gray days started. One morning, the 10th, there was a light scum of snow on the ground, and a week later there was a real snow, two inches or more. But things didn't seem too bad. Fanny had taken to reading, for want of anything better to do, and Richard brought home books from the pushcarts that he thought might divert her. There was even one book of poems by some American fellow named Bryant, and Fanny took a real interest in some of his stuff. Not all of it. The one called "Thanatopsis" didn't make good sense, although the book said it was real popular. Neither Richard nor Fanny could figure why. It didn't seem to matter, because now there were always spareribs to suck on, and though Fanny gave up the whole business of cooking, Richard didn't mind taking over. One thing different he did do, however; he found an old iron skillet in one of the alleys. It was all full of filth and rust, but a good red brick broken small scoured it up in a hurry. After that they had spareribs the way they should be—fried. They both thought they could never get enough of them. There were days, however, when Fanny was not pleased—those were the sauerkraut days. Kraut was so cheap that one could buy it on market a big kettleful for a dime, but when there was kraut Fanny wrinkled up her nose. Richard generally induced her on those nights by buying a little beef or a couple pork chops. There were even nights when they felt real cosy once their supper was over, both of them trying to read by the light of the single lamp and both of them disinclined to go to bed and so start another day.

In fact, Richard often wondered whether this wasn't about the way his father and mother, and all other people for that matter, had started out their married life. Maybe this was the way it had to be—a new family just needed everything under the sun. Then, with the months and years, most of those needs would be taken care of, and a man and wife could settle down and be content. It wasn't a bad way to begin, once you thought about it for a little while. Not a bad way at all.

IN DECEMBER they were probably more miserable than they had been in November. More snows fell and the streets were icy, so that horses went down, particularly some of the big dray horses that had to try pulling up the cobblestones from the Landing. When the river began to go icy, the steamboats practically stopped. One or two got through from Pittsburgh and Wheeling, and probably a few more from downriver, where the conditions were not yet quite so bad. People on the streets went in greatcoats and roundabouts now, and they shuffled along somewhat woodenly, as if they were afraid of falling. They did fall, and they sometimes broke bones.

In their little house Richard and Fanny froze, and there was simply nothing to do about their plight. Sometimes now, when the slaughterhouses shut down for a while, there was no free hog meat available, and to make matters worse there was almost nothing that could be picked up from the market gutters. Richard walked his rounds dutifully, shivering in a big brown suitcoat that he had found thrown away in an alley. Fanny was perhaps worse off because she tried to get along in the house with only a flowered kimono. She said she couldn't get into her dress, and there seemed just no way to keep her warm. The kimono was not an alley acquisition, but it was almost as bad; Richard had found it in a store that sold cast-off garments. The kimono had been torn under both arms, and Fanny refused to try to mend it. She couldn't without needle and thread, but that was not the trouble—the trouble was that she was just not interested in mending it.

As Christmas approached Fanny began to speculate whether her father and mother would invite them both up for Christmas dinner. In any event she said she wouldn't go. She couldn't get there anyway, not unless her father borrowed a horse and wagon and came down after her, and that didn't seem probable. Fanny didn't want to see her father and mother—she said they would stare at her, and be certain to ask her when last she had been to Mass. In simple truth Fanny was herself worried about that. She really didn't know what good Mass would do her, but it was an obligation, and there was just no way for her to go. Richard agreed with her—there wasn't. But he did feel bad because she felt bad. The baby, Fanny said one day, would have to be baptized by a priest so that they could be certain that it wouldn't go to hell if it took sick and died. Richard wondered about that, without saying anything. The more he thought about it, the more he decided that religious opinions were very strange. The Protestants couldn't get along with the Catholics, and the Jews couldn't agree with anybody. And they all claimed that they knew and practiced the truth. There had to be an error somewhere. Maybe the Shakers had it right, or at least people like the Shakers. Insofar as he knew, the Shakers didn't baptize. Of course, without children, there was just no one to baptize, and maybe that was the reason that they didn't practice the rite.

There was an invitation for Christmas from the Gillespies, and John Gillespie did volunteer to drive down and bring Fanny up to the house. One late afternoon when they were closing up the shop John came up to Richard's anvil and just stood staring for a while. Richard wondered what was on his mind, and it seemed that it took a long time for Fanny's father to find any words. "Guess you'll be coming out to the house Christmas," Gillespie finally said. "I'll come down and git Fanny. Guess she ain't in very good shape to walk all the way up." Richard didn't promise, but that night when he told Fanny her face went a little black. "They want to do something, they could bring down my old quilt," she said. "They don't seem to care whether we freeze to death or not."

"They don't know how cold it is in here," Richard pointed out. "They never been down here."

"They never been down here, and I'm never going back up there," said Fanny bitterly. "You can tell him as much. They don't own us."

Richard made the blow as soft as possible, and it seemed to him that Gillespie was relieved. "Guess maybe she don't feel like it," he said. "When's her time up? Not for a while yet, is it?"

"March," said Richard, and as usual he flushed. It didn't seem decent to talk about Fanny's condition with her own father. "Course," he added, "she might come early."

Gillespie simply nodded his head and walked away.

So that was Christmas, and the day when it came was just like any other day, except that there was little work done in the town. The bells rang in the morning and the horses stood hitched out in front of the churches, although now some of them were hitched to sleighs. Richard envied some of the horses the warm blankets their masters threw across their backs before they went in to services. The thought occurred to him that it wouldn't be too hard to steal one or two of the blankets, but he buried it in the back of his mind. They'd get through all right. January would likely be about like December, and February maybe about the same. Then it would be March again, and with March things should be better. Particularly as soon as Fanny's trouble was over. They'd be able to breathe again then, and the world would look a whole lot brighter.

THE RIVER went solid, and some people were even bold enough to walk across the ice. And some of the hardier souls built tiny shelters on the ice and cut holes to fish through. The shelters were never too far from shore, but they were probably over pretty deep water. Now the town sometimes got gray with wood and coal smoke, and the smoke smelled good, particularly since it was evidence of warm fires somewhere. But there were few horses that came to the Red Star to be shod. A few wanted caulks, but there was never much more than three or four dollars a week to take home. John Gillespie was pretty good about dividing up the spoils, Richard had to admit that, and on Saturdays of those weeks when they had done a little better John generally managed to find an extra dollar. But there was one thing very wrong—Asenath wasn't on market anymore. Richard noticed that one Saturday, and then he made a business of going back the next, and the next, to see if she'd be in her stall. There just wasn't any stall, and finally in a sort of panic he decided to see if he could find the place she lived.

He found it, and it was just the way that Asenath described it, a sour tenement that seemed to be full of Italian families. There were kids on the street all around the place, little roly-poly, dark-eyed, and dark-skinned kids who didn't seem to mind the cold too much.

Richard thought of asking them where Asenath lived, but decided they wouldn't even know her name. Inside the front door there was a narrow rickety staircase, and from the dark second floor the staircase curled up another flight. It wobbled a bit when Richard walked up. By this time he had gotten a little accustomed to the garlic smell of the place. Asenath had said that she lived on the third floor, and the third floor had a rather long hallway with several doors on either side of it. Richard knocked on the first, and in due time the door was opened a crack and a fatty woman stood there looking at him. "I want to find the lady who works down on market," Richard told her after he got over being tongue-tied. "You know, the big lady." And he held out his hands in an attempt to indicate girth. That brought no response at all; the woman gobbled something in a language he couldn't understand and finally slammed the door in his face. Richard tried the second door, and the third, and the fourth, always with much the same experience. At the fourth, however, a little bright-eyed boy stood behind his mother, and he seemed to understand a little bit. "She seeck," he said. "She no feel goood. She seeck."

"Where does she live? In what room?"

The boy came out into the hall after that, and grabbed Richard's hand. He seemed not in the least to be afraid, and as they walked back down the hall he kept on jabbering. But this time he jabbered in Italian.

The room he pointed to was on the left, right at the front of the building, and once Richard hammered on the door, the youngster ran back down the hall to join his mother, who had been standing watching. No one came, and Richard knocked again, and again. "Asenath," he started calling. "Asenath, it's Richard Robinson."

That finally brought a response. There was a sound of furniture moving in the room, and in due time Asenath came, her eyes blinking. She stood there immobile, as if she were made of tallow, and Richard thought she looked a good deal thinner. "Don't tell me it's time," she almost groaned. "I thought you said March."

"I did say March," Richard agreed, "I guess I just wanted to make sure that I knew where you lived. That's all the reason I came."

Asenath stood again, her eyes almost uncomprehending. "She's gettin' out, ain't she?" she finally asked slumberously. "She ain't just sittin' around or layin' in bed?"

Richard had to admit that Fanny didn't get out much. She really didn't get out at all, but somehow he didn't want Asenath to know that.

And again Asenath stared, holding onto the edge of the door. "Reckon I'll be ready when she's ready," she said finally. "I ain't feelin' up to much right now myself."

"You got a cold?"

"I got a pain in my belly," said Asenath. "Ma was around, she'd know what to do, but I don't know where she's at."

Richard felt very uneasy. "I hope you get better," he finally got out. "Real fast."

Asenath nodded her slumberous eyes. "Reckon I will," she said. "If I don't they can carry me out and put me in the ground."

And with that she thrust the door shut, and Richard stayed only long enough to hear her pushing chairs out of the way again.

But he felt better—now that he had found her he felt better. Asenath would likely be all right in a week or two, and she had taken part in so many births that she'd know just what to do. The miserable thought had once or twice occurred that he might have to help Fanny himself, and his only experience had been in seeing cows drop their calves. It very probably wouldn't be like that at all, and in any event he didn't want to have anything to do with it. It just didn't seem decent.

IN THE MIDDLE of January there was a great snow, one that stopped most of the traffic in the streets. It also stopped anyone from coming in to the Red Star. People tried to walk in the horse tracks down the middle of the streets, and they fell and floundered, yet managed somehow not to hurt themselves too much. No teams pulled up and down the Landing hills now, nor was there any reason. Probably the high-toned burghers, those who lived in the big houses out on the hills, didn't suffer too much. Richard had heard that some of those houses had fireplaces in almost every room. It would take a mountain of wood to keep that many fires burning, and it would take some servants working full-time to carry in the wood. The probability was that the rich men could afford such servants, and maybe pay them good wages in the bargain. At least they would have enough to eat.

At home things were painful. Fanny rarely moved now, because she said that whenever she got up she shivered so hard that she couldn't get warm again. Some days she just stayed in bed; bed was probably the warmest place to be. Richard had brought down her old quilt from the Gillespie house—one day he just got brazen enough to ask John Gillespie if Fanny could have it. John hunched his shoulders, but the next day he brought the quilt over to the shop, and that night Richard carried it home. Fanny didn't even bother to say thank you.

There was, in all the misery, some one thing to be happy about: Asenath was back on market. Not every Saturday, but some Saturdays. Richard couldn't make out what she was selling and was afraid to ask her. All that the stand showed was a number of little packages wrapped in brown paper, stuff that looked like meat paper. Richard had to wonder what sort of meat it could possibly be. The mystery, however, ended one Saturday when Asenath called to him as he went by, and Richard was glad to respond. Richard wondered what she wanted, and thought she meant to ask about Fanny, or might even have some word about Ruth. It was neither—Asenath, after fumbling around and stammering a while simply said that she needed money to pay her rent. Could Richard let her have a dollar or two. It would just be a kind of payment in advance.

At the moment he had thirteen cents in his pocket, and he had to tell her that in a shamefaced way. But Asenath didn't show any emotion; she simply stared cowlike while she pushed one of her packages at him. "It's ten cents," she said and held out her hand.

"What is it?"

"Horehound drops," said Asenath. "Good an strong 'cause I made them myself. Good for colds."

Richard decided not to tell her he didn't have a cold. He had counted on the thirteen cents to get them through the weekend, but now he gave Asenath his only dime and kept the three big pennies jingling in his hand. "I'm sorry," he said. "Things are sort of slow."

"They ain't slow, they're dead," said Asenath. "I ain't had anything decent to eat since last Tuesday. An' then it was only bread and cheese."

That afternoon Richard made another trip up to the slaughter-house, and this time there was some pork in the barrels. He was choosy—he pushed aside all of the ribs that had been trimmed too well. Once he got his bucket full, he staggered back through the snow, afraid that Asenath might be gone. She wasn't—she sat hud-dling over a charcoal brazier that the Syrian next to her had kindled. "Got something for you," Richard had to shout at her. "You like spareribs?"

Asenath finally muscled herself to her feet, but when she saw the pork bones her eyes got big. "Holy Gawd!" she said. "Where did you ever get all of them?"

Richard didn't tell her. "Just thought you might like some," he said. "Take whatever you want."

"I thought you said you didn't have only thirteen cents."

"Fellow gave them to me," said Richard. "Take what you want."

Asenath took generously, but there were still enough spareribs left so that Fanny and he could have a good supper.

After that, whenever the slaughterhouse butchered, and it wasn't every day since the Cincinnati market was full of pork, Richard kept Asenath supplied. He began to wonder after two weeks or so whether he wouldn't really be paid up by the time Fanny came. He should be—the pork ought to be worth something.

And so January finally dragged through, and people talked about the groundhog seeing his shadow on the second day of February—and he did, and then February was cold again, and kept the river frozen. It seemed as if it had been a white city for months, not just one or two months, but almost forever. There were foot-paths along all the streets now, frozen, rutted footpaths, and here and there people had brought out their house ashes and scattered them on the icy snow. The same thing was true of the streets—some-how the wagon wheels had smashed the snow down hard. Every night some young bucks hitched up and raced their cutters up and down the hills; at least people said they did. Richard had never seen them. And every Monday morning dutiful housewives hung their wash out to freeze—they said it got whiter that way. Richard wouldn't know—they never washed clothes, or even pretended to wash themselves. It just wasn't that kind of winter.

Now that it was February he became more apprehensive. Fanny

was big as a barn, and her ankles were swollen, so that sometimes he had to help her across the room. She wasn't reading much any more either; most of the time she just sat and stared. Richard brought home all the gossip he could, but Fanny didn't seem to be interested. Out on Mount Adams a peddler had been killed when he was kicked in the head by a mule. And people said they bet Kentucky niggers were getting across the ice every night. It was a likely story—there wasn't any place for them to go once they got into Ohio. And a person never saw any of them, only those who were always in Cincinnati. A few of those even bragged about the fact that they were free men and had papers to prove it. Most of them, though, were hired from Kentucky families on the other side of the river. Once there was even a story about the ice going out, and no one knew how it started, because when people rushed down to look at the river it was just as solid as ever. Fanny seemed to listen to all such stories, but she must not really have heard because she never offered any comment. Richard pitied her. She had been such a beautiful girl, and now she was something of a mess, her eyes dull, and her satiny hair dirty and kinky. Once or twice he offered to brush it out for her, but she said she had no brush and had broken her only comb. But on one night she didn't protest, however, when he tried to untangle the skeins with his hands. For a little while he even forgot that she had become so savage.

It would be only another month, only one more month, and then she'd be good as new again. A little wobbly at first, maybe, but that would last only a few days. And February might turn warm, so that they'd all be more comfortable. It did sometimes, and when it did a person felt that he could breathe again.

That night, lying in the dark, Richard thought he heard a steamboat whistle. Maybe spring would come early. If it did, it would be the biggest kind of blessing.

FEBRUARY 17 was a cruel day, near zero, and with a blast of west wind sweeping down through the valley. Richard was frozen by the time he got up to the Red Star, and all the way he kept wondering whether he had brought enough stovewood into the house. Fanny hadn't ventured out after any for months now, and though he had enough packing boxes broken up, most of the outdoor pile was half covered with snow. He had visions of her venturing out, and falling, and not being able to get back into the house. At least he knew that there was extra warmth for Fanny in bed—he had surrendered his brown overcoat for use as an extra blanket.

As matters turned out, there was not any sense in his having come up to the Red Star, for there was just nothing to do, and all morning the big outside doors flatted in the wind while John and he hung over the forge in the attempt to keep warm. Out on the edges of the shop one could see his breath like a white plume. Dinnertime came, and John Gillespie didn't even have the courtesy to tell him to come over to the house and get warm. Richard had thought he might today, but although John might have if he alone were concerned, he was evidently afraid of his woman. Mrs. Gillespie didn't any longer give Richard the courtesy of a nod. It seemed strange for her to feel that way—he thought it was usual for married people to have children. But she evidently had something in her craw.

There was one fellow came in for caulks that afternoon, a big countryman in a red muffler on his way back up Mill Creek, and besides that nobody stopped. At four John started banking the forge and said they might as well go on home. Richard agreed, but he huddled over the forge for a long time before he ventured out. When he did he discovered that it hadn't gotten any warmer, and that the wind was still blowing. Sometimes it blew so hard that he had to stagger down the icy ruts, and he was frozen through long before he came to Elm Street.

Fanny seemed the same, about the same, but when he went up to the bed and asked her how she was she only groaned. Even then Richard wasn't too worried—lots of times Fanny didn't even try to answer him. He kept telling himself that there wasn't anything different at all, all the time he got in more stovewood and thawed the pump in the neighbor's yard so that he could draw a bucket of fresh water. But when he got back with the water Fanny was groaning again, and for the first time his heart jumped. Not tonight, pray God not tonight. And it was a whole month early. His nerves taut, he approached the bed and stood staring down at her. "There ain't nothing the matter, is there?" he heard himself ask. "You don't feel any worse than usual, do you?" For answer Fanny did manage to open her eyes and blink at him a little. "You better get her," she managed to get out. "That woman you were telling me about. You'd better get her."

Richard felt weak as a cat, but it did no good trying to talk to Fanny anymore, because she was groaning again. He took one quick look at the stove to see that it wasn't too hot, then grabbed the piece of discarded horse blanket he was wearing for a coat, and rushed out the door. It was already almost dark, and although there were lamps in a good many of the houses, there was almost nobody on the streets. Richard ran, stumbling across the drifts and ruts. His chest began to pain him from the icy cold and he could feel his heart pounding, but there was no stopping now. If Fanny thought she was going to have her baby, then Asenath had to get down to the house as soon as she could. And if Asenath weren't home, or was sick, then—but he wasn't able to conclude the thought. Fanny could depend upon nobody in the world except him, if Asenath couldn't come, and he knew he wouldn't be able to help very much.

It took an eternity to get to the rickety wood tenement, but there it was at last, and in another two minutes he was climbing on all fours up the shaking stairs. The smells in the house were the same, old urine and onions and garlic, and just the general smell of decay. Richard felt his gorge rise, but it was no time to be squeamish. As it was he had a time finding Asenath's door in the dark hall, and finally had to feel along the wall until he came to it. There was no light in the room.

Richard hammered on the door, and after a while punctuated his hammering with shouts. Let people think what they wanted to, he didn't care. No one came out into the hallway, however, and after a time Richard tried the knob. The door was locked, but now he thought he heard Asenath lumbering around inside. There was finally proof—the cracks in the woodwork proved that she had lighted a whale-oil lamp or a candle at least. Asenath took her good-natured time, but she did finally appear in the door, and she still had the lamp in her hand. Richard could have embraced her—Asenath was frowsy and dull-eyed as usual, but she was Asenath and she was reputed to know something about babies. Asenath looked at him slumberously, but she didn't say a word, and after a time he managed to get out his reason for coming. He had thought she'd know, just by seeing him. "I guess it's time," he said. "I guess she means to have it right now."

Asenath stood in the lamplight, her eyelids fluttering. "How long?" she asked. "How long's it been going on?"

"I don't know. I was at work, and when I come home, I found her that way."

"Her water broke?"

"I don't know what you mean."

Asenath only nodded. "Ain't no hurry," she said finally, and turned back into the room, where she slowly started gathering things. Richard didn't know what went into the stack, but there were a lot of folded pieces of cloth, and a knife and a scissors, and string, and even a bar of yellow soap. Asenath kept looking around, as if she didn't know just what she wanted, or had forgotten where she put things. She even took time to slice herself a piece of bread, but Richard noticed that she had nothing to put on it.

"We'll have to hurry," he interrupted her. "I wouldn't want it to come while we weren't there."

Asenath only sniffed. "Got all night," she said. "Might not come till morning."

Richard felt the sweat on his forehead turning to ice. "Well, she's all alone," he said. "She might think nobody's going to be around to help her."

Asenath was not to be hurried. The pile of supplies she rolled in a big towel, and she ate another slice of bread before she even started to put on her coat. Richard could have beaten her if he had dared—he had never seen a woman take any more time to do things. But Asenath was like that, had always been like that. It had been Ruth who was able to get things done.

Out in the street Richard wanted to hurry, and tried, but Asenath moved like a sleepwalker. It was probably good that she did—if she had gone down, there was no way Richard could have gotten her back onto her feet. Down Sycamore they went, and over Seventh, and then down Elm until they finally came to the alley and all the while Richard was shivering so hard he wondered if he'd ever be able to make it. They did, finally, going in the alley and around the corner of Mrs. Tarlbot's house until they came to the one-room shack that served as his own. The first thing he saw was that he had left the door open a little when he had run out. It must be terribly cold in there, even in the bed.

Asenath went right to the bed the minute they got there, and without hesitation reached her hand down under the covers to feel Fanny's belly. After she did, she only sniffed again. "She ain't even near havin' a baby," she said when she came over to the stove. "That all the fire you can get in that stove?"

"You mean she isn't going to have it tonight?"

Asenath sniffed again. "Maybe she will and maybe she won't," she said. "All I know is I want to get warm a little bit. And how about a bucket of water. You got one to put on the stove?"

Richard got the fire going, and added to the woodpile, and when he came back from the yard a second time saw that Asenath had lifted the water bucket onto the stove top. For a while they stood there shivering together, and then Asenath put her coat back on. "Guess you might as well go on," she said finally. "Ain't nothin' you can do here. You might as well go."

That came as a surprise—Richard hadn't counted on going anywhere. And he had nowhere to go. He told Asenath as much, and she promptly got hostile. "I don't want you around," she said. "Wherever you're going, you might as well go right now, before it gets too late."

"You think it will be born tonight?"

"It'll be born," said Asenath. "I don't know when, tonight, or tomorrow, or some other time. You should have knowed that when you put it in there."

Richard didn't know whether he felt more miserable or cold. He kept looking around the room, hoping against hope that he could find something to throw on before he had to go back out in the cold, but, as he knew, there was nothing except his piece of horse blanket. He'd likely have to walk to keep warm, and maybe as a last resort he'd go back up to the Red Star and get the forge going. But only as a last resort—the Gillespies wouldn't like that at all, and he didn't like being beholden to them.

IT MUST BE below zero, maybe pretty far below zero. And he was walking on wooden feet—he had been walking on wooden feet for hours. It seemed he had been up and down through the City a dozen times, clear down to the Landing and past MacCready's, where there was a big padlock on the door as he thought there would be, out north almost as far as the canal, across Broadway and Sycamore and Vine and Race and Elm and back again. Almost all doors were locked, although he did manage to get into St. Peter's. It wasn't much warmer in the church, but the sanctuary lamp was glowing, and he was protected from the wind. Richard tried sitting in one of the pews, but it was terribly cold hunched up there, and he decided he'd better move if he didn't want to freeze to death. Down near the waterfront again he spent his last dime on a bowl of bean soup in a woebegone all-night place. There were three drunks sprawled over a table in there, and the proprietor, a lanky balding man who said his name was Joe, didn't seem to like it that Richard wanted only bean soup. "What you need's this," he said, and held up a brown bottle. "Drink all you want for another dime." When Richard shook his head and turned back to his soup, Joe seemed disgusted. After a time he went back to the corner and started shaking the drunks, but they were too far gone to come to life. They wouldn't stay warm in the place, but they wouldn't freeze to death, and after a time Joe seemed to have reconciled himself to that fact. "Dam' cold out there," he said when he came back behind the counter. "What you doin' out? Don't you have no place to go?"

Richard stuttered a little bit, and finally decided to tell Joe the truth. "My wife's havin' a baby," he said.

At that Joe's face went even longer. "Jesus Christ!" he said. "She picked a night. Five below outside."

"I guess she didn't pick the time," said Richard. "I guess there just ain't nothing you can do about babies."

Joe looked disgusted and swabbed up some bean soup with his towel. In the lamplight they looked at each other, Richard's spoon poised, Joe with the towel thrown back over his left shoulder.

"Women!" Joe said finally. "Cause o' all the trouble in the world. Fellow plays around with them a little bit, an' next thing he knows he's up to ears in you know what. I know—I been through it."

Richard went back to his bowl, but Joe saw no reason to let him alone. "How old is she?" he asked.

"I guess she's twenty," said Richard.

"What'd you mean guess. Don't you know?"

"She's twenty."

"You ain't that old yourself, are you?"

"Last birthday," said Richard.

"Where you live?"

Richard didn't want to say. "Farther up town," he said. "Over near Elm."

"What is it, first baby?"

Richard nodded, and Joe seemed satisfied. "They do it every time," he said by way of consolation. "Just when a feller gits things goin' a little bit, his woman knocks him in the head with a baby. Do it every time."

"I guess they can't help it," said Richard. "There's just nothing they can do about it."

That seemed to make Joe angry. "What d' you mean nothin'?" he asked belligerently. "That's the way they want it. Ain't a single woman ever been born as has the sense God gave little green geese. That's what they want—to have babies. Didn't you ever see 'em, the way they kiss and coo and act like the little pissants is somethin' special. Just dolls, that's what women think they are, an' that's the way they treat 'em. Ain't a single one o' them has enough brains to blow her own nose. That's the way they want it." And Joe punctuated his remarks by swinging his towel and slapping it down across the counter. Richard wiped his mouth with his hand. The moment Joe saw that he grabbed up Richard's bowl and carried it back to the stove to fill it again.

"This one's on me," he said when he brought the bowl back. "You ain't got money in your pants to pay for it because you got a stinkin' woman who's havin' a baby. I know—I remember. I was over in Pittsburgh when I went through the same dam' thing you're goin' through tonight. An' I was just your age—twenty. Maryann was her name—she was a good-looker with big black curls. Only she didn't have good sense. Just as soon as she got up again, she started makin' eyes at a riverman, an' when I knowed that I said good-bye to Maryann. That's when I come on downriver to Cincy. Been here ever since."

Richard thought he'd better not ask questions, and didn't. The bean soup kept his mouth occupied, and he thought Joe should be content with that.

"That's what you'll do if you got good sense," said Joe, and draped himself across the counter. "Go on downriver a piece. And when you do, show that you've learned your lesson and stay away from 'em. You let another female hook you, and you can tell your-self you need a good kick in the ass."

Richard bent over his soup, but with Joe hanging over the counter he thought at last that he'd better say something. "How long's it take?" he finally asked.

"How long's what take?"

"Having a baby. How long's it take."

Joe didn't really answer. "You can stay here all night if you want to," he said. "No reason you shouldn't—there won't be nothin' doin' on a night like this. Just go on over along the wall and pull a couple chairs together and stretch out. Maybe when you wake up it'll be morning."

"It won't take that long, will it?"

Joe only whistled. "They make it last a long time," he said lugubriously. "Just their way o' makin' a man feel like hell. They could likely have 'em in fifteen minutes if they wanted to, but they just don't want to. Go on, go over along the wall and get a couple chairs and stretch out."

Richard thanked him, and did. The chairs felt icy cold, but it wasn't too bad once he got stretched out on them. For a long time he could see Joe walking up and down behind his counter and snap-ping his towel, then finally he shut his eyes, and that was the last he knew. When he woke up Joe himself was hunched over a table asleep, and outside it looked like gray morning. Richard tried to be as quiet as possible as he got his legs under him. It was time to go home.

ASENATH GOT UP from her chair and met him where he stood right inside the door, staring at the bed with the covers drawn tight over it.

"I done what I could," Asenath said slumberously. "I guess she just didn't have enough strength. But I done what I could."

Richard felt his heart race. "You don't mean that—" he man-aged to get out, and could not finish his sentence. Asenath stood in front of him nodding her head, and acting as if she didn't want him to look. "She just didn't have enough strength," she kept on saying. "I told you to make her keep on walking. She just didn't have enough strength."

Richard knew that he ought to scream, but somehow he couldn't. But he felt like screaming.

"How about the baby?" he finally managed to ask.

"Big little red-headed boy," said Asenath. "He had the cord tied around his neck. I kept on slappin' him a long time, but he just wouldn't breathe. Fine little red-headed boy."

Richard cried then, and Asenath finally came over and put her arms around him. "I done what I could," she kept on saying. "You can believe me or not, but I done what I could."

There was just nothing else to say, and nothing else to do. It was only that the world had come to an end.

FANNY AND the baby would be buried in the Potter's Field without benefit of any religious ceremony, but because the ground was too hard to dig, the bodies would be kept on ice until the weather broke. Mrs. Tarlbot took care of all that—she was the landlady to whom they had been paying six dollars a month rent. It was too much and Mrs. Tarlbot knew it, and now that they could pay rent no longer, she wanted their things cleared out in a hurry. Richard promised her—vacantly, without the least notion what he was talking about. The Gillespies should have the things, of course, or at least the right to sell them, since it was with their money Fanny had bought the bed, rocker, chairs, lamp, and the poor carpet on the floor. That was all they had possessed, unless one counted the iron pot, the skillet, and bucket, and a few pitiful odds and ends of knives and spoons.

Richard knew that he should talk to the Gillespies, and he had in a way, for he had asked Asenath to go around and tell them that Fanny was dead. Asenath had never reported back, and two days later Richard himself went up to the Red Star. He had expected John Gillespie to be furious with him, but Gillespie was not at all. He was not angry but broken, so much that he even limped when he walked back and forth across the smithy. "She wasn't a bad girl," he kept telling Richard. "Fanny wasn't a bad girl. She was high-strung and a little headstrong, but she wasn't a bad girl. She wasn't a bad girl atall." And Richard saw the two big tears drop out of his eyes and streak his cheeks. Gillespie picked up a hammer, and then put it back down again, and then he repeated the action, as if he really didn't know what he was doing. He seemed to want to say something, and not know how to get it out.

"It wasn't yours anyways," he finally managed to say, and now the tears were falling unashamedly. "It was that red-headed feller—he was the one that did it to her. She was crazy about him, but he ran off downriver after he had promised he was going to marry her."

Richard stood like a post. He couldn't at first realize the full import of what he had just heard, but if he did understand John correctly it made matters a little different.

"He said he was a good Catholic too," said John Gillespie. "Course, he couldn't get to church very often, not when there were too many boats down at the Landing waitin' to be unloaded, but he knowed all the right things to say. He had been brung up right."

Richard thought he'd let it go at that, without further inquiry.

"I guess all the stuff that's left in the house is yours," Richard finally said. "It's not much, but it was all bought with your money."

John Gillespie shook his head and wiped the tears out of his eyes.

"Don't even want to set eyes on it again," he said. "Neither does my woman—we don't want to set eyes on it. All it would make us do is remember."

Richard managed to get away soon after that. Nothing had been said about his continuing at the Red Star, but he knew that nothing needed to be said. The job at the Red Star was done, and all John Gillespie's grandiose dreams of building up the shop were finished. He'd go on struggling along there, of course, but the Red Star was running downhill and it would soon be out of business.

Kicking through the snow on his way back down Race Street Richard suddenly realized that he was going no place, that he had no place to go. He was finished in Cincinnati—the City had been unfriendly to him. The idea of going downriver, or up river, sounded appealing, but at the moment there was no traffic either up or down river, and he wouldn't get very far if he had to go on Job's mare. And he couldn't walk up Mill Creek Valley and beg a job with one of the farmers—the farms were sleeping in February, and they'd keep right on sleeping. That meant that there was but one place in the world left—home. He'd have to go back home, and if he did he'd very likely discover that he wasn't wanted there either.

Chapter 7

IT WAS A bright day, and at high noon the sun sowed a million diamonds in its path. Curiously, once he got away from the city streets, Richard began to feel better, although his stomach was gnawing. There was no way to stop that—he hadn't a penny in his pocket. He remembered then how he had started down to Cincinnati the same way, and of how John Cheeseman had fed him in Lebanon and then at parting given him a silver dollar. He needed another John Cheeseman, and he needed him before too many hours went by.

There were farm teams and travelers on the pike, at least some. One man was snaking logs with a yoke of big oxen, and Richard remembered the corduroy he had helped put down. The logs seemed to slide easily over the icy snow, and the fellow driving the oxen seemed to be content that the beasts should take their time while he occupied himself with his corncob pipe. Then there was a stage full of people, and it was driving hard for Mason and Lebanon, the four horses running quite easily. Richard examined the tracks after they went by—as he expected, the horses were wearing caulks. That explained how they could run so confidently.

Two hours after the sun was past the meridian he decided that he'd have to try begging. Other people did it, and it wasn't at all uncommon. But he hated himself when he went to the back door of a good-looking white farmhouse that stood near the road. He had picked the house because it had three chimneys that were trailing good blue woodsmoke. That meant that whoever lived there was at least rich enough to keep warm.

Nobody answered his knock at first, and then, finally, he heard the kitchen door opening and a tiny white-haired woman shuffled out onto the porch. She didn't seem to be afraid, but the moment she got out in the colder air she threw her apron up so that it half covered her head. Richard liked her looks—she had sharp, inquisitive eyes, and a long thin nose.

"I'm hungry," he told her immediately. "You got anything I can do for something to eat?"

At that she looked him over very carefully. "Don't appear like you're starvin'," she said. "When'd you eat last?"

"Yesterday," said Richard promptly. "It wasn't much, only a couple crullers. That's all I've had in the last two days."

That reply seemed to make her more considerate. "Sakes alive!" she said, and walked around him. "Sakes alive!"

"I don't want much. And I'm willing to work."

After that the woman scampered back inside without another word, and in two minutes reappeared with a seventy-year-old codger who helped himself along with a blackthorn cane. "There he is," she said, as if Richard were some animal on exhibit. "Think maybe he could do it?"

The old fellow wasn't committing himself. "Think maybe he could if he wanted to," he said. And very boldly he reached out his hand and squeezed Richard's biceps. "Think maybe he could," he said again after he seemed satisfied.

The old woman still wasn't sure. "How come you're on the road?" she asked sharply.

"I been down in the City," said Richard. "I'm on my way home."

"How come you got no money in your pockets?"

"I been working down there. In a blacksmith shop. I just ran out of money."

The old woman still walked around. "Sounds like a likely story," she said, but her words were not venomous—she just seemed to be thinking out loud. "What we want's somebody to help take a chist upstairs," she said. "Papa could likely do it hisself if he didn't have a bad leg. Think you could do that?"

Richard assured her that he could, and without another word she walked back in, and was immediately followed by her husband. Richard didn't know for sure, but it seemed that that was his invitation to enter, and he went along. The old woman stood at the door and shut it behind him.

Chapter 7

"You want to work first or eat first?" she asked the moment she turned. "Won't take you long to get it upstairs."

"Work first," said Richard promptly, and without ado she turned around and led the way through the kitchen and into what must have been the sitting room. There was a good stove in there, and it was hot, so hot that the room steamed. There were potted plants on boxes under the two windowsills.

The chest was not in the sitting room—it was in the front room, and it wasn't a chest but a chest of drawers. The moment he saw it Richard began to wonder if it would go up any staircase—it was just too big, a rosewood monster that still had the drawers crammed full. That could easily be remedied, of course; they'd have to take the drawers up separately. After that they could struggle with the frame. That was theory—the fact was that only two of the four big drawers at the bottom could be pulled out. And from the weight of the piece of furniture it seemed as if they must be full of rocks. But at least two of the drawers were empty, and Richard set them aside.

The trouble actually was the old man, who insisted that he get at the top of the load to guide it while Richard lifted and pushed on the bottom. That meant one short step at a time, because the old fellow had to be certain that his game leg wasn't going to collapse on him. But that was the way they went out through the icy hall and up the flight that looked as if it must be fifteen steps long. The old woman followed along step by step, and she gave directions like a general. Richard ignored her, and he noticed her husband did too.

Once upstairs, it was easy, for the chest came to rest in the middle of a giant empty bedroom. It was terribly cold there, worse than the outdoors, and they were all glad when they could get back out and shut the door. Once back down the stairs and out in the sitting room, the old woman became more gracious. "That was my daddy's," she said. "Come all the way from Virginy when he come over in 1809. And what it's got in is his law books. That's why it's so heavy."

"Was he a lawyer?" Richard asked.

"He was in the Legislature up in Chillicothe," said the old woman fiercely. "Lawyer down in Virginy, an' the best lawyer in Ohio. That's where I was born, down in Virginy. There ain't no other state like Virginy, and there ain't never goin' to be one."

She looked fierce, and Richard thought he'd better not contest the point. So they stood for a moment, in a sort of tableau, until she finally came to her senses. "Guess maybe you want to eat now," she said. "All we got's ham an' liver. There's some old popovers too—you can eat what you want of them. Got apples inside."

"I'll take anything," said Richard. "Anything you want to give me."

"His name was Aldergate," said the old woman. "That was my name too 'fore I was married. Ever hear of it?"

Richard had to confess that he never had. He was actually thinking of ham more than anything else in the world.

"Elijah B. Aldergate," said the old woman. "Mark it down in your mind, so's you'll know it the next time you come across it. The B is for Benson. Elijah Benson Aldergate."

And without another word she disappeared in the direction of the kitchen, where after another minute or two Richard heard pans clashing.

The meal was good and there was enough of it, so that he ate like a hog, the two of them sitting at the table and watching him. Once or twice the old fellow reached out and got a piece of ham fat and sucked at it, but the old woman sat quiet until she suddenly remembered that she hadn't poured the coffee. She got up immediately and brought a mug of the black stuff. It tasted as if it had been brewed for days; it was so thick it could almost have been spread upon bread.

Richard shook hands with both of them before he left, even though they hadn't suggested he take some bread and what was left of the meat with him. They both came out to the back porch with him, and they both waved when he turned before he started up the road. Richard had told them that he'd remember them always. After Cincinnati, he was perfectly willing to ask God to let them into Heaven without examination.

Unfortunately, however, the hours spent with the Applegates, or whatever their name was, had drained a lot of sunlight out of the day, and the sky had gone so dull that it appeared it might snow. Richard hoped not—he wouldn't want to be caught on the road in another snowstorm.

IT WAS NIGHTFALL before he got to Mason, and in Mason the town was sealed up so tight that it might as well have been a picture on the wall, all its houses blue-black and with tiny pinpoints of yellow to show where there were lamps or candles behind the windows. The town smelled like good wood smoke and that was heartening, but without money there was just no place to get in out of the cold. And it was cold, and seemed to be getting colder as the night sealed down tight. Richard kept looking at the barns as a possible place of refuge—the only trouble was that most of them were too far away from the pike. People didn't like it if they saw somebody going into one of their barns. Of course, there weren't many people out looking, not on a night like this.

Richard walked clear through the town and back out on the pike again, and then decided to go back. After Mason he'd have to take his chance on bedding down in some shed or barn on one of the farms, and most of the farms were pretty well back from the road. It seemed better to see what he could do in Mason. There was a little place that passed for an inn, but there was no sense going in there, of course; however, the inn barns sometimes held quite a lot of horses. Sleeping in the hay there, he'd count on the horses to help keep him warm. Or, if not warm, then warm enough to stay alive.

He was loitering down the little lane that led past the place that called itself the Black Hawk when the back door suddenly opened and a woman came out on the step with some dishwater to throw out. She saw him, stood for a moment as if scared, and then hurried back inside. Richard knew what she'd do next—she'd scream for help, and the men would come out. He decided to run—and did. Back of the stables was an open field, and once in the open field he knew that nobody would be able to see him. He circled south, and in due time came back to the pike. He felt a little warmer after his run, but not warm enough, and he soon felt the sweat turn icy on his body. That kept him moving, but moving futilely. There was just no place to go.

The barn, when he finally found it, was nothing much, just slab sides and a roof. It smelled like pigs, but there must have been horses there once too, for it had a haymow, and Richard climbed up and buried himself in the hay. He thought he'd get warmer after a time—it generally happened that way. He didn't get warm, but he did stop shivering. That was at least something to be happy about.

Lying there in the dark, the hay covering everything except the tunnel he had left for his head, he began to think for almost the first time, as if the leaden weight he had carried on his shoulders had become a little lighter. He had made a fool of himself, as big a fool as anybody could imagine. And after almost two whole years in the City he was no richer, and probably not very much wiser than he had been when he went down to Cincinnati. Worse than that, everything else had changed, and likely everybody. He wasn't sure his mother and father would welcome him back home, although it was probable that his father would be more gracious than his mother. And Ruth was either with the Shakers, or Asenath had been mistaken and nobody knew where she was. If she was with the Shakers, then there was a chance that she might already be converted to that funny religion. Ruth had a level head on her shoulders, but so did a lot of other people, and they almost always got converted to some religion they didn't know anything about. Of course, there might be a God. If there was, nobody really knew anything about Him, because people thought all sorts of things. The Indians had had a god too—they called him the Great Spirit, or something like that. And it was a safe bet that the black people over in Africa, and the yellow people away over in China and Japan had gods. People couldn't all be right, not unless they decided to agree, and if one thing was sure, it was that men could never all agree about anything. They couldn't agree about how to plant crops, or build houses, or even shoe horses—little things like that. And then, by paralyzing themselves, it seemed as if a lot of them would get together and say they knew the last word about God. It was enough to make a fellow laugh.

Ruth was somewhat the way he was—she thought the way he did, at least most of the time. She could never go Shaker. That didn't mean, however, that she might not be in Shakertown. And if she was, then it would be pretty hard to find her. The Shakes had too many big houses—Families, they called them—and all the women dressed alike and kept themselves locked in their rooms most of the time. It was really something like a big prison, Shakertown was. They walked like prisoners, and they didn't talk much, and they worked so hard they were so tired at night they didn't want to do anything but sleep. Frankly, it didn't seem like much of a life, and it looked as if a person had to lose a good piece of his mind before he even wanted to try it.

It was cold, cold, and he didn't know whether he'd be able to make it to morning or not. If not, he'd have to get up and get out on the road again. There wouldn't be any teams or people out there at this hour, and there'd be no chance of getting a lift in a farm wagon. But if he walked, walked all the rest of the night, he might be up as far as Lebanon by morning.

That was the last he knew, and when he did finally wake up there were roosters crowing out somewhere near the barn. A few moments later he heard a fellow come out with a couple milk buckets—they kept clanking together as he walked. Richard lay still—it wasn't the time to get up right now. They'd see him, probably, when he did finally decide to move, but they wouldn't be so kind as to open the door and invite him in for breakfast. Nobody did that—fellows on the road were just fellows on the road, and everybody was glad when they were gone down the road, and so lost forever.

AFTER MASON, RICHARD debated whether he should go on to Lebanon, or cut off on the pike that led north through Union Village and on to Red Lion. The Red Lion road was a good deal shorter, although not so well traveled, and it would go within a long mile of the Robinson farm. But there was no chance of work up that way, not unless he would be content to work on the farm for nothing, while Lebanon offered at least the faint prospect of employment. The real reason for his choice, however, was probably that the nearer he got to home, the more disheartened he became. It would be all the same, chores from first light to dark, and never a penny in his pocket. There would be enough to eat, of course, and a good place to sleep. There would also be his mother's constant moping and nagging—she was a good woman, but so good that she knew she was invariably right. And—and this was perhaps the largest of all reasons—she had definitely said that she wouldn't live in the same house with Ruth. And every time Richard thought about Ruth, a little of the old dream came back. Ruth wasn't Fanny and she wasn't Mrs. Bentley, but she had always seemed to have a great deal more sense than either of them. In fact, she seemed to have a great deal more sense than he did himself. And if Ruth were with the Shakers—and he found himself hoping mightily that she had gone no further than Shakertown—then she might be found and lured back into the world. The large chance was that she would be glad to come. But—and this was always the nub of the matter—she couldn't come to the Robinsons' if his mother was dead set against her, and they couldn't start out on their own without a penny in pocket. It was a pretty mess, and the summation of the whole problem seemed to indicate that he had no option except to go on to Lebanon and see if he could find work there. If he couldn't, then—but he never got on to the conclusion of the "then." The trouble was that he couldn't find a conclusion.

He plodded on towards Lebanon, and as good luck would have it, a mile or so up the road he was overtaken by a red-faced fellow who was driving a pair of big grays in front of a jolting farm wagon. The man stopped as soon as he came abreast, and motioned with his hand. "Goin' up toward Leb'non," he said. "Might as well ride."

Richard climbed up, and the next minute the fellow had flopped half of a horse blanket over his legs.

"Out on the road early, ain't you?"

"Guess I am," said Richard. "You going all the way to Lebanon?"

The man nodded. "Where you been?" he asked.

"I was down in the City," said Richard, and realized how important that sounded.

"Didn't walk all the way up, did you?"

"Guess I did. Course, I stopped to sleep last night."

The man nodded his head and a couple drips of mucus came out of his nose and fell onto his blue wool muffler. Richard understood by something in the nod that the fellow knew that he had slept out in a haystack during the night. It wasn't contempt, not quite, but it was awfully close.

"You don't know John Cheeseman, do you?" he asked in an attempt to give the man something to think about.

That proved a more congenial topic. "Guess ever'body knows John," said the man immediately. "Best dam' farmer in the county. Why, you know John?"

"Not very much," said Richard. "You got a good team, haven't you?"

The fellow nodded without saying anything. "What did you do down in the City?" he wanted to know. "Things is slow down there, ain't they?"

"I guess so," said Richard. "Least, they was slow in what I was doing. I was a blacksmith, but it was pretty slow through the winter."

The man nodded again. "Sent me some of my hogs down," he said. "Fellow was buyin' them up to drive down to the slaughter-houses, but he didn't want to pay nothing for them. I let him have six or seven."

The conversation was ended again, but the wagon kept jolting along and the few farm buildings crept by at funeral pace. A little way up the road the man fished in his pocket for a long time and finally came up with a plug of tobacco. He had a time biting off a hunk. "Got lick-rish in it," he said when he saw Richard looking at him. "They make it that way. Want a chew?"

Richard didn't. Nor was he certain how far he could trust the fellow, but he decided to try. "You don't know no jobs open up in Lebanon, do you?" he asked, and tried to seem indifferent. "I'd like to catch on as a blacksmith if I could."

The man shook his head, and again the drops descended onto his muffler. "Don't know o' a thing," he said. "There's old Ike Potter on Main Street—you might go around and ask him. And there's Bill Hinkle's place—that's right on the pike. We'll pass it going in."

"Where do you take your own horses?"

"Potter," said the fellow. "Bill's almost as good, at least I reckon he is. But Ike's better. Once he puts shoes on, they last a spell. Go around and see Ike. Ask 'em both before you get out of town. That's what I'd do."

At the Francey Tavern the man pulled in the horses at the horse trough and threw the reins down. "Reckon it's about time for somethin' to keep us warm," he said. "You feel like snortin' a spell?"

Richard didn't want to admit that he didn't have a penny in his pocket. "Guess I'll just go on," he said.

"You can get free breakfast in here if you buy a drink. Allays cheese and stuff set out on the counter."

"I ain't hungry," said Richard. The thought struck him that he shouldn't be talking that way—he knew better. But out on the road it seemed the right thing to do.

The big farmer only stood and looked at him. "You come on in and git warm," he almost ordered. "Don't want nothin' to drink, you can stand by the fire. Tell you what—I'll buy you a drink, you can eat somethin'. And then I'll drink down whatever you order after I finish mine."

After that Richard agreed. The tavern was a tavern only in name, but there was a good fire in the single room, and Richard promptly moved up to it and tried to get warm. Before he knew it the big farmer he had been riding with came over with a glass of whiskey in his hand and stood beside him. "Go on up and order," he muttered. "Ask for a glass o' wine or somethin'. An' then move down the counter an' help yourself to anything you find."

Richard did. There was a woman behind the bar and she looked sharp—she was likely the mother of the little girl who kept running up and down through the place. "I guess I could stand a glass of wine," he said, and tried to make himself sound casual. "What kind you got?"

The woman only looked at him—disconcertingly. "I got dandelion an' elderberry," she said finally. "An' I got some peach brandy. Which do you want?"

Richard thought the peach sounded mild, and chose that, and in another moment he had the little glass in his hand. The stuff burned his lips like fire, and he had sense enough not to get any of it in his throat. They had made a little wine at home, not much but a little, but it had never tasted anything like this.

"You're hungry, eat," said the woman indifferently, and the next minute she had a big broom in her hand. From the workmanship Richard knew it was a Shaker broom—they had had one exactly like it at home. The Shaker brooms were made heavy, and they always had a lot of straw in them.

Richard ate, trying to be dainty. There was yellow cheese and white cheese on old blue plates and there was also a big mound of souse. The gelatinous souse had too much vinegar in it, but it was good, and the cheese tasted like manna from heaven. Unfortunately there was no bread—bread would have made the stuff taste twice as good.

The farmer came up to him after a little while, his glass empty. "You want me to, I'll put down the rest of that," he offered. "Brandy, ain't it?"

"Peach," said Richard.

The fellow threw back his head and let the brandy slosh down his throat. "Dam' good," he said the moment he was finished. "Costs a little bit more, but it's dam' good."

Back out in the cold, they climbed on the wagon again, and they both felt better. "Ain't only two–three miles further up the pike," said the farmer. "Git there along about nine or half-past."

Richard nodded. Now that they were getting close to Lebanon, he knew he'd have to decide what he meant to do. The sorry conclusion was inevitable—he'd do the only thing he could do: ask everybody in town if they knew of any jobs. The sorry conclusion was also inescapable that they'd likely all say no. And in that case there would be nothing to do but go out the west road, and try to get home.

BILL HINKLE'S PLACE came first—it was right out on the edge of town. It looked a lot like the Red Star, and it also looked as if it didn't have any more customers than the Red Star. There was one sorrel horse hitched to the rail out in front, but it didn't seem to be waiting to be shod. And the big doors were closed—that was probably because of the weather.

"You tell him I sent you," said the farmer as Richard climbed down. "Tell him Hank Jaffers sent you. And then when you get done in there go on up to Ike Potter's on Main Street. Ike don't want you, I don't know who in hell will."

Richard went through the small door and after a moment was able to pick up shadows in the darkness of the shop. There was a giant of a man at the forge, Bill Hinkle probably, and he was hammering hot iron, though for the life of him Richard didn't know what he was making. Probably something the little fellow in a black hat and coat wanted, and probably something that he didn't have to have. It looked like a big foot scraper or something that was destined to scrape ice or snow.

Neither of the men paid the slightest attention to him, and Richard finally had to go up to the forge. After that Bill knew that he was there, but didn't take the trouble to inquire what he wanted. The iron didn't seem to want to come right, and after a few minutes Bill carried it back to heat it again. Richard thought that was his chance, and took it. "Guess I'm looking for work," he managed to blurt out, although Bill still wouldn't look at him. "Don't have nothing, do you?"

At that Bill did look, and opened his mouth to laugh. He had a satyr's face and a mop of dirty yellow hair that hung across his low forehead. "Ever hear anythin' funnier 'n that, Enoch?" he addressed the little fellow in the black greatcoat. "Here's a feller asks whether I'm takin' on anybody. Jesus Chree-ist!"

The older man didn't seem to think the situation very funny. He said nothing, but he kept fidgeting as if he was anxious to be away. "How much longer you think it'll take?" he asked, and pulled out a large silver watch and looked at it.

"Take as long as it has to take," said Bill.

"How long's that?"

"Maybe half hour. I don't know. The dam' thing won't bend right."

Richard stood—and watched. He never did really learn what was being hammered, but it seemed to be some sort of frame for two iron wheels. Probably some sort of child's toy or go-cart.

"You ain't got nothing then?" he heard himself ask, and again knew he shouldn't talk that way. Somehow it seemed necessary when he was talking to fellows like Hinkle.

Bill stopped for a moment and looked around. "All I can do to keep on eatin' myownself," he said. "Some days it's so bad that all I can get is fiddlin' jobs like this."

"You want it to fit the wheels, you got to bend it a little more," Richard suggested.

For answer Bill handed him the hammer. "Want to try it," he asked, and seemed to expect Richard to refuse. He was obviously surprised when Richard took the hammer.

It was a tough job because the frame was so heavy that it didn't want to make a U-turn properly, but Richard finally got it so that he could slip the wheels into place. Bill stood by indifferently, but the little man in the black coat seemed to be satisfied. Better than that, he fished in his vest pocket and finally found a quarter dollar that he offered to Richard. "Guess it's worth that," he said, and in the next moment he handed Bill a big round half dollar. "You want any more, you'll have to whistle for it," he said, and without further ado picked up the contraption and went out to his buggy.

Richard followed him, and after a moment's indecision turned up the street to see if he could find Ike Potter's. The quarter dollar made him feel a great deal better—somehow it restored his confidence.

Chapter 7

IT WAS THE SAME at Ike Potter's, and Ike had a big shop with two forges. Like Bill Hinkle's place, the smithy was empty, and both Ike and his helper were inside the little office trying to keep warm beside an iron stove. Ike was old and white-headed, and he was perfectly willing to talk—in fact, he talked too much. Business was bad, he said, very bad. Farmers didn't seem to be bringing in their plows; they'd all wait until the last minute and then want the whole kit and caboodle done at the same time. The trouble was there weren't too many horses moving during the winter. Lots of the people kept them in their stalls and only took them out once a week for exercise. No, Ike didn't know any place to catch on. It was always this way in the winter, but this was the worst in a good many years. What Ike had always thought he ought to do was shut up shop and go down South for the winter. Only reason he didn't was that it was too damned far. He had a daughter living in Tennessee, a daughter named Floribelle. Down South they trained the niggers to do their work for them. Floribelle had a few darkies of her own, and she was always telling about them in her letters. Got lazy and sassy sometimes, and you had to beat them to make them work.

After that, Richard saw doomsday written large above the Lebanon skies. He hated to get out on the west road because he hated to come back home like a dog with its tail between its legs. But if that was the way it had to be, then that was the way it had to be.

The quarter went that noon to a little eating place on Broadway, he got the value out of it—he had two pork chops and a big plate of boiled potatoes. He felt so good when he started on the west road that he thought he wouldn't have to eat again for a week.

THE ROAD led out of town right past the town graveyard, and now it would be only four or five miles before he was home. Curiously, the nearer he got, the more he realized that he didn't want to go home. It would be different if he were coming home rich, or comparatively rich, or at least with a new-found place in the world. But to be nothing, nobody, to have not a single copper in pocket—that was like gall in the mouth. He had been rich—he had once had a hundred dollars. And then, by the most unlikely chain of events, he had lost all of it. In a way he was responsible, of course; he had been weak and had permitted Fanny to tempt him. After that everything that had happened seemed inevitable and inescapable. Thinking back on Cincinnati, the only person he had really loved, or at least the person he had loved best, had been Asenath. Whether or not she was a good midwife he didn't know, but he was certain that she was a good woman. Rough, unkempt, unlovely—she was all of that. But Asenath seemed something like a rock—in her slumberous way she was unassailable. She stood at the edge of the ocean of life, and she was beaten by every wave, but she never flinched. He had never realized that anyone of the Berzinskis, anyone but Ruth, might show such good qualities.

It was early afternoon, but on the pike between Lebanon and Monroe there were few travelers. Richard had been waiting for someone to come along. It wasn't that he was too tired to walk the rest of the way, but his shoes were pretty well beaten, and the stitching might be loose because his feet seemed to be getting a bit wet. It wasn't too much, but he knew that as soon as he stopped they'd be cold. There was something of a shoemaker's outfit at home, a last and hammer and awls and thread with good beeswax on it, and he might be able to resew his shoes that night. And then again the thought struck him that he mightn't be there at all. His mother might not be glad to see him, and she might even turn him away from the door. Richard felt his mind churn with a hundred vagrant thoughts, all concerned with his mother. He loved her—in a way—but once he was past ten he had never loved her as he had loved his father. His father worked on and on and kept his mouth shut; his mother was always complaining, whether there was anything to complain about or not. There was nothing that ever suited her, nothing that was ever done right. She did keep a trim and tidy house—one could say that for her. And she was a good cook, and always cooked enough. But a person wanted a little more than that—he wanted peace, particularly when he was home. Nobody could ever seem to relax in the house, not at least for a very long time. His mother would sit in her rocker, even when they were all tired at night, and seem to be inventing things that in her mind had to be done immediately. The cat must be put out or the dog brought in, someone must go out to the well and draw a bucket of fresh water, there was wind coming in the west window and the curtains ought to be pulled across the glass. Both he and his father were used to her whims, and they jumped, of course, while all she did was sit by the fire, her knitting needles in her hands and her mind busy with a thousand things beside the knitting.

It was about three miles now, and then he'd have to turn north. What he really should do was not go home at all, just go on down to Shakertown and ask them to take him in for the night. For the night or maybe longer. They would—they were always feeding and sleeping travelers who were caught out on the roads. And they didn't seem to ask any pay—he had never heard of anyone paying them anything. All in all, they did seem to be a decent group of people. Not their ideas, of course; some of their ideas were downright foolish. But if a person could just let such thoughts go in one ear and out the other, then Shakertown might not be a bad place to live. Perhaps in time they'd even let people marry and live together like they should, and then Union Village would be a better place. With children running around, everybody would be happier, and then in time the forty-five hundred acres they owned might be added on to and the five hundred people in the Society might become five thousand. And then it would seem like a different world, with people getting along with each other and not trying all the time to cut each other's throats.

Curiously, the home fields and hills looked a lot better than anything else that he had seen. And the junipers, big and little junipers, so dark green and pointed in the snowy fields—he hadn't seen anything he liked quite as much as those. For some reason he couldn't understand, this was cedar country—cedars was what almost everybody called them. All the hills had cedars and the farmhouses were more often than not surrounded by them. They looked as if they ought to have some good use, unless their only real purpose was to add beauty. One thing he did know—birds liked them to build nests in. The branches were so sticky and prickly that big birds and cats would have a hard time getting through them.

It was only about a mile now, and he began to remember little pieces of poems and things he had once learned to make time go faster. Even the plot of *The Vicar of Wakefield*—he had brought the Vicar along home with him but he had left all his other books behind, and now he'd bet that he'd regret being so foolish. Up in Warren County there just weren't too many books to be had, and without books, or at least something to read, he was going to feel lonesome. He'd like to show Ruth how well he could read—he could read a lot better than she could now. Before, she had always been a little better than he was.

And there the little road turned off, the road home, from the Lebanon Pike up to the corduroy. Well, it wouldn't be long now. His father would be surprised—he'd hold out his big hand and shut his eyes. And his mother would have a number of things to say, maybe too many. The trouble with his mother was not that she talked too much, but that she talked sharp. She probably didn't mean half the things she said, not at least in the way they sounded. He could see the Berzinski cabin now, and when he noticed the dead chimneys his heart jumped. Ruth should be there, where she would be available. And it seemed strange to have all the Berzinskis gone—he had gotten used to having them around. Sometimes they could hear the Berzinskis shouting at each other clear up on the Robinson hill.

Strangely, he had an impulse to go into the Berzinski place, to see how the cabin looked without the family in it. What the place really needed was a warm fire to make the chimney smoke. He had a good notion to go in and build one. That way he could get warm before he blundered on home, and he could even take off his shoes and dry his feet out. It wouldn't take more than an hour or so, and then maybe he could wait until it was dark and suppertime before he went up the road. His father might even still be out in the barn, and they could go in together. That way his mother might not have to try to say anything too tart.

Richard swung the door and it creaked, but it did come open. It was dark in the cabin, but it wouldn't be dark if he could get a fire going. He felt for his block of matches—he still had them. Well, it wouldn't take long. And maybe then, sitting in front of her own fireplace, he could reason out what to do about Ruth.

IT WAS GETTING dark and it would be a lonesome and bitter night. Casting about for something to burn Richard inevitably discovered the straw doll propped into the window recess. He didn't recognize what it was at first; then when he did he fondled it for a while before he put it back in place. It had to be Ruth's, although he could not remember ever having seen it before. And there was plenty of straw on the floor to burn. Wood was a little harder to find, at least in the house cabin, but the second cabin with its old mangers and cow stalls supplied him with all he needed. Once the fire was going he swept the hearth with a handful of straw and lay in front of the flames. It was so luxurious lying there that he went to sleep—it seemed that he was the warmest he had been for days.

It was hard to know what time it was when he woke up, but when he did he canceled all thought of going home. The Robinsons were always in bed by eight, and it was probable that their fire was already banked up for the night. That wasn't the real reason he didn't go up, however; the real reason was that he was afraid. At any rate his homecoming could wait until morning. All he really wanted was something to eat, and he racked his mind to think of something. He finally did—it was probable that there would still be some hard field corn in the Berzinski cornfield. Walking that far in the dark and snow, however, was not to his mind, and he decided to starve until morning. It wasn't too bad just to lie in front of the fire, and before he went to sleep again he built it up bright. There was still part of an old stump in the fireplace and he had built his fire against it; now he more carefully arranged his wood so that he could make certain that the stump would catch. That way there would still be a glow in the morning, and the morning was sure to be so cold that he would need warmth more than anything else.

Lying there in the ashes and the lambent light that flickered across the cabin beams, Richard went over the whole thing in his mind again. There was no sense in staying at home, and he wouldn't unless he discovered his father in failing health. And if his father weren't, if it looked as if the Robinson place could run along without his being there, then the best thing would be to try to find work in one of the towns, in Monroe, Red Lion, Blue Ball. Or go even farther, to Franklin, Springboro, Middletown, or back down to Mason. Lebanon was a possibility, of course, but not for getting into one of the smithies. When things opened up—and they generally opened up in the spring—he might even catch on building something. Or he might get out on one of the farms, and that's what he'd rather do, but only if they paid cash money. That wouldn't solve the whole problem, however—money wouldn't. He'd have to learn if Ruth were really in Shakertown, and if she were, then he'd have to get her out of there. They wouldn't need much to start, maybe only enough to eat on. And there seemed to be no good reason why they shouldn't come right back here, to the miserable Berzinski acres. The place had evidently not been sold, and the probability was that the Berzinskis would never make any further claim to it. But first he'd have to go home, whether he wanted to or not. That was the key to the whole business: to go home and be convinced that he wasn't needed there. After that he'd go over to Shakertown and make some discreet inquiries. He winced a little when that thought crossed his mind—no one made discreet inquiries in Union Village. The place was sealed in silence, and from all anyone could see from the outside there were only dead people buried in the houses.

He fell asleep again soon after that, and woke up only when it began to be gray dawn. Outside there were a few faint sounds, the usual crackling noises of the winter forest trees, and what sounded like distant crows. There was even a bell, faint and far away, and that would have to be in Union Village. Why it was ringing he didn't know, but maybe it was only a sign that the new day had begun.

NO ONE CAME to the door, but old Mose, the red setter, ran up from the barn and leaped all over him. Richard rubbed his silky ears—Mose had always liked that. He knocked again, and finally had to give up—his mother, if she was in the house, had likely seen who stood at the door. Richard went out to the barn then, walking in the steps his father's boots made in the snow. His father was forking out the stalls, and he was so busy that he seemed not to know that Richard stood behind him. Richard had just about decided that his father didn't mean to recognize him when Abraham turned a little and almost jumped with fright. The next minute he was crying and had Richard securely tied in his arms. Neither of them said a word—they just stood there, the tears leaking down their cheeks and their arms around each other. "Your mother know you're home, son?" his father managed to get out.

"I was up at the house," Richard said. "Nobody came to the door. I thought maybe she was out here."

A funny look flickered across his father's face. "She don't hear so good no more," he said. "You had your breakfast?"

Richard didn't know whether to say yes or no. "Guess I could eat something," he said. "Last thing I had was out on the road."

Abraham started to lead the way to the house. "You just come on up," he invited. "How far'd you come this morning? Where you been all this time?"

"I been down in the City," said Richard. "I been learning how to be a blacksmith."

Abraham didn't seem to like that. "Ain't nothin' beats farmin'," he said. "See them geese over there? Your Ma hatched them out last year. Didn't lose any either, 'cept maybe one or two. But we got seven left."

Mose barked at the geese and they hissed at him, completely unafraid. Richard's eye took in the chickens too, and the fact that a couple of the ewes looked big. There'd be new lambs before long, probably before the cold was out of the ground. They never liked to have lambs born too early. It was the same with pigs, or almost the same. The trouble with nature was that she was too prodigal—she just seemed to break her neck to have all sorts of things born, in season or out of season.

They were at the house now, and Abraham swung the door. "Mamma," he started calling. "Where you at, Mamma?"

There was just no place for Mrs. Robinson to hide, and she had to appear. It seemed she had been sitting in front of the fireplace, and it seemed that she didn't know that Richard was around. But she didn't kiss him—the Robinsons almost never kissed anyone.

"He's been down in the City," Abraham announced. "Learnin' how to blacksmith. And he's hungry."

That made Mrs. Robinson start to the kitchen. "There ain't a plenty," she kept grumbling. "There's cornbread and some syrup left over from breakfast. And there's cold gravy."

"Couldn't you fry up something?" Abraham asked. "Cut a couple slices and I'll eat one too."

"Won't be too long till dinner," said Mrs. Robinson. "Why? Ain't he et yet this morning?"

Abraham didn't seem to want to agitate the matter and Richard kept on assuring both of them that the cornbread would do quite well.

They sat and looked at him, but it seemed that his mother never completely relaxed. Richard tried to ask questions just to get them to talk. Why had the Berzinskis pulled out? And just where did they go? Were they all gone, or were some of them still around? And what was going to happen to their land now? Would it be sold for taxes, or were the Shakers going to grab onto it? The upper field was all right—it drained pretty well and had always produced pretty good crops. That would be a good field for the Robinsons to have—it was almost right across from their place. Or didn't his father think that he wanted to take on any more land?

The answers when they came were noncommittal, although it seemed that old Abraham was talking with a halter on his tongue. Nobody knew why the Berzinskis had left or where they were gone. And he guessed the land would be sold for taxes—it was probable that the Berzinskis had never paid any taxes. No, he didn't think he wanted the place. And it was probable that the Shakers wouldn't want it either—it was getting a little far out for them since they generally tried to get all their acres to lie together.

"Never have figured out how they manage what all they got," Abraham said. "Must be something what all they believe."

"Person would have to be crazy to believe any of it," said Richard's mother vehemently. "All that shakin' and falutin' around don't make no sense to nobody."

"They're real good farmers," said his father. "Ain't no better. Part of what they're farmin' right now was only an old cattail swamp. Drained it with ditches—that's what they done. Nothin' wrong with it now."

They sat. They sat and stared, and it seemed that no one could find anything to talk about. Richard told them about MacCready's place down near the waterfront, and then about the Red Star. He told them nothing about the Gillespies, and absolutely nothing about Mrs. Bentley. If they knew what was behind him in Cincinnati, they'd go straight through the roof.

"Guess maybe we better be thinkin' o' gettin' along on out," said Abraham after a spell of silence. "I mean, if you want to come on out with me. I don't fork out the stalls every day, not anymore, but they get bad after a while."

Richard got up before his father did. It seemed strange not to be master of himself, to be waiting upon the wills of other people, even if they did happen to be his father and mother. And it was quite apparent that his mother was still angry. It was after they were out in the barn, however, that his father came straight to the point. "You fixin' to stay on a while here or not?" he asked bluntly. "What do you have in mind?"

Richard didn't really know what he had in mind, but he thought it best not to say so. "I guess maybe for a while," he said. "Maybe in a little while we could begin to think about plowing."

Abraham only whistled at that. "Not for a long time yet," he said. "Can't trust March. Won't be till April at the earliest. Why? You itchin' to get your hands on a plow?"

"I guess I could help. If I'm still here."

What he wanted to ask was if his father knew anything about Ruth, but it seemed a touchy subject. He twisted it around in his mind, but there was no way he knew to be indirect about the question, and finally he just blurted it out. "You don't know what happened to Ruth, do you?" he asked directly. "Ruth Berzinski?"

That made his father uneasy. "You know she went Shaker, don't you?" he asked. "Don't know why, but that's what she done."

"She still over in Union Village?"

Abraham just shook his head at that. "All I know is that Mamma said she come to the back door one day some months back. Had on her Shaker clothes, but she wasn't wearin' any cap."

"What did she want?"

"Wanted to know if she knowed anything about you," said his father. "I guess Mamma didn't treat her very well. Told me she sent her away without tellin' her anything."

"She didn't have anything to tell," said Richard as quietly as he could. He wasn't really quiet—his heart was racing. If Ruth had dared ask his mother anything, then Ruth desperately wanted to know what had become of him.

"Maybe I'll just mosey on over there this afternoon," he said after what was a long pause.

"Over where?"

"Shakertown. She wants to see me, and I want to see her."

Abraham just shook his head. "Never find her," he said. "If she's over there in one of them big houses, only the angels would know how to find her. And maybe she ain't there at all anymore."

They changed the subject after that, and in two minutes they weren't talking. The stalls were cleaned out and the horses petted—it was still old Nellie and Jack in the stalls. And before they left the barn Richard looked around. Everything seemed shipshape—the harness had been oiled and was hanging on its proper pegs, the plow and harrow were shiny, and there was plenty of clover hay in the mow. Better yet, there was a large crib full of corn out in the barn-yard, and the rats hadn't been able to get at too much of it. It seemed that the Robinson place was prosperous, about as prosper-ous as it had ever been.

That was the way Richard thought it should be—that was the way he wanted it.

IT WAS HARD walking in the winter woods because the snows were deep and unbroken, save for the scrawls of animal tracks. Under the great trees the shadows were blue and sometimes violet, and the old raspberry canes were definitely purple. Richard took his time—he almost had to take his time, because he was continually floundering. He had thought of going around by the road, but this was the shorter way, and he didn't want to go around by the road. The path to Union Village, the only path they had ever used, led through the woods, and on through Jehovah's Chosen Square, and this was probably the way Ruth had come when she went there.

But today Jehovah's Chosen Square looked deserted by both man and God—it lay sepulchrally white except for the beech leaves that the winds had scattered like a mosaic over the snow. Richard plowed on, unafraid of being discovered. Now that he had had a good dinner, his muscles felt taut again, and he was ready to chal-lenge the world. What he'd do in Union Village, once he got there, he had no idea, since no rational thought entered his mind. It would be futile to ask for Ruth directly. He thought of a subterfuge, of going to each of the big houses in turn and saying that he had a mes-sage for Sister Ruth. Then, if there were any Ruths, they'd probably ask Ruth who, and he'd manage to get out something that sounded a little like Berzinski. And if they asked further and inquired who the message was from, he'd say Asenath. If that didn't get results, then he didn't know what would.

It got no results at the North Family—that was the big brick house that was first in his path. The man who met him right inside the front door took him to somebody called an Elder, and the Elder only shook his head and led the way to a little office at the front of the building. Once there, he got out some sort of ledger and ran his fingers down the names written in it. "I don't know Sister Ruth," he said finally. "What you should do is ask at the main office. You know where that is?"

Richard didn't, and the Elder directed him: the office that was occupied by the Trustees was right down in the middle of the village. He should ask again when he got down there.

Richard meant to, but on the way down he had to pass a good many of the shops, and when he came to the blacksmith shop he turned in. There was a sprinkling of men and boys inside the open doors, some of them farmers who were paying to have their horses shod. And the blacksmiths themselves didn't look like Shakers—they all had on good leather aprons and only one of them wore a winter Shaker hat. Richard made himself at home. It was a good shop—he saw that at once, three forges, clean floors, more tools than a person could shake a stick at. The blacksmiths seemed to know their business too—they wasted no time. One of them was making hinges, evidently for some kind of shed or cow barn, and he curled the metal and hammered the parts together so easily that it looked like baby work. It wasn't baby work—Richard knew that much. He stayed there a long time watching the fellow, and at last the man looked up and smiled. "Think you might be able to do it?" he asked provocatively. He was surprised when Richard answered, "Know I can. That's what I been doing."

After that it seemed there was a bit of camaraderie between them, and when Richard asked, the man actually told him his name. Just John Runkle, nothing fancy like Brother John Runkle. John had his sleeves rolled up to his elbows, and his muscles looked as hard as rock. Richard wanted to ask him questions, but didn't know how. There was no sense in asking him if he knew where Ruth was. Runkle very likely didn't know where his own wife was.

"Guess there wouldn't be any chance of catching on here," Richard finally ventured. "I mean, doing what you're doing?"

Runkle looked up at that and smiled. "You don't belong to the United Society, do you?"

"Not yet," said Richard.

"Thinking of joining?"

That was a hard question to answer, and Richard hesitated. "That's what I might do if I could get in here," he finally lied. "Guess maybe you got all you need. I mean blacksmiths."

Runkle only smiled again. "You come up just as soon as you join," he suggested. "Tell the Elders that's what you can do best."

"What Family you live in?"

"Center," said John Runkle. "Nearest the shop."

"You don't know Sister Ruth Berzinski, do you?"

At that Runkle only shook his head and went back to his hammering. "There's Sister Ruth Nordhoff," he said finally. "She wouldn't be the one, would she?"

Richard shook his head, and when Runkle got busy again, he blundered back out into the light. But he did stop at the Center and ask, and the Elder there did the same thing, looked up the name in a book where he seemed to have everything written down in order. There was no Sister Ruth except the one whose last name was Nordhoff.

Richard went to the Brick House next, then to the South. That left the Hill Families, the Square, and those that were on the south pike. There was only one big house down there, although there were some other smaller Shaker houses. Richard knew that they were called Gathering Orders, although he didn't know what that meant.

He was somewhat upset when he went back home the same way he had come. He'd find her—if she was in Union Village he'd find her, although it looked now as if it might take a long time. He might even go over and join the Society for a while. He would in a minute if they paid cash money—he'd like smithing in the big blacksmith shop where everything was in apple-pie order. But it would be silly to do that if he would finally have to leave without a cent in his pockets. It began to look as if there was just no way out of his dilemma except to go to one of the nearby towns and see if he could find work.

But in doing that he would never find Ruth.

AND THERE the matter stuck.

Richard marveled at how easy it was for him to pick up the daily round of activities again. He gathered eggs and milked cows, curried and fed the horses, even threw grain to the chickens and geese. Once a week he swept the floors—there were a few rag rugs scattered around, particularly the large one in front of the fireplace, and they were hard to clean. He even helped his mother with the dishes, although she would not trust him to wash them. Somehow the days wore through, what with running up to the attic for something his mother suddenly remembered and had to have immediately, running out to the barnyard a dozen times a day, splitting wood for the fire, shoveling off the walks whenever there was another snow, and getting up from his chair many times at night to pull the curtains, hunt the big needle, find the scissors, or almost anything else. If there was one thing certain, it was that Mrs. Robinson's kind was forever busy. One could tell by the way she knit her brows, but when she also took off her eyeglasses she had come to sudden resolution. "Richard, get up and get me the big butcher knife," she would suddenly demand. "Not the little one, the big one. Out in the second drawer. I can tell from right here that that begonia needs to have its soil dug up again. It's so tight the plant can't grow."

The food was good, and it was plentiful. One thing neither of them had to do for Mrs. Robinson was cook—she simply would not tolerate either one of them messing around in her kitchen. "Got to eat a peck o' dirt before you die, but I don't want it to be dirty dirt," she would generally say. "You been out in the barn." Or, apropos of nothing, she would suddenly bawl out, "That water bucket needs to be filled again." And if either Richard or his father would remark that he had just filled it a half hour ago, she was sure to come back with "That last water had scum on it." But the food was good, very good, and the smokehouse was still half filled. Richard counted the items one day: there were still six hams, probably as many sides of bacon, some slabs of salt side that were frozen stiff, and, of all things, a quarter of beef. Since they never butchered any of their own cattle, Richard knew that his father must have traded for the quarter, probably with the Taylors, who lived up the road a mile or so. He wondered why his father and mother had never cut into the beef, but when he examined the quarter one day he had his answer. It was frozen so hard that it would have taken a big ax to break into it. So they ate pancakes and corn cakes, sausage and more pancakes, sauerkraut and smoked side, hominy and hawg, and endless loaves of bread. There was always honey for breakfast, their own honey, and Richard remembered that there had always been honey. It was good with biscuits, little round, flat, hard biscuits that had a habit of appearing miraculously. If there was any trouble with their meals, it was that they simply ate, without the least attempt at conversation. It was only "Gimme a little more of that sausage, Ma" or "Pass the beans down this way again." The beans were always brown beans, and it was always a late summer task to shell them out and hang them up in cloth bags. If there was one thing that his mother watched, it was that she'd never be short of beans. She always complained about them—they weren't the same kind of beans they had had down in Virginia when she was a girl, but it was quite apparent from her eating that she found no fault in them.

It was best at night, after the big lamp was lighted and it was getting on towards eight. Old Abraham always got up and brought the Bible from the table in the corner then, and he could always find the place where he had left off the night before. He was reading Isaiah at night now, and he read very well, not in the least the way he talked. Looking at his gray head every night, Richard thought many things. One, and the most agonizing, was that his father was getting old—he had been fifty-four his last birthday. And that meant that his mother was getting old too—she was just a year younger than his father. They both showed it. Their hair was gray, and sometimes white in patches, and their faces had lines that would never be eradicated. People did live to be a whole lot older than that, of course; sometimes way up into their sixties, and even seventies. But it wasn't usual for folks who had had to work hard all their lives. First the back would give out, and then the legs, and finally a person wouldn't be able to see to do anything anymore, even with good store-bought glasses. And by thirty or forty his teeth would be gone. Happily Richard's father and mother had kept some of their teeth— they could both still bite an apple, and they both had at least one good jaw to chew on.

His father and mother always sat in the two maple rockers, one on either side of the fire, and the cat would always be at his mother's feet, and old Mose at his father's. And then his father would find the place, and clear his throat before he began, and when he did wonder would begin to fill all the room. "Sing, O barren, thou that didst not travail with child," his father would read, his voice full and rich as if he himself might be some old Hebrew priest. And it was better when he came to a good passage, because then he would always take a deep breath and try to make his voice even stronger. "Fear not, for thou shalt not be ashamed; neither be thou confounded, for thou shalt not be put to shame, for thou shalt forget the shame of thy youth, and the reproach of thy widowhood shalt thou remember no more." His father would pause after a passage like that and look over his eyeglasses at both of them before he went on. He always made Richard feel uneasy. Mrs. Robinson, however, kept on knitting or whatever she was doing; she said that the Lord wouldn't mind because He had said He didn't like idle hands.

Once in a while after that they'd repeat the creed, all of them mumbling, which was a godsend to Richard because he really didn't know it very well. He couldn't understand it either, and he didn't dare ask either his father or mother what it really meant. It had three parts: one for the Father, one for the Son, and one for the Holy Ghost, who were said to be three persons in one. That had confused Richard from earliest childhood. There was just no way to be three persons in one. But when one was talking about religion, one didn't ask questions.

Ordinarily, though, they just said the Lord's Prayer after the Bible reading. And then somebody would put out the cat, except in the worst days of winter, and someone would bank the fire. Mrs. Robinson never did any chores—it was enough for her to fold up her handiwork and put it on the table in the corner. It went right on top the Bible, and that's where it had gone for more than twenty years.

Richard had to sleep in the one little room upstairs. It was icy cold, and in summer it was sometimes miserably hot. It had no window, but the frost knew ways to come in through the cedar shakes, and when the wind was blowing hard there might be a sift of snow on the floor. But the chimney went right past the head of the bed, and the chimney ordinarily helped to moderate the temperature. At any rate, there were enough covers, even a goosedown quilt. Once he got warm, Richard didn't mind if it was zero outside. And it was sometimes zero, sometimes even worse than zero.

All in all, it was a good life, really the only life he had ever gotten used to. Now, however, it seemed something was lacking; he was torn so badly inside that he couldn't really take pleasure in anything. And he was letting day after day go by, and really doing nothing. From the looks his mother gave him, and from the way she ordered him around, he knew that she thought she had the upper hand again. She might even think that he had forgotten about Ruth. He hadn't forgotten, and he never would. It was maddening to think that she was over in Union Village, just about a mile away from him. And it was more maddening to know that if he found her, he wouldn't be able to offer her anything. There was but one conclusion: he'd have to get out again, and look for a job. Then, when he had some money in his pocket, Ruth and he might be able to start out together.

HE TOLD his father what he meant to do, and he knew that his father would tell his mother. Richard realized that he had when his mother got frostier again, but he pretended not to notice. After all, he wasn't going far, not clear on down to the City this time. He tried Monroe, and there was nothing there. In Blue Ball the only shop he found was that of a German shoemaker. Red Lion was little better: it had a tavern and a church and not much more than that. He'd have to go farther, probably to one of the larger towns. At least he wasn't starving poor any longer—his mother made no protest when he told her that he'd like to take some bread and meat with him. He did have to walk, however; his father didn't want anything to happen to Jack or Nellie, since he said he couldn't replace either of them. That was the simple truth—he couldn't.

Then one day there was Franklin, sitting on the Miami River and the new canal. It had the usual inn, and a good many shops, maybe six or seven of them. Richard found the blacksmith's without any trouble, and the old fellow even consented to talk a while. He couldn't hire anybody on—he didn't have enough trade for that. Sometimes, though, he got busy, generally on Saturday mornings. He wouldn't mind turning over a quarter dollar or two if Richard wanted to come in on Saturday mornings and help him out. Richard only shook his head after that and said he lived too far away. "Tell you what you do," said the old fellow as he was going out the door. "You go on down the street a piece until you come to Whitney's. Thorpe Whitney. He's got a sign out in front with his name on it."

"What's he do?"

"Does ever' dam' thing. Buys and sells anythin' there is to buy and sell. Got the place stuffed so full you can't even get in through the door."

Richard waved good-bye and went on down the street. There

were some good brick houses, and some women out sweeping porches who looked sniffles at him, but he saw no sign that said anything about Whitney on it. He tried to ask a sour-faced woman with a shawl over her head, but all she did was turn back towards her house. "Don't need no tramps around," he heard her say. And then, "Go on back where you come from."

Richard didn't—he kept looking for Whitney's. When he found it, he discovered it was nothing but a little yellow brick building with some sort of wood house that seemed to be tacked on behind it. There was a big cedar tree in the front yard, and the sign was hanging from a limb of the cedar tree. "Everything Bought and Sold," the sign read, and under it the name Thorpe Whitney. The words were hardly legible; they looked as if they had been burned into the wood.

Richard got the door open finally and had to wedge his way inside. As the old man in the blacksmith shop had told him, there was everything for sale in Whitney's. Washbowls and pitchers, a raft of old furniture, some of it with the legs knocked off, buckets, leather bags, harness and bridles, scythes and hay rakes, a miscellaneous assembly of knives, forks, and spoons, hair ribbons, shawls and bonnets, jars of goose grease and camphor, bunches of herbs, even withered looking geraniums hanging upside down. Richard dared hardly move, really dared hardly breathe. The whole tumble-jumble looked like it would crash down to the floor if anyone so much as touched it. He didn't touch anything, but he did manage to wedge himself in from the door. There was nobody in attendance, and it seemed there would be no one in attendance, for no one had answered the little bell over the door that he had tripped when he entered. There were voices, however, or at least one voice that was coming from somewhere in the shop. The girl—it sounded like a girl—was singing, and she had a good voice. Richard waited, and whistled. The girl kept on singing. Finally he went back to the door and rang the bell with his fingers. He made it tinkle a long time.

That brought her, and she seemed to know the shop so well that she didn't have the least bit of trouble walking through the aisle. "Didn't know you were in here," she said, and laughed. "What you want? Looking for something particular or just want to look around?"

She staggered Richard—she was so efficient that he didn't know what to say. She was a big girl, and she was really pretty, her hair done up and her eyes as clean as if they had been washed in morning dew. He thought he had never seen a prettier girl in the whole world.

"Well, you want anything?"

But this time she laughed, as if she knew he was a greenhorn.

"I was looking for whoever owns the shop," said Richard. "You don't own it, do you?"

"Might as well own it," the girl said. "Leastway, I'm the only one who's ever here. What do you want?"

Richard decided he might as well tell her. "What I'm really lookin' for's a job," he said. "I don't suppose there'd be anything like that around here."

"There was, I'd have it," said the girl. "What kind of job you want?"

"I'm a blacksmith," said Richard. "Learned down in Cincinnati. I can shoe horses about as well as anybody."

The girl laughed at him again, and didn't seem in the least embarrassed. "Where you from?" she asked suddenly. "Don't come from around here, do you?"

Richard didn't know whether to tell her or not.

"You wouldn't know where it is," he said. "I lived on a farm all my life. Except when I was down in the City. It's way down in the country. Near Shakertown."

After that the girl just looked at him for a long time.

"Wish I could forget it," she said. "I was in the Shakers almost all of the year before last. Finally couldn't stand it any more and had to run away. And I'm damn glad I did."

Richard was shocked at her swearing.

"I don't suppose you knew Ruth while you were there?" he half asked.

At that the girl seemed to stiffen a little bit. "What Ruth?" she asked. "What was her last name?"

"Her name was Berzinski, but she didn't look like no foreigner. She wasn't as big as you."

The girl just stood and stared at him. "My Gawd!" she said finally. "I never thought I'd ever set eyes on you. Ruth told me all about you. She wasn't very happy down there and she thought you'd come back. You never did."

This time it was Richard's turn to stand and stare. "I was over there a couple weeks ago," he said. "In Shakertown. Nobody knew anything about her, nobody I asked. Is she still there?"

The girl made a gesture with her hands. "Not if she's got good sense she ain't," she said. "I was Ruth's best friend. I'm Clema Porter. I wanted her to run away with me when I run, but she wouldn't do it. She acted like she was afraid, but I think now she was really waiting for you. But she wasn't very happy."

"How long ago? I mean, when was it you ran away?"

"Way back before Christmas last year," said Clema. "We were in what they called the Gathering Order. You know where that is?"

"Know about where it is."

"It's the one for women, not the one for men. Called the West Frame. On the south road, the one that goes over to Monroe. My Gawd, how I hate Monroe. I almost froze to death there the night I run away. Had to sleep in a barn."

Richard fooled with a couple old horsewhips that had been threaded through the neck of a big brown jug. "You think she's still there then?" he finally asked.

"I don't think anything," said Clema. "Only I think if you've got good sense you'll get down there and get her out of that damned house. There's an old goat named Samantha runs it. She don't like Ruth. She didn't like me either. Ruth and I were just alike. We couldn't stand all that goody stuff."

Richard didn't know how to leave, and took a long time doing it. Clema at last got him to the door, where he stood ringing the bell. "You tell her about me," Clema kept saying. "She thought I was a fool for running away, but I told her Uncle Thorpe ain't so bad when he's not drunk. That ain't often, but he does manage to come to his senses once in a while. I wanted her to come right here with me."

Richard finally got out of the store, although Clema insisted on shaking his hand before he left. He knew by that that she wasn't a real lady. But she was a nice girl, a girl he thought he could get to like an awful lot. One thing was certain—Clema wouldn't put up with any nonsense.

ON THE WAY back from Franklin that afternoon it started to rain, and it was a dreary, oppressive rain that ate into Richard's very soul.

His clothing was soaked in no time, his shoes began to be heavy with mud, and the rain was so cold that it penetrated to his very skin. Curiously, there was no one and nothing on the road; it seemed that all men and beasts had read the weather signs, and retreated indoors. Here and there Richard passed a farmhouse over which gray smoke was bending down across the roof, and once or twice there was some sort of miserable roadside tree or shed that offered a moment's respite. But there were no two ways about it—the way to get home, eventually, was simply to plod on. One thing was certain: there would be no visiting in Shakertown that day. It might be just as well—it would get dark early, and it seemed to him that the time to ask after Ruth would be in the morning. Well, he would go on home and travel around to Union Village the next day. By that time his clothes would have had a chance to dry by the house fire.

He reckoned without his mother, and his mother, when he finally came in through the back door, seemed to be upset. "Don't know where you think you been, but you took your good-natured time about it," she accosted him the moment he came through the door. "We don't have such fancy ways here at home. When there's work to be done, there's work to be done, and there ain't nothing to do but do it." And with that she almost slammed the potatoes she had been carrying in her apron down on the table. As was inevitable, they rolled, and a good half dozen of them fell on the kitchen floorboards.

Richard said nothing for a moment, and then he asked, "Where's Papa? He out in the barn?"

"Generally is at this time o' day, ain't he?'

Richard went back out, although the little rest had made him feel stiff. All the way home he had thought only of getting in by the fire, but that could wait. As his mother had indicated, when there was work to be done, it had to be done.

His father, as always, greeted him with a fugitive smile. "Got ever' thin' done but feedin' and beddin' down," he said. "Maybe you better give Nellie and Jack some oats as well as corn. Feels like it's goin' to get chilly."

Richard did. After that he grabbed the big milk pail and started back for the house, leaving the task of shutting the barn doors to his father. And once in the house again he avoided his mother and built up the fire. He took off as much as he decently dared and hung the wet coat and woolen shirt on the backs of hickory straight chairs that he brought over to the fire. That done, he sat on the hearth and managed to get his boots off. It was then he noticed, ruefully, that he had made tracks clean across the room, and likely across the kitchen as well. He'd have to wipe those up, just as soon as he got a chance.

The rain turned to ice while they were eating supper, and although it was black dark out they could imagine that everything was casing hard. They'd likely have to have hot water to pour down the well in the morning—they might even have to pour hot water over the handle of the pump to get it thawed. Even the barn doors might be frozen shut. But in a way it was pleasant to hear the sleet outside—it gave them an added sense of security within. It was a good supper, hot boiled eggs and fried potatoes, with what was left over from the dried apple cobbler they had had the night before. A person could say anything he wanted to say about the Robinsons, but nobody could say that they didn't set a good table. Richard realized again that his mother was some kind of magician in getting things together. She could whip up almost anything out of a little flour, grease, and sugar, and her jar of yeast was always fermenting on the kitchen shelf. Every week she added a little potato water to it, and every week there was more than enough for Saturday's baking. And down in their dirt cellar they still had plenty of almost everything left, and it was near the end of winter. There were cabbage heads down there and a half bin of potatoes, and there were even mounds of turnips and wrinkled beets. However, Richard had noticed in the kitchen that they'd need another barrel of flour before long. And the sugar barrel was no more than a fourth filled. They could get the flour they needed from the Shaker mill but it would be more troublesome to get the sugar. They might have to go clear to Lebanon after that.

"Well, did you?" Richard heard his mother ask half angrily, and realized suddenly that he had been daydreaming.

"Did I what?" he had to ask.

"You'd pay attention once in a while, you'd know what I was talking about," she said, and broke a piece of bread into her potato grease. "Get a job anywhere? Just what I asked?"

Richard caught the hint of displeasure in her tone. "I went to Franklin," he said. "They didn't need no blacksmith up there. It was the same as Lebanon and Monroe and Red Lion."

"You don't think people have been sitting around and waiting until you got there, do you?"

Richard mopped up his own greasy plate—it was a rule in the family. "There ought to be somewheres I could catch on," he said dismally.

At that old Abraham lifted his bushy gray eyebrows. "You don't have to," he said. "You can stay on right here. There's plenty to be done around the farm, and it'll be more than we can take care of in spring. I'll let you have a calf, a few pigs, and sheep for your own."

It was almost a generous offer, and Richard knew it, but it wasn't exactly what he wanted or needed. The animals would mature finally, and he'd be free to sell them and keep the money, but it wouldn't be much money. Not enough.

"What I really need's a place of my own," he said finally. "It wouldn't have to be a lot. Even the Berzinski place would be all right."

"Beggars can't be choosers," said his mother calmly, and got up to bring over the coffee pot.

Richard took no umbrage at her remark. It was a well-known fact that beggars couldn't be choosers, and he might have said the words himself.

"What I need is a way of getting a start in life," he said. "Maybe in a year or two I ought to get married, and I can't without having a little bit of money. That's what other people do. Get married, I mean."

His father slowly stirred his coffee with the handle of his table knife. "I was past thirty," he said. "And so was your mother. You don't have to get married just as soon as you come of age. There ain't no law you do."

"Thirty-two when you was born," said his mother. "Young folks was different in those days. Then didn't anything come easy."

Richard decided it was fruitless to quarrel. It was a well-known fact that both his father and mother had worked too many years at home—they had always moralized about it. And when they finally started, they had had next to nothing. Even his baby crib had been nothing but an old tin foot basin—at least, that was what they had always told him. It might have been the way of the world then, but he frankly didn't think he could be satisfied with it now. And he couldn't be satisfied with little more than cornpone every meal, as they said they had been.

They all cleaned up the supper mess together, and after that it was almost time to read the Bible. But that night old Abraham didn't seem to have as much conviction in his voice, and Isaiah sounded somewhat dreary. Happily they only repeated the Lord's Prayer, and that Richard could say. It was not a night to struggle with the Creed.

THE WOMAN who came to the front door of the West Frame was tall and scrawny, and she stood there in a Shaker cap staring at him with gimlet eyes. Richard thought he had never seen a less well-favored woman in his life. She didn't have curves in the right places—she looked as if she might have been shaped out of a thick board.

"I've got a message from Cincinnati for Ruth Berzinski," Richard said, and tried to make his voice very casual so that the woman wouldn't get suspicious.

The woman asked who as if she hadn't heard, and Richard repeated his exact words. After that she just stood and stared a while before making up her mind. "You'd better wait," she said finally, and shut the door in his face.

A long five minutes passed, and then finally there were sounds on the other side of the door. This time it was a big woman who looked like she was made out of dough. She had tiny pig eyes under her Shaker cap, and almost no nose or chin. And her look was not investigative, but seemed downright accusing. "Maybe I didn't hear right, but I don't know what you want," she said. "We don't buy nothing from peddlers."

"I want to see Ruth Berzinski," said Richard. "I've got a message for her."

The woman seemed to hesitate a long time. She had on a white muslin apron over her gray Shaker dress, and she reached down and wrapped her hands in the apron as if she were trying to hide them.

"What's the message?" she asked finally.

Richard was a little nettled, but tried hard not to show his mood.

"I wasn't supposed to tell no one but Ruth," he said. "It's a family message."

"Who from?"

"Her sister Asenath," said Richard.

"She ain't here no more," said the woman. "The Berzinskis have all gone away." And with that she started to swing the door shut, as if that ended the matter. Richard had anticipated the action and had his big foot in the door. Once she noticed that, Samantha seemed not to know what to do.

"I met her down in Cincinnati," said Richard. "Asenath, I mean. She told me to tell Ruth just as soon as I got home."

Samantha just stood and stared. "I don't even know who you are," she said. "For all I know you just made it all up."

Richard stared back at her, but if he thought he could daunt Samantha he was badly mistaken. With the assurance of heaven, Samantha had nothing to fear on earth.

"You did, didn't you?" Samantha asked finally. "You just made it all up. And Ruth Berzinski ain't got no sister. Leastways none by the name of Asenath."

This time Richard shoved his shoulders through the crack in the door.

"You just go get her," he told Samantha. "You want to listen, you can. But I'm not supposed to tell nobody but Ruth."

Samantha held the door, and Richard couldn't get inside the house.

"Won't do you no good," said Samantha finally. "Ruth ain't here. I don't know who told you she was."

And with that she did manage to get the door closed, and Richard heard it being bolted. He stood on the porch for only a moment longer, long enough to notice the face in the window when Samantha pulled the curtain a little to see if he was gone.

In a way he was satisfied—the ugly old woman had known about Ruth, and that meant that Ruth had been at the West Frame, whether she was now or not. Richard decided on a subterfuge—there was a dense woods on the south side of the road, and he thought that by pretending to walk towards Lebanon and then cutting into the woods and coming back he would be able to see if anyone came into or out of the West Frame. He had forgotten the ice storm—it made the woods treacherous, even if it did sheathe most of the briers.

But the long vigil did him no good at all—the West Frame house was frozen in silence. No one went in, and no one came out, and the only sign of life was the tall curl of wood smoke over the roof. How long he waited there he didn't know, perhaps two hours at the least, and after that he was so cold that he just had to start back home. There was no sign of life on the Lebanon Pike as he walked east, save only the sound of singing from the Shaker schoolhouse. It seemed as if a dozen or so girls were warbling a two-part song, and it sounded pleasant. So pleasant that it really didn't seem to represent anything Shaker.

AFTER THAT Richard proved how little he knew about Shakers by haunting the south road. People who knew the Shakers better could have told him that throughout the winter the big houses became sepulchral, as if all the converts had been buried for the winter. Folks who knew better than that knew that the great Families were veritable beehives of activity. There was always work in plenty: seeds to sort and package, wool and flax to spin and weave, brooms and chairs to be made, candles to shape, caps and garments to be fitted together, summer straw hats that each man braided, boots and shoes to be made or mended. There were a hundred crafts, some of them very particular. In the East Family there was even a man who had some experience in drawing teeth, in the North one who made a specialty of shaping ox yokes. Sister Mercy Parmenter of the South was such a good hand at embroidery that she was not only tolerated but encouraged to fashion pigeons, pansies, and polka dots in every conceivable color, and some of her art work had even been sent back to the Eldresses in the First Ministry at Mount Lebanon, New York. Brother Garmen Streichofer could weave chair bottoms better than any others, although he had a hundred imitators. And Sister Amanda Small, who lived in the Brick, knew German, and was called in from time to time to decipher German letters.

However, to a person passing on the roads, there was no evidence of activity in the many Families at all. And Richard Robinson belonged to those who had been only road passers, and now, watching daily from his covert on the south pike, he saw nothing happening in the West Frame. There was one good reason: he always waited until the morning chores were done before he started for the woods, and by that time Ruth had walked east on the road and was safely in the school. Richard ordinarily went home when the sun had half completed its slant down the western sky, and so he passed the schoolhouse before Ruth started home. After two weeks of fruitless watching he would have sworn that no such person as Ruth Berzinski existed. He could just as well have taken oath that no one lived in the West Frame at all. There was little evidence that anyone did, although six or seven times Shaker teams and wagons had pulled into the lane that led around to the back of the house. What they brought Richard never knew, but he conjectured that it was some sort of supplies, because there were generally fewer barrels or boxes on the big wagons when they went back up to the Village.

Richard tried to be home every afternoon in time for the barn work, and he refused to answer his mother's questions, or answered them in such a way that she got little information. No, he wasn't looking for an outside job, not exactly. And yes, he was minding his own business. And he wasn't bothering anybody. No, he wasn't thinking of going away for good. Not exactly. No, he hadn't asked other farmers whether they had a cash job he could do. No, he hadn't even thought of setting up some sort of traveling blacksmith shop that could be pulled around to the farms. But it was a good idea. Or almost a good idea. The only trouble was that a blacksmith needed a lot more equipment than a scissors grinder or even a butcher.

So the days passed, and March grew old. By April most of the frost would be out of the ground, although there might be throwback days. But the spring flowers would begin to come up in the woods and the skunk cabbage would appear in the wet places. After that people would have to start looking for pokeberry shoots and dandelions, and it would be a little late to strip sassafras roots. The great flocks of wild pigeons would be flying again, sometimes so many of them that they would blacken the sky. And then the peach buds would start to swell, and the wild plums would bloom in their thickets. It would be time to hope again.

Time to hope again, but unless things changed there would be nothing to hope for. And once it was time to plow—and by April it would be high time in all but the wettest fields—there would be no chance to waste so many hours loitering in the thickets along the Lebanon Pike. It began to look as if that enterprise was fruitless anyway—one could wait a lifetime and not see the person he was waiting for.

Chapter 7

FROM THE SOUTH woods there had been no sign of Ruth. There had been no sign of anyone else in the West Frame either, neither the tall slatternly woman or the pudgy one made out of dough, nor anyone else who might be living there. On the third of April, a Thursday, Richard decided that he would stand his last vigil, and he did, fruitlessly. It was a good thing that he had so decided, because that night his mother raised a storm when she finally discovered that there were only a dozen quarts of flour left in the flour barrel with the baking to be done on Saturday. Richard had known that for days, and had wondered why his father, who was ordinarily so forehanded, had done nothing about the shortage. But that night at prayer time, and after the Creed, his father did announce that they would be going to the mill the next day. The mill meant the Shaker Mill; the flour there always seemed whiter and finer than other flours.

"Don't suppose they'd take a load of corn in exchange, do you?" his father asked, and Richard didn't realize for a moment that the question was addressed to him.

"Course they'll take a load of corn," said Mrs. Robinson defiantly.

"What d'you think, Richard?"

"Suppose they would," said Richard. "I don't know. I don't see why they shouldn't."

His father seemed lost in thought for a few moments. "I know the big miller over there," he said finally. "You know, Brother Benjamin, or whatever they call him. Trouble is, I ain't sure he's still there. Ever'thing will likely be all right unless one of them Elders is pokin' around."

Mrs. Robinson threw down her knitting. "Always borrowing trouble," she said. "Can't borrow it one place, you borrow it another. Keep on doing that an' you'll be dead afore your time."

"Well, they ain't no reason why they would take corn. They don't need any corn—they always have too much of it."

"You don't take them corn, what else you got to take? It's all you got—you'll take corn, or you'll stop eating white bread. It's just as simple as that."

They took corn, a whole wagon load full of the stuff, and that meant a lot of shoveling from the crib. The empty flour barrel stood in the front of the wagon bed, and Mrs. Robinson had seen to it that they dumped the last few quarts of flour into one of her big stone jars before they carried the barrel out. "You see to it that they bolt it fine," she kept admonishing. "You see to it they bolt it fine."

"Allays do, don't they?"

"Well, I don't want it like cornmeal. You keep your eyes open and see to it they bolt it fine."

It was a relief to get away from the house. It was a fine day, the water sluicers running, and the road difficult until they got down to the Lebanon Pike. After that there was more stone, and Jack and Nellie seemed to be able to draw better. At the Shaker schoolhouse it seemed to be the noon recess, and there were girls playing on one side of the yard and boys on the other. They all were running like young colts, and it was a joy to watch them. Richard had a momentary nostalgia—it had been fun to go to school when the days were good. Those kids were doing what he himself should be doing— learning. He had made all sorts of promises to himself, but ordinarily he was tired at night, and his father and mother didn't like to have the lamp or candles burning after they went to bed. But it had been weeks since he had read any print, and he was getting out of practice.

The road led north, past the South Family and the Center Families, and on to the cut off to the mills near the creek. Evidently the sawmill was operating because they could hear the rasp and chuckle of the machinery inside. And evidently it had been going for days, for there were stacks of rough lumber piled near the mill. It looked as if the Shakers were thinking about building again, perhaps some more big barns.

The grist mill lot was muddy, and there were three teams hitched to the rail along the platform. Abraham Robinson carefully backed in between two of the other wagons so that he could get right against the platform. After that there was nothing to do but mosey inside. Richard couldn't understand his father—old Abraham just took his place with the other fellows near the door and seemed to be content to stand watching. Richard thought his father should make a business of hunting up the miller, or at least communicate with somebody. The great stones kept turning around and the giant wooden arms and levers kept bending and unbending like big grasshoppers, and nobody seemed to be concerned in the least. Richard's practiced eye saw that the blacksmiths had been at work also—there were a good many iron contraptions that would require a pretty piece of work to turn out at any forge. Some of them looked almost too heavy to handle.

"Guess maybe you ought to tell somebody what we're here for," he suggested to his father, and when Abraham couldn't understand because of the noise, Richard shouted the same words at him. At that the big farmers all seemed to turn and stare for a moment. Richard stared back—he couldn't for the life of him figure that he had done anything wrong.

It seemed an eternity—and it must have been a full hour—before Abraham did move, and then it was only when he saw a squirrelly-looking fellow come out of what must be the office. Richard didn't know what was being said, and had to move over to find out. Once in a while his father or the floury little man would look back at the door and point, and then they'd turn back and go on talking. It didn't seem that they were quarreling, but there did seem to be some sort of disagreement. "Cost you a dollar," he heard the Shaker fellow say when he walked up. "Don't need any corn, not this year—not like a couple years back when we sent a whole passel to the Irish—but we'll take it. Even trade for the flour, but the grinding will cost you a dollar." And after that the fellow smiled, as if he were giving Richard's father a bargain.

His father took his time about answering. "Never cost a dollar before," Richard heard him say. "Don't know why the price has to go up. Never did before."

"Costs money to run the mill," said the Shaker, and took his white hat off his head. He was as bald as a stone, except for the tiny fringe of yellow hair over his ears. Richard thought he looked something like a dwarf, particularly when he smiled so that his lips came up to meet his nubbin of a nose and his eyes squinted.

"It's all water power," said Abraham Robinson. "Don't cost nothing to use water power. The good Lord gives you that."

The Shaker didn't seem to mind. "You make up your mind whether you want to do it that way," he said, and started to walk away. Abraham grabbed him. "I don't have no money with me," he had to confess. "Didn't bring none because I wasn't countin' on it's costin' a penny. Never did before."

That made the miller look quizzical. "Tell you what I'll do, Brother," he said finally. "I won't give you a full barrel."

"How much?"

At that the dwarf smiled again. "Maybe you better trust me," he said, and this time he did hurry off until he was completely lost behind the machinery.

Richard walked across the room and stared down at the water in the race tumbling over the heavy wheel. It was a pretty sight and it made him think of the many times he had come to the mill with his father before.

The man from Monroe got his flour and pulled out. After that the red-faced farmer in a broken straw hat pulled his team up and carried away a whole mess of coarse ground corn. Richard knew that the only thing it might be good for was chicken feed. The third farmer, a tall man with eyes as hard as agates, finally got fixed up— it seemed all he had wanted were two middle-sized sacks of meal. He might have had them for the asking an hour ago, if he had just been a little more forward.

Then, finally, it was their turn, and suddenly they were very busy. "Just pull your team around to the back of the mill and throw the corn in the crib," the dwarf directed. "Can you wedge the barrel out and put it on the platform, so's I can use it?"

Richard did, but it was a job because the corn had bound it tight into the corner.

"You want me to come back here after I shovel out the corn?"

"Yea, Brother," said the miller, and again his eyes sparkled. "Back in, same way you did before."

Richard's father didn't come back with him, but that was all right because they had only one scoop shovel. The corn didn't go into a crib after all; it went into some sort of wooden chute that carried it down under the mill. Richard couldn't see, but he figured there was a good tight room down there, probably so tight the rats couldn't get in.

It took most of a half hour, and by the time he brought the horses around to the platform again the barrel of flour had been rolled out and was waiting. It was full to the brim. Old Abraham stood beside it, and he seemed to be busy jawing with the dwarf, who was himself busy slapping at his long apron. "You say you don't understand it, and yet you keep on being Shaker," Richard heard his father say. "It don't make sense."

The dwarf didn't seem to be disturbed. "You don't know any

better," he came back evenly. "Makes sense to me to let the Elders worry about such things. They got a lot more book learning than I have."

"How do the Elders know?"

The miller looked hard after that. "Guess maybe you don't believe in divine inspiration," he said. "Guess maybe you don't even believe in God."

"I believe in God same as you do."

"Then maybe you don't believe in revelation."

"What revelation you talking about? I believe in the revelation of the Bible."

"Think God stopped acting way on back in the Bible, that's what you mean. Think He don't act now."

"Course He acts now," said Richard's father, and raised his voice. "All a man has to do is look out at his fields. Guess there's God in most everything that happens."

The miller nodded his head. "That's as far as you go," he said finally. "We go further. God sent down His son Jesus Christ, and then He sent down His daughter, Mother Ann. An' neither one o' them knew at first, but they heard God talking to them, an' then they did what they had to. That's all there is to it."

Abraham just stood shaking his head. "Don't make no sense to me atall," he said. "Don't make no sense atall."

"You think on it, Brother," said the dwarf. "Pray on it. And when you do, maybe the light will shine. And then you come around, and we'll make a place for you in one of the Families."

After that they got the flour in the wagon and covered it with a piece of burlap the miller had provided. But it was a lonesome ride back to the Village and down the pike to the south road because Abraham Robinson had his head down. He seemed to be thinking so hard that he didn't want to talk, and Richard wisely left him alone.

So they came to the Lebanon road and started east, and now they were both driving like wooden men, saying nothing to each other. And then Richard saw a woman come out of the schoolyard and start towards them, and there was something about the way she walked that made his heart jump. She was still too far away to recognize, and she was dressed in a long Shaker coat and had a dark bonnet on her head, but even at that distance Richard thought she was the right size and height to be Ruth. "You drive," he heard himself shout, and the next moment he had thrown the reins into his father's lap, and had jumped off the wagon and was running. He felt the hot tears lace his cheeks—it was Ruth—it had to be Ruth. And now it seemed she was running too, and when they met and threw their arms around each other they were both crying. How long they stood there in the road Richard didn't know, but he did know that he was not even aware that his father had driven way down the road. By the time he came to his senses and looked, Abraham Robinson was far down the road. It was too late to run and catch the wagon.

RUTH SAID she couldn't talk—somebody named Samantha would know if she didn't come home in time. Richard had wanted her to cut into the woods with him so that they would be safe from interlopers, but Ruth didn't want it that way. She said it would have to be some other way, but they thought of everything, and nothing would do. Ruth couldn't really come down and let herself out of the house after everyone had gone to bed—it was too risky, since there was always the chance that somebody in the Gathering Order wouldn't fall asleep. And Samantha had her own room on the ground floor. Nor could Richard very well come to the schoolhouse, either at noon, or after school was dismissed. What she proposed was perhaps bolder—she'd find a way to get away on Saturday and meet him in Jehovah's Chosen Square. In the afternoon, when there was a chance that the day would be warmest. And then they'd walk back into the woods together. No, she didn't know where her family had gone. Richard told her about Asenath, but wisely said no more than that Asenath had had a stand on market. Ruth had nothing to tell, nothing except that she had been teaching school because the old teacher was going to die.

And they looked at each other, and Richard pulled Ruth into a clump of elderberries at the side of the road. After that he took off her bonnet and cap, so that her black hair tumbled down over her shoulders. She didn't seem to mind. She kept looking at him with wide blue eyes, and he understood the question. He was too ashamed to try to answer it, at least right then. No, he hadn't been able to get together enough money. It would be even more difficult to tell her that he had had enough, and then had lost everything. And he wouldn't tell her about Fanny, not, at least, for a long time. And he'd never tell her about Mrs. Bentley. That episode was a bad dream; he could almost conjure himself into believing that it had never happened.

There was really not too much need to talk. "I love you so much, Richard," Ruth kept on saying. "I was afraid that you wouldn't ever come back. I love you so much."

Richard held her tight. "I love you so much too, Ruth," he said, and looked deep into her blue eyes.

"I was afraid you wouldn't ever come back."

Richard told her about Clema Porter in Franklin. And, that done, he told her about how he had come to the West Frame, and had been turned away at the door. And how he had watched for over two weeks from the south woods.

"I was in the schoolhouse every day," Ruth kept on saying. "I was in the schoolhouse all the time. I can read real good now. Did you ever hear of a writer named Washington Irving? I got his book. You'll like it, Richard."

Richard wasn't too sure. "I read a good bit down in Cincinnati," he said importantly. "Oliver Goldsmith. *The Vicar of Wakefield*. And I read the newspaper. They put out lots of them down there."

Ruth nodded her head. "I found a *Western Star*," she confessed. "Right on the road one day—it was laying right in the snow. I still got it."

Talk wasn't important, however, and after a time they stopped that nonsense and just held each other. "I went to your house," Ruth confessed once. "Your mother wouldn't let me in. But I couldn't stand it with the Shakers any longer and I wanted to know if you had come back home."

Richard nodded his head—his father had told him that. "She don't mean things," he said to defend his mother. "She's not really hard-hearted."

Ruth released herself from his arms at that. "She don't like me," she said, and this time her eyes blazed. "And I don't like her very much. Not any more."

Richard tried to get her to come back to his arms, but she wouldn't. "I've got to get home," she said, and corrected herself,

"I've got to get to the West Frame." And with that she started walking out of the little screen of elderberry bushes where they had found covert. Richard grabbed hold of her wrist and held her for a moment, but Ruth finally pulled away. "You can wait until Saturday," she said. "Right after noon—just as soon as I can get away."

"What if it rains or snows?"

Ruth smiled a little at that. "I'll be there no matter what the weather's doing," she promised. "You be there too."

And with that she was gone, and Richard watched her swinging down the road until she turned into the West Frame and was gone.

He didn't walk home that night—he was transported by angels. At least he could never afterwards remember walking home. All he remembered was that his mother met him at the door with a sour face. "Guess maybe you don't care whether your father ruptures himself getting the flour into the kitchen all by himself," she said angrily.

That brought Richard to his senses. "He get it in all right?" he asked.

"Of course he didn't get it in. It's still out in the wagon, and the wagon's in the barn. Can't let flour set out in the weather till it gets wet or moldy. You ought to know that much."

Richard hitched the team and brought the wagon to the back door. Even then it was a job getting the heavy barrel of flour into the kitchen, a worse job because the door frame was too narrow. However, the flour finally was pushed, dragged, and maneuvered into place. It was always a job, but they had struggled through it a dozen times before.

However, his mother did not recover her poise. All that night she sat stiff as a statue, and this time her hands were not busy with any needlework. She seemed to be staring straight out ahead of her, as if she was looking for the end of the world.

Chapter 8

IT WAS A gentle day, benign with sun. There was a prickle of leaves through all the trees, and on the border of the woodland there were in places bright blue flowers. Someone had turned a few sheep into the Chosen Square, and they were thinner and whiter than usual, for they must just have been sheared. Ruth stopped and watched a while, and when she stopped walking the woods was completely quiet, save now and then for the sharp stab of a redbird's call. Ruth listened hard, thinking that in the complete silence she might be able to hear Richard's feet sluffing through the leaves, but there was no such sound at all. Ruth was not dismayed. He would come—he said that he would come. But she had thought that he would be waiting for her.

Truly, in her heart she knew she needed him, and she hoped that he needed her as well. Not that she had been bitterly unhappy. She had been happy at times—it was a joy to teach the children, and she had learned most of their personal stories. Poor, defrauded little minds and bodies, they were being cheated of everything a child had a right to expect. Now there was nothing for them except the schoolroom, and despite Elder Phineas Riegel's mild protests, Ruth tried to keep it bright and cheerful for them. She had cut out birds and butterflies from whatever colored paper the Elder could supply and had pasted them right on the walls and window frames. Some of the Christmas rings were still hanging from nails—the girls had protested when she had told them that it was time to take the rings down. Ruth had agreed—it was a shame to take anything away from them. Now that the weather was warmer they were no longer so hideously muffled up in their heavy winter clothes, but their dresses were still far too long, and their shoes much too heavy to run in. Ruth had let them take the shoes off so they could run as children were expected to run. And that too the Elder had disapproved of, and he had laid his long finger along his long nose and shaken his head. Ruth had ignored him, as she most generally ignored him. In her opinion he was not a bad man; he was simply not a really good man. At least he did not satisfy her definition of good.

It had been hard to get through the winters, what with Samantha continually harping in the West Frame, and Elder Phineas coming in to the schoolroom almost every afternoon to try to convert her to the Shaker faith. They went round and around, and although Ruth couldn't use the big words he was forever using to confound her, nothing in her heart agreed that what he said was right. He was always talking about the blessing of Almighty God, and pointing to Union Village as proof. Ruth agreed—it did look like a blessing. But children were a blessing too, and in Ruth's mind Almighty God, the only kind of Almighty God she could understand, would want children to be born. And Elder Phineas was always referring to Mother, or sometimes Holy Mother. Ruth had been interested in what he had had to say about the woman whose name was Ann Lee, but it seemed he didn't know too much. She had been born in England, and she had married there, and had a family. Her children had been sick and had died. Her husband, her earthly husband, hadn't been much. And then, suddenly, it had come upon her that she was meant to save the world. Gradually she had begun to understand that she was really the female Christ, because God was both male and female. And then some people had believed her, and they had all come to America, and tried to settle in New York. But they had left there because they were mistreated and had gone up what was called the Hudson River until they found some acres they could settle on. They had called their place Mount Lebanon, and later some of them had gone off to other places in New England. One of the names was Canterbury, or something like that, and one Enfield. And then, a little later, but Mother Ann was dead by that time, the Shakers (for that's what people called them) saw what they called an "opening" in the West, and had sent out missionaries. That was when some farmer named Malcolm Worley had given them his farm on Turtle Creek, and then Richard McNemar, the preacher of the church there, had joined them, and after him most of the members of his congregation. After that they had branched out again, up in Ohio and down into Kentucky, although when they had tried to go into Indiana it seemed they had not been blessed. But that was the way Union Village had been started, and that was why it was here now. Only now it had more than four thousand acres, and had its big orchards and grainfields and everything.

Elder Phineas had told it all a dozen times over, and to his mind Union Village was proof positive that Almighty God had held His hand over the United Society and blessed it repeatedly. Or continually. Ruth wasn't quite so sure, but she was puzzled. She didn't think the world might be coming to an end, as the Elder seemed to believe, and she didn't think there should be an end of human families. But one thing was certain: most of the people in Union Village did seem to be able to get along without much worry. They got sick, of course, and they died. Ruth had seen the Shaker cemetery—Elder Phineas made a business of taking her up there one day when school was out. Nothing—nothing to mark the graves at all. The dead bodies were just wound in sheets and put into boxes and covered over in the ground, and after a few years it was hard to know just where the dead people lay. That didn't seem decent either, but it probably didn't matter. Only it seemed as if most other people did put up stones to mark the places. Ruth had seen the cemetery at Lebanon when the Families had made their visit to the world, and it had stones. It was even said that the daughter of Henry Clay was buried in one of the graves—she had died in Lebanon when the Senator was on his way back to Washington. Frankly, Ruth didn't quite know what that meant, but it seemed important because people talked about it. She had heard Henry Clay's name several times. It seemed that he had come from Kentucky, the same state as her father and mother, and he had made a business of having his own coach driven back and forth to Washington.

It was time for Richard—it was way past time for Richard. He couldn't have forgotten; something else must have delayed him. His mother, probably. Ruth decided to walk through the woods to meet him—she knew pretty well which way he'd come. And one place was as good as another, only she'd have to be certain that he didn't pass her.

And that made her wonder about a good many other things. Richard had gone away to get some money, and now it seemed he had no money. He had probably been careless and had it stolen.

They hadn't really had much chance to talk, but she'd find out today just what was the matter. Now that it was spring again, it was time for them to find a place so that they could get a start in life. By May things would have to be planted, both in the fields and garden. That is—if they could find a place with a garden. Fields were probably out of the question. So, for that matter, were gardens, or the shabbiest kind of house. Ruth thought of the Berzinski cabin, but she didn't like that idea. Not very much. There was good garden soil there, and if they just could get their hands on a horse and plow they'd likely be able to make ends meet. But what she really wanted was something new, something, at least, that was not too much stained with evil memories from the past. That was the trouble with her own home—she'd never be able to erase things from her mind that she wanted to forget. They could make the cabin livable, of course, and it had a good well. And—she reddened—it would be pleasant to know that there was a baby coming. No matter what the Shakers said. It couldn't be a sin. What Elder Phineas had always said was that it was living in the Adamic Order, which was inferior to Church Order. And as long as men and women just came together to have children it wasn't sin. Only that's the only time they could— to have children. Otherwise it was sin, the blackest kind of sin.

She stood still to listen—it seemed there had been some kind of sound in the woods. She heard, and saw, a red squirrel, and after that the flapping wings of a couple wild turkeys almost startled her out of her senses. But there it was again, a soft sliding sound, as if someone were walking. Ruth turned and ran in the direction of the sound. It was Richard—it had to be Richard; there was just no one else it could be on this golden day in April.

THEY HAD KISSED each other unashamedly—and more than once, they were so hungry for each other. And now they sat together under a giant beech, the sun rays slanting down through the new pinkish green leaves. Richard was telling of Cincinnati, and Ruth was having trouble keeping up with him. It seemed sometimes as if he were confused, couldn't rightly remember what had happened. He had worked in a blacksmith shop, for an old fellow named MacCready. And then he had worked in another blacksmith shop, for another old fellow named John Gillespie. And he had made two or three dollars a week, and had kept his money in a little stone jar that he buried under the dirt floor. It had counted up finally, until there were almost a hundred dollars. All silver dollars. And then something happened so that he had lost it all, and he hadn't a penny in his pocket when he started back home.

Ruth reached out her hand and patted his big muscular forearm. "It don't matter," she said. "It don't really matter. All it means is that we'll have to wait a little longer."

For some curious reason Richard had seemed to turn a bit red, as if he were blushing. Ruth reached up and kissed him again. "It don't matter," she said again. "I can go on teaching in the Shaker school. Only there won't be any school in just a little while. Soon as it's summer."

"I been trying to get a job," said Richard. "I don't know what's the matter. I'm a good blacksmith—I can do anything anybody else can."

They sat and stared out through the woods, neither one of them seeing anything. "What I don't understand," Ruth said at last, "is how you lost your money. Did somebody steal it?"

"No, nobody stole it."

"Then what happened to it?"

This time Richard seemed to be fiery red, and it seemed his tongue was tied. Ruth wondered what had happened to him.

"There's something I got to tell you," he said finally. "I didn't lose the money and it wasn't stole. I had to get married. That's where it went."

This time Ruth sat stunned. For a few seconds she tried to tell herself that she hadn't heard the words correctly. She could feel her heart racing; it seemed to be thumping so hard she thought she might faint.

"You never told me," she said at last, and her voice was very small. "Why did you have to get married?"

This time Richard blurted it all out. The second blacksmith had had a daughter named Fanny. And Fanny told him that she was going to have a baby, and so he had to marry her. And she had had the baby, and both of them had died. Asenath had been the midwife who delivered the baby and Asenath had done her best, but it hadn't been enough. And that was where the money had all gone.

They sat again, both of them speechless.

"Was it your baby?" Ruth asked at last.

"It wasn't my baby," said Richard fiercely. "It had red hair. Only she said it was my baby."

"Was there any reason she could say it was your baby?"

He pulled an old branch out of the leaves and started stripping off the twigs.

"I guess there was," he said miserably. "Sunday afternoon. It was one Sunday afternoon. She almost made me do it. But it wasn't my baby—my baby would have been born in March. This baby was born in February. That's the reason I know it wasn't mine."

Ruth got up then, and walked a little way off into the woods. She couldn't think—her mind seemed stunned, dead. This was the way it happened then; once out of sight, out of mind. And all the dreary months she had been waiting, and hoping, and assuring herself that Richard would be true to her and would come back for her as soon as he could. This was the way it happened. The Adamic Order. Or whatever Elder Phineas said was worse—she couldn't remember the name for it. And what was done could never be undone. He had come back all right, but he wasn't the same Richard. He didn't belong to her anymore—he belonged to some other woman. A woman who was dead.

Almost imperceptibly she started walking back in the direction of Union Village, without really knowing what she was doing. But when she came to her senses, she knew that that was what she had to do. It was the only way she could walk—Union Village was the only home she had. And probably the only home she could ever hope for. Elder Phineas had been after her for months to sign the Covenant, and that's probably what she'd have to do. And then, as soon as she did, Elder Phineas said that he would transfer her to the East Family, because it was nearest the schoolhouse. And then Sister Lena would die, and she'd be the only teacher, and that's the way she'd grow old, until finally it came her time to die.

Ruth stopped for a while in the center of Jehovah's Chosen Square. It all seemed so peaceful—the white sheep grazing on the fresh grass, the great wall of trees sealing the holy ground on all sides, the high clouds floating through the April sky. It would be like this through all the tomorrows—at least, that's the way she hoped it would be. She'd never have any babies of her own. Other people would have babies, probably lots of babies. And she'd help raise them, and teach them, and love them—and then they'd all go away from her, and after a time forget her. It seemed a shame, but there was just nothing she could do about it. Nothing at all.

RICHARD HAD expected Ruth to cry—that's what women were supposed to do. To cry as if her heart were broken, and then finally to subside and say that she forgave him. And it hadn't happened that way at all; she had simply acted stunned. And then she had gone away and stood under a tree for a while, before she finally crept off through the woods. He hadn't expected that at all. He had heard men say that no man could understand women. All the men he had known, generally farmers or fellows in the blacksmith shops, had acted as if women were, if not crazy, then irrational. It seemed they cried a lot and chewed the rag, and then generally wilted and were forgiving, even when they hadn't been offended. His mother wasn't exactly like that—she generally acted angry or morose. Almost as if she had eaten sour apples. But that was the reason he had liked Ruth—she hadn't been like his mother or Asenath or Mrs. Gillespie, or even Fanny. Ruth seemed to have good sense, to be long suffering and level-headed. For some strange reason, living with the Berzinskis hadn't hurt her—she hadn't been a real Berzinski. The sudden thought struck him that maybe she wasn't really a Berzinski—but that, of course, couldn't be true. She was a Berzinski all right, but some sort of a throwback. Sometimes calves or colts were like that—they seemed superior to either of their parents. Maybe people were the same way.

Walking back home that afternoon, through the day that had started well and no longer seemed bright, Richard wondered just what he was expected to do now. He couldn't very well go after her, at least not down to the West Frame. He might be able to wait for her at the schoolhouse. But there was a good chance that she wouldn't want to see him, that he was forever ruined in her eyes. That was why he hadn't said anything about Mrs. Bentley; if she knew that, she'd really turn against him. The trouble with women was that they just didn't understand men; they were supposed to, but they didn't. They expected men to be as pure as they were. But they were never tempted—they just didn't know what it was all about. All women wanted to do was have babies, and men had babies only as a consequence. That was the main difference between the sexes, and that's all there was to it.

Coming in from the old cornfield Richard noticed that his mother was already out in the yard. She generally wanted the chickens and geese fed early, no later than three, and it was perhaps after that time now. Well, her mouth would be full of stones, and they'd likely have nothing but fried mush for supper. And the moment she saw him Richard knew that his conjecture was true: his mother's face seemed to turn black. "High time," she said surlily. "Seems all you can do when there's work to be done is go gallivantin'. Don't seem to think your father might need you for something."

Richard went right past her and on up to the house. His father was sitting at the kitchen table drinking a cup of cold coffee. "Soodling at it," he always said, and no one knew where the word came from. But that's what his father always called it: "soodling."

"You want me for anything this afternoon?"

His father seemed surprised. "Don't know why I should," he said. "Ain't done nothin' myself. Guess maybe we better think about gettin' the plowin' done—that's all."

Richard knew the plow point would have to be sharpened again—it had battered against too many stones. It was getting a little late to take it over to the shop in Union Village today, but that's what they better do Monday morning. That is, unless his father had something else he thought needed doing a lot more.

"You know what I been thinking?" he asked his father. And went on immediately, "I been thinking about plowing up the Berzinski field. No reason why we shouldn't."

His father only shook his head. "No use gettin' into more trouble than we're in already," he said cryptically. "Don't belong to us, and we got no call to plow it."

"Maybe you ought to buy it," Richard suggested. "I mean the high field, the one right across from us. That's all we'd want."

His father didn't even answer that remark. Somehow the Berzinski place seemed poisoned, although the fields certainly hadn't been at fault for all the Berzinski doings. But that's the way people thought, no matter how irrationally.

"You don't mind, I'll take the plow over Monday morning," Richard said again, and again his father didn't answer.

Richard wondered about his mood, but he said nothing. Maybe

the two of them had had a quarrel, his father and mother. They never did quarrel, they never had quarreled, but that was no proof that they couldn't. And his mother hadn't been acting like herself. She had always been fiercely protective, fiercely defensive, but of late she had become belligerent, picking quarrels without excuse. It made living with her a bit difficult.

"There ain't nothing the matter with Mamma, is there?" Richard asked. "I mean, she ain't sick or anything?"

This time his father did raise his head. "Guess maybe she ain't feelin' quite as peart as she should," he said. "Says there's somethin' inside her that hurts. She don't know what it is."

And with that Abraham went back to soodling, and Richard went into the other room. The fire had almost died out on the hearth, and would have to be rekindled because it would likely turn cool by evening. Richard went back out to the woodpile and brought in a great armload of wood. The thought occurred to him that things would likely seem better after they had all had their supper and were settled in for the night. Perhaps everybody was just worrying too much without real reason to worry. It was curious in a way: his anxiety was that it might be hard for him to make up with Ruth, and their concern seemed to be fear that Ruth would come running after him. It was like an arithmetic problem that couldn't be solved anyway you tried it, by short division, long division, fractions, or any other way. The answers were just not written down in any standard table.

THAT SATURDAY NIGHT Samantha was particularly obnoxious, and Ruth was in no mood to trifle with her. It seemed that there had been a "duty" of cutting up seed potatoes that afternoon, so that Ruth's absence was particularly noticeable. There were new faces in the Gathering Order now, Charity Baines and Margaret Barkley and a sloe-eyed girl named Bessie Something or Other. And some of the older faces had been transferred after their owners signed the Covenant and Samantha had given assurance of their good conduct and professed piety. Lucy Hawks was one, as were also Naomi Spinsterwald and Clementina Richards. The new women Ruth thought objectionable, particularly Charity and Margaret; they were both elongated specimens who seemed to have been nurtured on walnut juice. And they were both trying their hardest to ingratiate themselves with Samantha, so that the three of them formed a sort of claque. Ruth judged that they were all equally old, somewhere in the late forties. It was evident that the two older newcomers were both from broken-down farms because their hands were hard and they were both efficient in the kitchen. The third woman, the one called Bessie, looked like a tramp, and that was the way she acted. She had curves in the right places, and she was always slurring her words as she tried to honey up to Samantha. Samantha on her part seemed to be afraid of her, at least of what she stood for.

It was while they were eating supper—and Ruth was making a brave pretense of being interested in the fried hominy and old pork gravy—that Samantha deliberately became offensive. "I don't know why some people think they should eat," she announced loudly. "Them as don't work got no call to come to the table." Ruth looked up after that, and from the eyes turned in her direction she knew that Samantha had previously been berating her. The sloe-eyed girl grinned out of the side of her mouth, but she hid her grin behind her hand. Ruth decided to let the remark pass, and bent down again to pretend interest in her plate. Samantha, however, didn't mean to let her have any peace. "Well," she said again, and again her voice was too loud, "where was you this afternoon? Allays runnin' off when there's a job to do. Where was you, Sister Ruth?"

Ruth felt herself getting angry. "It's none of your business," she heard herself say. "It just isn't none of your business."

With that Samantha seemed almost to choke. She clapped her hand to her mouth, pushed her chair back, and glared down the table. "It's my business to see that you're fitten for the Society," she said angrily. "What the Society expects is that everybody pitches in when there's work to be done. Where was you, out pickin' posies?"

At that some of the women sniggered, and then looked down at Samantha to make sure that she understood their support.

This time Ruth pushed back her chair and stood up from the table. "I work all week long," she said quietly. "I teach in the school all week long, and that's a whole lot more than you do. I don't have to cut seed potatoes—I got other work to do."

Samantha's eyes got red. She just sat and stared, seemingly unable to find appropriate words of condemnation. They came, finally.

"You're a goin' to hell," she said judicially. "That's what's a-goin' to happen to you—you're a goin' to hell."

And with that Samantha stomped out of the kitchen, and went down the hall to her room. She was even careful to slam the door behind her.

After that there was no more supper. And, despite the fact that the dishes were done up as usual, that night there was no evening service. For a while the women just seemed to stand around and stare at the walls, and then, when the clock pointed to half-past seven, some of them got candles and went upstairs to bed. Ruth didn't—she sat in the kitchen because it was warmer there, and after a time everyone was gone except the sloe-eyed girl. Ruth ignored her, and the two sat at opposite ends of the table staring at each other. Ruth, however, wasn't seeing anything; rather she was really seeing over and over again what had happened in the woods that afternoon. Over and over her mind told her to pull herself together. It had happened to other women—a hundred thousand times. She knew that, but the difference was that she had trusted Richard. Well, the other women had probably trusted other men—it was as simple as that. Men were children: they had to be directed every minute, and they simply could not be trusted. No, said the other half of her mind, that wasn't true. She didn't want a man like that. You can't always have what you want, said her critical mind. You either have to be content with what you can have, or you have to be content with nothing. Well, said her positive self, I don't want—

"What's the matter?" asked the sloe-eyed girl. "You thinkin' about something?"

Ruth let her repeat the question before she got up and stared at her. The girl was pretty in a way, although she looked a good bit used. But she moved like a tiger—everything about her seemed to flow sinuously. And her tight shirtwaist wasn't tight enough; it was so loose that her breasts jiggled. She very likely knew it.

"I don't want to talk," Ruth finally said.

"You ain't worried about what she said, are you?"

Ruth remembered Samantha's diatribe and had to smile—a little. "I wouldn't stay here if I was you," she said. "It's no place for a person like you. Go back where you come from."

And with that she went out from the kitchen and through the parlor and up the stairs to bed. One of the new women still had her candle burning by her bedside, and Ruth put it out before she got under the cold covers. Her mind kept going round and round, fruitlessly. What she had told the new girl was true for her too—she shouldn't stay in Union Village. If Clema Porter was running some kind of store in Franklin, she could go to Clema. Somehow, however, she didn't want to—Clema wasn't exactly the type of person she admired. There was one other choice possible, a choice that made the gall come into her throat—she could join the Society and so be transferred to the East Family. Elder Phineas had promised her that, a hundred times over. It wouldn't necessarily be for life—she could leave any time she wanted to. But she'd have to sign the Covenant, and she didn't know what was in the Covenant. Perhaps Elder Phineas could explain it all to her. And then, if she did join, she'd be out from under Samantha's heels. That would at least be some sort of blessing.

It didn't seem like a very great one.

ON MONDAY and Tuesday Elder Phineas did not appear at the schoolhouse, and those were two hard days with Samantha. Both nights Samantha must have searched through Scripture, because what she read had to do with being obedient to the powers in constituted authority. It made sense, a little sense, but only a little. The powers in authority weren't always good, and it did seem funny if God wanted them to have lots of help in doing anything they wanted to do. Both nights Samantha had looked hard at her before they knelt down to say the Lord's Prayer, and both nights Ruth had stared back. And she hadn't said a word of the prayer.

On Wednesday afternoon, just when she had finished sweeping out the schoolroom, Elder Phineas did come, and he had another book with him, a big yellow book that was called a Lexicon. Ruth hardly acknowledged the gift when he laid it on her desk. Elder Phineas must have noticed her mood, for he seemed just a bit uneasy, and at last he went back and sat down on one of the benches. "Everything all right, Sister Ruth?" he finally asked. "You don't act like you're feeling good. Is everything all right?"

"I guess it is," said Ruth, and belied her words by starting to cry. She hated herself for her weakness, but she couldn't control herself. When she did finally get the tears wiped onto her school apron the Elder was standing beside her again. Like almost any man he didn't seem to know what to do. "You don't have to tell me about it if you don't want to," he said when she looked up. "But that's what I'm here for—I mean, so you can tell me any of your troubles."

Ruth stood silent for what she knew was a long time. "It's about the Covenant," she heard herself say. "I don't know what's in it, and I don't want to sign anything I don't understand."

After that Elder Phineas went back and dragged the bench nearer to her desk.

"I can't tell you all the words," he said, "but I know pretty well what's in the Covenant. There's nothing to be afraid of. Those that join the Society must consent to surrender all their personal property. They must not be slaves or own slaves. They must not engage in trade, or be in partnership with anyone who does. They must promise to be obedient to the Elders and Deacons. That's about the sum and substance of it, and you can see most of it doesn't have anything to do with you."

Ruth stood silent. "It's the religion," she said after a long time. "I don't think I understand the religion."

Elder Phineas smiled paternally. "If you'll not tell anyone, I'll tell you a secret," he said. "I don't understand the religion either. I don't think anybody does. It's like that with all religions—nobody understands them. Maybe God wants it that way."

"But I don't understand about the woman," said Ruth. "That's the part."

"You mean Mother?"

Ruth nodded her head.

"I don't know what's so hard about it," said the Elder sadly. "Do you understand about Jesus Christ?"

"I think that's easier."

"Why easier? All we have to bear witness are the words of Scripture. That's all we know. Nobody living ever saw Jesus Christ in the flesh, and very few people who lived then ever heard Him speak. Yet we all say that He was the Son of God. For Mother there are still a few living witnesses."

Ruth had to acknowledge to herself that there was some logic in the argument. Perhaps it had been this way back in Bible times, right after Jesus Christ left the earth. Most people didn't know about it, and most people didn't believe it after they heard. Only His disciples believed it. In a way it was the same with the Shakers—only the disciples like Elder Phineas believed that Mother Ann came from God.

They stood and paced the room together, and Elder Phineas was persuasive. He'd bring over a copy of the Covenant, and she could read it word for word if she liked. And if she signed the Covenant, and then later regretted that she had done so, she could always leave the Shakers and go away. But she couldn't take any property with her, only the clothes she wore. Some people did leave, but it wasn't a good thing to do. The world was an evil place, and it was rushing to its doom.

They must have stayed in the schoolroom for a good hour because the stove started to crack as it got cold and the long shadows began to creep across the schoolyard. After that long hour Ruth thought that her mind was quieter. Not completely convinced, only not so restless and upset as it had been. Perhaps it was all destined that it should be this way. And Elder Phineas had assured her that life with the East Family would be a great deal better than life in the Gathering Order. The people there were more stable—they had left their cares behind them. And she would have no duties in the Family—it would be enough that she taught the school. Except in summer—in summer she could work in the garden if she liked. That would be good for her—she's get a lot of sun in the garden.

Ruth nodded her head as if she agreed to everything. A bit of perversity made the idea jump into her head that she'd better run off to Clema that very night. She knew she wouldn't, but the thought had leaped like lightning across her brain.

That night Samantha ignored her, and Ruth ignored not only Samantha but everyone else. The sloe-eyed girl tried to be friendly, and Ruth at last broke down and talked to her. She had been transferred from Watervliet, where she had gone after she had had trouble with constables in Dayton. And she didn't like it here, not a little bit. Maybe she'd just take off and go on down to Cincinnati. What did Ruth know about Cincinnati? Did she know anything?

Ruth flushed when the girl mentioned Cincinnati, but she said nothing. Yes, she knew too much about Cincinnati. That was where Richard had lost his soul, and that was where Bessie Blair would lose hers if she was so imprudent as to run down to the river. Cincinnati was likely about like Sodom and Gemorrah, and when the world came to an end it would very likely be destroyed by fire.

Chapter 8

ELDER PHINEAS was as good as his word—he was back the next day with a printed copy of the Covenant in his hand. And it said exactly what he had said: a person must be obedient to the Deacons, the House Elders, and the Ruling Ministry. There were always four Elders, two on the women's side and two on the men's, in each of the Families and in the whole of Union Village. But the Ruling Ministry was in Mount Lebanon, New York. And no one could be a slave or own slaves, or engage in private trade, or be a partner with anyone who did. The worldly business of the Society was conducted by Trustees, who were themselves subject to the decisions of the Ministry. Any member could leave the Society any time he liked, but could not sue for the restoration of any property he had brought with him. All members were to share all things in common.

Elder Phineas explained a few other things that were not in the Covenant. Women were always supposed to wear their caps, and men were expected to shave once a week, although some of the members had claimed that beards kept them from catching colds, so that last rule might be changed. Elder Slingerfield, who it seemed had been appointed by Mount Lebanon and so was first in the Ruling Ministry, had forbidden the reading of newspapers and magazines. And there was a good chance that pork would no longer be served on Sundays. Beyond that there were few prohibitions, but in general nothing was done for show. Flowers were not planted unless they had medicinal value, because they were only for show. And every man was expected to braid his own summer hat out of available straw, and most hats were so well made that extra ones had sometimes brought a high price in the world's market. Nothing unseemly was tolerated. In the Family Rooms, where the members of the separate Families often gathered for a time after supper, the men sat in chairs on one side of the rooms and the women on the other. It was the same in the Meeting House—there was no dancing together. And when there was a great call for seasonal work, everyone was expected to pitch in and help. But there were outings too: once or twice a year members who wished might be loaded up in farm wagons or sleighs and taken out to some town in the world, generally to Lebanon or Middletown. Some of the members seemed to like that.

Now, was there anything else he might explain?

Ruth shook her head, and after a time Elder Phineas pulled a goose quill and a small vial of ink out of his coat. Her hand shook as she signed the Covenant, but for some reason she seemed to feel a little better when that ceremony was concluded.

"Guess that's all there is to it," said Elder Phineas. "I'll make arrangements with Eldress Anna and Eldress Mary and you can come down to the East tomorrow night. And you won't have to bring anything with you except the clothes you're wearing. We got a God's plenty of everything down there."

Ruth thought guiltily of her two Washington Irving books and of the copy of *The Western Star* that she kept hidden in the attic. She'd bring them all down to the schoolhouse tomorrow morning—that was the simplest way to keep possession. And that's where she'd keep everything else she wanted, particularly the jars of flowers that the children were always picking along the roadsides for her. And perhaps she'd stay after school and read, maybe as much as an hour a night, because she had to keep reading, whether the Shakers wanted her to read or not. Already she was forgetting some of the words Washington Irving had used in his *Sketch Book*. She never had understood all the words written by Diedrich Knickerbocker, and perhaps she never would.

They went out the schoolhouse door together and parted at the pike. After that Ruth loitered home. It was a pretty day outdoors, even if it was starting to get dark. The wild plums were blooming in the thickets, and there were bushels and bushels of violets. And the birds were singing—a person could always tell it was spring by the way the birds sang. They were even building nests in the crotches and thickets.

That observation made her feel bad again. That's what she had thought she might be doing this spring—thinking about a nest. Once she joined the Shakers she would have to give up that thought forever.

THE EAST FAMILY dwelling was commodious, although it was not so large as the North, South, and Center dwellings. At that time the East housed perhaps no more than forty or forty-five members of the Society, but the East Family did not believe that virtue was in size only. The East Family garden was perhaps better than those of the other Families; at least it always raised more than enough to bring the Family through the winter. And the East prided itself upon its broom room, loom room, and cheese room. That was perhaps a foolish pride, and was the accidental result of having Brother John Shawkey in brooms, Sister Melissa Argentuile to rig and manage looms, and Sister Carrie Carmody in the cheese room. All three were experts, and knew it. So did everyone else in the East Family, and so did many imitative and envious people in the North, South, and Center Families. The Gathering Orders and Mill Families ordinarily stood outside these family feuds; they all had their own virtues, and were superior to what they considered bickering.

Like the other Family houses, the East contained some twenty rooms on the second floor, and of these ten and ten stood beyond the two center stairways that were used one by the women and one by the men. The great kitchen and dining room, the work rooms, shop rooms, Family Room, rooms for the Family Elders, and what was called the Office occupied all available space on the first floor. And the East, like all the other Family establishments, had its own great backyard earth cellar, necessaries, horse barns, cow barns, pig houses, and sheep shelters. It also had a great orchard, and like the garden, the orchard was very fruitful.

Beyond foolish pride, however, the East really had nothing to boast about. All the great Families contained experts in various crafts, and all had gardens and orchards that were roughly comparable. To be very truthful, life was about the same in one place as in another, and there were always accidental excellencies everywhere that came to light, were marveled about for a few weeks or months, and were then forgotten. One thing else, however, the East might have been able to boast about at this time: the members never spoke openly, but almost all believed that their ruling Elders were superior to those of the other Families. Elder Phineas Riegel, First in the Ministry on the men's side, was known and respected throughout Union Village. Elder Arnold Peabody, Second Elder on the men's side, was liked, but had not the respect of Elder Phineas. And, similarly, Eldress Anna Martin, First in the Ministry on the women's side, was so calm and sincere that she was everywhere admired. Eldress Mary Garfield, Second in the Ministry, was a good woman, but she couldn't shake a stick at Sister Anna. So, with Elder Phineas and Eldress Anna in the same Family, there was every reason that the East could give itself a few airs.

Elder Phineas came down to the schoolhouse for Ruth the night after she had signed the Covenant, and he must have prompted Eldress Anna, for when the two of them reached the East dwelling it was Eldress Anna who took charge. Ruth was to be assigned to the room with Sister Carrie Carmody, and might, if she liked, on Saturdays help in the cheese room. That was not the reason for Sister Carrie's selection, however; Elder Phineas and Eldress Anna had talked over the situation very carefully, and had decided that Ruth must be with someone stable. And while Sister Matilda and Sister Hortense came to mind, both were rejected because they were too old. Sister Hortense was mild and pious, so much so that she might get on a young woman's nerves. And Sister Matilda didn't seem to be able to get rid of some sort of rash that kept her scratching, so much so that she was sometimes bloody. Every known salve had been tried, and even flaxseed poultices, and nothing had as yet helped. But Sister Matilda was a lovely woman, and her convictions about Mother were very deep.

At that it seemed that Sister Ruth wasn't very fortunate at first. Eldress Anna herself took her down to the cheese room to meet Sister Carrie, but as ill luck would have it Sister Carrie was at that moment so busy that she could hardly take time to look up. After that, Eldress Anna had no choice except to conduct Ruth to the second-floor room where she was shown her bed and then left alone. Eldress Anna thought that on the whole that might be wise—Ruth would need a little time to make necessary adjustments. But it did look as if the girl needed some new clothes. And her shoes seemed a bit muddy and run over—she might have to have a new pair of boots. Eldress Anna had heard stories about the woman named Samantha at the women's Gathering Order. Some people said that Samantha worked the girls too hard, particularly in the garden. There had been a few complaints, but nothing serious. Except for the girl who drowned herself in the mill pond—that had been very serious. Poor little thing—it was a pity that she had been so unhappy.

That afternoon Ruth had a whole hour to herself to stand and stare. That was exactly what she did—she stood at the window and wondered why she was in this God-forsaken place. Outside the window it was April, and she could see blossoms on some of the plum and peach trees. She remembered then that there would be Johnny-jump-ups in the woods, and likely Dutchman's breeches and blood-roots. When she had been a little girl, she had always gathered bouquets of bloodroots and Dutchman's breeches, but the flowers had never lasted halfway home. Now she no longer gathered them, but she did like to see them hiding down between the leaves. In the spring woods it was good just to be alive. The rivulets and creeks would be slurring along, and the blackbirds preening themselves and wallowing in the shallows. And there definitely would be other things: hickory buds swelling, and oak and ash buds, and all such things.

Well, she would try to behave herself and conform as well as she could. Happily she'd be able to be away all day long, and would simply have to eat and sleep here. Except in summer. In summer she'd likely wish her life away, counting every forlorn day as it dragged slowly towards her liberation in the fall.

IT WAS on the eleventh of April that the sad news came that Sister Lena Gaspar was dead. She had been the first, and only, teacher for many years, and her service had started way back in the reign of Elder David Darrow. There had been no schoolhouse in those days. The schoolhouse had not been built for many years after. Lena taught both boys and girls for almost ten years, and then, after a proper separation of the sexes had been managed, she bestowed her wisdom and love upon the girls. Known as a stern disciplinarian, Sister Lena had also been known for her loving heart, although for good reasons she never handled or fondled the girls in her care. But she did see that they were properly dressed and fed, and she did teach them all to come up to her high standards before she released them. And that was not before they could read the New Testament, and were able to handle numbers clear up through square root. Lena also required that they have a great deal of practice in writing with goose quills and even steel nibs before she approved them, although the ink made from oak galls was never quite satisfactory.

Now she was dead, dead after she had been in the new school-house only some sixteen years. The news went through the Village with wings, and it was down in the East Family the very night she passed away. Brother Matthew Barker had stopped in at the South on his way home from Red Lion and everyone in the South had worn a dismal face. The women were even then washing and wrapping Lena's body, and the coffin box had been sent for. Sister Lena would lie in state in the center hall of the South Family, and all who wished to say farewell to her were to assemble by two o'clock the next day. As usual there would be an hour of remembrance in the Family Room, and then those who wished might follow along to the grave. Since it gave every prospect of being a bright and warm day, the Elders at the South thought it might be a large funeral.

Ruth heard the news first from Sister Mary Ivy, and for some reason her heart skipped a beat when she heard it. Then, at about seven, Elder Phineas himself came around and knocked on her door. Eldress Anna was out in the hall with him, both of them standing like statues in the wan evening light. "We'll be starting up about one o'clock," Elder Riegel told her. "You can let the girls out for the afternoon, right after they eat their noon lunches. And you come back home then."

"We'll all go in a body," said Eldress Anna. "It's only fitten. Not all of us, only about twenty, mostly them that was taught by Sister Lena. But you'll have to go because you're the new teacher, and it wouldn't look right if you didn't."

Elder Phineas nodded his head up and down in assurance. "Sister Ruth will be glad to go," he told Eldress Anna.

"You can wear a black armband if you want to," said Eldress Anna. "You don't have to, but you can if you want to." And she pushed a hand up under her cap and seemed to scratch at her white hair for a moment.

Ruth felt just a little miserable after they were gone, but she didn't say anything to Sister Carrie. And Sister Carrie didn't seem to want to know what had happened outside the door. She sat before the window in the wan April light and simply stared out at the greening fields, as if her thoughts were worlds away. Ruth stood uncertain for a few moments in the center of the room; she would have liked to talk a little, but it didn't seem that Sister Carrie was in the mood. In fact, Sister Carrie rarely, if ever, talked, and when she did her speech was never more than a few words. "It won't be such a pretty day tomorrow," she might say. "I saw sundogs this evening." That had been perhaps her largest remark, but when Ruth had made that observation the reason for some comment of her own Sister Carrie had closed up like a clam.

Ruth had never learned her story. Sister Carrie looked as if she should be in her late thirties, and she was not ill-favored. She stood tall and straight, and she had the reputation of being the best cheese-maker in the Village. She acted, however, as if she were full of hidden bruises, bruises that were incurable. Ruth would have liked to know more about her, but Sister Carrie volunteered no information, and Ruth was afraid to ask if she had ever been married or had children. One thing Sister Carrie did drop one day: she had once lived somewhere over east. Since Ruth had no very adequate idea where the places that Sister Carrie mentioned were, the information did her no good.

It was a bad night for Ruth because she dreamed, and when she woke in the morning she did not at first remember that she was to dismiss her girls at noon. The thought, when it came, made her feel a little sick. She had never attended a funeral, and had never seen a body laid out. The fact that she did not personally know Sister Lena Gaspar didn't help very much. She'd have to be there: have to walk up to the South with all the others who were going, then stare down at the body and afterwards take part in whatever kind of service the Shakers had. And she'd have to follow the wooden box to the grave. The idea was a bit disgusting and a little frightening. It didn't help that she herself was the new teacher—twenty or thirty years from now the same thing would be happening to her. Only it would be different people who would be burying her—Elder Phineas and Eldress Anna and all the rest would likely be dead themselves by that time. She didn't want life to be that way—there was something wrong about it.

As she had been directed, Ruth let the girls eat their lunches on the school ground before she let them go home. They weren't very happy to have the holiday; they seemed to know that the afternoon would be taken up with some kind of work. All the way back to the house that sheltered the children's order, Mary Brooks and Felicity Jackson held her hands. The East Family was only a little farther on, but after she left the girls Ruth walked very slowly. She kept on debating possible excuses, but none seemed very good. She had a terrible headache. Or she had sprained an ankle and couldn't walk. Or she hadn't known Sister Lena Gaspar. No reason she could think of would stand approval. No, she'd have to go, no matter what. But, she told herself, she wouldn't have to look. And when they finally came to the graveyard, she'd stand in the back of everyone else so that she wouldn't be able to see.

There were two yucca plants that stood out near the front gate of the East Family yard, and Ruth stood for a moment caressing their stiff spears. They'd bloom in summer, bloom with tall towers of white blossoms. It was a wonder that they hadn't been up-rooted—once a year they were in defiance of Shaker taste. Probably they stood only because they were wild, and had not yet been noticed by the House Elders. She was a bit like that herself—she was too wild ever to make a good Shaker. She liked simple things too much, the things that grew in fields and woods.

THE COLD BODY lay in its pine coffin in the center hall, and it was wrapped in a fine white sheet. Everyone had to pass it on his way to the Family Room, but Ruth hadn't looked—it seemed profane to stare down at a dead body. One thing she had noticed out of the corner of her eye, however. Sister Lena Gaspar's hair had been almost white. And she hadn't been any more than fifty or fifty-five years old.

In the large Family Room there were nearly a hundred people, for good-sized delegations had come down from the Center, Brick, Square, and North Families. There was no one from the Gathering Order—at least Ruth recognized no one. She had thought that Samantha would be there of a certainty, but it would have been hard for Samantha to waddle that far.

They sat on straight chairs that had been taken down from the walls and arranged in a large deep circle, and when all the chairs in the room were taken, members of the South Family started carrying in more chairs from other rooms. Almost everyone was middle-aged or old, and everyone was sitting with his hands folded in his lap and his head bent down. The South Family members who were carrying chairs tiptoed. But that was the only sound, except for that made by a few pestiferous bluebottle flies. Ruth had thought that some of the mourners would be crying, but no one shed a single tear. One old woman did sniffle, but that was probably because she had a cold.

Then, after what seemed an eternity, some old man who must have been the oldest Elder present got up from his chair and stood in the center of the ring. He just stood there, for what seemed an intolerably long time. Then, finally, he said five words: "I guess we can begin." That was all, and after that he went back and sat down again. Ruth hadn't the slightest idea what was supposed to begin, because nothing happened.

Then, her head down, she heard more words, and sneaking a look over her left shoulder she saw a white old fellow who looked eighty. "She was a gert good woman," said the old man wheezily. "Yessir, that's what Sister Lena was—she was a gert good woman."

After that it seemed as if the dam broke. The white old man was hardly back onto his chair before there was a different voice, and this time across the room from Ruth. "I'm Charley Buckley from over at the Mill," said the voice. "Sister Lena taught me my numbers, and she used to slap my fingers with her ruler when I did something wrong. That's why I learned, because she slapped my knuckles. I can still read a little, but not very much because my eyes is weak."

Off to Ruth's right a matriarchic woman labored to get to her feet, a woman so old that she looked as if she might blow away. "Guess ever'body knows me, Sister Annie Bickeldorfer," she said. "I been here in Union Village since it all started. And I remember Sister Lena when she come. She was just a little girl then, only about ten years old. Her pappy was a drunk, an' that's why her mother brung her. 'N' I remember when she first started to teach school. Had real black eyes in those days, and allays carried her school things in a brown bag. She was strong as a mule then. Couldn't nobody hold a candle to her in them days—couldn't nobody."

There was a bit of a pause after that, and Ruth's eyes saw a couple people helping Sister Annie get back down on her chair. Then from behind her there was another voice, a strong one. "We're all a-goin' to miss her," said the woman's voice. "That's all I got to say—we're all a-goin' to miss her."

The young man who stood up next kept fumbling with his black hat. He looked young, probably in his early thirties, and his face was so red that he must work outdoors. "Sister Lena knowed all the hard words in the whole Speller," he said. "Tried to teach 'em too, but we never learned 'em. That made her mad, an' she'd make us stand up in the front corner with our faces to the wall. I used to hate her when I was little, but I don't hate her any more, because all she did was what she had to do."

Ruth was wondering how Sister Lena had ever taught boys, when she heard the first voice again. "She was a gert good woman," said the voice. "That's all she was—a gert good woman."

After that there was another woman's voice behind her. "Guess maybe she's with the saints in Heaven," said the voice. "Maybe she's with Mother herownself."

The man who talked next looked in his sixties, and announced himself as Brother Charley Kemper from the North Family. Ruth knew that he could never have been one of Lena Gaspar's children, but the old fellow seemed to want to honor her nevertheless. "Sister Lena Gaspar knowed all the fractions an' all the tables," he said. "What they used to do ten–twenty years ago was get her to measure up the acres in the new fields the Trustees bought. She could do it 's well as anybody. One of her favorites was to make all her kids learn how much three an' a half dozen eggs would cost at seven an' a half cents a dozen. Didn't nobody leave off school until he could do it neither."

After that there was the sharp twang of a woman's voice. "She had a gift to learn things," said the voice snappily. "Mother gave her the blessing."

After that somebody got up who said he was Brother Harrison Oliver. He looked old too, maybe in his fifties. "One thing I didn't much like about Sister Lena was that she didn't believe in the Instruments when they talked with tongues," he said. "Allays said it wasn't no language atall, only sounds they made up as they went along. Elder Brubaker didn't like it neither, an' he called Lena in an' told her not to say that to nobody anymore."

"Well, maybe she wasn't always such-a-much," said a middle-aged woman sharply. "All I can say is that if I had what Sister Lena had, I'd be glad to get out of this world and go to Mother."

That seemed to be all, and a full minute went by. Then the younger man who had talked about the Speller got up again. "Well," he said, "she's with the saints in glory. They're all likely sittin' somewheres this minute an' listenin' to the angels sing."

Everyone seemed to conceive that as some sort of benediction. Ruth had thought that Elder Phineas from the East would likely say something kind, but he didn't. Neither did any of the other Elders. Finally the old man who had started it all off got up again, and simply motioned with his hands that they should all get up. They did,

and started to file out the door of the Family Room and turn
straight down the hall so that they'd go right past the coffin. It was
two and two, and they filed to left and right to pass the pine box.
Whoever was leading the procession didn't stop. At the road they
turned north, walking rather sharply. Ruth was with an old woman
who was huffing and wheezing, but she kept her legs moving. Then,
after what seemed a reasonably long time, they slowed down and
turned into a little lane that cut across an open field. There was a
big oak tree over in the field, and Ruth saw a mound of yellow dirt,
so she knew that's where the burial would be. Sister Lena's body
wasn't far behind the procession. The carpenters had nailed down
the lid, and now four men were carrying the wooden coffin on their
shoulders. Ruth hung back, as she had promised herself she would,
but she could see that the pallbearers were putting the coffin down
on ropes. After that it was soon over—the coffin slid into the
ground, and the members started back out through the graveyard.
Nor were there any farewells at the pike; the North, Square, and
Mill Family members simply turned north, and the East, South,
Brick, and Center members went south.

Ruth walked woodenly, in company with some middle-aged
woman whom she had seen at the East. Nobody was talking; no one
seemed to notice that it was a bright April day. Lena Gaspar was
simply gone and would soon be forgotten, although now and then
kindly remembered. But that was the way of life, and death was
nothing to worry about. Beyond this world's travails were only the
Shining Mountains, and there the saints dwelt in some sort of super-
nal bliss with Mother, the angels, Jesus Christ, and Almighty God.

AFTER THE FUNERAL Ruth had a hard time pulling herself together
again. She thought it would help if Sister Carrie Carmody were not
so totally uncommunicative, and on an April evening three days
after the burial she discovered that Sister Carrie could talk. It was
something about cheese that Ruth asked her, for she was dreading
helping out in the cheese room, and when she asked, Carrie didn't
answer her question directly. "There's no use worrying about it,"
she said. "I don't want you to come down to the cheese room on
Saturdays."

Ruth felt a little hurt. "It won't hurt me none," she said. "I could learn."

"I don't want you learnin'," said Carrie. "You do, you'll get just like me. And I don't want nobody to get like me. You go on outside and work in the garden."

After that there was a momentary pause and Ruth thought the conversation concluded, but for some unknown reason on that mild April evening Carrie seemed to want to talk.

"I been down there fifteen years now," she said emotionlessly. "I been down there so long I'm just like a big hunk of cheese myself. My God, how I hate that room and everything that's in it."

Ruth came to attention. "Aren't you happy here?" she asked. "I thought you were. Aren't you happy?"

Carrie grunted. "The only people happy here is those that have cheese for brains," she said. "Them that can't think. Person thinks, it does something to him. Every time. It does something to him."

"You don't believe it's all true then? What they say?"

Carrie grunted again. "We was doin' right well over in Amanda," she said. "Had us a good cabin right down under the hill, and a cow, and a couple pigs, and some chickens. Didn't have no babies—that was the trouble. For some reason I couldn't have babies. Then Virgil—he was my man, an' he got religion at a camp meeting—decided that we'd have to do something or we'd be damned. Guess he thought maybe that God had it in for us. So he heard about the Shakers, and like a big ninny he kept talkin' to me until we joined."

"Where is he now? Your husband, Virgil?"

"He's up in the graveyard," said Carrie without feeling. "They put him in the South because they decided we'd better be separated, and he got kicked by a mule three years afterward. Took in one side of his head."

Ruth didn't laugh even though Carrie recited her story so tonelessly that it seemed she had little feeling about it—nothing but a sort of vague regret. The past was past—and irrecoverable. And the future promised nothing. That left only the gray present, a perpetual round of days when she worked mechanically to keep from thinking.

"Why don't you go away?"

"Where to?" Carrie asked. "Who'd want me now? I'm over forty. Who'd want me?"

It was a hard question to answer, and Ruth saw no reason to lie. No one would want Carrie, just no one. And there was nowhere to go. Given a little luck, she might catch on as a servant in some big home, but that wasn't a likely probability. Ruth had faced that moment of fear herself, and had bitterly realized that no one would want her.

"You don't believe in what the Shakers say at all then?" she found herself asking repetitiously.

Carrie got up and went over to the window. "I guess I can stand it," she said at last. "Ain't nobody bothers me, not very much. And I just keep my mouth shut and pretend. But I don't take any part in the dancing on Sundays. And I don't believe what they say about the woman they call Mother. Near as I can figure, she was just like the rest of us. Had a hard time in the world for a long while, and finally got weak in the head. It ain't hard to do. You keep on imagining things, and finally you get a notion they're true. Only they ain't. But you don't know it because your brains is blasted."

Ruth went over to the window and stood beside her—it was the only escape for both of them that seemed possible. It was evening, but the birds were still fluttering around in the trees. And it was too early in the season, but there was a goldfinch among the sparrows and blackbirds. Ruth watched while the goldfinch swooped out to the garden where the potato rows still showed hummocky in the late light. Somehow she found herself hoping that the finch would find a place to go.

"I won't come down to the cheese room on Saturday then," she said quietly, and put her hand on Carrie's shoulder. "I guess I'll have to tell Eldress Anna."

"I'll tell her," said Carrie. "You tell her an' she won't know what to make of it. If I tell her, she won't ask no questions."

They went to bed soon after that—it seemed the only thing to do. Sleep offered one sure way of escaping the world, probably the only way. In the morning they would both feel less rebellious.

Chapter 9

THE PAIN in Mrs. Robinson's insides was really the reason Richard went to work for Ike Potter on Saturdays, since it set up a chain of circumstances and events that eventually led to the blacksmith shop. Things had gradually gotten worse at the Robinson house, and now there were days when Mrs. Robinson didn't get out of bed at all. Or got up very late. She was cross as a hatchet and almost as sure to bite if one said anything or did anything that wasn't exactly in compliance with her wishes. And since Richard and his father had to keep on eating, it was obvious that someone would have to try to cook something, and their intrusion into her kitchen made Mrs. Robinson furious. A hundred times they explained over and over that they were just boiling potatoes or frying corncakes. But Mrs. Robinson insisted that the whole house smelled like burnt grease. And they weren't cleaning up the skillet properly— it had to be rubbed out with sand before it was washed. And they shouldn't feed old Mose pancakes on the kitchen floor—it made spots. The complaints were constant, but so unfortunately were Mrs. Robinson's pains. It was something inside her, right down in her middle. She couldn't say just what.

Richard's father was a little more precise when they sat over supper at night. The trouble was, he whispered, that Mrs. Robinson's bowels wouldn't move anymore. She'd tried a few things, but without results. Apples might do the job, but it wasn't apple season. Maybe if the Berzinskis were still living down the road, the old woman would know what to do. There had to be something, snake-root or jimson or something. Trouble was that when you didn't know what to cook or make up into tea, you'd very likely use the wrong thing. Maybe somebody ought to go over to Lebanon and see if there was a doctor over there. They could maybe pay him in kind, with a piece of bacon or a half ham, or something.

Richard didn't think much of the idea when his father mentioned it, but toward the end of the week his mother seemed to get worse, and on Saturday morning his father gave him a dollar and told him to saddle up Nellie and ride her over to Lebanon. There had to be a doctor in the town.

Unfortunately Nellie cast a shoe on the pike coming into Lebanon. Richard went back a piece but couldn't find the iron, and finally rode Nellie on in without it. Once in town, he lost no time in asking people if they knew where any doctor lived. They did—but most of them smiled. Doc Grafton was down on Plum Street, and his office was right in his house. The house had been whitewashed, and it had a couple lilac bushes out in the front yard. Doc might be a little hard to find—if he wasn't to home, then he'd likely be up or down the street in one of the taverns. The Golden Lamb would be the best bet—Doc liked to booze up there because there were always high-falutin' fellers in the Lamb.

Richard found the house all right, and he dutifully knocked at the front office door. No one came, but somebody did let a dog out the back door. It came tearing around the house, growling and snapping as if it meant business, and Richard had to kick at it to keep it away. It wasn't too big a beast, but it made up for its size in meanness. For a while he had to stop knocking and devote all his energies to kicking. And then, finally, a big black woman did pull the door open. She just stood there, a red handkerchief wound around her woolly head, and she didn't make any effort to make the dog behave.

"I want to see the Doctor," Richard yelled at her. "He to home?"

The Negro mammy looked inscrutable, but she didn't say anything.

"I want the Doctor," Richard yelled again. "Is the Doctor at home?"

This time the Negress backed away from the door and half motioned for him to come in. Richard did, in a hurry, glad to escape the animal.

After that he waited—for a long time. There was nothing in the office except a maple desk and a couple splint chairs. The desk had some old yellowed books stacked upon it, and it also supported a sheaf of yellow papers. Richard was just curious enough to start examining the books when the Negress came back in for a moment. "He's in bad," she mumbled. "That's where he's at—he's in bad."

"Well, can he get up for a little while?"

"Ain't no fire burnin' unner you, is they?" asked the Mammy. "You wan' to see Doc, you'll have to wait till he gits heah."

Richard waited what must have been almost an hour. Finally then there were scuffling sounds out in the house, and eventually the door pushed open and Doc wobbled in. He looked uncertain on his feet, and his eyes were bloodshot.

"Well," he said disgustedly. "I thought there was somebody in trouble." And after that he looked as if he meant to retreat back into his house.

Richard got up and moved over so that he could grab the old codger if he tried to get away.

"It's my mother," he said rapidly. "We live out in the country. She's hurtin' inside. Has been for two weeks now."

Doc's eyes looked bleary. In fact, Doc looked almost totally incapacitated. His beard was a scrubby gray along his cheeks and chin, and his thin gray hair showed pink patches of scalp. His eyes looked hurt, and they were so watery that it seemed almost as if he had been crying. It seemed, however, that his brain was working, that he was thinking so hard that he simply stared into space.

"Ain't no fluxion, is it?" he wanted to know.

Richard didn't have the least notion.

"Her bowels won't work any more," he said.

"Don't have no liver spots on her face, does she?"

Richard didn't think so.

"She passin' water all right? Ain't no blood in it, is there?"

Richard didn't know, and Doc was disgusted.

"Where's she hurt?" he asked, and roughly punched Richard in the stomach. "High or low. Up here, or down here," and every suggestion was accompanied by a punch.

Again Richard didn't exactly know, and Doc said "Jesus Christ!" in a disgusted way. "Trouble with you dam' farmers," he grumbled. "Never know what's wrong with you, and always runnin' around here an' wantin' to be cured. How about rhubarb—you got any in the garden?"

Richard was again about to say he didn't know, when he did remember that he had seen red rhubarb stalks pushing up through the debris along the garden fence. "I'm pretty sure we got rhubarb," he said. "How do you want her to take it?"

Doc looked at him as if he were a fool. "I want her to eat it," he said. "Three times a day, maybe four or five. Stewed. You know how to stew rhubarb?"

"Guess she does."

"Put some honey in it," said Doc. "Dam' stuff's sour without honey. Now how about white walnut? You know where there's a good white walnut tree?"

Richard promised that he did. There was a fine butternut tree over in the old Berzinski field.

"Scrape the inside bark," said Doc. "Take you an ax or a drawknife or whatever you got out there. Scrape the bark down, not up. Scrape it up an' she'll puke her head off. Scrape it down an' the stuff'll go the other way. Make some tea out of it."

Richard nodded his head eagerly. "You want me to come back an' tell you how it works?" he asked.

Doc looked disgusted. "Course it'll work," he said. "Always does—no reason it won't this time. She gets cleaned out, you stop the butternut an' the rhubarb or her bowels'll run away with her."

After that Richard fished the silver dollar out of his pocket and Doc's eyes began to shine. It was quite obvious that he knew what to do with a silver dollar, and he even became so genial that he sniffed at the April air when he let Richard out the door. The day had started to turn warm, and the perfume of the lilac blossoms was on the air.

AFTER THAT Richard took his time riding Nellie up to Ike Potter's blacksmith shop. Because the day was so fine, there were lots of people on the board and brick walks, and the street was full of buggies and farm wagons. Lebanon, he thought, was really a magnificent town, with its giant elm trees arched over the streets and its great two- and three-story buildings. There were many imposing stores and shops, some of them soliciting business with signs on their windows. But the Golden Lamb Tavern was undoubtedly the finest building in town, and if Richard had had even a dime in his pocket he might have ventured in. He had always wanted to go into the Golden Lamb, but had always been afraid to.

He wasn't sure what story he would tell Ike Potter, but he thought that Ike would understand about the shoe and perhaps even let him put on a new one himself. It wouldn't cost much, not if he did the work, and the Robinsons could drop in and pay Ike the next time they got over to Lebanon. His heart sank, however, when he saw all the rigs and teams hitched outside the shop, so many that he had a hard time finding a place to tie Nellie. As he had expected, the place was crowded, but there was no one helping Ike, and one of the anvils had no one working at it. Richard warily edged through the crowd of farmers, trying to get near enough to ask Ike if he could heat up some iron and put a new shoe on Nellie. Most of the fellows were bundled up too warm, and they were sweating so much that they had begun to smell. Ike had to keep shoving his way around on most occasions, but not when he was carrying hot iron in his tongs. The farmers got out of the way whenever he came near them with hot metal.

Richard finally got his chance to ask, and when he did Ike just waved his hand at the shoes on the wall. He was going back to his forge then, but something made him turn in a hurry. "Ain't you the one who was in here once before?" he yelled across the crowd. "Said you knowed how to shoe horses?" Richard nodded his head eagerly, and Ike yelled, "Well fer Christ's sake, get busy. Way it looks, you can stay on all day."

Richard threw off his coat after that and rolled up his sleeves and the minute he did he himself became the center of a clamoring crowd. Most of the fellows were polite enough—they just asked, but some actually grabbed him. One tall and heavy man with high cheekbones even led a big team of gray farm horses right into the mob. "I been waitin' since Ike opened up this mornin'," he said, and acted like he dared anybody to challenge him. "Three hours—that's how long I been waitin'."

"Hell," spat a little man with a nose that lay in his whiskers like a red apple, "Ike promised me Friday. I was in here yestiddy an' Ike promised me. You ast him."

Richard somehow managed to get through them and went out to get Nellie. By the time he brought her back the first farmer was tying up his grays to the hitching rack. Richard ignored the act. Nellie would stand—he was pretty sure she would stand without tying, and all he wanted to do was get the shoe on her foot. He had promised his father he'd be back to plow just as soon as he could be.

Somehow, once they saw what he was doing, most of the farmers held back, but the man with the grays seemed to be angry. "I got to git on back home," he kept on saying as he got into Richard's way. "Only reason I come in was to get shoes on the team. Ike told me I'd be first."

Richard pared Nellie's hoof a little, measured and shaped the shoe, then found nails and hammered it on. The job was done in ten minutes and as soon as it was finished he had the farmers on his back again. By the time he led Nellie back out to tie her, he had made up his mind—he'd help Ike out a little bit. Maybe until noon—then go on home. The farmer with the big gray field horses came first, and the team took a long time. After that there was a good bay that unfortunately had a cracked hoof, and after the bay a sorrel that had to be tied because she started kicking. Richard had almost finished with her, and was thinking about getting back out on the pike when his ears became conscious of what the loafers were talking about. One fellow had evidently mentioned that he had been cheated by the Shakers, and almost immediately he had provoked a hive of bees. Nobody, it seemed, had any use for the damned Shakers. They talked angrily, interrupting each other, and even pushing each other in the chest now and then. The Shakers were all morphodites—that is, the men were. And they castrated the boys who came in, just like a man would cut pigs. Knowed they did. An' when some one of their women did get pregnant, then nobody ever saw the baby. Took it out an' buried it in their graveyard at night. Ought to be run clear out of the country, once and for always. All it would take would be fire—all their barns would go up with fire. Not the big buildings—they were all brick. But they had to have the cow barns and horse barns and things like that to farm, and they'd never get along without them. Damned shame that they hadn't been run out twenty or thirty years ago.

The talk was circular, endless, and at times angry enough, but it didn't seem as if it was too dangerous. Just talk—most of the fellows were evidently mad because the Shakers were too successful farmers. There was some talk of their big harvests, and even some suggestion that there might be some sort of magic connected with them. One thing was certain—Shakers always thought Shakers came first. Fellow could take a load around to their grist mill when they were grinding their own wheat or corn and find out they wouldn't do a thing for him. No sir, they all ought to be run out of the country.

It was after noon, and Richard was covered with sweat. Ike had come over once or twice to see how he was doing, and Richard had dutifully gotten down into his pants pocket and handed Ike the money paid him. It looked as if he'd be able to get away within another hour, and he had made up his mind to do just that, when there was a commotion out in the street, and a string of swear words a mile long. Richard was surprised when he saw the looks on the farmers' faces—they all seemed a bit apprehensive. "Told you," he heard one of them say to another. "That's Mike. Has to be—ain't nobody else can cuss like that."

It was Mike all right. Richard looked out towards the light in the street and saw a giant shadow. The man carried a whip in his hands, and when he strode into the shop he started flipping it around playfully. The lash caught a few legs and must have stung one face, because one of the farmers put his hand up to his cheek. The next moment Mike had gone over and grabbed Ike Potter. "I got Jennie," he said while he held Ike by the shirt. "Want her fixed up right away—I got to get out of here."

Ike looked as if he didn't know what to say or do. "I can't take her until I get this job through," he said. "Won't be but a little while."

For answer Mike brought the whip down hard, and Ike jumped and cried out. Worse than that, the horse Ike had been working on started rearing, and Mike started after the horse. Richard had hot tongs in his hand, and when Mike raised his arm to lash the horse Richard instinctively swung the tongs. It crashed against Mike's upper arm, and with that the whip flew, and Mike seemed to fall to one knee. Never as long as he lived would Richard forget the face he saw before him when he turned—it was an evil face, full of lust and murder. "You stupid son-of-a-bitch," he heard Mike roar, and the next moment he lunged at Richard. Richard hit him over the head with the tongs as he came in, and the next moment the two of them rolled.

Chapter 9

THE FIGHT had been going on a good quarter of an hour, and they were both bruised and bloodied. Mike Sloan had been somewhat beautiful in a white-ruffled shirt when he had come into the shop, but now the ruffles were torn to shreds and Mike's green coat looked as if he had been dragged through a pigpen. More than that, he had bruises on both cheeks, and one eye was sealing shut. As for Richard, not even his mother would have recognized him. The left eye was closed, his upper lip was badly cut and swollen, and his knuckles were running with blood. At that, he had given a pretty good account of himself. He didn't know it but he was the first man in the history of Lebanon who had ever stood up to Mike Sloan, who because of his savage nature and fourteen-stone weight had everyone pretty well cowed. There was some evidence of the hate against Mike in the circle of onlookers who had retreated to the edges of the shop and had even climbed on Ike Potter's worktable; these worthies, their numbers swollen now by those who had seemed to come running from everywhere in the town, cautiously helped Richard as much as they could, particularly when he was down flat on his back. Then, it seemed, a tumult of bodies would roll over both combatants and tear them apart. There had been good need of their help one time in particular, for Mike was known as a gouger and made a business of conspicuously hardening his right thumb nail by holding it over candleflames in all the taverns.

Now they faced each other again, both of them ranting, and both faces not really able to see well any more. Mike looked as if he was crouching again, getting ready for another of his savage rushes, a tactic he employed twenty times before. Each time Richard had gone down, for Mike was agile and there was no way of standing up against his weight. Happily Richard had generally managed to roll free, but that luck couldn't go on forever. A few farmers in the crowd yelled warnings, but the shouts did no good whatsoever, for Richard knew as much as they knew, and didn't know how to meet the rushes. This time he waited until the last moment, and then leaned to one side, but as ill luck would have it he tripped over a piece of wood. He went sprawling on his hands, and the next moment Mike was on his back, his hands clawing at his face. Richard bit through one of Mike's fingers and Mike released his hand in a hurry. They both got back to their feet, crouching in front of each other, their eyes glaring. Like roosters in a barnyard they pawed around for position, neither one quite sure what the other would do. One of the farmers held out a heavy hammer for Richard to grasp, but he didn't see it; his eyes didn't dare be distracted for a single second. Mike crouched again, always the preliminary to his rushes, and this time Richard simply threw himself under him when he came. They both staggered back to their feet, their positions reversed. Mike came in immediately, and Richard hit him right in the mouth, so hard that his hand felt paralyzed. But he knew that Mike had lost a front tooth because he spit one out on the floor. "You simple son-of-a-bitch!" Mike sputtered as soon as he had finished spitting blood into the dirt. "By God, I'll kill you."

He might have, but he never got a chance, because the crowd at the door pushed in across the floor and a tall white-whiskered man in a bottle-green coat marched in between them. He just stood there for a moment, his buggy whip in his hand, and then he stood facing Mike like some angry schoolmaster. "I've told you and told you," he said caustically. "By God, if you won't listen, I'll disinherit you. That's what I'll do—I'll disinherit you. I won't have fighting every time you go out into town. You hear me—I won't have fighting." And with that Judge Sloan turned to the sheepish farmers and commanded them to go home where they belonged.

Richard somehow managed to get over to the trough where they quenched the hot iron, and he was still trying to wash the blood off his face when Judge Sloan came over and stood beside him. He didn't know it at first, but his one good eye finally took in the tall man in the beaver hat and he felt his legs tremble. He supposed he was going to be arrested, and perhaps thrown into jail.

"I don't know who you are, and I don't care," he heard the Judge say. "All I know is that you've earned this." And with that he held out his hand, and it had a twenty-dollar banknote in it. Richard had never possessed one in his life, and he had seen only one or two others like it. "Come on—I want you to take it," the Judge said sharply. "You've earned it. Might be the only way that boy of mine will ever get any sense into his head."

Richard took the note and watched the Judge as he turned his back and marched out of the shop. The place was strangely quiet now; if the loafers hadn't gone home, they were all outside. And there were no horses left on the floor—they had all been dragged outside the moment the fight began. Through the big door Richard could see sparrows flying through the sunlight out in the April day, at least half see them. He began to wonder if both eyes would seal up before he got home.

He had to find Ike Potter before he left, and Ike was outside, standing strangely quiet beside a big black horse that someone had just driven in. Ike looked up a moment, and Richard thought that he smiled. "I guess I better be gettin' on home," Richard said apologetically. This time Ike did smile. "You come back on in every Sat-day," he said. "Anytime else you want to, but every Sat-day. Maybe you'll be good for business."

Richard finally got on Nellie's back although it was a struggle. But it seemed as if the people in town thought him some sort of hero, for as he rode down past the Golden Lamb and turned west he noticed knots of people pointing at him from the sidewalks. They didn't say anything, just pointed, and sometimes even the women-folks stared at him. He began to get the idea: they thought he was something of a hero because he had stood up to Mike Sloan. Perhaps no one else had ever dared. Well, it was nice to be a hero, but it did hurt a lot. His face felt like it had been through a lard press, and his arms and chest were evidently covered with bruises.

But he had twenty dollars in his pocket, the first twenty-dollar bill he had ever owned in his life.

IT WAS WORSE than he thought at home—worse, and better. Richard didn't go in to see his mother, but his father came out to the living room. Richard saw his face—it looked horrified. "Nellie didn't run away, did she?" his father asked.

"She didn't run away," Richard answered.

"What happened?"

"I got in a fight," said Richard miserably.

His father just stared after that, and Richard told him about the rhubarb and white walnut bark. He'd go back out and get them both in just a few minutes. The rhubarb first. And then his father could boil the rhubarb and put some honey in it while he went over to the Berzinski field and tried to get some of the white walnut bark. It had to be scraped down, not up, and then it had to be cooked into tea.

"Who was it, Doc Fellows?"

"I don't know what his name was."

"He take the whole dollar?"

"He didn't give me no change," said Richard.

His father seemed not to like that. "Never did cost more than fifty cents," he said. "Must be an expensive doctor. Doc Fellows never took no more than fifty cents."

Richard went out and got an armload of rhubarb, and since his father was back in with his mother when he came back to the house, he cut the stalks up and put them into the big kettle. The thought did occur to him that it would take days for his mother to consume the mess, but perhaps his father and he could down some of the pieplant too. He had eaten it before, and he didn't think too much of it. But if whatever his mother had was catching, then it might be prudent for both him and his father to take necessary precautions.

He cut a slice off the last loaf of bread and spread it with good yellow butter before he got the ax and started for the woods. Cutting the bread he remembered that they'd have to do something about that too—Saturday had always been baking day. And some more butter would have to be churned. He had never baked bread, but he did know how to churn butter. He didn't like the job.

From the position of the sun in the sky and from the way the shadows fell in the woods he judged that it must be about three o'clock. Perhaps a little after. There'd be light for another good four hours, and they'd need it all to get everything done they had to do. The white walnut bark shouldn't take too long a time. It didn't make sense that it had to be scraped in a particular way, that it would make a person vomit if scraped up, and cause him to have a mighty purge if it were scraped down. Well, the doc should know—he seemed to understand his business even if he had been a little drunk. Richard started swinging the ax and made a foot-wide gash in the tree. The outer layers of bark came off all right, and sure enough, underneath there was an oozy shell of white. He remembered then that he had forgotten to bring any container for the scrapings. He'd have to put them on a piece of outer bark. But the tree didn't scrape well, and it was an awkward way to use an ax blade. Down, down, down,—probably the easier way to scrape. The bark didn't pile up very fast, and it didn't come off too well. They'd probably have to put in some honey when they boiled it too. And it might be a good idea if they all took a few doses of white walnut along with the rhubarb.

Back home once more, he got the small kettle and put the walnut scrapings on the stove in a quart of water. The honey could come later—long sweetening didn't have to cook. The house seemed very quiet; his father and mother didn't make any sound at all. Richard would have liked to look into the room where they likely sat before the fire, but he didn't think he dared. It might be that they were both asleep, and that would be a blessing.

The eggs and the feeding and the milking and stabling down for the night took what seemed to be hours, and he was so stiff and sore that he didn't enjoy a single minute of the work. There would be supper to get too, and it would probably have to be some more cornmeal cakes fried on top the stove. That wasn't too hard a job, and the cakes were easy to make, just a little lard, a little milk, and a lot of meal. Happily they wouldn't run out of those things—they had them in plenty. Meat would taste good, but meat would mean going to the smokehouse. And the smokehouse was sacred—only his mother had ever been permitted to take things out of the smokehouse. It was her rule—she said that she had to go slow so that things would last through the winter.

It turned out to be a not entirely bad night after all. About sundown his father woke up and came out into the kitchen, and after that it seemed things were more normal. They lighted the lamp and had the corncakes and coffee, and that too was usual. Richard thought while they ate that he would try to get an opportunity to ask his mother how to make bread. It had to be made one day and baked the next—he was pretty certain of that. And if things turned out all right, he'd try to make it by lamplight after supper.

However, things didn't turn out all right. His mother tried to eat a dish of rhubarb, and vomited. It was the same with the white walnut stuff—she couldn't keep it down. His father got a little tense after that, and kept on asking how Richard had scraped the tree. Had he done it the way Doc directed? Richard said he had, but his father only shook his head.

There was no family worship that night; Abraham Robinson seemed to be so much worried that he had forgotten. And Richard set no bread. His mother had her eyes closed and only moaned a little from time to time. She was still sitting in her chair and moaning when he finally went up to bed. For the first time he felt a little frightened—it might just be that they'd have to ask the doctor to come out to the house.

THERE WAS no bread baked and there was no garden planted. They ate corncakes. Some of the barn work didn't get done, the eggs were ungathered, and there was nothing to do with the milk so that a little of it was fed to the cats and the rest poured into the pig trough. And although both Richard and his father coaxed, Mrs. Robinson refused to try more of the rhubarb or white walnut. Day and night the fire burned in the April room, and day and night Mrs. Robinson sat in her chair with her feet propped up on a footstool and a heavy quilt spread over her.

Richard knew that his father was worried, and on Tuesday he sent Richard back into town with his last silver dollar. This time Richard didn't get to see the doctor—the old Mammy said he was sick. Sick meant drunk. He did see a young fellow who had been graduated from Eclectic Medical Institute in Cincinnati and was trying to get a start in Lebanon, and the young fellow only shook his head. "Seems like her bowels must be bound up," he finally declared after he had heard all the symptoms. "Maybe she's got a kink in them."

"Would it help her to walk?"

"Might, and might not. She still able to walk?"

Richard said he didn't know. He did know in a way—he knew that if his mother had made up her mind that she was going to stay in her chair, that's where she would stay. Richard didn't spend the whole dollar—the young fellow took fifty cents—but he came home no wiser than when he had trotted over to Lebanon. And, as usual, there was work to be done.

That night he went up the road a piece and told the Taylors about the trouble they were having, and Miz Taylor (that's what everyone called her), a thin and sallow woman with haunted eyes, was properly sympathetic. "I'll do anythin' I kin do," she kept on saying. "Trouble is I don' know what to do. But I'll do anythin' I kin do."

Richard promised to come and get her if his father knew of

anything. But Mrs. Taylor had a pack of young-uns, and she wouldn't be able to be away from home very long. Maybe not at all.

That night—it was still late light when he got home—he took his father's suggestion and rode over to Union Village. He passed the East and the South Families, and went right to the Center—it was the largest building. In the Center supper was over when he got there, and most of the members were in the Family Room, but now and then someone walked up or down the hall. Richard had to accost four or five of them before anyone seemed to understand what he wanted. Finally an old gaffer seemed to, and in due course he led Richard down the long hall until he came to what was called the Dispensary. As good luck would have it, Sister Laura was in the little room, and after the old man left Richard told her what he needed. His face got red when he had to talk to a woman about his mother's bowels, but there was no help for it, and he did it. Sister Laura didn't seem to be shocked. "I don't know, I don't know," she kept on saying. And then, "I'm not allowed to be a doctor. Not for anybody on the outside. I mean, not for people who aren't believers."

"You just tell me what to do, and I won't care whether you're a doctor or not," Richard said vehemently. "Trouble is, we don't know what to do."

After that Sister Laura seemed very thoughtful. She was a rather beautiful woman as she stood in the lamplight in her knitted cap and white collar, and the thought crossed Richard's mind that he would have liked to have had her for a mother. She seemed patient, kind, and thoroughly intelligent, so much so that he found himself wondering how she could be a Shaker.

"I don't think I know what to do," Sister Laura said at last. "You say you've tried white walnut. Have you tried speedwell and tansy? They're good for most everything."

Richard confessed they hadn't tried either, and immediately Sister Laura started to make up a little package of each for him. "I put in some camomile too," she said, when she handed him the paper and her smile was like a benediction. "She'll have to want to keep the tea down," she said, again with a smile. "The sick person has to want to recover."

When Richard offered to pay her Sister Laura seemed insulted. "We're not that kind of people," she said quietly. "Things we can do for the world, we want to do, and we do gladly. You make some tea soon as you get home—boil the water and steep it. Then let her spoon it down slowly. Is she still able to hold a spoon?"

Richard thought she was.

"If she's not, you soak a cloth in the tea and put it in her mouth," directed Sister Laura. "And we'll hope she gets well. I think she will."

Richard loved her gentleness; she had caused him to revise his whole opinion about Shakers. At the mill he had never thought they were that decent.

However, his elation didn't last long after he got home. He cleaned out a kettle and steeped the tea as he had been directed, but he might as well have made it for the man in the moon. His mother seemed so weak she couldn't talk, but when he carried the cup in to her, she simply pushed it away with a feeble hand. After that his father took the cup of the camomile and tansy and tried to hold it to her lips, but she refused to take it into her mouth and the tea simply ran over her chin. Seeing that, Richard remembered what Sister Laura had said: she'd have to want to get well. It seemed that that might be part of the trouble—his mother was simply beyond all desire to go on with life.

IT TOOK a long time for Mary Robinson to die, and there was no one to help her. Or almost no one, certainly no doctor, wise woman, minister, or priest. Day and night Abraham Robinson sat in before the fire watching and nodding, and day after night and night after day Mary sank nearer and nearer ultimate forgetfulness. Richard like a coward escaped, although his torture as he drove the team of oxen in front of the plow was perhaps worse than his father's. The birds were flying and singing out on the high hills and the sun was on his back, but with the turn of every furrow he remembered that there were a hundred things that had to be done back in the house. If it hadn't been for old Mose he would have felt panicky, but Mose somehow stiffened his spine. The old red setter would have moments when he remembered his youth and galloped a hundred feet or so after a rabbit, but that was generally the end, and after that Mose would come back to the furrow again. Richard always petted him—Mose seemed to be his only living link to reality.

So Wednesday passed, and Thursday. On Wednesday Richard

killed a chicken and tried to boil broth for his mother; on Thursday he put all compunctions behind him and boldly entered the smokehouse and brought out a ham. The ham pleased his father but his mother ate none of it. Nor had she even consented to sip the chicken broth. Then, on Friday morning, Miz Taylor hallooed from out in the road, and Richard went out to meet her. John was on his way in to Lebanon, said Miz Taylor, and if Richard liked, she'd come in and set a spell until John came back about one–two o'clock. Richard insisted she come on in. There was really nothing that Miz Taylor could do for his mother, but Richard knew she'd tidy up the kitchen. And likely rearrange his mother's pillows and quilt. There was something about a woman's hands that seemed to know what and how to do—it was almost as if they were ministering angels. Miz Taylor had few front teeth left and her elongated body looked like it jangled at the joints, but her spirit was pure gold and everybody who ever met her knew it. So Richard went back out to the fields as soon as he got Miz Taylor established, and when he came back in at noon she had ham frying and a batch of bread rising in his mother's big crock. Better than that, she had redded up the whole big room— the crocheted rugs had been shaken out the back door, the floor swept, and the clutter of furniture pulled apart so that a person could walk through the room again. The three of them ate together that noon, and Miz Taylor wolfed the ham, snagging it with her side teeth and pulling hard with her fingers until she got a mouthful. Richard decided then that she'd take the rest of the ham home with her—it was probable that the Taylors had been out of meat for a month. When he told her that—that they had no use for the rest of the ham because they were getting tired of it, she started crying and finally got up from her chair and came over and kissed him. Richard didn't relish the kiss very much, but he did love the woman's spirit. From all he knew about him, John Taylor was the same way, one of the workingest, doingest men in the whole township. The only trouble with the Taylors was that their ground was sour, but that was really a blessing in disguise because if it hadn't been sour someone else would have grabbed it. The Taylors had been up on the woods patch for years, and they had had kids and made do. Even God in Heaven couldn't have expected any more.

That night Richard even began to hope a little again—his mother seemed quieter and appeared to be sleeping. He tiptoed around the kitchen for a long time, and when that wouldn't do, he managed to sneak into the living room and get his *Vicar of Wakefield* book. Then, sitting at the kitchen table and chewing at what was left of the ham—Miz Taylor had insisted that he take off a couple slices before she carried the rest of the ham home—Richard read again of the tribulations of good Dr. Primrose. It was a sweet and gentle book, and he found himself thinking that the man that wrote it must have been sweet and gentle too. That was really what he would like to do, write something for people to read. The only trouble was that he had nothing to write; all he knew was what they did on the farm, and maybe a little about Cincinnati. And the only kind of people he knew weren't like Dr. Primrose—nobody would be interested in folks like the Berzinskis and Taylors and the Gillespies down in Cincinnati. People in books always came from far countries, and they were always people of importance.

The oil burned out of the lamp and Richard got a candle to throw light on his book. He knew it was after nine, but he couldn't rightly see the clock through the kitchen shadows. He had rarely stayed up as late as this—it made the morning too hard. And now he'd have to tiptoe when he went in to bed, and the floorboards would likely creak and perhaps Mose would rouse himself to see why he was stirring around. It wouldn't be right to wake his father or mother, not at this hour. Perhaps the best thing to do would be only to put his head down and sleep at the kitchen table. He had done that once or twice in his life, and he hadn't felt too bad the next day. Besides, it was a warm night and he really didn't need a blanket.

Dr. Primrose kept on trusting in God, and the candle kept on burning, and Richard kept on reading—and then a rooster crowed and he came to his senses. A little watery light was leaking in through the window, and he felt shivery and very uncomfortable. The fire would be out in the living room too, and both his father and mother would be cold. He'd have to fix it after a little, just as soon as he got awake. Probably, however, it would be better not to stir it up—if they were sleeping, it would be better for his father and mother to go on sleeping. What he really wished was that Miz Taylor would come down again. What he really wished was that Ruth would come in. But that was like reaching for the sky. He knew that she had really joined the Shakers because he had watched from the woods one day and seen her come out of the schoolhouse with her pack of girls. They had all gone east, not west, and after leaving the children at what was called the Children's Order, Ruth had gone on to the big East Family house. He couldn't understand why she had done a thing like that—gone Shaker. Ruth had a good mind, and more than that she was a woman—she could never be content with other people's children. He had hoped that she'd get over being mad, and then he thought he might be able to talk to her, but it seemed that she hadn't. Women were really awfully hard to understand. They had notions—all of them had notions. The real trouble seemed to be that they couldn't understand men.

Unfortunately he knocked a tin dish down off the table and his father woke up and cried out a little. Richard carefully picked up the dish, then tiptoed over to the door so that he could look into the room. As he had expected, the fire was completely out. And his father was really stirring—he had managed to get one leg out from under the blanket covering him and was trying to get his bearings and make his old bones work. Richard went over to the woodbox and got some kindling to start the kitchen stove, but before he could get it going his father half limped out into the kitchen. Richard thought there was something wrong in his face—it seemed frozen into something like a mask of horror. And his father wasn't walking, just standing a step or so inside the kitchen and looking at him.

"Ain't nothing the matter, is there?" he heard himself ask. And then, when his father didn't move, Richard went over and put his arm around his father's shoulders. "Ain't nothing the matter, is there?"

It was then that he saw the big tears rolling through the stubble on his father's cheeks and in that moment he himself felt as if he had been stabbed.

"I guess she's gone," said old Abraham. "I don't think Mamma's with us no more. I guess she's gone."

Richard left him propped up against the kitchen table while he himself went in to look at his mother. She wasn't breathing—at least the quilt didn't move. And her eyes were closed, and she seemed all huddled together. Richard finally found courage enough to reach out his finger and touch her cheek—it was icy cold. It was then that the tears started down his own cheeks, and by the time he came back out to the kitchen he was crying unashamedly. Now that she was dead, he remembered his mother in life. Not the way she had been in recent months, but the way she had been for years before. When he was no more than a baby he had been always with her: they had made garden, slopped the pigs, fed chickens, churned butter, and done everything together. And there had been happy times, times when all three of them had hitched up the horse and gone to Monroe or Lebanon. It hadn't been Nellie in those days but a big brown colt that his father had finally traded because he had too much spirit. And it had been his mother who had taught him his first letters. On winter days sometimes, when his father was out in the barn, they had made cakes and built woodblock houses, and done everything together. His mother had been beautiful in those days, and she had been very proud—she had told him a hundred times that she had been one of the Hendersons from Virginia. He was really a gentleman, or should be, and she expected all sorts of things from him when he grew up.

Now it was all gone, shattered, shattered like a maple tree shatters its leaves in an autumn wind. All the old days were dead now, all the good times, the whole irrevocable and irrecoverable past. Dead, dead, dead. His mother was dead, and in a little while the old man half lying over the kitchen table would be dead too. And then he'd be all alone, all alone. Jack and Nellie and Mose and everything he loved would go, and there'd be nothing left. Perhaps the answer was the one Ruth had found—perhaps he should go over to Union Village and join the Shakers. That way he could always be sure of belonging to a big family, and he'd never have to worry about things anymore.

He came out of his depressive mood when his father looked up and asked if the coffee was ready. Richard jumped for the stove. The coffee was ready, the animals would have to be taken care of, and somehow they'd have to manage to get through the day.

THE MINISTER was a tall, cadaverous man that Miz Taylor sat under in the hill church a mile or so up the road, and the Taylors brought him with them in their farm wagon when they came down to the house for the funeral. The Taylors had done more than that—they had asked the Rafe Peterses to come down and help with the burying. And it had been the Rafe Peterses who supplied the coffin, a good solid oak box that had been meant for a barn manger. At least the wood had. Somehow Rafe Peters hadn't used the wood, and when Miz Taylor told them that there'd have to be a coffin, the Rafe Peterses surrendered the wood and put the box together.

The service was right at the house—it could have been in the white hill church, but somehow Richard's father hadn't wanted it there. No good reason, only the one that the Robinsons hadn't gone to the hill church. Perhaps once or twice, but no more. Abraham Robinson never said as much, but Richard inferred from words his father and mother had dropped from time to time that Mrs. Robinson thought she was a little too good for the hill church congregation. Not a single person who worshiped up there could look back to Virginia; they were all Kentuckians and plain folks from southern Ohio who were just like the Kentuckians. And all of them shouted in church, at least a little, and not a single one of them believed in election like the Robinsons. And that prime error made them just a little less than respectable.

Miz Taylor had cleaned up the living room and even pushed stuff out of the way in the kitchen, and now, on Monday afternoon at exactly two o'clock the gangly minister got his black book out of his pocket and stood up beside the oak coffin to read. Richard had heard the words before but didn't know where they were found in the Bible. "I am the resurrection and the life, sayeth the Lord. He that believeth on me, though he were dead, yet shall he live; and he that liveth and believeth in me shall never die." The preacher snapped the book shut then and stood holding it in his hands while he stared at them. Richard found his glance uncomfortable, very uncomfortable. However, what the preacher had to say when he began to speak was not bad. He hadn't known Mrs. Robinson, and so he couldn't really say if she had died in the faith. But he understood that she had. And if she had, then her sorrows were now all over, and she would be waiting on resurrection morning to greet all the people who had known her and loved her on this earth.

There was a good bit more like that, most of it directed to the Taylors and Rafe Peterses more than to the Robinsons. And, just when it seemed that he would never stop, the preacher said amen— a real short prayer—and put his book into the pocket of his shiny black coat.

They walked up the road behind the farm wagon bearing the

coffin, the preacher first, then Richard and his father, and behind them the Taylors and Peterses. Mercifully the road was good enough—it hadn't rained for a spell. The weeds were already green along the rail fences, and there were a few early posies, though what they were Richard didn't know. It seemed almost as if it weren't real, as if they were just walking in time, or out of time. But the Taylors' home went by, and there were some of the kids hanging on the front fence, and then, shortly afterward, the white hill church, and then, after a hard climb through ruts, the tangled little graveyard. Blackberries smothered almost everything there, but the Peters had the grave dug, and they had supplied the ropes for the coffin. That made it all come back, what had happened in Cincinnati, and Richard remembered Fanny and felt a lump in his throat. Fanny the way she had been at first, when her figure wasn't swollen and she hadn't been cross all the time. And that brought the rest of it back—the fateful Sunday afternoon when they had lain together in the violets up along Mill Creek. It had been just about a year ago.

The box was being put down on the ropes now, and John Taylor went over to help the Peterses lower it into the grave. The men had braced themselves and seemed to have a good hold on the ropes. And then, as they started to lower the box, the preacher picked up some of the clods and dropped them on top the coffin. "Earth to earth, ashes to ashes, and dust to dust," he said solemnly. And finally, when the coffin was at rest, the preacher held up his hands a little, and said "Let us pray." Afterward Richard couldn't remember the prayer, not exactly, but it was something about those that died in the Lord having rest from their labors and having their works follow after them. After that the preacher again held up his hands and actually seemed to be holding them out towards Richard and his father. "The Lord bless thee and keep thee," he said. "The Lord make his face shine upon thee and be gracious unto thee. The Lord lift up his countenance upon thee and give thee His peace."

Afterward, stumbling a little over the other hummocks in the blackberries, the hot tears coursing down his cheeks, Richard knew that that was what he'd really like to do and be. A preacher. But he couldn't be a preacher—he hadn't a chance. Preachers had to know a lot and go to school for a long time. There was just no way he could do it, no way. He had his father to take care of now, and his father might live a long time. And after that—

Chapter 9

There was no end to the "after that." The future was like a big cocoon or wall of silence, and what would come out of it no one could guess.

THE PLOWING went on, day after day, and it was slow and patient work. Richard insisted that his father do some of it, particularly on Saturdays when he rode Nellie in to Ike Potter's blacksmith shop. Ike was generous—he generally gave Richard half of everything he took in, and sometimes added a quarter or a half dollar. It was good to be in Ike's shop and participate in the friendly brawl that seemed to go on every Saturday. It was good also because he was a marked man after his fight with Mike Sloan, and all the old farmers and gaffers seemed to defer to him. The younger men were more backward; they seemed always to be assessing Richard's brawn with furtive looks, and they would glance away the moment he looked at them. But he knew, and in his simple-mindedness he was very proud. Saturdays were always a colored shuttle of impressions: fine and fancy Lebanon ladies parading down the streets, sometimes with parasols; fancy steppers that the dudes brought in to be shod, even when the horses needed no work; farmer talk of floods and droughts and grasshoppers and how the blackbirds followed along and ate up half the seed; garden seeds placed out in front of the stores with proper scoops and labels; women in sunbonnets washing steps and porches along the streets; runaways on the pike, and stages pulling up at the tavern—all that sort of thing. Lebanon was excitement, challenge, a part of the big world. On Saturdays it had its own market, and there almost anything could be bought, all sorts of cheeses, bunches of young onions, mounds and prints of home-made butter, eggs by the basketful, even homemade bread and crullers cooked in hot lard. Richard loved the market stands and in the nooning he sometimes paraded along the street and looked at the wares, but he never bought a thing. He did have some hankering after a tin dipper he saw one day but he didn't buy it—it cost a whole dime. The fellow selling the tinware said it wasn't overpriced, not at least in the Cincinnati market, but Richard tried futilely to cheapen it to a nickel. They didn't really need the dipper at home for the water bucket; the one they had was badly dented, but it would do. It had for more years than Richard could remember.

On Saturdays he sometimes thought he was happy, and he even gave himself airs as he strutted along the Lebanon brick walks. The rest of the week, however, once he was back into the lonesomeness of the hills he doubted his happiness. There was just too much to do; his mother, for all her waspishness, had performed miracles around the place. Now there were geese and chickens to feed and eggs to gather, the house to be kept somewhat respectable, and there was always the inevitable duty of preparing something to eat and cleaning up afterward. They ate fried potatoes until they were sick of them, they ate pancakes, corncakes, something that passed for biscuits and something that was decidedly not bread although it had been intended to be bread. They ate meat, ham, and bacon, and the supply in the smokehouse was getting low. They ate young onions from the garden and they tried cooked dandelions and found them bitter and gritty. And that was about all they did eat. At the table Richard's father was ordinarily very silent, and he never had one word of praise for the food, even though it was sometimes good. Abraham Robinson seemed to be living in the past, he seemed to be mechanical in everything he did in the present, and he definitely had no hope for the future. One Sunday, almost the first Sunday after the funeral, Richard asked him whether he'd like to shave and go up to the white hill church, but his father seemed to be dazed by the suggestion. Richard asked again, and this time old Abraham simply shook his white head. "Guess not," he said finally. "We don't have nothing we have to do at home," Richard told him. "And that preacher seems to be all right." But Abraham was imperturbable, and Richard finally left the house and took Mose out for a walk. After that he took Mose out almost every Sunday morning. And always, or almost always, they'd walk back into the woods and end up right against Jehovah's Chosen Square. The Shakers weren't using it to dance in, not yet, but they'd be at it in July and August. In May the weather was too uncertain, and from the Square it was a long way back to shelter.

So the days passed, and the weeks dragged through, and the seed corn was gotten into the ground. The winter wheat looked promising, and as usual they planted a little barley. However, weeds began to take the garden, and neither Richard nor his father had enough energy left over to do anything about it. Richard did chop at some of the big Jimson weeds, but it was a halfhearted effort and the Jimsons recovered. Actually he thought the brown chickens ought to be able to take care of the weeds; they got out of their pens and scratched up everything else in the garden.

And—fight the thought as much as he would—the mind flash was recurrent that what the farm really needed was a woman. And to Richard the idea of a woman meant only one person—Ruth. He could make a business of asking her again, now that he knew where she was in Union Village, but he was both ashamed to and afraid to. Ruth wasn't a true Berzinski. All the rest of the Berzinskis would have cussed him out to his face, and then begun to forget what they were cussing about. But not Ruth—she didn't explode that way. When she was hurt she was silent, and she kept right on being silent, for a long time, or forever. Richard had known that from their schooldays—he had once been so imprudent as to tell Ruth that she was dumb when she couldn't get a problem right on her slate. After that he had to walk home alone for a month and it wasn't until he gave her a jarful of tadpoles that she forgave him. He never knew why she had so wanted the tadpoles.

Well, he could try to get into the East Family to see her. Or wait for her after school—it hadn't yet been dismissed for the summer. That was probably the better idea. She'd likely be walking with the little girls she was teaching, but she could send them on ahead. There was a chance she wouldn't, of course. In that case he'd be tongue-tied; he didn't mean to beg for forgiveness in front of a pack of little girls. And there was the other idea that had sometimes teased his mind—he could hunt for another girl in Lebanon. Most of the females over there were stuck-up, of course, and they wouldn't want to come to a hill farm. There was one girl, Annabel, who sometimes stopped in the blacksmith shop for a minute or two—she was Ike's granddaughter or niece or something and she lived right down the street. Annabel wasn't exactly pretty, not pretty the way Ruth was, but she was shapely and she wriggled her hips when she walked. Richard didn't know how old she was, but she looked like she was sixteen at least. That was old enough to get married. Only Annabel seemed somewhat giddy, for all her vacant face. She'd look with her big blue eyes when Ike said something and seem not to know what he was talking about, and half a minute later she'd be laughing out loud. Richard didn't much want Annabel, but she'd be better than nobody.

By late May they got the last of the corn into the ground, and had a little time on their hands. The pigs had farrowed and the young chickens would soon be big enough to be fryers. The sheep hadn't been sheared as yet, and they were hot and losing some of their wool, but the Robinsons had waited a long time for the itinerant who ordinarily took care of the job for them. He was an old fellow, so old that he didn't look as if he'd be able to stand bending over the sheep for a whole day, but there probably wasn't any better hand in the country. All he generally asked was his noon meal and a dollar, and then at sundown he'd just go back out to the road and disappear. But this year he hadn't come, and he might be dead.

That night, when they again had little more than fried potatoes for supper, Richard asked his father about the shearer, but Abraham seemed not to understand what he was talking about. "We used to eat a lot better than this," Abraham said finally. "When your mother was alive we used to eat a whole lot better than this." And he got up and took what was left on his plate and scraped it into the slop bucket.

Richard only stared. He'd have to ask Ruth again—there was no other way around the problem. He had probably waited too long; school might now be out for the summer. And he didn't relish the idea of going over and butting into the East Family's business. They might not even let him see Ruth—they'd probably know what he was about. But he'd do it that way if he had to; he'd march right in and ask for Ruth Berzinski, and then, if they didn't call her, he'd have to figure out some other way to get in touch with her.

SCHOOL WAS OUT—no one came out on the school grounds to play during the nooning. When he knew that, Richard boldly stepped out from the screen of leaves that had hidden him. He felt relieved in a way, now that he knew he wouldn't have to face Ruth, and he picked up some young walnuts that had fallen under a roadside tree and started throwing them at marks. That excitement over, he decided to go into the school ground and get a drink from the pump. Lots of people did that, so that there would be no danger if he were seen. He had drunk from the well before, and it was good water.

His drink done, for some perverse reason he started for the schoolhouse door, thinking that if it were unlocked he'd go in and see what kind of room the Shakers had given Ruth to teach in. The outer door was unlocked, and inside there were two doors, one for the boys and one for the girls. Richard opened the right-hand door, and it was just as he had imagined it—a large empty room with three windows. There was a part of a slate in front, and it had been scrubbed clean. That was all save for the teacher's desk and the benches the kids sat on. That inspection over, he decided he might as well see the other room, and he nosily twisted the knob and started in. The room was just like the other, benches and teacher's desk, and some empty brown jars on the windowsill. He had just decided that this must be Ruth's room when he saw her—she was sitting in the back corner near the window and she had an open book on her lap. And she looked like a real Shaker, with white cap and collar, and a long brown dress that came clear down to her shoes. Ruth didn't look up at first, and then when she did he thought she gasped. Richard just stood there, uncertain what to do. There was a lump in his own throat, and although his brain told him that he should say something, no words came out of his mouth.

Ruth got to her feet, and carefully marked the place in her book before she put it down on her chair. She too seemed not to know what to do. Her hands kept picking at the sides of her long skirt as if she was trying to straighten it.

"What do you want?" he heard her say, although his heart was beating so fast he wasn't sure she had really said anything. "You want something?"

Richard kept staring. "I just thought that maybe you wouldn't mind talking," he finally got out.

Ruth looked at him soberly. "I don't know what about," she said. "I'm sorry about your mother."

Richard was amazed that she knew, but the Shakers generally knew everything. Sometimes when people died in the surrounding countryside they carried food in and did things like that.

"I guess she just had to go," he said. "She was real sick. A long time."

That was the end of that, and now they both stood and stared. Ruth finally went up the side of the room and changed the position of two of the stone jars on the windowsill. Somehow Richard got the idea that she was fighting to retain control of herself.

"I just wanted to talk," he said again, and moved a few steps toward her. "I don't know how you feel anymore, but I know how I feel."

Ruth let that pass without comment, but she did come towards him. "We could take a walk," she suggested. "I'd like to see the flowers in the woods."

Richard felt a little better after that, and even managed to step out of her way when she started for the door. Once out in the woods he thought his tongue would be looser; it was always easier to talk in the woods. And that's what they were both used to, and the woods was where they had had their best times together.

Today, however, they went into the trees right across the road, and neither one of them knew that patch of woodland. There were little ravines running south, and fern fronds in some of the ravines, and there were lacquered yellow flowers in all the clearings. It seemed like old times again when Ruth stooped and picked a few of the flowers. They traveled circuitously, avoiding the raspberry and blackberry brambles, and as usual the birds began to protest their intrusion. High overhead a few black crows circled and cawed, and from somewhere nearer the whiplash of a redbird kept flicking through the trees. So, silently, they went clear through the woods and finally stopped in a tiny valley where a little brook trickled through the sunshine.

"What do you want to talk about?" Ruth asked then, and raised her head to look at him.

"I guess I just wanted to know if you forgive me," he said. He still didn't seem to have full control of his voice; it was almost as if someone else were speaking.

Ruth hung her head a little. "I'll never forgive you," he heard her say. "Some things are unforgivable."

Richard was silent for a long time after that. "I don't think it's right for you to go on like that forever," he protested.

"What you did will go on forever. I can't forget it."

"You might forgive it even if you can't forget it."

"I think it's the same thing," said Ruth. "If I could forget it, I could forgive it. I can't forget it."

After that they just stood and looked down at the little stream. There were minnows darting through the ripples, and from the meadow atop the rise on the other side of the stream they heard a cow low. The day suddenly seemed stagnant, stagnant with light and with the inner darkness in their hearts. Curiously Richard felt not so much ashamed as angry. It wasn't right for her to be like this, and he told her so.

After that Ruth herself simply stared at the water. "I tried," he heard her say. "I tried to forgive and forget, but I guess I'm just not that kind of person."

"You didn't have to turn Shaker," he said. "There wasn't any sense in your doing that."

"There's no sense in a lot of things," she answered.

"You don't believe it," he pointed out. "You don't believe what the Shakers say."

Ruth didn't answer right away. "I might," she said finally. "I don't know enough yet to know whether I believe it or not. It's not so different from anything else when you think about it. And it does something to people. I never knew people could be as kind and sweet as the Shakers are."

Richard decided that he wouldn't be dragged into that argument. He couldn't be—he didn't know enough to argue that the Shaker faith was wrong.

"I guess that it's just that I need you so much," he said. "We always knew that we belonged together. Ever since we were kids."

"And you forgot the minute you went away."

That was unfair, and Richard had to answer. "I didn't forget," he said vehemently. "I wasn't the father of the baby. She just said I was."

"You gave her reason to think so."

That made him angrier. "You don't know what it's like to be a man," he said. "You think they're made just like women. They ain't. Men lose control of themselves."

Ruth refused to comment on that opinion. "They've been good to me," she said. "They took me in, and fed me, and waited for me to make up my mind. And I've got a job to do, and I like doing it."

"You can't go on teaching forever."

"I can go on until I die," she said. "That's about as much of forever as a person ever gets in this world."

"They're not your children. You'd never have any children of your own."

"It don't seem to matter," she said. "I love them, and they love me. That's all that matters."

"Then you mean it's all over between us?"

This time she touched him. "I don't know, Richard," she said sweetly and grasped his hand. "I need time to think. Maybe after a while I'll want you a whole lot more than I want you right now. I'm not sure if I ever will or not. But I want more time."

That didn't seem fair and he told her as much, but she didn't answer him. Instead she started back up the little hill, and when he saw she meant to go back through the woods he joined her. Strangely the thought kept coming into his head that she wasn't the old Ruth at all. She seemed almost a stranger, a beautiful stranger. She seemed to be older, a lot older, than she had before, and she was more sure of herself. He had thought that she didn't like the Shakers at all, and now she was telling him that they were the best people she had ever known in the world. The whole thing made him mad, and he kept biting his lips as they worked their way back through the briars.

At the road, however, she told him that he'd better go on alone. He was almost eager to, and he didn't look back as he strode down the Lebanon Pike. Women, women—he couldn't get the idea of women into any proper focus at all. There had been Mrs. Bentley and his mother and Fanny, and now Ruth. There was also Miz Taylor and Sister Laura, who had given some herbs to try to make his mother well. But Ruth was different—she wasn't like any of the rest of them. Probably because she was a Berzinski.

That was it, he consoled himself—it was probably because she was a Berzinski.

RUTH REALLY didn't like herself very much. And the reason she didn't like herself was that she doubted that she had said, or done, the right thing. She hated herself, in a way, for what she had done and said; she hated herself, in another way, for what she had not done and said. The regrettable circumstance was that she had prepared her case in her own mind, and that when the time had come, she had failed to find the right words. As a matter of simple truth, she was puzzled both by Richard and by herself, and as a matter of larger truth, she was no longer sure of anything. She had thought for years that the greatest goal in life was to marry and to have a home and children of her own, but the girls she taught had proven to her that her love need not be saved for her own children. And Sister Carrie Carmody, her roommate in Union Village, had somewhat altered her views of marriage. Marriage in Carrie's opinion, and she had been married for more than ten years, was rarely successful, since married mates were rarely compatible. Women, said Carrie, were neater, cleaner, more inclined to take pains and to use diplomacy to gain their goals; men were dirty, crude, and too often inclined to resort to brute force. Women could endure privations and miseries better than men; men resorted to the bottle as soon as things began to go wrong. It was women, not men, who kept homes together. It was women, not men, who brought children into the world, who taught them, watched over all their pains, bruises, and sicknesses, and who finally sat back in silence while their fathers boasted about their accomplishments. Carrie's husband, Virgil, had been a locksmith, and a fairly good one, but he had gone to pieces when he had discovered that there was little call for locksmiths. That—and the fact they didn't have any children—was why they had eventually gone over to the Shakers. And though Carrie really hated what she was doing, making cheese almost every blessed day of her life, her life in Union Village was a great deal better than any she had had before.

Ruth had listened, dutifully and impressionably, but she had not believed Carrie—not entirely. She wondered, however, if the simplicity of the Shaker life and the joy she had found in the classroom might not have weakened her will. It probably had, but that was not the only reason she had changed. She had begun to believe that what the Shakers said might be true, that life in the Spiritual or Church Order might be superior to the Adamic Order as the Adamic was superior to the conventional lusts of the world. Men were not intended to be beasts—not if they were the children of Almighty God. It might be that God was testing every single person, that only the regenerate might gain Paradise. It might be true that God had sent His prophets to men, and sent the Christ in both the male and female forms. No one could prove it was not true. And it did seem as if God had blessed the Shaker community in fullest measure. It might be almost time for the day of the Lord to come, for the heavens to be rolled away and the earth to be consumed by fire. A person could go crazy thinking about things like that, but they might be true.

Even at that, it seemed as if men and women had been made to live together, and Ruth had to admit that she had never met anyone she had liked as well as Richard. But how to forgive what he had done in Cincinnati. It wasn't true, what he said—that men and women were different, that men simply couldn't control their lusts. The right kind of man likely could. And if a man couldn't, then one came to the inevitable conclusion that he wasn't the right kind of man. And if a woman became confused and made a mistake in choosing a mate, then it was likely she'd be in the same kind of mess. That wasn't true marriage—simply to endure from day to day. If that's all marriage could offer, then it wasn't good enough.

Ruth had a good notion that things weren't going well in the Robinson household. While she lived, Mrs. Robinson had done all the kitchen and house and garden work, and now the two men, Richard and his father, were likely in some sort of mess. That was no reason, however, why she should sacrifice herself. One didn't marry a man simply to help him clean up the kitchen or bake bread. One didn't marry for any real reason except children and companionship. She needed both, children and companionship, but that was what the Shakers were giving her, and she liked their simple and pious ways. In the Family Room at night, after they had all left the table and kneeled down at their chairs to thank God for their food, there was always the greatest peace and quiet. The older people always sat nearer the stove, and even when the stove was no longer needed they kept their accustomed seats. That meant that the younger members would go down nearer the window. But it was all like a big family, and whenever anyone spoke everybody else listened. Ruth liked the looks of the men across the room—they were rubicund and tired, but they looked contented. There was old John Stringwater, in his eighties, and Matthew Colson, in his late seventies. Those two did nothing but feed the chickens, but they always made a long business of it and seemed to be out almost the whole afternoon. Then there were the farmers and the barn men and the mechanics and woodcutters and those that were employed at particular crafts. Harry Dodge built looms and kept them in repair, and John Pogle made things out of copper and tin. And then, finally, there were the young men, who were ordinarily just learning some craft or business. But they all looked the same when the long day was over, and when they spoke there was never a sharp word. "Brother John, you get all the corn planted?" someone would ask, and be met by some slumberous answer such as "We didn't get the far field yet.

Got all the rest." Or it might be, "Sister Lucy, when you goin' to bring us in some more apples? They all gone?" And Sister Lucy Parkinson would smooth her dress and answer slowly, "All the old apples is gone. Guess maybe they'll be makin' kitchen sauce out of some of the new ones afore long." It was like that, the lamplight on the center table growing stronger as the outside light faded, and everyone just sitting at peace for a spell before the move came to go upstairs to bed. On some nights, though, one of the Elders or Eldresses would step in and offer prayer, and they would all stand while the words were being said. Eldress Anna had the largest gift of words and seemed to know the most—she could embellish her prayers by all sorts of Scriptural references. But Elder Phineas seemed to know the most about Mother, and he generally referred to her when he dismissed them for the night.

There was something quaint and homely about it all, and in a way it was a good life. But today, kicking through the schoolgrounds on her way back to the pike (she had had to go into the schoolhouse to hide her book away), Ruth also had some sharply negative thoughts. Surrendering to the Shakers was in a sense just another way of giving up everything she had always dreamed about. Life was probably meant to be a struggle, and the people who didn't want to struggle probably had no business to keep on living. It would probably be better if she didn't make up her mind too soon. Richard would likely come back again—once more. After that she was pretty sure that he wouldn't come again, for he had his pride too, and he wouldn't want to be a beggar. She'd have to make up her mind, and she'd probably have to make it up in a hurry, in a week at the most. Life with the Robinsons wouldn't be bad, in fact, it would be almost what she had always dreamed about. Old Abraham, Richard's father, might be bothersome at times, but all the old people were bothersome—they couldn't be otherwise. And he wouldn't live forever. And then they'd be alone with a place of their own, and they could keep on getting books and learning things and teach their children what the world was all about. That is, if they knew. It seemed as if a lot of people never found out.

THE FOLLOWING Saturday noon Richard was putting the last shoe on a piebald nag that belonged to Mrs. Lacey when Ike came over and stood idly watching him. Richard got the wrong notion in his head—he thought that Ike might be critical of the way he was doing things. That made him a little nervous, and he did bend a nail he was pounding home. But that wasn't it at all—the moment he had taken the piebald out and hitched it to Mrs. Lacey's buggy Ike told him he might as well come down the street with him. It wasn't far to his daughter's house and no one would have to stay to watch the shop. "Chicken noodles," said Ike, and patted his stomach. "That's what she generally has, chicken noodles. You like chicken noodles?"

Richard would have liked the hide off a mastodon. "Guess so," he told Ike. And then, prudently, "She don't know I'm coming, does she?"

Ike only smiled. "Don't make no difference," he said. "I told her you might. There's always enough."

Richard went over to the trough and washed his hands a little. That done, he tried to slick back his hair, but it was long and shaggy and it didn't slick very well. Always before his mother had cut it once a month, and now it was beginning to hang down the back of his neck again. And his shirt was dirty, and he likely looked a sight. But Ike was dirtier than he was—in fact, Ike was always dirty. Some of the dirt might have been underlaid by liver patches and so looked dirtier, but there was plenty of it on Ike's hands and face nevertheless.

They strolled down the street and their eyes blinked in the sun. There was a good yellow-red brick house next to the shop, a tall house with green shutters, but after that the structures were all thin frame and Ike's daughter lived in the third of them. The place looked too skinny to have a good kitchen to eat in, but Ike boldly led up the brick walk and made a clatter as he climbed onto the porch. And Ike was unceremonious—he went right in and almost left Richard standing on the porch watching a robin in a maple tree.

Once back in the kitchen, however, Ike assumed better manners. "This here's my daughter," he said, and pointed to the middle-sized woman at the stove. "Name's Mabel. That other one over there in the corner I guess you know. She's the one that's allays down at the shop, Annabel."

Mabel wiped her hand on her apron and then held it out for Richard to grasp, and when she saw that Annabel came across the floor and did the same thing. Richard stood like a lump, afraid to move. The table was set with four places, and he thought again that he was unexpected and unwanted because the fourth place would undoubtedly be for Ike's son-in-law.

"Go on—set down," Ike commanded, and pointed to the plate at the far side of the table. "Guess that's where you want him, ain't it, Mabel?"

Mabel said it was, and the next minute brought over a big tureen full of chicken noodles, which she squashed down in the center of the table. Annabel had to run to get the bread plate out of the way.

Ike asked a sort of blessing, although no one could distinguish the words in the mumble. Then Annabel kicked Richard's foot and said "Excuse me." Richard was properly impressed by her fine manners and got his big boot out of the way. He did notice, however, that Annabel kept looking at him; and despite the fact that he tried to keep his eyes down on his noodles, he couldn't help noticing her from time to time. She wasn't bad; in this light she looked a whole lot better than she did in the blacksmith shop. Her eyes were probably too far apart, and they were definitely too wide open, but she had a good nose, and her lips were wide and full. Today she had a green ribbon tied in her copper hair, and the green was the same color as her blouse.

"Guess you're the feller that put Mike Sloan in his place," he heard Ike's daughter say. And the next minute she had reached out and was feeling the muscle in his forearm. "It feels like it's rock," she commented, and looked up at Richard admiringly. "Annabel, come on over here and feel this feller's arm."

Richard expected Annabel to say no, but it seemed as if she had been waiting for the invitation, for she pushed back her chair and came around the table immediately. "My Gawd," Richard heard her say, and the next moment she was smoothing his arm with the flat of her hand. That might have gone on a long time, but Ike found a fly in his soup and lifted it on his spoon and put it on the table. Mabel pretended shock, but she seemed to think Ike should go on with the soup. So did everyone else.

They ate prodigiously, three bowls apiece. The clock on the wall crawled uphill until it passed one, and still they sat and soodled their coffee. "How about that feller as was after you last month, Annabel?" Ike blurted out casually. "He come around anymore?"

"I don't want Annabel going out in his buggy with him no more," said Mabel. "He ain't no good—he's a Dutchman."

Ike assumed a philosophic pose. "Lots of good Dutchmen in the world," he said. "Cincinnati's full of them. All they got down there—Dutchmen."

"Well, she can't go with this one," said his daughter. "Can't even say his name right. It's Sigrid or something—only he don't say it that way. How's he call it, Annabel?"

"Sigurd," said Annabel. "He's all right too, no matter what you think."

Ike pretended indifference. "Well," he said finally, "guess Annabel is growin' up. First thing you know, she'll be runnin' out on you."

Annabel's mother shook her head. "Not till she's seventeen," she said. "That's what I was when I married John. Seventeen."

Richard fidgeted. There'd be three or four wagons or rigs at the shop waiting when they got back, but Ike pulled out his pocketknife and cut a hunk off his plug of tobacco. "Guess maybe she better be lookin' around," he said, and patted Annabel on the rump as he went by her. "Can't wait too long. If you do, you get crowded out."

Both Annabel and her mother shook hands at the front door. "It was right good," said Richard as he tried to get off the porch. He wished Ike would wait for him—Ike was already strolling down the walk under the maple tree.

"Well, you come back," said Annabel's mother. "Anytime you want—you come back. Don't need no handwritten invitation."

Ike moseyed down the sidewalk, evidently trying to put off work as long as possible. "Dam' nice girl," he said casually as he stepped over a fishworm on the walk. "Ain't no nicer girl in Lebanon than Annabel. Ought to hear her read. She reads so that all the words run together."

Richard made no comment. But Annabel did seem like a nice girl, he had to admit that. And if she could read so that all the words ran together, then she could read a lot better than he could. He still had a little trouble, although he could find his way through *The Vicar of Wakefield* pretty well. Trouble was that the book was wearing out.

Chapter 10

B Y JUNE Union Village was a great green and gold beehive of activity. The farm teams were always in the fields now, and the women in the many gardens, and those who drove down the pike from Red Lion must have imagined that they were going through a populous city. It was a good time to be alive: the green shoots growing, the drivers hallooing to their teams in the fields, the acrid smell of sweat in the air at all the noonings. There were even those who became so intemperate as to talk during the meals. But, no matter what happened out of doors, the spinning wheels continued turning and those who worked at the looms kept hammering out their endless yards of cloth. Most of the seed peddlers were back home from their long journeys, some clear into other counties, and the sale of good stout brooms had been greater than that of the year before. And now a great deal of the pieplant had been sealed into jars and carried to the basements, and there had been the annual gorge of fresh dandelions. On sunny days the children ran through the yard of the Children's Order like young colts, and it was difficult to get them to pull weeds in the garden. For it was full spring, the orchards had bloomed, and the sun lasted the whole day through, so that the nightly gatherings in the Family Rooms no longer required lamplight, particularly not since many were so tired that they sought their beds before the bats began to fly.

Best of all, there were Union Meetings every Sunday, and the white Meeting House had been scrubbed half as clean as Heaven. And it was like Heaven there every Sunday morning, for there was a great deal of energy in the dancing now, and some of the younger members even tried to improvise new steps. But the older members still held to the square step and the shuffle, and their faces glowed as they moved up and down and made the peculiar humming noise in their chests. Unfortunately the gallery was full of interlopers almost every Sunday, and some of these fancy Dans and giddy Nellies in floppy hats and flounces had no manners, so that they would laugh and point and in general make a nuisance of themselves. They were tolerated only because the Ruling Ministry thought that it was a part of the Shaker creed to bear witness to the world. If only one re-generate might be saved from the burning, then that single salvation would justify the disdain of all the rest. And no one could tell which of the new converts—and despite the fact that the winter Shakers had all gone away, there were still one or two who came into the So-ciety every month—no one could tell which of the new converts had first witnessed the ecstasy of salvation by coming in to look at a sin-gle Union Meeting. So the troops marched dutifully up and down the roads to the Meeting House, and in July and August they would be marching farther, clear over to the Chosen Square.

Unfortunately, however, it seemed that this year there were to be no visits of holy and mighty angels. Sunday after Sunday the Elders waited for someone to go into rapture and to talk with tongues, but no one did. And no one fell down as if struck by lightning, or was propelled by invisible forces up and down the Meeting House floor. Mount Lebanon knew that there had been a slackening in the spirit, and Mount Lebanon, as usual, sent its annual messages to the soci-eties in the West, to Pleasant Hill, South Union, Whitewater, Water-vliet, North Union, and to the great congregation at Union Village. "To All and Several" those messages would be addressed, and they would go on to warn against any blighting of the holy spirit that had shaken the Society in earlier days. The messages would be read in Union Meeting by the First in the Ministry, the ruling male Elder at Union Village, and they would be listened to with bated breath. The messages spoke of "sackcloth and darkness" and they spoke of "Anti-Christ" and enjoined obedience to the ruling powers. They re-peated also that Christ had made His second appearance on earth, and that it had been despised by the profane and adulterous genera-tion. The messages were frightening, but hopeful, and after they were read there was never any more dancing. Somehow, despite the warmth and the birds calling outside the Meeting House, the days always seemed to be blighted when the Ministry at Mount Lebanon wrote to its children in the West. The green fields seemed not quite so green any more, and the sky was no longer a limpid yellow. That mood wore off, of course, but it took time for the regeneration of smiles and a little laughter. It was not easy to forget that life was a serious business, and that the day of the Lord would come as a thief in the night.

All in all, however, Union Village was a happy place. Not happy—rather tranquil and contented. The wheat and barley got tall in the sun, the young corn was cultivated by a hundred plows, the flaxseed had been scattered over the harrowed ground by young women with scarves tied around their heads, and on rainy days the field laborers gathered in the barns to repair harness and wagons while the women scoured jars or helped in the kitchen. No one ever complained about compulsory idleness, and in fact rainy days were sometimes the best of all because of the enforced gatherings. Outside on the main road travelers might be floundering up or down, their horses and capes streaming with water, but in the silent houses women were mending quilts, crocheting rag rugs, or simply cleaning and tidying their rooms. And in the shops, of course, work went on as usual. The great saw snarled in the lumber mill, the carpenters kept turning their spools and spindles on foot lathes, and the joiners marked and notched and drove their pegs cleverly so that maple or walnut would be held together for all time.

It was a good life, a very good life, with God's plenty for all. God's chosen people might be few, but they waited patiently for re-demption. And God in His chosen time would speak, and the blessed would pass into life eternal.

WHEN WASHINGTON IRVING wore out, Ruth complained to Eldress Anna that she needed something to do, and Eldress Anna, after a few moments of cogitation, turned her over to Deaconess Zelda, who was in charge of the kitchen. Deaconess Zelda was fifty and stout, and she had a way of looking at a person as if her gimlet eyes were boring right through her. But Deaconess Zelda could move, and she did move. There were a hundred things to do and think about in the course of the day, and Deaconess Zelda seemed to have everything catalogued. That first day the job she assigned Ruth was a heavy one: there were still some pieces of meat in the smokehouse that should have been moved to the icehouse weeks ago. Ruth should go out there—Sister Martha was in charge. She'd know what to do—she had been doing it for years.

Actually, it was the first time that Ruth had even heard of the icehouse, but she did know where the smokehouse was, and when she went out the back door she saw two women carrying hams, one dangling from each arm. Ruth traipsed along after them and so in time came to the icehouse, which was over near a tiny runnel that ran below the garden. Standing in the open door Ruth could see shadowy shapes inside, their breath blurry in the frost. She waited dutifully, and in due time the two women who had been carrying hams came back out. When they started across the yard again, Ruth followed them, and from that time on she did exactly what they did. The smokehouse was still a quarter full of meat, and to Ruth's nose some of the meat seemed to be a little spoiled. She wondered if she should say anything about the odor, but decided not to. It was none of her business, and Deaconess Zelda and Sister Martha very likely knew about it anyway. The two other women looked at her as if they wondered why she was there, but they said nothing, not even a word of greeting, and after that Ruth simply followed along after them. But it was heavy work carrying a huge twenty-pound ham dangling from each of her arms, and after a time it was dirty work too, for some of the grease rubbed off on her long skirt. Over to the icehouse they all struggled and dumped the hams down on stacks of pond ice, and then back again, and to the icehouse again until it seemed the weight was driving their feet into the ground.

Curiously, that job made Ruth's mind stagnant—it was almost as it had been in the old days in the Berzinski cabin. She began to wonder just how much she really wanted to be a Shaker, and decided that if she had to give up the school she wouldn't want to be a Shaker at all. It was all right for Martha and Lily and Hannah (she had heard the two other women called by those names), but it wasn't what she was cut out for. That negative thought made her wonder if she had gotten so soft-handed that she couldn't stand work anymore. She decided that that wasn't the reason for her disdain. And what they were doing was important—if the hams and bacons couldn't be saved, then they wouldn't be eating meat much longer.

That night, back in the room with Carrie, she tried to clean up her dress, but the grease wouldn't come out with cold water, and the dress would have to be sent to the washhouse. That made Carrie ask her what she had been doing, and when Ruth told her Carrie laughed. "You should try making cheese if you're so finicky," she said. "That's all you get down there in the cheese room. Grease and slop. Did you ever smell me at night?" Ruth had, but she didn't say so. Carrie sometimes smelled like a cheese herself. She generally washed a little before she went to bed, but the odor was pervasive, and it had taken Ruth a long time to get used to it. In fact, she never had gotten used to it.

It was better after that, however, helping Deaconess Zelda was. Deaconess Zelda didn't want her in the kitchen proper, and so Ruth was sent out on what Zelda herself thought might be fruitless missions. To find wild strawberries, for example—Zelda said they sometimes grew in the grass on the edges of woods, but Ruth had a better notion because she had picked wild strawberries all her life. The strawberries gone, Ruth picked bundles of fennel, marjoram, parsley, sage, tansy, coltsfoot, and peppermint. After that Zelda wondered about chokecherries and then raspberries, and almost at the same time said that the blackberries would be ripening. Had Ruth noticed in her forays through the fields? Ruth had, and in time she dutifully brought in great wooden buckets full of raspberries and some blackberries. There was even a curious demand in July— Deaconess Zelda wanted young fuzzy butternuts to pickle for the Christmas feast. That was a harder task, getting the butternuts, and for the first time Ruth's offering was small. There were butternuts in plenty, but they were up in the trees, and there was simply no way to get them down.

And so the summer wore away. In the first days of August Ruth went down the road one afternoon and made another visit to the schoolroom. Somehow when she went in there she had a curious feeling—it was almost as if the walls spoke to her and told her that she was forsaken. She felt a bit vague and dizzy for a little while, standing there in front of her teacher's desk. And then she managed to get herself together again. It might not be the way she had planned her life, but it was the best that life could give her. She had thought that Richard would come back again, and she had half planned what she would say to him. But he hadn't come, and she had worn out her eyes looking up and down the roads. Now, she was fairly sure, he would never come. And for the life of her she couldn't think what she had done wrong.

She didn't go straight back to the East that afternoon; she went across the road and poked through the dense brush in the south woods until she came out on the little stream again. There were cows in the tiny valley now, switching flies as they stood in the shallows. Even that seemed to be some profanation of the spot—she hadn't planned for it to be that way. The stream should be lonely and silver as it had been before, and she would stand exactly where she had stood before and look down at the water. And then she'd try to remember all the words that they had spoken to each other. And maybe then she'd know what she had said wrong.

She took a long time getting home that afternoon, and when she finally came in she went right up to her own room. Lying there in the halflight she heard the first gong for supper, and ten minutes after that the tears started coming in. She decided she'd skip supper—it would be far too substantial for her appetite. What she'd really like to have was no more than a piece of dried bread and a cup of mullein or sage tea. But she couldn't ask for those in the kitchen; if she did everyone would think that she was sick. And she wasn't sick—only drowsily uncertain how much longer she wanted to go on.

ON THE FIRST Saturday after they had gone down to Annabel's house, Ike waited around at noon and seemed to think that Richard knew he was expected to go along down for dinner again. Richard didn't know, and Ike finally had to tell him to get a move on. "I don't feel right about it," Richard protested. "She told you to come on back, didn't she?" Ike asked. "Mabel. Ain't that what she said?"

Richard had to admit that she had said something like that, and rather hangdog he washed up a little and followed Ike down the street. As before they blundered right into the house, and as before there were four plates set at the table, and on the stove a big pot of what Mabel said was barley soup. Ike seemed to smack his lips at that, and so did Richard when the soup was served. It had big chunks of meat and onions in it, and it tasted about as good as any soup he had ever eaten. Today Annabel had a brown ribbon in her hair and wore some kind of yellow dress with green buttons. And her hair was frizzed.

They ate, and tried not to stare at each other. Charles was out teaming again, said Mabel. That's where he always was, either on his way down to the City or on his way back. Sometimes he didn't come home for two or three days hard-runnin'. And when he did, all it seemed he wanted to do was sleep. Ike grunted, and went on slurping soup, and that was the end of that.

Then Annabel got finished, and asked Richard if he wanted to go out in the backyard and see her rabbits. She had six of them in a cage. Richard had never heard of caged rabbits before, but when he saw them he knew they weren't his kind of rabbits. The poor things looked hot because their box was in the sun. Annabel giggled when he told her so. "What do you do with them?" he asked. "They ain't good for nothing, are they?" "They're good to eat," said Annabel. "You want you one next Saturday, all you got to do is say so."

For some reason the idea was abhorrent to Richard. "Guess not," he said. "I ain't sure I'll be here."

That made Annabel pretend to be sad, and she reached out and took hold of one of his hands. "You don't know how much we want you," she said. "It's awful lonesome here. It's lonesome for me in Lebanon. Seems like I never have nothing to do that Mamma will let me do."

Richard fell into the trap unwittingly. "What do you want to do?" he asked.

Annabel looked out across the box-elder tree. "Guess what I really want is to see something," she said. "All the other girls go out driving, but I never get a chance."

"You could walk," said Richard. "Lebanon ain't that big."

"I don't want to see Lebanon, stupid," she said, and slapped her hand on his chest. "I want to drive out into the country, like all the other girls do. Maybe clear down to Mason, or over along the Miami River. There's an old Indian fort over there, but it's pretty far."

Richard debated silently, and finally decided that he didn't want to drive Nellie in to town just to be kind to Annabel. But it wasn't because he found her distasteful. Annabel was as neat as a pin, and she was clean, and she had good manners. And he was getting used to her looks. He still doubted that she could read as well as Ike said she could, but she might be able. She talked pretty well.

"Tell you what," he said finally. "Maybe someday I'll borrow a rig somewhere. I won't promise, but if I get a chance, I will."

That was almost good enough for Annabel, and she seemed reasonably happy. And just as soon as they were back in the house she blurted out the news so that both her mother and Ike knew.

Ike only sniffed again. "How about that other feller?" he asked. "You give him the gate?"

"She ain't allowed to go out with him," said her mother. "He's a Dutchman."

"Plenty good Dutchmen in this world," said Ike, and Richard remembered that it was almost the exact conversation of a week ago.

"They ought to stay home then," said Mabel. "Don't know what they want over here anyway."

"They want Annabel," snorted Ike, and laughed explosively.

On the way back to the shop, however, Ike became more serious. "Tell you what," he told Richard. "What Annabel needs is to get out of that house once in a while. I'll drive my own rig down next Saturday, and you take her out for a little ride in the afternoon. Take her on down the pike a piece. Or take her on over where you live an' let her see the Shakers. She'd like that."

Richard didn't promise. He'd lose money by taking Annabel driving, and he certainly didn't have any intention of taking her out to the farm. Or to Shakertown. That last might be dangerous—there was a chance that Ruth might see them.

"Well, what about it?" Ike wanted to know. "I'll bring down my rig if you'll take Annabel out for a little drive."

Richard finally consented. There was always the chance that the next Saturday might be rainy, and if it weren't, he'd stay out only about an hour. They could head north from town a little piece on the stage road, or maybe go south towards the City. But they'd never get anywhere, not in an hour or two.

All that week he worried himself about the matter. He needed new clothes, at least a decent pair of pants. But he couldn't shoe horses in a decent pair of pants. The two ideas were incompatible— one didn't shoe horses and take a girl out driving in the same clothes, even if Ike did think so. But there was no help for the matter now, and Annabel would have to be satisfied with the only pants he owned.

Saturday came bright and warm, and today Annabel's hair was falling around her shoulders. She looked real pretty that way—there were curls and ringlets in her hair and it looked like old brass. Richard thought there was something different about her face too—it seemed composed and assured. But there was something wrong also—today there was hardly any conversation at the table. Ike didn't even ask about the Dutch fellow. And, for some curious reason, today the meal was fried chicken, as if it was a special occasion.

Both Ike and Mabel came out on the front porch to see them off, and Mabel even brought out a laprobe that she said was to keep the dust off Annabel's dress. The laprobe was heavy and would be too hot, but they obliged Mabel by pulling it over them before they drove away. Richard swung Ike's horse around and headed back for the pike, and once at the pike he turned north and thought he'd go on until he found a decent country road. There wouldn't be much to see on a country road, but it would be quieter, and he could give the horse her head. It would be pleasanter going on that way.

"IF YOU could have anything you wished for, what's the biggest wish you have in the whole world?" asked Annabel suddenly, and brought Richard back to his senses.

They were on top a long hill, passing a big white farmhouse with an equally big barn out behind. And the farmyard was full of chickens, and a collie dog had come out to the fence to bark at them.

"I don't know what you mean," said Richard. "Nobody can have the things he wishes for."

"I know that, silly," said Annabel, and managed to snuggle one of her hands into the loose knots his hands made on the reins. "But if you could, I mean. What would you wish for?"

Richard's mind raced. Fanny used to try to get him into traps by asking senseless questions like this, and he was not about to commit himself. "I guess twenty-five dollars," he said. "Asked any more, I know I wouldn't get it."

"Oh, silly!" said Annabel, and managed to slap him again. "I mean, what would you really wish for."

Richard refused to answer. "There's lots of things," he said at last. "We need all kinds of things at home. Ought to have a new plow, and harrow, and maybe even a whole new wagon."

"I didn't mean things like that."

"That's the only way I can think," he said. "Why? What do you want to know for?"

Annabel pouted. "Maybe just because I wanted to know," she said.

"Ain't no sense in wishing for the moon."

"There's no sense in wishing for things like a plow and wagon either," she said. "All it shows is a lack of ambition. It proved you don't have any gumption."

"Don't know what I'd do with it if I had it."

"You don't want to shoe horses all your life, do you?" asked Annabel directly. "If you do, you got bats in your head."

"What do you think I ought to want?"

Annabel found a handkerchief somewhere and wiped her face.

"What anybody else wants," she said. "You ought to want to be rich so that somebody else could shoe your horses for you. You ought to want to be like Judge Sloan."

Richard remembered the dapper man who had handed him a twenty-dollar bill. He had never told anyone about that, and the bill was at home in the bottom of a box.

"I wouldn't mind being rich," he said slowly. "If I was rich I'd find me a woman that had diamonds in her ears and a great big pearl necklace. And I'd have a couple of my front teeth knocked out and get gold ones put in."

This time Annabel looked at him as if she hadn't realized he was a complete ninny. "I was being serious," she said. "All I want's a nice house. And maybe some kind of rig and a team of horses. And then I'd marry and have three children, two boys and one girl, and I'd take French lessons. And we'd never have noodle soup again, not once in my life. That's what I'd do."

The talk flagged. They were going through a long cut in the side of a wooded hill, and it was dark and cool in the tunnel of leaves. And quiet—it was so quiet that they could not even hear any birds. Annabel pretended to be cool, and snuggled a little against him, and Richard obligingly let her snuggle. She was well padded, and he liked the feel of her hips against his.

"You know what?" he asked suddenly, and she suddenly opened her eyes and looked at him as if she expected something. "What?" she asked languorously.

"I bet we're lost," said Richard. "I never saw any of these places before."

After that Annabel seemed to retreat to her side of the buggy, and she was still sitting well away from him when they at last found Lebanon again. Richard jumped out to help her down, but she was already on the walk going into her house by the time he got around the buggy. He knew then that she was peeved, perhaps not really mad, but just a little hurt. It didn't surprise him. Mrs. Bentley had been the one woman in his life who had always been cool and sure of herself; all the others, even Ruth, had seemed to have whims. And Annabel was perhaps no better than most of the rest of them.

Ike seemed to expect some momentous announcement when he took the rig back and hitched it under the sycamore tree, but Richard tried to pretend he was busy, and Ike gave up after a time. Richard caught his glance a few times after that—it was inquisitive, but it was also almost accusing. He began to wonder what Ike had expected. Perhaps nothing more than any other silly old grandpa. Like women, they were most of them all alike.

THERE WERE other occasions, although Richard took oath that there would be no more. Ike skipped a Saturday, and then made Richard go with him the next because he said that Annabel was having a birthday, her seventeenth. What Ike didn't say was that he had made a slight miscalculation—the birthday wouldn't be for another two months. So they ate something that Ike's daughter called chowder. It looked horrible but it tasted all right, and since Ike had been foresighted enough to bring his buggy down to the shop, Richard was more or less pressured into taking Annabel out for another afternoon ride. He put a good face upon it, and even assumed good manners—he handed Annabel up into the buggy as prettily as if he had practiced. Annabel needed to be handed up about as much as she needed to be skinned; she was a strong and rather athletic girl, and she was decidedly out of place in pretending languor. Once settled in the buggy—and she had managed to take most of the middle of the seat—Annabel said that she wanted to go out east of town.

So east they went, and they were soon in a few hills. Richard thought of the old Indian fort, but he didn't know exactly where it was, and so they just drifted along as usual, except when Annabel got giddy and waved her handkerchief to cows and sheep out in the fields. That lasted a few miles, and then they finally broke down and said a few things to each other. No, Annabel didn't have her rabbits anymore—her mother had sold them all to some boy. And yes, Richard admitted that he and his father had a complete farm, with sheep, cows, pigs, and even geese. No, they never planted much wheat. Mostly corn. And some hay, of course; there had to be hay for the horses and cows.

Then, when things seemed to be going along fairly well, Annabel said what she really wanted to say. Asked rather. Out of a clear blue sky, there was the sudden question, "I don't know why you don't like me. Why don't you?"

Richard felt a tiny bit of a shock go through his nerves, but he pretended to be very busy with the reins. "I never said I don't like you," he said, and managed to control his voice. "I like you all right."

"You don't act like it."

"I guess I don't know how to act around women," said Richard. "I never had a sister. Maybe that's why."

Annabel snuggled a little nearer, although that was almost impossible. "Do you think I'm pretty?" she wanted to know, and bent her head around in front of Richard's face. "Do you?"

"I think lots of women are pretty," he said gallantly.

That made Annabel pretend to be furious. "I'm not talking about lots of women," she said sharply. "I'm talking about me. I don't think you ever knew lots of women. You don't act like it."

Richard drove, and whistled between his teeth. The tall cedars were stately on the high hillsides, and now and then there was a big barn or house nestled down under the trees. And there were lots and lots of sheep in the pastures. It was a high, white day, with the cumulus riding at the top of heaven.

"Well!"

It was Annabel again, and he had to force himself to turn to her to avoid being impolite.

"I like lots of girls," he said. "I mean I have. I don't know many girls now."

"I bet you don't know any girls now," said Annabel. "Besides me. And I bet you don't like anybody well enough to get married."

Richard drove on again. Ike's horse was a good trotter, and

when she picked up her feet it was a little hard to go on talking. But Annabel was urgent, and he had to make some kind of answer.

"Tell you the truth, I ain't never thought about it," he said. "It takes a lot of money to get married. Farmers don't make much money."

"You could go on working with Grandpa."

"I know I could. But I don't make much, only maybe two dollars a week. Can't live on that."

This time Annabel used both hands to grab his right arm. "I don't think you know what you're talking about," she said. "Or you don't want to. Farmers get all their living from the farm—everybody knows that. And they don't have to work very hard for it either. God just gives it to them."

Richard had to smile. Her face was stern, but it was very pretty, and the wind had brought color into her cheeks. But it was her eyes he liked, deep dark blue eyes that looked like pools of deep water. She was a pretty girl, a really pretty girl—there was no doubt about that. Now, when she was more earnest than he had ever seen her before, she looked as if she ought to be kissed into docility. He made the mistake and kissed her, and after that Annabel needed to be kissed a hundred times. And some of the kisses were long and wet, and Richard forgot all about the horse. Luckily the horse had been well trained and held right down the center of the road.

"I don't think you know what you're talking about," he said when he had straightened up and come back to a semblance of rationality. "I mean about farms. You don't know what you're talking about. Nothing comes easy."

Annabel too seemed to have returned to reason. At least she sat erect. "I could do wonders with a farm," she said. "You think I'm afraid to try, you're crazy."

"I bet you've never seen a farm. I mean really seen one, inside all the barns and stables and sheds. You don't know how much there is to do."

Annabel snuggled again. "Take me out," she half begged. "I want to see your farm. Take me out, will you, Richard."

It was the first time she had ever called him by name, and he rather liked to hear his name pronounced like a caress. He hadn't really meant for it to come to this sort of decision. He couldn't very well take her out because of his father, and he didn't want his father to get the wrong notions. But it might be all right some Sunday, he guessed—that would be the best time. He could drive Nellie in in the morning, and they could cook some sort of dinner together. And then, about three o'clock when he had showed her all about the place, he could bring her back into Lebanon and be home before late dark. It would probably do no harm. But he wouldn't want Ruth to know. Not that there was much chance—Ruth was probably gone forever. But he wouldn't want her ever to know.

"Well, will you? You act like you think I'm not good enough."

"It's my father," he temporized. "He's an old man, and I have to take care of him. My mother's dead—she died two months ago."

Annabel seemed to get serious. "I don't see how that matters," she said. "I'm not afraid of your father, and I don't see any reason he'd be afraid of me."

Richard thought of telling her that his father might get the wrong kind of ideas into his head, but decided he'd better not. Annabel would be insulted, and he really didn't want to hurt her. She was a fine girl, maybe a really fine girl, and she did seem to have ambitions. There was only one trouble—everytime he looked at her he remembered Ruth. It was only a trick of mind, of course, but right in front of his eyes Annabel would turn into Ruth. And they weren't in the least alike, but it was always Ruth and not Annabel that he was thinking about.

"Tell you what," he finally promised. "I can't take you out to-morrow because if it's good weather I might have to plow corn. But I will some Sunday. I'll come in and get you about nine o'clock in the morning and when we get home we'll have to get dinner. Will that be all right?"

Annabel evidently thought it very much all right because she bent her head up so that he had to kiss her again. It rather got on his nerves, all the kissing, but she seemed to expect it, and so he obliged her. But he knew, no matter what she thought, that she'd never make a farm woman. She'd never be able to get used to the lonesomeness. A person had to learn how to get along without trying to talk to the lilacs in the yard and the rhubarb along the garden fence. Some farmer's wives never did learn, and they went sort of crazy. That would be an ugly thing to happen to Annabel.

Chapter 10

IT WAS mid-August and they were marching again, marching in Jehovah's Chosen Square. The sheep had grazed the long grass down, and the rains had packed the ground reasonably hard, although it was still a bit springy underfoot. And now for consecutive Sundays they had danced and hummed in the great square of forest trees, and the windy air of the early mornings had been like tonic to their starved souls. Ruth was almost glad for the dancing, although about all she did was skip and shuffle in the closed ranks. Almost glad, but not completely. The Square meant too much to her—it was closely associated with better days from her past life. She wasn't furtive with her eyes because she knew that none of the Sisters knew her secret, but she was always looking back towards the east screen of trees. Richard and she had come through the beeches and oaks a dozen times together, and they had always talked soft because there seemed to be something mysterious about the holy ground. And now, by some sort of cataclysm, those days were gone forever, and all she could do was wheel and shuffle in the close-packed ranks of Sisters who evidently thought they were dancing before the Lord. Well, they were, in a way—the Divine Soul was likely in the sky and trees and even in the crows that kept flying over and cawing their heads off. Ruth bit her lips a little at that thought, but it was the only way she could think of God. There really wasn't any truth in the things the Shakers said about the woman they called Mother. She might have been a good woman—Ruth didn't really know, but she was certainly not the second Christ. There just wasn't any good reason for thinking so.

The men were half racing up and down now, and the older people were dropping out and going over to sit under the trees. Just as soon as the women started the fast shuffle, that's what all the old women would have to do too. But when they dropped out, they wouldn't go where the men stood congregated. The men always went to the north side of the Square and the women to the south. Ruth decided that just as soon as she had the opportunity she'd drop out too—only she'd go a little farther into the woods, clear off to the east. Those were the woods she knew, and she thought it would be good to see them again. What she wanted to do more than anything else was wander lonesome, kicking through the leaves, perhaps picking a few daisies or heads of phlox, or whatever offered. It wasn't right to live starved lives, the way the Shakers did. Things that were beautiful were meant to be enjoyed, and it was no sin to love flowers and plants and red squirrels and things like that. Religion was never supposed to be melancholy; one didn't worship God by pretending that He had made a botch of creation.

But it was not going to happen today, the opportunity she had hoped for. The men were making a block again, and the women were grinding along at diminished pace. It took Ruth a while to know what was happening. Then she saw the big man who was First in the Ministry of the men's side in Union Village, and he seemed he had something he meant to read because he was standing off to the north in front of the group with his hands up. That was what it was all about; just as soon as the dancers stopped the big man took off his hat and said he had another letter from the Ministry at Mount Lebanon. Ruth couldn't catch all the words, but she didn't try very hard. It was always something about holy and mighty angels—always holy and mighty angels, not any other kind. According to the Elder they had now begun their work again. The Ministry at Mount Lebanon asked that all believers should consecrate themselves so that they would become acceptable instruments of the Lord.

The Elder talked on a little after that, but Ruth couldn't hear him and didn't try. What she was really thinking about was that day in the woods with Richard. She had probably been a fool, or had as least acted like a fool. He had meant well, and she had had no reason to hate him because he had been forced into marrying some girl in Cincinnati. She'd never be completely able to forget that, of course, but in a long life one had to train oneself to forgive a lot of things. She had really acted like a fool and he probably would never come back.

They were dancing again, and Ruth had to pretend to shuffle. Over on her left was old Sister Mitterhauser, her face sweaty and gray locks coming out from under her cap, and on her right was a tall woman with hawk eyes who smelled and flapped her arms a little as if she'd like to take off into the trees. Ruth couldn't smile, but the smile crossed her mind if not her face. It was all ridiculous, completely stupid and ridiculous. People with good sense sat in their church pews on Sunday morning, and listened to what was called a sermon. And the Catholics heard mass, although Ruth hadn't the slightest idea what that was. Probably something about as bad as

Jehovah's Chosen Square. It wasn't so bad dancing in the Meeting House—there were chairs there for the old people when they got tired—but it was ridiculous to dance out in the woods. The woods were too sacred—one went through woods on tiptoe, and never even talked loud. It was enough just to look and listen, not bumble in one's chest and snort every time one had to draw another breath.

Next time they came here she'd run. Just wait ten or fifteen minutes, then go over into the front trees, then work her way to the east woods. And after that she'd travel—she didn't know how far. No one would miss her when the Family marched back to the East, and she might be able to stay away all afternoon. Then, when she finally had to come back, whoever saw her would only suppose that she was coming in from doing some outside chores or visiting the necessary.

Ruth felt better after that. She even reached over and told Sister Mitterhauser to drop out and sit down a while. Sister Mitterhauser did, just as soon as they marched down to the south side of the Square again. Ruth wondered about her a little, just as she wondered about all the rest of the people in the Families. Sister Mitterhauser looked as if she should be somebody's grandma, and she should probably be thinking about serving Sunday chicken and dumplings to her family. That was probably the trouble, that she no longer had any family and had been forced to turn Shaker. There wasn't another good reason to be Shaker, not in the world.

IT WAS a fine late-August day, and in the early morning there was a white ground mist over all the land. It smothered the head-high fields of corn and made islands of farmsteads. But it would be hot later, probably very hot. Driving Nellie indolently and not caring very much when he got into Lebanon, Richard had time to indulge in many long thoughts about Annabel. One of them was perfidious to Ruth—it was that Annabel would very probably make a good wife. She seemed loyal and steadfast, and he thought that she would very soon acquire a great deal of competence in doing all the things that had to be done on the farm. She'd even probably like doing some of the things: making butter, taking care of the garden, dressing chickens, things like that. Annabel had what she had claimed he himself didn't have: gumption. He wasn't sure exactly what she had meant by the word, but he supposed it meant something like standing up for what a person thought were his rights. Richard half agreed with her—he very probably didn't have gumption. People with gumption didn't stop to stare at things—they were forever pushing. That might be the only real way to get ahead in the world.

Cutting into Lebanon and turning north past the Golden Lamb, Richard noticed that the sun-lacquered streets were full of people who were all dressed up in their Sunday clothes. Churchgoers probably—some of them even now climbing into rigs and surreys that stood at the hitching blocks. He felt a bit ashamed when he saw the way they were dressed, some of the women in white ruffled dresses and wide hats, and with satiny ribbons and flounces that shimmered in the sun. The men were more somber, most of them in black, but some of them wore top hats and swung silver-mounted canes. He couldn't help wondering if he'd ever be able to afford such finery. The world was a big place and it had lots of different kinds of people in it, but most of them seemed to like to parade. There must be something the matter with him that he didn't. He liked things that were solid, not just for show. Solid iron or solid maple or solid cherry or walnut. And solid brick and stone. Some of the Lebanon houses were like that, and they gave character to the families that lived in them. Out home too many things were make-do, slabs of boards nailed over holes, wire holding up rusty gates, things like that. It was the same way inside the house—the rockers were broken on a couple of the chairs and too many of the dishes and crocks were chipped and dented. Out home they seemed to think that anything was good enough; here in Lebanon the people probably thought that nothing was good enough.

Richard slowed Nellie as he turned right on Plum Street and went by Ike's blacksmith shop. It was only three houses now, and he let Nellie walk in. He wondered how Annabel would be dressed. Bright as a penny probably, with no thought of how rough her clothes should be for the country. That was the only way he had ever seen her—she had always been bright as a penny. It was probably a good characteristic, and he certainly didn't object to it. Green was her color, he had noticed that, green or blue, and she almost always wore a string of beads or a locket. Actually she looked rich—a stranger would never guess that she came from this mean little house on Plum Street. The Johnsons didn't have any land at all; there wasn't enough out back that they could even put in a decent garden. And the land sloped off to some sort of thickety creek or run, so that even the little they had wasn't manageable.

Annabel did not come out on the porch, and Richard had to hop down and go in. Once he was across the porch, however, he saw her—she and her mother were standing right beside the center table. Annabel had on green just as he expected, and she was holding some sort of little green hat in her hand. The hat had long wide ribbon ties, and he guessed that she'd make a bow under her chin.

"I'll bet you thought I'd never come," he said when he got in through the door. "I had all the chores to do first."

Neither Annabel nor her mother seemed to care about that. They both stood silent, as if apprehensive about something. Richard didn't have to wait very long to discover what it was. "Papa's out in the kitchen," said Mrs. Johnson. "Guess maybe you'd best go out and say howdy-do." Richard thought she made a wry face, but that might have been imagination.

Annabel took his hand and started to lead him out, and Richard thought she was shaking a little. He found out why—at the kitchen table there sat slumped a big black hulk of a man. His hair hung down over his neck and was even in the way of his eyes. Richard thought his eyes looked mean. "This here's Richard, Papa," said Annabel, and her mother immediately put in "Richard Robinson. He works for Grandpa on Saturdays."

The big man at the table didn't get up, but he did hold out his hand. He also burped, and pulled his hand back to wipe it across his mouth. "Heard of you," he said, and looked away. "Seems to be all Annabel's talking about. What do you do, farm?"

Richard thought it was a pointless question. "We've got near a hundred acres," he said. "Ain't all good for farming—some of it's too hilly."

Johnson only scowled. "Ought to get you a good team an' a good heavy wagon," he said. "Can't make any money out of farmin'."

Richard didn't debate the question. They stood like dummies, and Johnson finally reached for another hunk of bread and smeared it with apple butter. "Well, I guess we'd better be going," Richard told Annabel. "It'll take us a while to get out there."

They went back out unceremoniously, and Annabel's mother

followed them out onto the skinny front porch. "You take care, Annabel," she kept saying. "Don't step in anything. You know what I mean."

Annabel evidently did because she giggled. Once out into the sunlight she seemed more like herself and she swung her hat merrily as they went down the walk. This time Richard didn't hand her up into the buggy; she climbed up energetically and as usual plopped herself right down in the middle of the seat. And this time her mother evidently didn't think of providing any kind of laprobe.

Richard breathed again as soon as he was away from the house. He definitely didn't like Annabel's father, and he thought her mother must have had a hard time of it in the world. Mabel Johnson stood at the edge of the front porch until they were out of sight, and when Annabel waved back she didn't even return the greeting. Like a lot of other women he had seen in his life, Mabel Johnson was probably what was called a happily married wife.

THEY CUT UP in the buggy, and it was a good thing that Nellie knew the road. Once out of Lebanon Annabel was a chatterbox, and she asked a thousand questions. She also was embarrassing because she pointed at every house and every person they passed. Who were those people—did Richard know them? When were lambs born, and pigs, and calves? How many were there out on the farm? Had Nellie ever had a colt? What did a person do out in the country when he needed a doctor? Did Richard still have all his teeth? She had all hers, but did Richard? Was he putting up anything? Why not? It wouldn't stay warm all the time, and when winter came they'd be glad to have some stuff in crocks.

Richard noticed that she had used "we'll" and not "you'll." He didn't mind—she had a right to think that way if she wanted to. He had tried to imagine what it would be like if he were married to Annabel. She wouldn't be like Fanny—he would bet a large part of his soul that she wouldn't be like Fanny. For one thing Annabel would turn out to be a doer. She wouldn't need books to read; she'd just go from morning till night using her hands and feet. But—and this was one of the first things he had thought of—they'd find it awkward living together in the farmhouse because of Richard's father. Abraham Robinson couldn't be turned out of the bedroom he had occupied for years, and that meant that they'd have to put a bed in the far corner of the living room, since Richard couldn't expect Annabel to climb to the loft. That would crowd the living room, but it could be done. Only they'd have to be careful not to make too much noise at night.

They were going up past Berzinski's old double cabin now, and Richard felt a little twinge in his heart. He brought the reins down and made Nellie trot again. "Won't be long till we get there now," he said. "That's the last house."

"It don't look much like a house," said Annabel.

Richard didn't comment. They got on the stretch of corduroy and climbed the far hill, and there on their left in front of them were the Robinson buildings. This morning, for all the sun's light, they looked mean and ugly, the house much too small, the barn somewhat in need of repairs. Richard had meant to nail the boards back where the farm horses had kicked them off their stalls, but he had never gotten around to doing it.

"Well, guess that's it," he said, and waved his hand. "Don't look like much, but we like it all right."

For some reason Annabel didn't say anything. She just sat and stared, and she was still staring when they turned in to the lane. Richard thought her face looked puzzled when she turned towards him. "Does anybody else live up this road?" she asked, and she seemed a little frightened.

"Taylors," said Richard. "And the Rafe Peterses. And there's a hill church up there a little piece farther on."

Annabel just kept looking. Richard had known that she might be disappointed because the Robinson place didn't look anything like the big farmhouses down on the pike.

"It's not bad when you get used to it," he said. "Fact is, you get so you sort of like it."

Annabel was brave. "I didn't know it'd be this lonesome," she said when he helped her down from the buggy. "It's so quiet. There's nobody around."

"Nobody but the birds," said Richard. "Only when the wind blows in winter you know it. Gets so bad sometimes you can't even talk outside the house."

It was a little better when they went into the kitchen. Richard had cleaned up fairly well, and had even swept the floor. And

Abraham Robinson came out from his chair before the fireplace and held out his hand. Annabel took it and kept looking at him, as if she couldn't believe he was really alive. "Took you a good long time," said Abraham finally. "It's past dinnertime."

That at least provided them with a reason to do something. Richard sliced potatoes and Annabel found one of Mrs. Robinson's old aprons and tied it around her middle before she got a crock and started on what she called a cake. She had a time because she didn't know where anything was, but they did manage to find eggs and lard and sugar and soda and flour. Annabel said she had wanted a dark cake, but there was no chocolate in the house. There never had been.

It was better when they finally got down at table, although there was no meat. But the bread and butter and fried potatoes tasted good and Annabel jumped up from time to time to look at her cake in the wood stove. It didn't rise properly, but it did come up a little, and they decided to let it in the oven until they were finished with their coffee. Instead of cake Richard went out of the house and down into the dirt cellar and finally came back with a jar of what he said were peach preserves. There was a little green mould on the jar, but the preserves tasted good on bread. They sat a long time drinking coffee and answering Annabel's questions as best they could, and in consequence they ate too much, so that the hot cake was ready before they rose from the table. Like pigs they even ate some of that.

Then it was time for dishes, but Richard hadn't put any water to heat because he had decided that they wouldn't do dishes. Annabel didn't seem to be able to understand that, and Richard had to argue with her. The dishes always had to be done, had to be done just as soon as the meal was finished. Otherwise the kitchen was no longer usable.

"I just thought you'd rather go out," Richard said. "I can do them tonight."

So they went out, and old Abraham got his cane and came along with them. Mose was waiting at the back door and barking, and they walked two and two, Richard and Annabel first, then Abraham and Mose. Annabel didn't like the pigs in the pigpen, and she seemed disappointed that the cows and sheep were all out on the hills. She did like the horses and the oxen, and Richard let her throw them armfuls of hay. Then it was time for the geese and the chickens, and Annabel was afraid of the geese—they were too big and strong and they hissed. By that time they had left Abraham and Mose behind—they had stayed in the barn, probably with the oxen. Richard knew that his father spent a lot of his time talking to Midge and Frank.

"Guess maybe you want to see the garden too," said Richard when they came back out of the henhouse. "Ain't much this year—my Mom always took care of it. Guess maybe Papa and I don't know the right sort of things to do."

"That would be my job," said Annabel promptly. "I mean, what I think I could do best would be take care of the garden."

The garden was on a gentle hillslope northwest of the house, and to get to the gate they had to go around the fence that was supposed to keep out the chickens. Richard was ashamed when they went through the gate—the place was more grown up with weeds than he had remembered. There was a fair patch of corn, and he knew approximately where the cabbage row was supposed to be, but he couldn't find the redbeets at all—they had been completely smothered under a blanket of chickweed.

"Don't much matter," he said, and stood up suddenly so that all the blood drained out of his head. Annabel was standing in front of him, and suddenly over her shoulder he thought he saw something moving in the field of corn behind the barn. Whatever it was was between the cornrows three or four hills in from the edge of the field, and it looked like a person. And the colors were too dark to tell for sure, but Richard thought that the person was dressed in Shaker gray. Whoever or whatever it was just stood there for what seemed a long time, and then slowly began to dissolve in front of his eyes until it was swallowed by the corn.

"What's the matter, Richard?" he heard Annabel say.

"Ain't nothing the matter. I just stood up too fast."

"You look like you saw a ghost," she said. "Your face is green."

That was an impossibility, and Richard knew it. His face might have gone a little white, but it certainly was not green. However, he felt his pulses pounding madly, and he wondered how he could get Annabel back in the buggy so that he could drive her into Lebanon.

"You'll have to take your cake with you when you go," he said when they were coming back out of the garden gate. "Papa and I never eat cake."

Annabel looked just a little puzzled. "You mean it's time?" she asked.

"Guess it's time if I'm going to have you home for supper," he said. "What time do you eat?"

"Eat sometimes at four o'clock when Pop's home," said Annabel. "What time is it?"

Richard looked at the sun and knew it was after three. He fairly dragged Annabel to the barn, pushed her out of the way when she wanted to help him hitch, and promptly drove her out of the yard without another thought of the cake. In fact, he never even let her say good-bye to his father. The thought that he didn't dare say out loud, that he didn't dare even think out loud, was that it had been Ruth in the corn. And if it had been Ruth, then Ruth was in trouble and by God he'd find out what the trouble was just as soon as he came back from Lebanon.

ON THAT BRIGHT Sunday morning when the layered fog lay like cotton over the fields it was announced at breakfast that the Ruling Elders had again ordained that there would be dancing in Jehovah's Chosen Square. They were eating hominy that morning, and for hominy made palatable by cream and maple syrup Ruth had simply no appetite. She felt her heart skip, however, when she knew that they would again be in the Chosen Square. She'd get away as soon as she could—it looked as if it would be a bright day in the woods. What she'd do after she escaped from the dancers she had no very adequate idea, but she did know that she would not come back until night. So, when Sister Agnes passed her the heavy plate of cheese, she didn't pass it on to Sister Agatha as she customarily did, but carefully chose two large pieces and laid them on her plate. It might be a harder trick to provide herself with bread, but if no suitable opportunity offered, she decided that she'd simply bend over the table and pick up two slabs before she left the room.

As usual on such mornings when the Society had been told to march all the way to the Square, there were some complaints in the hall, particularly from those older members who couldn't march a mile at the rapid pace the Elders always set. The Chosen Square was way beyond the white Meeting House—in fact, it was back in the fields halfway up to the North Family. Ruth heard two old women sputtering as she walked past them—she knew by the way they favored their bunions that they had no business marching. It was the same when she got back in her own room; Carrie Carmody fairly exploded the moment she came through the door. Carrie had a reasonably adequate vocabulary, particularly a negative one, and she wasn't afraid to say sometimes that she thought the Ruling Ministry must be made up of fools. "They ought to know," she kept on saying. "My Gawd, they ought to know that's too far for people to trot just to stumble around under the hot sun. Sometimes I think—" and she broke off without actually saying what she thought, so that Ruth had to prod her. "I think they're all idiots, that's what," said Carrie firmly. "They don't do anything all week except just sit on their behinds up in the Meeting House. That's all they do."

Ruth wouldn't argue the matter. She had thought about the Ruling Elders a few times herself, and like Carrie she had wondered what they really did with their time. The House Elders were different—they generally kept an eye on everything that happened in their Families, and they knew what all the Deacons and Deaconesses were doing. But the Ruling Elders, the two on the men's side, as they called it, and the two on the women's side, must just sit and look out the windows and think holy thoughts. It didn't seem like a very profitable way to pass time.

Carrie grumbled, but she was ready at half past nine, and they went down to assemble with all the others in the lower hall. Eldresses Anna and Mary kept counting as the women came down the stairs, and in the front hall Elder Phineas Riegel and Elder Arnold Peabody seemed to be counting the men. It was cool and dark in the hall, but outside the sun was blazing down, so that Ruth knew it would be hot marching. She should have left off one of her petticoats—three would be too many for such a hot day. Maybe she'd take off one—or even two—and hide them as soon as she got into the woods. But the woods might be cooler, particularly the thick woods where the sun hardly even slit down between the trees. Ruth looked at the big clock on the wall, but the hands said that it was already nearly a quarter until ten, so that she knew she didn't have time to go back to her room and change.

Then, at ten minutes to ten exactly, they were off, and the minute they went out the door somebody started one of the hymns. It had a good catchy tune and they could tramp to the music. Ruth

didn't know the words—all the Shaker hymns were alike. All they
ever talked about was Mother and being good and obedient children
so that they could come to Mother in Paradise. Elder Riegel seemed
to be setting a fast pace, and already some of the older people were
falling out and dragging along behind. Right down the center of the
road they kept plodding, and one of the teamsters on the road saw
them coming and politely pulled his wagon off to the side of the
pike until they got by. The sun was hot, and it seemed there were no
birds flying. But the cornfields looked cool—the corn was past head-
high. And off to the left and immediately south of the Center Family
was a field of blue flax that was pretty. Then, just before they got to
the Center, that Family started out to the road, and Elder Phineas
politely stopped the East line until the Center had all gotten onto the
pike.

It was only a little way after that until they came to the lane
leading back between cornfields, and once in the lane they stopped
trying to march together because the ground was hummocky. Ruth
went ahead at her leisure, and lots of impatient Sisters passed her.
The thought occurred to her then that it might be more sensible not
to go all the way to the Square; if she hung back, she could probably
get off the lane and go back through the corn until she reached the
woods. It was such a good idea that she tried it, but there were too
many stragglers, and some of the people in front of her started
turning around and shouting for all of them to come on. Ruth did.
It would probably be better to go all the way to the Square—she
didn't know the south part of the woods very well, and she did
know the part that bordered the Square. She'd have to endure a few
hymns before the dancing started, and one of the Elders would
probably have something to say. That was the way it generally happened, even though practically no one could hear the Elders when
they spoke out in the open. But it was no loss—they always said the
same thing anyway.

Ruth maneuvered so that she could get into the outside line in
the women's block. Sometimes that wouldn't work, and it wouldn't
if somebody started some of the fancy maneuvers that made the files
go through each other. But it wouldn't matter because everyone always had to go clear down to the end of the lot before he turned and
countermarched, and at the end one could always pretend he had to
stop a while or go into the woods. And Ruth didn't much care if

anyone saw her, or wondered about her. She had thought of telling
Carrie what she meant to do, but at the last moment she hadn't because Carrie talked too much. No, she'd just go off when the opportunity offered and spend the day any way she liked. And then, when
she came in at night, if anyone wanted to question her, that would
be his privilege. She could always say that she had gotten a little
sick, or felt faint.

Elder Michael was talking now, and they were all standing piously and swatting their hands at honeybees and flies. It didn't seem
to matter that nobody could hear—they were used to that. And
Elder Michael wouldn't talk long—he never talked long. Ruth
thought that she would be a little ashamed if Elder Phineas knew
what she meant to do. He had been good to her, and she liked him
as much as anyone. But he wouldn't understand—none of them
would understand. All that most of them wanted was to discharge
their duty and march back home for dinner. And probably sleep
through the afternoon. They wouldn't understand what a privilege it
was just to walk in the woods.

They were forming ranks to dance now, the men on the left, the
women on the right, everyone an arm's length away from anyone
else. Then the bumble started and soon everyone was making that
raucous noise that sounded like a hive of swarming honeybees.
Their feet moved, and they marched, up and down a few times
rather sedately, and then faster as they all got used to the pace. Mm-
mmmmmmmmmmmmmmmmmm went their throats, and then some
idiots started singing, and then they Mmmmmmmmmmmmm-ed
some more. Ruth kept on watching for her chance. It was a little
early to fall out, but some of the older people were already doing it.
Well, she'd wait a little while, perhaps five minutes longer. Then it
would be Mmmmmmm and out into the woods, and anyone who
wanted too much to know what she was about might have his long
nose scratched by blackberries.

IT WAS A golden day, a glorious day, and the farther away she got,
the more glorious it became. It was surprising how far the noise of
the Shaker humming carried—she could imagine she heard it
when she was clear back in the hickory grove. No matter, no matter
now—let them bumble until their noses dripped. Her stupid

petticoats came off and were hidden under a scrubby hawthorn. Ruth piled leaves over them and then took a line on two big hickories so that she could find them again before she went back. She'd have to find them because there was no way of replacing them, and Eldress Anna was a stickler for petticoats. And it wouldn't be until late fall that she'd be able to replace them—in Shakertown everyone got two complete sets of clothing every year, and that was all. And one set was supposed to be in the washhouse every Monday morning.

Now that she was alone, Ruth realized that she really had no plans for the day. Well, she'd walk east, and south. Probably before the day was over she'd go east clear as far as the road. Nostalgically she thought she'd like to see her old home again, although there was something inside her that told her that she really didn't want to see it. She wondered what had happened to them all, particularly what had happened to Rachel. Richard had said that Asenath was in Cincinnati, and that seemed strange. But Asenath was the bull-headed one—she never said much, but she did just about what she wanted to, and little else. There had probably been a fight before they had gotten to Cincinnati; Ruth didn't know, but she thought that Asenath had perhaps said that she wouldn't go down into Kentucky. Somehow, irrationally, Asenath had always said that Ohio was better than Kentucky—the Kentuckians were always fighting and feuding all the time.

Ruth wandered carefree, and now and then providently felt for the bread and cheese in her pocket. It had made a big bulge, but she hadn't minded, and happily no one had asked her what she was carrying. Somewhere, she knew, she'd sit down and eat her noon meal. Maybe down by one of the pools in the little creek that trickled through the woods—that would be a fine spot. And then maybe she could take off her shoes and stockings and wade a while, the way she had done when she was a little girl. Or simply lie on some moss on a shelf over the bankside and watch the dragonflies stitching up and down over the water. She kept telling herself that that was what she would do, and that then she'd be perfectly happy, but for some unknown reason she kept on delaying finding the spot. She wouldn't acknowledge as much to herself, and she kept on fighting down the thought, but it kept coming back—she wasn't really happy, and just being in the woods didn't make her so.

She went over it all again in her own mind: Richard had said that he'd come back and marry her just as soon as he could. And then he had married some girl in Cincinnati because he had had to. That was the cardinal offense—that he had had to. It didn't help a lot that the girl had died and her baby with her—he shouldn't have had to marry her in the first place. And then he had slunk back home like a dog with his tail between his legs, and he had had the nerve to think she'd still want him. And she didn't and wouldn't, not ever.

She did eat her bread and cheese, and afterwards couldn't remember eating any of it. And she took off her shoes and stockings and waded, and the water was really too cold when it came up to her knees. She couldn't remember that it had been this cold when she was a little girl. Then she had gone barefoot most of the summer, and she was in and out of the water a dozen times a day.

She sat on the bank in the sun and made herself very still so that the birds and animals would come about again. They didn't. The woods seemed strangely sterile, almost lifeless. Looking down at the moss she could see that ants were busy threading in and out of the green fibers, but they didn't offer much companionship. Then she did see a bluejay flash across one of the branches, but it disappeared almost immediately. There was something wrong, and she didn't know what it was. It seemed that she didn't want anything anymore, didn't want to go back to the Shakers, didn't want anything else. If only Richard hadn't made such a fool of himself. He was a greenhorn, that was the trouble—he didn't understand what the world was all about. If she had been the one who had gone to Cincinnati, she would never have lost her head over any man. And his shabby excuses. She didn't believe that at all, that men couldn't control themselves as well as women. Goodness knew women wanted things too: they wanted to be loved, and they wanted babies, and a home, and a kitchen to cook things in, and all sorts of things like that.

It must be about two by the sun, and she would have to think about starting back in another hour or so. First, however, she'd like to go a little farther, perhaps clear on back to the Robinson cornfield. She knew it would be a cornfield because it always had been—it was almost the only place the Robinsons could plant corn. She could walk through the corn and not be seen. Somehow, once she had made that resolution, she felt better, and when she got her black stockings and shoes back on she started to walk fast. And now, for some strange reason, the woods seemed to come alive. She saw red squirrels and gray squirrels, and once she saw a big yellow fox that was standing on a stump and sniffing. Ruth froze in her tracks and watched him while he stood there, and while she was pretty sure that he knew about her, he didn't seem to mind. Then, finally, he was gone, but he didn't go towards the Robinson farm because he had probably heard old Mose barking. Ruth wasn't sure, but she though she had heard Mose herself.

It was good once she got in the corn, and she went down the north end of the field, although she was careful to hide herself by sheltering herself behind three or four of the cornrows. For some reason her heart was racing, and she felt as if her cheeks were flushed. That couldn't be true—it was probably only that the sun was hot. But it wasn't hot in the corn, so that shouldn't be the reason. Then, far ahead of her, she saw the old barn with its gray boards, and now she was certain old Mose was barking. The Robinsons were probably out—it was getting near to the time they'd be thinking about doing chores. Well, she'd sort of like to see them again. She had always liked Richard's father—he was a gentleman. And, if she could, she'd like to see Richard. Not that she had any further designs on him. Only simply because he had always been something like a big brother to her. He would be still, if she hadn't made such a fool of herself when he had come after her and they had gone down into the south woods.

She froze—there were people in the garden. Richard certainly. And a woman—no, it was only a girl. Ruth couldn't see her properly because the weeds were too high, but she looked as if she were almost as tall as Richard. And her hair was copper-colored, and she had on a little green hat. There—she saw Richard straighten up, and he seemed to be looking in her direction. Ruth made herself very still, and then when he kept on looking, she lowered her head and started sneaking back through the corn. And now her heart was racing again, and she couldn't stop it.

The nerve of him. She couldn't believe it—that he should have found a girl so fast. There wasn't anyone like that in the whole neighborhood, and he had probably brought her in from Monroe or Lebanon. But the colossal nerve he had. He must be as hard-hearted as a stone—he didn't seem to have any common sense at all.

The corn cut her, and she managed to scratch herself badly in a blackberry snarl as she hurried out of the Robinson field. Her jaws were set, and she was very angry. She'd like to know who that hussy was, and she'd like to tell her a few things. The most important one was that she was making a fool of herself if she thought she could trust Richard. That was all—a complete fool of herself.

RICHARD NEVER whipped Nellie, and he wouldn't whip her today, but he did try to keep her jogging. And Annabel didn't seem to mind—she sat well away from him on her side of the buggy, and seemed to be content just to stare at the fields as they went by. Sunday afternoon was very still, and there was little sign of life on the farms. Even the cows were lying down under trees in corners of the pastures, as if they too were waiting for nothing but time to start the long file home. And the road, which had never seemed that long before, went on and on interminably, and felt a great deal more rutted than it had been in the morning.

But at last Lebanon, and at long last Ike's blacksmith shop, and the row of skinny white houses.

Annabel hopped down the moment he pulled Nellie in. Richard thought she wasn't going to say anything, and it was quite pointed that she didn't ask him to come inside. For a moment she just appeared to stand beside the buggy and stare at him, and the thought jumped into his mind that she was saying a silent good-bye. As she poised there, her big blue eyes looking right through him, Richard couldn't help a tiny spasm of regret. It hadn't been what she had expected—the farm had disappointed her. And she was saying good-bye, saying good-bye forever.

"I'm sorry if you didn't have a good time," he managed to get out.

For a moment she didn't say anything, just stood and looked, almost as if she wanted to cry, and then, without a word, she turned around and ran up the walk. Richard had Nellie going before Annabel went in through the door. He was sorry in a way that he was such a clod—it did seem as if he owed Annabel more than he had given her. Maybe she could find a way to go back to her Dutchman now, Sigerd, or whatever his name was.

He never remembered how he got back out of Lebanon that

day—he had been thinking too hard. And his thoughts were like a knot of tangled string, and he couldn't find any way to unravel the knot. There were a few options, none of them good. The first was that he could just go back home and do nothing. If it had been Ruth in the corn, then she might come back again, or never come back. Or he could go home, and without doing any of the chores or milking, set out through the woods after her. There was a chance that she'd still be there, waiting for him. There was a larger chance that she wouldn't be. Or, and this was the thing he really didn't want to do, he could drive right down the road to the East Family and demand to see her. Whoever was in charge would either let him see her, or not let him. And it might just be that if Ruth were there she wouldn't want to see him. In that case he would have some kind of answer, not a very satisfactory one, but an answer nevertheless.

He drove for the East Family, and Nellie was never slower. The sun looked now like it might be as late as five o'clock, and if so he would likely surprise the East Family at their supper. It wasn't much on Sunday nights—he had heard that. But it would be good just to see Ruth again, to know that she was safe.

Turning into the East yard he noticed the two yuccas in bloom beside the front gate, and wondered why the Shakers tolerated them, since insofar as he knew they were good for nothing. The lane led straight back to the barns, and Richard knew there was no place to tie, but that was all right since Nellie wouldn't wander away. And he'd have to go to the front door, since that was the only way strangers were ever admitted. His legs felt rubbery, and he was shaking a little, but he did walk back around the big house and climb the three steps leading up to the door. No one came when he knocked, and after a time he realized that if the Family was at dinner, no one would come. After that he turned the knob and went in. It was dark and cool in the hall, and it took a little while for his eyes to adjust to the gloom. His ears told him that everyone was back in the big room by the kitchen where the family ate, and he started walking in that direction. Perhaps he could just stand in the door and see whether Ruth was sitting at one of the tables.

"You want something?"

He jumped when he heard the voice behind him. Standing there was what looked like a white old woman, her dark dress indistinguishable in the dark hall. All he could see were her cap, face, collar, and white hands. But she didn't seem to be excited in the least; she just stood there and waited for him to speak.

"I wanted to say something to Ruth Berzinski," he said. "Do you know whether she's here?"

The old woman acted as if she had not heard him, and for a long while just stood again. "You mean Sister Ruth?" he heard her finally ask. "The schoolteacher?"

Richard nodded his head yes, and then, when he realized that she might not be able to see him, said, "That's the one I mean. The schoolteacher."

The old woman didn't say anything after that, just started to move down the hall in the direction of the dining room. Richard wondered if she meant for him to follow her, and finally decided that it would do no harm. A few people who had finished their meal were coming out of one of the far doors now, and they all went by like shadows, the women distinguishable by their caps and collars. Richard bumped right into a tall man—it seemed the fellow hadn't seen him at all.

They stood in the doorway looking, and Richard's anxious eyes swept up and down the women's table, and then looked again more carefully. Ruth was not at the table, and the probability was that she hadn't been. The old woman who had escorted him finally turned and held out her hands in a gesture of defeat. "I don't see her," she said. "I don't see Sister Ruth at all."

"Could she be up in her room?"

"I don't know. I don't think so. I'll ask Sister Carrie—she's the one that lives with her."

Richard crowded the door while the old woman went inside the dining room, watched while she went up to some rough-looking countrywoman and started talking. The two seemed to be a little agitated, because when the old woman came back to the door, the farm woman came with her. They made a cluster outside the door to the dining room, and the one who was called Sister Carrie seemed genuinely disturbed. "She didn't come back," she kept on saying. She didn't come back from the Square atall. I don't know where she is."

Richard's ears pricked up at the mention of the Square. That was how Ruth had gotten up into the woods, then—she had just run away from the Sunday morning dance. And that's where she'd still be, up in the woods somewhere. God knew what she was about, but if she had not come back to the East Family, then she probably meant never to come back.

He went back up the hall without thanking everyone. Out in the open once more, he looked at the sun—it would still be light a good two hours. He couldn't drive Nellie home, but he could drive her up the Red Lion Pike until he came near the Square. In fact, he might be able to drive her right into the Square and let her graze there. She'd be safe, and there was a good chance that no one would ever lay eyes upon her.

IT WAS BEGINNING to get dark in the woods, and the blackbirds were loud as they swarmed about the tall trees and tried to get settled for the right. Richard had walked fast, straight back to the hickory grove, then on beyond the hickories to the thicker woods that went on clear to the Robinson cornfield. But Ruth was not in the thicker woods, and he didn't really think she would be. The thought came to him to call for her, but he didn't because he had always hated people who shouted in the woods. And it was likely that Ruth wouldn't answer anyway. Something he had managed to do, however, was to get himself scratched raw with blackberries. It was hard to see the canes in the gathering dark under the trees. The sun was low in the sky now and would soon go under, but there would be almost a full moon in another hour or so. The moon might be even better than the sun.

He turned south, knowing that Ruth had often used the path beside the little creek. The woods were more open down there, although it was very dark under the low-hanging beeches. Perhaps that's what she was doing—perhaps she had simply crawled under one of the big trees and decided to bed down for the night. They had often crawled under the beeches together, but they had never spent a night there. But it was a lovely place to hide.

It took time to look under all of the beeches, and he didn't do a very good job of it. There were too many trees to investigate, and after a time he had to reorient himself. The sun was down now, and it was gray dark, but in the eastern sky there was the first glow of light from the rising moon. He thought again of calling, and almost did, but when he opened his mouth no sound came out of his throat. He just didn't want to do it, and Ruth wouldn't want him to do it.

They never called out in the woods—they always went silent as shadows. He wondered what the Shakers would be thinking about Ruth's disappearance. He wondered what his father would be thinking about his own. Old Abraham had had to go without his supper, although he had probably filled up on Annabel's cake. But the cows would be in misery and the chickens would have gone to roost without their corn. That didn't matter—not very much. The important business now was to find Ruth.

He thought then of the Berzinski cabin, and half decided that that was exactly where she'd be. It would be scary and uncomfortable in there in the dark, but Ruth didn't scare easily, and she had never asked for any comfort. He'd have to go along the creek until he came to the Berzinskis'. But if she were not there, then he'd be worse off than he was now. Better to scour the woods thoroughly before he blundered all the way over to the cabin.

It was useless, senseless—she was simply not in the woods. The rim of the moon was up now and it was tracing all the trees with light, but there was nothing to be seen. Richard made himself very still for a long time, his ears acute. He heard the leaves rasp a little under what must be some animal prowler, but there was no sound of a person walking. It was maddening—it was about like hunting for the needle in the proverbial haystack. There was a deeper and more impenetrable woods farther south—it was the one from which the Shakers generally cut their trees for lumber. For some reason Richard didn't think Ruth would be down there—the minute a person got off one of the wheeltracks through the Shaker woods he was in trouble.

Well, he'd start for the Berzinskis' and get that trip out of the way. Then, if necessary, he'd come back and hunt all night. There was a chance, of course, that Ruth had simply walked away, towards either Red Lion or Monroe. Or gone straight south on the pike that led down towards Cincinnati. He didn't think that she had done any one of those things, but there was no way of telling. Ruth was in a way unpredictable—she had a mind of her own.

IT WAS PROBABLY ten o'clock at night, and he was tired. The moon was riding high now, and the whole night was blue-silver, the tall trees etched against the sky. He had been to the Berzinskis' and had walked over every foot in the two cabins. There was no other place to hide. The horrible thought came to him while he was at the Berzinskis' that Ruth might have thrown herself down the well. He was almost afraid to look, but was happy when he did—the old half-rotten boards were still in place on the well-head. After that he felt better, no matter how discouraged he was. If only Annabel hadn't been at the farm. Ruth had likely made up her mind—she had been coming to him when she had seen Annabel in the garden. Life always seemed to arrange things like that; it seemed never to permit anything to be easy, plain, or simple. The flowers did bloom naturally, and the crops grew, but there was always blight, rot, murrain, and scab, worms in fruit, mold on the wheat in shock, smut on the corn. It seemed as if God just hadn't arranged things right. Or maybe—and this was a horrible thought—maybe He had contrived for everything to be a little blighted. That made man turn to Him for help. But the Shakers didn't believe like that, and there was generally little wrong with their wheat, corn, and apples.

He was going west again, walking softly along the little creek that led eventually back to the hickory grove. And then unbelievably, he saw her—she was sitting on the shelf above the largest pool. And she had thrown her Shaker cap away so that her long hair hung down around her face, and she seemed just to be sitting there and staring at nothing. Richard stood silent, sure that she hadn't heard his steps. He decided then what he'd do—he'd simply tell her that he had come to take her home, and he wouldn't put up with any of her silly nonsense. They could argue later, and it was probable that they would argue. But tonight they could both sleep on the floor in front of the fireplace, and tomorrow he'd take her up to the hill church. The preacher had to live somewhere nearby, perhaps in the cabin right across the road from the church. But before he married Ruth he'd have to go back and get Nellie—he'd do that right after the roosters started crowing in the morning. And a year from now, or maybe less than a year, they'd have their first baby, and after that it was hard to tell how many more.

He came out from behind the hawthorn tree that had sheltered him, and Ruth heard him and saw his ghostly shadow at the same moment. The next instant he heard her scream and saw her scramble to her feet. Then she was running, running toward him. "Oh, my God, my God!" he heard her cry, and that was the last either of them knew until they were in each other's arms.